MELTDOWN

BLACK GOLD CONSPIRACY

Albert L. Biele

An Old Line Publishing Book
Hampstead ◊ Maryland ◊ USA

Printed in the United States of America

ISBN-13: 9781937004729
ISBN-10: 1937004724

Cover Design by Christopher Saghy
Editing by Meredith Donaho

Old Line Publishing, LLC
P.O. Box 624
Hampstead, MD 21074
Toll-Free Phone: 1-877-866-8820
Toll-Free Fax: 1-877-778-3756
Email: info@oldlinepublishingllc.com
Website: www.oldlinepublishingllc.com

when, I pass a way, I want
this book, to go to meredith's
mother - Sharon Ditzel
With all my Love!
your Loving mother!
1-25-2012

I dedicate this book to my wife, Arlene, for her patience, encouragement, and the innumerable contributions she made in helping the author develop a plausible science-based story that highlights the perseverance and humanity we believe to be a prevailing virtue within all of us.

CHAPTER 1

Renowned geologist Tom Collins sat on a wooden stool in the providence of Guárico Venezuela, within the boundary of the Orinoco Oil Belt Assessment Unit, in a makeshift tent during the torrential rain storm, putting his final figures together on a geological study which had taken him to thirty-six countries over a two-year period. The program had been initiated for the purpose of developing new methods of locating and extracting petroleum from deeper wells.

The study was organized and developed by Tom on the premise of giving graduate students an opportunity to work in the field with some of the world's top geologists, but his real motive was to gain access to the international oil fields in an attempt to somehow correlate the extraction of oil with the recent dramatic increase in seismic activity.

He knew the oil companies would not have given him access to the fields if they were aware of his true intentions. If the findings confirmed his suspicions, they would be literally put out of business.

With the study completed, Tom was convinced the extraction of more than one quadrillion barrels of oil over the past 110 years had a definitive correlation with the dramatic increase of seismic activity. After finalizing his vertical computations taken from the data gathered through sonar instruments, he confirmed lava from the mantle was moving through thousands of new found cracks, progressively edging a pathway toward the service of the planet.

The Earth's crust seemed to be literally breaking apart. When Tom put the flow rates and data into a simulated computer program developed by the USGS, the final results confirmed his worst nightmare. Within a short period of time, the planet's temperatures would rise to levels incapable of sustaining life in any form. He continued to reenter the data hoping to find an error, but the calculations continued to confirm his original finding.

Tom flew back to the University of Pittsburgh where he taught geology and performed the majority of his research for the past ten years. He spent several weeks analyzing and reanalyzing all the information collected. The final results had not changed. He could not develop an accurate time table for when the molten lava would break through the surface of the crust without first monitoring its movement over predetermined intervals of time. He couldn't even determine whether the lava moved at a constant or accelerated rate of flow, but from the data previously analyzed, he was pretty much convinced that molten lava would break through the surface of the planet within a three to four year period.

Tom duplicated the report and sent the results to the International Geological Convention Center in Washington, DC, where he hoped to present his findings to the scientific world. He also mailed copies to three of his closest colleagues, and renowned scientist, asking them to meet him at his home in Gilford, Connecticut for a friendly get-together and to discuss the study.

He was well aware of the controversy the study would generate, but with the help of his colleagues and close friends, Tom believed he would be able to authenticate the findings in a more-timely manner.

Tom packed his bags, threw them into the car and headed home, anxious to discuss the matter with his associates.

As he drove into his driveway, Tom saw his best friend, Joe Solino, standing on his front porch with a big smile on his face.

"Glad you could make it," Joe said in a joking manner, "where the hell have you been?"

"Same old Joe," Tom said smiling, as he gave him a friendly hug. "Thanks for being here. What's in the bag?"

"I brought some good Italian wine," Joe responded, as they both walked into the house.

"Did you get my package?"

"Forget it," Joe quickly responded, "you're not going to rope me into this project, not today, not tomorrow, and not ever. Don't even give it a second thought."

"I spent two years flying around the world putting this damn thesis together," Tom snapped, "you might at least spend ten minutes listening to what I have to say. Trust me Joe; you're going to be interested in what I found."

Before Joe had a chance to respond, the door bell rang. "Who else are you expecting?"

"I invited John Mason and Phil Dayne to join us."

"What the hell are you having here?" Joe asked, "A scientific summit?" Tom smiled.

"Let me get the door," Tom said as he turned towards Joe. "Please don't go negative on me, I need their help."

Joe didn't respond.

Phil rang the bell a second time and walked in just as Tom reached the front entrance. "Hello Tom," Phil said, a big smile on his face. "Did you enjoy your vacation?"

"Vacation," Tom snapped, "I spent two years running around the world sleeping in some of the worst accommodations known to man. Between the sand fleas, the insects and the snakes, it was more like doing penance."

"If I can recall correctly," Phil said, "didn't you invite three young female graduate students on the trip? I assumed..."

"You don't believe I'd take advantage of my position, do you?"

"I was hoping more than believing," Phil said, slightly laughing.

John smiled as he followed Phil into the house, realizing Tom was seriously defending himself. "Relax," John said as he shook hands with Tom, "he's pulling your leg. So how have you been?"

"I'm a little worn, but happy to be home." Tom closed the door behind them.

Joe walked over, giving them a friendly pat on the back. "We should do this more often."

"Easier said than done," Phil said, "we never seem to be in the same place at the same time. I understand you're at the tail end of a major project."

"That's true," Joe responded, "we have been correlating recent seismic activity occurring in locations not known to have previous fault lines."

"We've also had our hands full at the USGS these last couple of years," Phil explained. "There's been a dramatic increase in seismic activity, and to date, we can't figure out what the hell is going on."

"I think I have the answers you're looking for."

"Relax, Tom," Joe smiled "they just got here. Let them at least sit down before you put them through the mill."

"Sorry guys, please come in and make your-self at home."

"How's the family?," Joe continued, addressing John.

"Their doing fine, the little ones are keeping me pretty busy, but I'm not complaining."

Joe and John walked toward the living room, while Tom and Phil remained in the foyer.

"Did you look at the thesis I sent you?" Tom asked.

"Yes I did," Phil sounded somewhat hesitant. "Do you really believe the extraction of petroleum over the past hundred years is the primary reason for the increase in seismic activity?"

"Two minutes ago you explained how things are heating up down at the USGS. Well, aren't you the least bit interested in what's causing these phenomena's?"

"I'm a volcanologist, of course I am."

"You did read the report?"

"Tom, I'm not disputing your findings, I need more time to examine your papers. Actually, there was one part of the report I was particularly interested in, the section which clearly identifies the deterioration of the tectonic plates."

"Those are the results, Phil," Tom said in a low voice. "What I'm concerned about is finding a resolution to the problem. The matter is serious, and I really can use your help on this one. Can I count on you?"Phil took a few seconds before responding. "Yes, of course Tom. After all, the USGS is short on answers, and your report may possibly fill in some of the missing gaps. I'm sure I can get them to assign me to your project."

"Thanks, Phil."

"Sounds like someone is having a good time in the living room," Phil smiled.

"Well, at least their laughing," Tom snapped. As they entered the room, John and Joe were sitting across from one other, laughing hysterically.

"What the hell is so funny?" Phil asked.

"Second year in college," John spurted out in between laughs.

"Remember the prank we pulled on John," Joe said, "when we set him up on a blind date."

Phil and Tom started to laugh watching John laugh uncontrollably.

"Well," Phil asked, "who was the girl?"

"Mildred Kursh," Joe said, still laughing.

"Yes, I remember her. She played on the women's basketball team. Six -five or six-seven."

"She's the one," Joe laughed.

"Yeah," Tom smiled, "I remember the incident."

"Anyway," Joe continued half talking, half laughing, "he spent the entire evening looking up. His head was bent at a forty-five degree angle the entire night." Joe couldn't stop laughing. "His neck hurt so bad, he had to take pain killers."

Even Tom started to laugh at this point.

"At the end of the night, when we drove her home, I told John there was something in the trunk he might need before he walked her to the door."

"In the trunk?," Tom asked, "what the hell did you have in the trunk?"

"Why don't you tell them, John?" Joe had tears running down his face.

Still trying to catch his breath, and unable to get the words out, John mumbled, "A four foot ladder." He laughed so hard that he had to leave the room just to calm down. They continued to talk about their college days and some of the crazy things they did, or as John explained, "got away with."

After catching up with personal events, John walked over to Tom and patted him on the back. "You did a hell of a job on your thesis, but why would you want me to be involved? I'm a hydro-geologist."

"Trust me, John. Your expertise and research in CO2 sequestration, ground-water modeling, site characterization, and remediation technology will prove to be an asset to the project."

John smiled. "I'm glad you found the study to be of some assistance to your project."

"The study turned out to be extremely helpful," Tom explained, "especially your conclusion relating to the subsurface injection practice. You state the deep well drilling has the potential to cause low-level induced seismicity events, but do most occurrences actually occur along previously faulted rocks?"

"Yes," John said. "It should be noted that most cases have been documented at waste disposal wells, oil fields and other similar sites."

"Your study on the injection of CO2 is particularly interesting. You not only claim it can affect formation pressures in rock units distant from the actual infection point, but even more importantly, you state increased activity is greatest in seismically vulnerable locations with preexisting faulting; and there lies the problem."

"What do you mean?"

"Well John, I predicated the study on the possible correlation between the extraction of oil and increased seismic activity. Somehow, oil seeped into large voids located within the crust during the initial cooling period of the Earth's surface. I believe, over millions of years, the petroleum formed a natural hydraulic system which stabilized the plates. I know that this is only a theory, but further statistics and investigation seems to add further support to my thesis." Tom paused for a moment and then continued. "The majority of oil extracted from the crust occurred over the past 110 years which definitely parallels the increase in seismic activity during the same period of time, but more so, over the past 30 to 40 years."

"It seems it would be extremely difficult to prove your theory" John said.

"It's the only thing that makes sense," Tom responded in a low voice. "Before the continents formed into the land masses they are today, millions of years ago, twenty or more plates violently moved into one other, fighting for position. I believe the numerous voids within the plates created weak points from the mantle to the surface of the planet which acted as a highway for lava flow, keeping the planet in a volatile state. In time, the Earth with its uncanny ability to protect itself, filled the voids with pressurized petroleum, causing them to stabilize; that is, until the beginning of the twentieth century when oil became a commodity for profit."

Tom paused for a moment as he went through some of his notes. "Look John," he continued, as he handed him a chart showing the world's annual oil production from 1900 to 2011. "You're looking at the quantity of petroleum extracted from the crust over the past one hundred and ten years. It shows an average of a 14% increase per decade, but more importantly, 90% of all petroleum consumption occurred since 1957, whereas, a whopping 50% of the 90% figure was consumed since 1984. Why is this significant?" Tom asked, not expecting an answer from John, "because the increase during that same period of time parallels the increase in seismic activity."

"Theoretically, a sound observation," John said, looking somewhat surprised. "But the extraction of oil and increased seismic activity may be coincidental."

"I predicate my conclusions on the scientific data gathered over these past two years."

"I don't doubt your findings, Tom," John said in somewhat of an apologetic manner. He had a great deal of respect for Tom, and had no intent to question his work. "I just want to understand what the scientific facts are based on."

"The evidence is partially based on your study," Tom explained, "where you yourself have confirmed that seismic activity, due to deep well drilling, is greatest in seismically vulnerable locations with preexisting faults."

John shook his head in agreement.

"Don't you see? There must be thousands of preexisting unknown faults that formed millions of years ago when the twenty or so tectonic plates collided to form the nine major plates that exist today. The location of these faults will remain unknown unless they become active again. There was a paper submitted by GeoScience recently, attributing several Asian earthquakes to seismic activity caused by deep water wells. And today, we are experiencing tremors where there are no known faults."

"I see your point," John said. "Not knowing where the faults are is a problem. You see Tom, to avoid drilling in geo-active locations requires the investigation of subsurface geologic structures, review of seismic activity in the area, well testing, seismic monitoring, and modeling of pressure buildup and fluid migration."

"We took in excess of eight hundred sonar readings of the Earth's crust, John, and converted the readings to vertical views of the underlying surface in areas where petroleum has already been extracted." Tom handed John the charts as Phil looked on. Joe excused himself.

"I'll be back in a few minutes," Joe said, "I have to call a friend." Tom just smiled as Joe walked out of the room.

"Anyway," Tom continued, "the thin blue lines on the chart indicate an absence of solid matter or cracks in the crust, and there are thousands of them. The red lines connected to the bottom of the blue lines have been identified as lava flow. This tells us these new found cracks must go all the way down to the planet's mantle. Now, I would like to note, the sonar reading you're looking at was taken two years ago." Tom paused for a moment as he reached for additional charts. "I made new sonar recordings at these same locations just two weeks ago. Note that the later chart confirms the vertical cracks have extended themselves in excess of one hundred feet closer to the surface of the planet."

"Look," John said, sounding somewhat alarmed, "you are absolutely correct. The elevations of the blue lines have been extended, and the red lines are not only extended, but they've seemed to have grown wider."

"What is happening," Tom explained, "is the molten lava is melting the crust sediment as it moves through the cracks. This in turn is enlarging the area of lava flow, and at the same time inserting increased pressure within the crust, which is not only extending the cracks toward the surface of the planet, but is creating new veins, or cracks along weak points in the crust as it ascends toward the planet's surface."

"Is this a prevailing condition," Phil asked, "or is it isolated?"

"The condition is not only prevailing on dry land, but there is a strong possibility that this phenomenon is occurring more abundantly on the ocean floors."

"I'm convinced," John said. "If you're putting a team together, you can count me in."

"Thanks John," Tom said in a low voice, "you're a good friend."

Just then, Joe walked in, smiling.

"OK Joe, what's her name?" Phil asked, as he gave him a friendly pat on the back. Joe did not respond. "You must be getting serious," Phil continued, "because we still don't know who she is." Joe just smiled.

"What's your opinion," Joe asked, "regarding Tom's two year thesis?"

"Pretty convincing," Phil responded.

"So you're convinced Tom's work has validity?"

"Yes."

"Interesting," Joe said in low voice; he wasn't surprised."I have a couple of good bottles of Italian wine in the kitchen. I'll be back in a minute."

Phil shook his head knowing, that for some reason, he was being totally adamant about becoming involved, but decided not to push the subject.

Tom knew that Joe would be a real asset to the project, and knew he had to somehow convince him to join the team.

Tom was noted for his published works on seismic activity. He was sincere, well spoken and exhibited a dominating presence, standing at six-foot-one, with glaring hazel eyes and a deep well-pronounced voice that almost demanded attention. His three colleagues and longtime friends were also published scientists, and well respected in their field of study.

Joe held a position as a professor at the National Institute of Geological Studies he was at the tail end of finalizing several important scientific projects for the university. Tom, being familiar with Joe's work, realized he was resisting involvement in the project because of his obligations to the university.

This project is too damn important, Tom thought, I have to get him to read the report.

Tom followed Joe into the kitchen as he continued to probe for a response regarding his theory. "Joe, just listen, this is important," Tom explained.

Joe did not respond.

"Did you at least go over my report?"

"I briefly scanned over the report," Joe said in a low voice.

"We've been friends for a long time," Tom snapped. "When did I ever present scientific papers that did not have at least some validity?"

"Tom!" Joe snapped, "right now there are only two major arguments associated with global warming- whether it is caused by man, or the planet is simply going through a natural process." Joe paused for a moment as he turned to face Tom, "If I read your report correctly, you're suggesting a third theory. You believe the extraction of petroleum caused the seismic plates to become unstable, and we're all going to die. I don't understand as we have had more snow this past winter and record breaking cold spells all the way down into Florida. Where the hell is the global warming?"

"One sign of global warming," Tom explained, "is increased precipitation, which is solidly documented. Also, the cold air blowing down from Canada and other northern regions does not necessarily prove global warming doesn't exist."

"You should have been a dooms day prophet," Joe said apprehensively.

"Is this a test?" Tom asked.

Joe laughed. He realized the ice caps and glaciers were melting, and personally participated in a report regarding warm winter temperatures recorded in Canada and other northern regions. He knew the excessive melting process taking place in those regions caused colder air to be blown down to the southern states.

"The documentation," Tom said, "confirms lava is moving closer and closer to the surface of the planet through voids and cracks in the crust, which I believe is being caused by the extraction of petroleum. It's the only known event that parallels the increase in seismic activity."

While holding a bottle of wine in one hand and searching through the kitchen drawer with the other, Joe's response was, "Where the hell is the cork screw? I'd like to release some of the pressure from this bottle!"

"Left top drawer, next to the stove," Tom shouted, as he reached for the wine glasses. "Joe! I'm dead serious; there is actually a correlation between the extraction of oil and increased seismic activity."

Joe and Tom had known each other since they were kids, spending most of their spare time collecting rocks. Tom's mom, Grace, could not open a drawer in the house and not find a rock. One time the boys spent two days moving a forty-pound rock two miles from its original location to Tom's garage. When Tom's father Jim came home that evening, Grace gently whispered in his ear, "I think you had better have a talk with your son, the rocks are getting bigger." Jim called his son into the garage, along with his inseparable buddy Joe. The father looked at the forty-pound rock, looked at the boys, and said, "Geology. If you're hooked on rocks, remember the word geology."

Now here they were, thirty years later, both renowned geologists, with Tom attempting to lure Joe into what had to be one of the most controversial theories ever presented in the field of geology. The repercussions, Joe thought, could be catastrophic. I'd be better off if I got drunk tonight, got up early in the morning and left before he wakes up. If he calls me later, I'll tell him I was incoherent.

"Tom! People are actually buying our books!" Joe snapped. "The guy who came up with the theory, 'the extraction of coal causes increased seismic activity,' is on welfare today."

Tom smiled, "You always did have a great sense of humor."

Joe walked back to the study where John and Phil were waiting. "Well, maybe we can open a pizza parlor or work for the Red Cross," Joe joked.

"And what if my data is correct?" Tom snapped.

"That's even worse than being wrong. We are talking about the Arabs, South America and the guy's who own the big ships that move this stuff around. There are the oil wells, the middlemen, the processors and don't forget the teamsters. Do you really want to tell these guys they have to stop taking oil out of the ground? Or maybe we can simply tell them they're going through a career change. Tom! We are not talking about billions; we are talking about trillions, maybe even ca-zillions. Do you hear what I'm saying? The scenario, right or wrong, is written in stone. We will either be unemployed or dead. You know, swimming with the fishes. This is a 'lose-lose' proposition. I have an idea, let's just not tell them."

"No," Tom said, "it's a 'lose-win' proposition. If I'm correct, there'll be no oil wells, no tankers, or middlemen, or teamsters, and for sure, a lot less people on this planet."

"You mean there'll be no us," Joe responded, shaking his head.

"You did review the study I sent you?" Tom asked again.

"Yes," Joe said. He stood quiet for a moment, while gathering his thoughts, already aware of the fact that "no" was not an option. He realized his best friend had never pursued an issue without first having the conviction there was a high degree of truth in his initial findings. Joe offered his normal indirect response of approval.

"OK Tom, the first thing we should do is buy bulletproof vests and move into an armored bunker."

"Thanks Joe, you're a friend to be counted on."

When they entered the study, Joe realized why John and Phil were invited. They were experts in their field, and certainly trustworthy. All four were old college buddies and shared a professional admiration for one other, which in time, grew into a strong friendship. John married his childhood sweetheart, Joan, who made delicious apple pies, which was visible around John's waistline. They had two beautiful daughters, Rose and Susan, lived in a house with a white picket fence, had a pet dog and attended church every Sunday. He was a happy-go-lucky guy with old-fashioned values, had a good sense of humor and was an absolute genius in his field of study.

Phil, on the other hand, had the adventurous nature of Neal Armstrong, the courage of a lion and the strength of a bull. At 6'2," and two-hundred-ten pounds of solid muscle, he was a man who could take care of himself. With long-wind-swept blond hair and deep set blue eyes, Phil was certainly the catch of the day, but at thirty-eight he was still a bachelor. He had narrowly escaped death at the Saint Helen's eruption, but was not deterred from accepting other dangerous assignments, when the cause was justified. Dedicated to his work, he preferred looking down the neck of a roaring volcano, or in some way, standing at the very edge of danger just to feel the adrenalin rush to his brain, but even he was not crazy enough to want to die.

Tom walked into the study with Joe close behind him. He placed the wine glasses on the table as Joe simultaneously poured wine into each glass. With a friendly smile, Tom walked toward his guest and lifted his glass. "It's good to see us all together again, thanks for coming. Here's to good health, good wine and a friendship that will last forever."

As they were toasting, Joe quickly added, "You mean to the death, which may occur a lot sooner than we think?"

Seemingly unaware of Joe's comment, Tom turned toward his colleagues in a concerned and serious manner. "Gentlemen, common knowledge tells us that the tectonic plates have become seriously more active over the past thirty years, and although the logarithmic Richter scale was invented in 1935, worldwide monitoring of earthquakes was not realized until the 1960's. We simply did not have the technology, or the distribution system to monitor worldwide earthquakes, so I was careful to take into consideration time periods when seismic activity was accurately measured and logged by the USGS and other scientific institutions.

Because there is a lapse in time from when the petroleum is extracted from the crust and the initial reaction it has on the planet's seismic plates, I calculated the total quantity of petroleum extracted between the years 1900 through 2010 for the purpose of establishing the quantities, weights and the volume of the voids that were created by the extraction process." Tom handed each a copy of his calculations. "Knowing that one barrel of oil," Tom continued, "equals 42 gallons, and weighs .136 tons, documented records confirm more than 1,000 billion barrels of petroleum have been extracted from the planet since the year 1900, which equates to the removal of 204 trillion tons, leaving in its wake an excess of 5,400 billion cubic feet of voids."

"That doesn't necessarily prove that the removal of petroleum was the catalyst for increased seismic activity," Phil responded.

"I agree," Tom said. "I know a lot of this stuff is old hat to you and Joe, but I think it's important to fill John in on some of geological background sections of the study. I'll be getting to the meat of the study shortly."

Phil shook his head in agreement.

"The number of earthquakes occurred between 1980 through 2010, with an intensity of 6.0 or greater, were derived from the USGS data bank," Tom explained, "which confirms the increase in seismic activity over the past thirty years is nothing short of alarming. From 1980 to 1989, there were a total of one-thousand-one-hundred-twenty-five earthquakes with an intensity of 6.0 or greater, 1990 to 1999, one-thousand-four-hundred-sixty, and one-thousand-six-hundred earthquakes between the years 2000 to 2010. That's an increase of almost fifty percent from 1989 to 2010.

"Now, look at this chart I showed you earlier, it shows the annual oil production in barrels from 1900 to 2010. Notice the increase in seismic activity parallels the increase in the extraction of oil. There are some in my profession that will tell you we are going through the natural process of change, and the removal of oil and the increase in seismic activity is coincidental; but gentlemen, look at the numbers and look at the chart. The quiet voices of geologists are saying the increase in seismic activity in the latter part of the twentieth century to the present is alarming. Right now there are a lot of theories, but no answers."

Tom paused for a moment, and then in a low voice, continued, "There are two facts that cannot be argued against: the major extraction of oil did not occur until 1950, which parallels recorded increases in seismic activity from 1980 to the present day. As you can see, I have allowed a thirty year span for cause and effect, that is, it takes approximately thirty years from when oil is actually extracted to when its effects are realized. Now, we can tell ourselves this is simply a coincidence, or we can examine the evidence. We can also interpret the sonar charts in several different ways, but the one fact that cannot be disputed is that lava is moving vertically through thousands of new found cracks, faults and voids in the crust."

"Well," Phil responded, "we may not be able to confirm the exact cause of this phenomenon, but we obviously know it exists. What I mean is that it could be some sort of tectonic plate weight distribution factor, or as Tom explained, maybe the extraction of petroleum caused preexisting fault lines in the crust to reopen."

"The main point here," Tom said, "is the condition not only exists but is progressing at a measurable time sequence, and according to a simulated computer program developed by the USGS, molten lava may possibly reach the surface of the planet within a three to four-year period." There were no more questions from the group, just silence. Four years seemed too abrupt and extremely unrealistic.

"In our bulletins," Phil said, "when there are dramatic changes or severe unexplainable occurrences on the planet, we tell the public that the planet is correcting itself, but in most cases, we really don't know what the hell is going on."

Tom knew that the oil companies were the richest entities in the world. They controlled the world's finances and politics, and in the past they had resorted to nothing short of murder to secure their holdings. He knew Joe was right; fighting the oil barrens was probably the same as committing suicide.

"I have another concern," Tom said, "not only is seismic activity going to increase in numbers and magnitude, but my data also revealed that this activity is heating up our oceans. That's right, global warming for the most part is caused by the increased lava seepage from the mantle to the surface of the ocean's crust. These cracks have been dramatically increasing over the past one hundred years, but more so in the past twenty years. The increase in ocean temperatures has, in turn, caused atmospheric temperatures to increase at an alarming rate. The ice caps are melting from the bottom up, not the top down. If we continue to ignore the evidence, this planet will chew us up, spit us out and start over all again!" Tom paused for a moment to gather his thoughts.

"Just recently," Tom continued, "the Woods Hole Oceanographic Institution identified a new type of ocean ridge that is spreading so slowly that the Earth's mantle is now exposed over large regions of the sea floor, noting that these conditions exist at the Southwest Indian Ridge in the Atlantic and Indian Oceans, and the Gakkel Ridge beneath the Arctic Ice Cap Glacier. The British Antarctic Survey has confirmed that there is an active volcano beneath the Pine Island Glacier on the West Antarctic Ice Sheet. It appears that the volcanically melted water beneath the colossal ice sheet lubricates its movement, assisting its gravity-powered journey toward the Antarctic Ocean.

The temperatures of the ocean waters, although increasing at an alarming rate, has been somewhat subdued by the severe melting of the ice caps and glaciers around the world. If you place a pot of water on the stove at full flame, that water will eventually come to a boil. However, if you continually place ice cubes into the pot, you will prolong any dramatic increase in temperature, that is, until you start running out of ice cubes. Gentlemen, that is exactly what is happening; we are progressively running out of ice cubes.

It must also be noted that ocean levels have raised more than one foot from 1900 to 2011, noting that sixty percent of that rise has occurred since 1992. The only way you can achieve a rise in ocean waters is when land-ice melts, because, as you well know, ice floating in water cannot raise ocean water levels because the water displacement factor is already compensated for."

Tom continued, "Another sign of ocean warming is a condition called hypoxia, or low oxygen, which has long existed in the deep ocean. There are areas in the Pacific, Atlantic and Indian oceans where hypoxia is spreading, creeping toward the surface, and in some cases, encroaching on the continental shelf within sight of the coast line. These areas are called dead zones because nothing can live in them. Even phytoplankton, which is microscopic organisms and one of the richest ocean food chains in the world, die when entering a dead zone. Can you imagine how the world would be affected if the ocean became one big dead zone?"

"You're not trying to cheer us up Tom," Joe responded, "are you?"

Tom just shook his head and smiled.

"OK Joe, I get the message. I guess the tough question is what are we going to do about it?" Tom put his elbow on the table and laid his hand under his chin. He looked like he hadn't slept in days. "I don't have all the answers, but I believe I have enough scientific proof to submit my thesis, and with your help, we will have the political and professional connections necessary to turn heads."

Tom turned to John with a concerned look on his face. "John? Your input regarding this matter is essential; however, it is important that you and your family remain in the background during whatever course of action we decide to take. It is important that you, and they, are not subjected to any retaliation that may be initiated by the oil companies."

John turned and twisted in his chair, seeming somewhat disturbed with Tom's evaluation regarding his participation on the project. Before he could respond, Joe interrupted in a calm and friendly tone to assure John that the decision had nothing to do with their friendship, or his loyalty to them.

"You're not out of the circle, John. As a matter of fact, by separating yourself from any direct involvement, you'll be our most valuable asset. We will need someone on the outside that we can rely on. Who else can we trust, and more importantly, who else can we rely on when things start heating up?"

John smiled, "Thanks guys, I was just clearing up a little indigestion."

Tom made a sigh of relief. He thought Joe handled that well. Everything seemed to be falling into place.

"I have decided," Tom continued, "to announce my finding at the annual meeting for geological studies at the convention center in Washington, DC. There will probably be a lot of controversial feedback in the beginning. The scientists that are employed by, or who rely on grants from the oil companies, will most likely attempt to discredit our findings. When the smoke clears, other notable scientists not influenced by big money will start to collaborate with one other to confirm that our data has substance. Once we have conformation from the scientific world, everything else will fall into place.

My papers have already been submitted to the committee. Joe and I will be flying down Tuesday. As soon as we have some definitive feedback we will call you."

"What about the oil companies?" Phil asked.

"It really doesn't matter what the oil company's position is or is not," Tom responded. "It's more important for us to convince the scientific community that we have a major problem on our hands. It's the only way we are going to get the political world to pay attention.

You must understand Phil, in just three to four years the planet could reach temperatures in excess of 200 degrees or higher. We are talking about the potential extinction of mankind!"

"No," Tom reiterated, "without resolution we will witness the end of civilization as we know it."

"I am not advocating we do nothing," Phil said, "but as far as the oil companies are concerned, dead men don't talk! Maybe we can do this incognito, or something along those lines."

"Thanks, Phil. I appreciate your concern. I just believe that the sooner the facts are on the table, the more time we'll have to resolve the problem."

Phil reluctantly agreed, but understood why Tom was pushing the issue. "I believe that just about covers everything for now. But if you need us for anything, just give us a buzz."

"Thanks," Tom said, "and thanks for your support."

"We're all going to die," Joe said with a smile, as he shook their hands and said his good-byes. "I'm just kidding, Tom."

After they left, Tom and Joe spent the rest of the evening going over Tom's data. There was an enormous amount of information to digest. Joe continually bombarded Tom with questions. It was almost as though Joe was trying to find a flaw in Tom's research papers, trying to find anything that could possibly postpone the confrontation with the oil companies. But as the hours passed, it was clear to Joe that there was no error to be found. Tom, as usual, had completed a thorough scientific study that indisputably proved that the crust of the planet was breaking up. Even if the cause could not be unsubstantiated, Tom had concrete proof that molten lava was moving through large newly formed cracks, from the mantle of the planet to the planet's surface, and unless contained, life as we know it will definitely cease to exist.

"Well, Joe, do you still believe that I'm being a little too rambunctious? It's not just the lava flows occurring beneath the oceans that I'm concerned with; it's the lava flows that are now pressuring their way to the surface of the planet that pose the biggest threat.

I'll concede the fact that it would be impossible to confirm the actual rate of lava seepage that is occurring within the crust. But the real question is, what the hell are we going to do about it?"

Tom was now addressing Joe in a rushed, but concerned voice. "Do we wait until a couple of volcanoes blow their gaskets, and then send out a general alarm regarding the facts? Or..."

"Tom," Joe intervened in a calm voice, "you're going to bust a blood vessel. Take a deep breath, or go breathe into a paper bag or something.

It's me, your best friend. I already said yes. Of course we're all going to die."

Tom smiled. "Sorry Joe, I'm just a little tired, and we are not going to die."

"That's what I like about you, Tom, you're just so realistic."

"The way I see it, we first break the bad news at the convention tomorrow, which most likely will put the oil companies out of business, and then in a burst of gratitude, the numerous owners of these oil companies will start sending us 'Hallmark Cards', thanking us for the good deed that we have performed. After all, losing an income of one hundred billion dollars annually is not the end of the world. They can always sell shoes or golfing equipment or..."

"Alright Joe, you've made your point. I appreciate the humor; however, I do believe that eventually, even the oil companies will see the light. After all, value and net worth are relative terms; that is, we have more or less relative to the net worth of others. Anyway, without the planet, there is no net worth."

Joe smiled.

"You have totally exhausted my ability to reason, Tom," Joe said as he yawned, "I have diagnosed myself as brain dead. Good night, Tom."

"Night Joe, and for what it's worth, thanks."

As Joe walked to the guest room he murmured to himself in a low voice, "We're all going to die."

The next morning, Tom and Joe headed out to the airport. They were now firmly committed to presenting Tom's work at the Washington Geological Convention. Both men were recognized as top scholars in their field of geology, and confident that Tom's work would be well received by their colleagues and friends.

CHAPTER 2

Tom and Joe arrived in DC late that afternoon filled with anxiety. They were hoping that things would go well. After checking into the hotel, Tom called room service and ordered dinner. They spent the rest of the evening reviewing their data.

"Don't worry Joe," Tom said in a confident manner, "once we make our presentation, everything will be on the table. There may be a few rough spots here and there, but when the overwhelming data supporting the facts are realized, even the big boys are going to have to concede."

Joe had a great deal of admiration and respect for Tom, but he knew that with his idealistic nature, Tom did not see the whole picture.

Joe, on the other hand, saw things for what they were. He knew that history dictated that big money didn't give a rat's ass for human life, especially when it came to profit. Tobacco companies knowledgeably sold products that caused terminal illness for profit, and with the politicians in their pocket, were able to hold off legislation for years. There were planned wars and skirmishes for the sake of profit, again at the sacrifice of human life. Pharmaceutical companies continued to sell drugs knowing that their negative effects were more damaging than the illness, and then there were the drug lords making billions sending people to the cemetery. If these big-money entities didn't give a damn about human life, why should the oil conglomerates be any different? As they shut the lights off and prepared to go to sleep, Joe's mind continued to analyze every scenario that could possibly occur. "Tom! Are you still awake?"

MELTDOWN

"What?" Tom answered half-asleep.

"Maybe we should rethink our strategy. There are a lot of past circumstances that may not favor this particular approach, maybe we should..."

"Joe, go to sleep, we have a big day ahead of us."

Joe did not respond. He knew that Tom was dead set on presenting his findings at the convention regardless of the consequences.

The next morning came soon enough, and Tom woke up first and jumped straight into the shower. As he walked out of the bathroom, he saw Joe lying in his bed, still snoring away. "Rise and shine, Joe," he said, giving him a gentle shove, "it's time to get up."

"Yeah, yeah," Joe murmured, "I'm up, I'm up." As Joe slowly rose from the bed, Tom picked up the hotel phone.

"Take a shower while I order breakfast."

Joe hesitated for a moment until he was able to get his bearings. He wasn't exactly a rise-and-shine type of a guy. He was more of a "hit the five -minute-delay button on the alarm clock repeatedly," type of guy. Joe eventually staggered into the bathroom and shut the door.

Five minutes later, there was a loud knock on the door. Ah, breakfast is early, Tom thought. He was a man who lived for breakfast and could not function without at least two cups of black coffee. Tom cheerfully walked toward the door with the tip already in his hand. As he opened the door, four large men dressed in black suits pushed into the room. Two of the men grabbed both of his arms and banged him into the wall. Tom broke into a cold sweat. His voice quivered as the words coming out of his mouth accelerated; he sounded like he had a speech impediment. "Who the hell are you guys? Who are you looking for? You have the wrong room! I'm a professor! I teach geology! What the hell could you possibly want with a geologist?" From where Tom was positioned, he noticed the package one of the men threw on his bed, recognizing it as the same package he had sent to the committee chairman at the convention center. His posture immediately changed to one of pure unadulterated fear.

One of the men, wearing dark sun-glasses, walked towards Tom's right side, putting his mouth as close as he could to his ear, and whispered, "I'm here to inform you that your presentation was rejected by the committee."

"Why would they reject my study before it was presented?" Tom gasped. The man grabbed Tom by the collar and violently banged him against the wall.

"Listen to me, this is not a request, it's a warning. Take all this crap back to Connecticut and burn it."

"It's not that easy," Tom explained, "there is..."

"Pay attention!" the man shouted angrily, still holding Tom against the wall. "You and your friend's lives are in danger. Do I make myself clear?"

Tom listened nervously. His mind was racing through dozens of scenarios, none of them good. Did I put my closest friends in jeopardy? What was I thinking? Too much science and not enough common sense; I should have done this alone. These guys are going to kill us. I've got to get those packages back. Maybe I should try a little common sense on these guys; after all, even if I back off, the present danger to the planet is not going to go away. Tom turned toward the guy that seemed to be in charge. His heart was beating a million miles a minute while the two other men continued to hold him against the wall. "Even if I back off," Tom explained in a nervous manner, "everything in that package is true; this planet is in real trouble. If we don't..."

Without warning, a ripping fist pounded into Tom's stomach with the force of a truck. Tom fell to the floor gasping for air.

The lead guy leaned over his body and whispered. "Pay attention! This is your last warning."

As the men walked toward the door, one of them turned toward Tom. "By the way, tell Joe that he made the list too..." The men walked out, closing the door behind them, while Tom lay on the floor.

When Joe walked out of the bathroom, he saw Tom curled up and immediately ran to his side. "Tom! What happened, are you OK? Was it the food? Let me call the hotel doctor." Tom was just beginning to catch his breath as Joe helped him onto the bed.

"No, no, don't do anything," Tom snapped, "just get me a glass of water." Tom sat up on the bed.

"How are you felling? Maybe we should really call a doctor...!"

"No---, don't call the doctor," Tom quickly responded. "I'll be fine."

Tom knew he had to tell Joe what happened, but he felt rotten inside for putting his best friend in such a dangerous position. His mind was searching for solutions, but he continued to ponder the same thought over and over, they even have his name, this is terrible.

"Tom, are you going to tell me what happened?" Just then, there was a loud knock on the door. "Coming!" Joe shouted.

"No!" Tom screamed. "Stay away from the door! Do not open that door!"

As Joe continued to walk toward the door, Tom exploded with a voice that could have raised the dead, "DO NOT OPEN THAT DOOR!"

"What the hell is the matter with you?" Joe snapped. "Are you sure you didn't hit your head on something?"

Just then, a nervous voice came from behind the door, "You ordered breakfast? I could leave it outside the door if you'd like."

"Tom, before this guy has a heart attack, I'm going to open the door so that he can bring the breakfast in. Is that OK with you?"

"I'm sorry, Joe. Yes, let him in."

~~~~~~~~~~

After Tom had explained to Joe what happened, a long period of silence passed between the two men. There was no 'I told you so's,' Joe knew Tom was hurting, not just physically, but emotionally. He wasn't about to say anything that would make him feel worse then he already felt. Tom, on the other hand, remembered all the advice Joe had given him at the house. He realized that it was his dumb-ass pride that now put Joe and the rest of his friends in an extremely dangerous position.

"Joe, I'm really sorry. You were right. I allowed my pride to interfere with..."

"Yeah, yeah, yeah," Joe interrupted, "you're sorry that plan A didn't work and that we're all going to die."

"OK, I accept your apology. Now let's talk about plan B."

"What's plan B?"

"I don't know, but it's got to be a lot better than plan A."

Joe had thoroughly examined Tom's work and was resolved to the fact that they did not have three or four years as Tom had said; rather, two to two and a half years at most. He wanted to recheck the figures that morning before telling Tom of his findings but, under the circumstances, it did not seem like the most important issue at the moment.

Joe walked back and forth with a concerned and worried look on his face while he pondered the consequences and severity of the problem. Tom, on the other hand, was hoping that Joe would come up with some sort of solution. Suddenly, Joe turned toward Tom in a quick motion.

"Tom! Pack your bags, we're heading back!"

"But Joe," Tom snapped, "what about the convention? I have friends on the board that may be able to help us. You remember Jack Cadwell and Lou Feldman."

"Tom, let me ask you a question. How was the package sent out, and who did you address it to?"
~~~~~~~~~~

"Over-night, return receipt," Tom responded.

"It was addressed to the convention committee, 'Attention Lou Feldman' right?" Joe asked.

"Yes, Feldman is the chairman of the committee."

"And who returned the package to you?"

"What's your point?"

"There are a lot of dedicated geologists in this world who would probably come to our aid," Joe continued, "but I can assure you Tom, none of them are on the committee.

The fact of the matter is that eighty percent of all grants for these geological studies are funded either directly or indirectly by the oil companies. The grants are in the tens of millions of dollars. Our good friends are not going to jeopardize those grants. Look at the positive side of things Tom, if we get through this crisis, you'll probably win the Nobel Prize."

Tom looked emotionally drained. He had planned on presenting his papers at the convention for months. Scientists from all over the world would be there.

This was just something he had to do. It was his opportunity to present his findings to some of the best minds in the world on what he perceived to be the most critical situation ever to face mankind.

"You must understand Joe. We do not have a hell of a lot of time! It's imperative that we attend the convention and resubmit the package. If we miss this opportunity to present our case, we could wind up losing months! We simply do not have that kind of time!"

"Calm down, Tom, you're going to break a blood vessel! I wouldn't be here if I didn't believe it wasn't a good idea. I just cannot help but to remember what Phil said to us that night before he left."

"What was that?" Tom asked.

"Dead men don't talk!"

"What is that supposed to mean?"

"What does that mean?" Joe continued, "it means if you leave this hotel room and head toward the convention center, you'll have a zero chance of making it there alive."

"I don't think so Joe. I don't believe that they would resort to murder. I believe that they were just trying to scare us."

"Pray-tell," Joe said with a smile. "You don't really believe that, do you? Listen to me Tom, there are people out there that would murder someone for five hundred dollars. In this case, we are talking about trillions! Even Vegas wouldn't take odds on this one."

Tom was truly upset. He was still pretty shaken-up over what the four men in black had said to him. He knew that Joe was right, and now feared for his life.

"This is a life or death situation."

Tom's mind moved from one negative thought to the next, continually contemplating the dangers they would be facing. He had a difficult time understanding why they were encountering such strong resistance when the ultimate goal was to save the human race from a total annihilation. Failure is not an option, he thought.

"We don't have a hell of a lot of time Joe," Tom said in a determined voice. "We can't back off."

"Tom! We're not giving up; we're just going to reassemble ourselves. I realize how important this convention was to you, but we can't accomplish a hell of a lot dead. Listen to me, Tom, I'm with you on this one, I just don't believe that dying for a cause that has not yet been established is a good plan."

Tom paused for a moment as he digested Joe's concerns. "I guess you're right," he said in a low voice. "I'm just a little frustrated."

"Trust me," Joe snapped "it's the only choice we have. And I believe that the sooner we leave the better."

Tom started to pack his bag. "Remember Tom, we're not quitting, we're simply going back to formulate plan B. "Do you remember that movie 'Jaws', you know, when they saw the size of the shark, and the sheriff said, 'I think we're gonna need a bigger boat'? Well, that's what we have right now, a big problem and a small boat."

As they approached the lobby of the hotel, Tom recognized two of the four guys that had threatened him in the room. He stopped cold for a moment.

"Is something the matter, Tom?" Joe asked.

"No, Joe. I was just thinking. Let's grab a cab. We have a lot to do when we get back." They got into a cab and headed straight to the airport.

Tom now realized that there was a lot more involved than just science. It didn't seem to matter that severe global warming was about to annihilate all of mankind. The main objective of these assholes is profit. It's alright if we destroy the planet, as long as we keep the bank accounts intact. They'll be the richest dead guys on the planet.

CHAPTER 3

Tom and Joe arrived at the Westchester airport late that afternoon, which was less than an hour's drive to Tom's house. They had already called Phil and John from a payphone to explain what had transpired, and instructed them not to call for fear that it may be traced. He assured them that he would contact them as soon as they had devised a plan.

There was a cold silence in the car as Joe pulled out of the airport parking lot. It wasn't because there was any indifference between Joe and Tom. They simply did not know what to say to each other. They were facing a life-or-death situation, and reminiscing about the old days, or any other type of small talk, would have been insignificant under the circumstances. Each had hoped that the other would come up with some sort of miraculous plan, or even an idea of what to do next.

Tom was somewhat more emotional than Joe, especially after the scare he incurred at the hotel. To him, it wasn't just about the pending disaster to the planet; it was the pending danger it presented to his friends and associates. Joe, on the other hand, saw things for what they were. Not that Joe did not have a heart or care about others, he simply dealt with problems in a practical manner, and knew that the problem at hand was a whopper. There was no room for failure. He knew that the best scenario was also the worst scenario. Presenting the findings and convincing the scientific world that the findings had merit was one thing, but finding a resolution to the problem seemed near impossible to Joe. How are we going to possibly stop lava from moving to the surface of the planet, knowing that such a feat has never been accomplished before?

Joe broke the silence, "Tom, we have to consider two important objectives. The first objective should be to get a lot more people involved; people that we can trust. We should approach environmental groups, politicians and other scientists that are not financially tied into the system. The more people that are involved, the less chance there is that the oil companies will resort to violence. The negative publicity will not help their cause. Their only course of action will be to discredit our findings. The competitive nature of this type of argument will attract governmental and private scientists from around the world. When the smoke clears, the only thing that will surface will be the truth. The questions are, is there enough time to stop any further damage to the Earth's crust? And, how the hell do we do that?"

Tom listened to Joe carefully this time. He liked his approach; it was a plan that could eliminate violence and at the same time draw attention to his work. Scientists from all over the world would surface, some probably already working on the same type of research. He knew that once they confirmed his calculations, they would agree with his findings.

"You're an absolute genius, Joe. It's a great plan." Tom had been emotionally drained when he first realized that he would not have the opportunity to present his papers at the convention. Now, once again, he felt that something might actually be accomplished.

"To answer your questions, Joe, time is running out. And no matter what the solution, we're going to need the full cooperation of the oil companies. No solution is possible without their participation."

As Joe turned onto Tom's street, they saw several police cars with flashing lights and two fire trucks sitting directly in front of Tom's house. The house, although still standing, was badly burned. They saw someone standing in front of the house talking to two policemen.

Joe parked his car next to the patrol car and shut off the engine. He then turned toward Tom. This time, Tom looked mad as hell. Joe could not remember him being that mad since the neighborhood bully, Kevin Storky, confronted him when he was twelve. Tom had beaten the crap out of Kevin, and sort of ended his reputation as being the toughest kid in town.

There was smoke coming out of Tom's ears. He had definitely crossed the line. He was no longer Tom the compromiser; he was the other guy that is within all of us, the guy that wants to get revenge. "I don't understand!" Tom shouted, "the oil companies have billions of dollars, and have more resources, scientists and engineers working for them than any other entity in the world! And you mean to tell me that they don't know? I just cannot believe it! They have to know! And if they know, why the hell are they trying to put me out of commission? I just cannot seem to grasp their intent. Are they just stupid, or is this just a fat-cat syndrome? What's their goal, to be the richest dead men on the planet?"

For the first time, Joe felt that Tom was really aware of the circumstance.

Joe and Tom got out of the car, and approached the policeman who was standing alongside Tom's neighbor, Bob Morgan, who turned toward Tom with a serious and almost apologetic look on his face.

"I'm sorry, Tom, I believe the house was totaled. There is absolutely nothing worth saving. The inside of the house was completely destroyed. If there is anything I can do to help, please don't hesitate to ask. You know that you're welcome to stay at our home as long as you wish."

"Thanks, Bob, I appreciate the offer, but I'm probably going to stay with a friend. Do you know what happened?"

"No, I didn't see anything," Bob explained. "There was this loud explosion. When I came outside to see what had happened, I couldn't believe my eyes. The house was totally in flames. Your fire-alarm system must have alerted the fire department because when I called they were already on their way."

The front door of Tom's house was missing. When Tom attempted to enter, the fire chief, who was standing just to his side, stopped him.

"The house may not be structurally secure. We'll have a team out here tomorrow morning to survey the damage. Is there a number I can call you at?"

Tom gave the chief his cell number.

"I'll call you as soon as I get the results."

"Thanks, chief, I certainly appreciate your help."

"Sorry about the house Tom, here's my card. If you have any questions, just give me a call."

After putting barricades around the house, the firemen left the scene.

Tom's neighbor said good-bye and again offered to help. However, before Bob reached his house, he turned back toward Tom.

"You know, there is something I forgot to tell you. Yesterday, there was a van parked in your driveway. It was some sort of pest-control company. At the time, I didn't think anything of it. The men in the truck looked like they were from one of those Arab countries."

"Thanks, Bob."

MELTDOWN

"Don't forget, if there's anything I can do..."

"Thanks again, Bob."

"What's the matter Tom, why are you looking at me that way?"

"I don't have a pest control service."

"You don't have a pest control service?" Joe said, seeming alarmed. "And he said that they looked like they were from one of the Arabian countries." Joe paused for a moment and then continued, "Is it possible that all of the oil barrens in the world belong to the same club?"

"Yeah," Tom said dryly. "And they're all suicidal. I have to tell you, Joe, none of this makes any sense me. What are the oil barrens going to do, build giant bunkers under the ground that are self-sufficient? That's where the problem is going to be, under the ground!"

"I know how you feel," Joe responded, "but there's nothing more we can do here. Let's head over to my place."

Before Joe got into the car, he noticed that there was a white van parked about 200 yards up the street. He wasn't concerned, and for sure, didn't want to get into a paranoid state of mind, associating every incident to a possible assassination attempt. He thought to himself, maintenance vehicles are commonplace in the neighborhood, so don't get paranoid on Tom, he already has more on his plate then he can handle.

When he pulled out, he noticed that the van did the same. Still not concerned, Joe made a few turns and then turned onto the New England through-way. The van was still behind him. By this time, Tom had dozed off. After he passed a few exits, Joe moved to the right lane and reduced his speed. The van also moved to the right lane. At this point, Joe was somewhat concerned. He decided to get off at the next exit, and then get right back on again. The van followed suit. He increased his speed slightly until he reached his exit, and then proceeded to Main Street, where he knew there were traffic cameras at certain intersections. Joe made a note of the exact time he passed the cameras. He then drove the car directly to the police station where his brother worked as a lieutenant in homicide. The van drove off. Joe parked his car, woke Tom, and immediately filled him in on what had just happened.

"Let's go into the precinct and explain to Bill what the hell is going on."

Joe's older brother Bill was married to a vibrant and full-of-life gal named Betty. They had four children: Bobbie, age five; Brian, age seven; Bruce, age ten and Billy, age twelve. Every towel and napkin in the house had the initials 'BS', exemplifying Bill's sense of humor. The two brothers were extremely close, and always happy to see one another.

They entered the precinct and walked up to the main desk. When the sergeant at desk saw Joe, he smiled.

"Joe Solino," the sergeant said in a loud voice, "how the hell have you been?"

"Pretty good, Frank," Joe responded, "how about yourself?"

"Nothing ever changes around here. It's always the same old crap, but I'm not complaining. Bill is going to be happy to see you."

"Is he in?" Joe asked.

Just then, Joe heard a loud voice behind him. "Hey Joe, so you finally decided to come and visit your big brother!" Bill walked over and gave Joe a big Italian hug.

"Good to see you, Joe."

"Good to see you too, Bill, how's the family?"

"The family's great. The kids miss you."

"Yeah, I miss them too. I'll have to make it a point to get over to the house."

"Hey, Tom," Bill said, "good to see you, how have you been?"

"Good to see you too, Bill."

"What's the matter Tom? You look like you're upset about something. Joe what's going on?"

"Tom's house was burnt down this morning, I mean, there's nothing left to salvage."

"You're not pulling my leg?"

"No, no, the house has been destroyed. The fire chief believes it was plastic explosives because of the intensity of the heat."

"I'm sorry."

"I don't know if it's the oil companies, or who the hell it is," Tom said in an angry voice. "I'm having a difficult time convincing people that the planet is going to self destruct in less than four years. I'm a geologist; I deal with facts and figures. I'm not a CIA operative, and I'm not Wyatt Earp. We should be concentrating on scientific solutions, and not running for our lives."

"That's what I like about you Tom; you never hold back, you just tell it like it is."

"I didn't mean to be so abrupt, Bill," Tom said, "I'm just having a bad day."

"OK Tom, just calm down and tell me what the hell is going on."

"Calm down!" Tom snapped, "I feel like I'm living in a nightmare."

"I'm sure we can get to the bottom of this, but I'm going to need some facts."

MELTDOWN

Joe proceeded to explain to his brother the events that had transpired in the past two days. He also told him about the white van that had followed them to the station.

"I ran the van through the traffic cameras," Joe said, as he handed Bill the exact time the cameras made the recordings. "Maybe you can retrieve the plate number of the vehicle and possibly identify the driver."

Bill looked visibly upset; he wasn't happy to find out that his brother and Tom were on a possible hit list.

"I'll take care of it, Joe. That was quick thinking on your part. I can understand why you're so upset, Tom," Bill continued, "don't worry, we'll find out who's behind this. Just write down anything that may be pertinent to the case. Officer Jones will take the information, and remember, the smallest detail could very well be the most significant."

"Thanks Bill," Tom said, "I really do appreciate your help."

While Tom followed Officer Jones to his station, Joe and Bill went to his office where they had a general conversation about the family and some of the local matters.

"How should we handle this situation, Bill?" Joe asked.

"Why don't you take Tom home and get some rest," Bill said. "I have a good friend that works for the FBI. I'm going to explain the situation to him and then get back to you. You take care of the technical end, and I'll take care of the guys that are giving you a hard time."

"Thanks, Bill."

"As soon as I have something, I'll call you. Here, take these two police cell phones, and whatever you do, don't use the house or personal cell phones. The number for this line is on the back of the cell. If you call, use this phone only, its untraceable."

"Ok, Bill and thanks." Just then, Tom walked in.

"Did you give the officer the information?" Bill asked.

"Yes."

"That's good," Bill said. "If you remember anything else, just call it in."

"Why don't you guys head out and I'll get back to you."

"Thanks again," Tom said.

"Don't worry, Tom, we'll get to the bottom of this."

"Thanks, I appreciate the help."

~~~~~~~~~~

After Joe left the precinct, Bill directed a couple of patrol cars to follow him home. He also directed the cars to patrol the neighborhood, and
~~~~~~~~~~

assigned one patrol car to park in Joe's driveway over night. Bill wasn't taking any chances. From experience, he knew that this wasn't just a couple of guys trying to harass them. These guys had to be part of a well organized syndicate, with one goal in mind-- to stop them from presenting Tom's study.

Bill seemed a little puzzled. They could have knocked these guys off anytime they felt like it, so why are they procrastinating; why are they buying time?

He also believed that the oil companies could be involved, but didn't quite understand the logic. It just doesn't add up, if the oil companies had the facts, they would simply agree or disagree. At the very worst, they would attempt to disprove the findings and be done with it, and why would they bring in 'hit men' from the Middle-East?

Whether Joe's pursuers were connected to the oil companies, or some other unknown group, wasn't really important at this time. All he knew was that some organized syndicate was trying to kill his brother, and somehow he had to stop them. "I had better call Pete," Bill muttered to himself.

Peter Marchel was a top-ranking FBI agent and long-time friend of Bill Solino. They worked on several cases together in joint operations. When off-duty, the men would also socialize and attend sporting events together at the school their children attended. Bill's wife Betty and Pete's wife Sara grew up together and had been best friends since they were kids.

Bill and Pete had a great admiration and respect for each other. Not just because they shared the same profession, but also because they shared the same values. Both were dedicated law officers with a high degree of integrity. Bill knew that Pete was trustworthy and reliable, someone on whom he could rely.

Bill was really proud of his brother for putting his life on the line for a cause that he believed would save millions of lives. As a police officer, he knew the courage it took to lay one's life on the line to save the life of another. He never dreamed that his brother, a geologist, would ever face such a circumstance. Bill made a personal vow to himself to do whatever he had to do to protect his brother and Tom.

It was ten p.m. when Bill called Pete. He spent an hour on the phone filling him in on his brother's circumstances. At the end of the conversation, Pete not only understood the seriousness of the case, but he thought there might be a strong connection with a major investigation that the FBI was presently conducting. In the past twelve months, scores of insurgents had entered the country illegally. They belonged to a radical religious group that went under the name of the "The Last Jihad". The group had cells in just about every country in the world. They had only one agenda: to cleanse the world of infidels in preparation for the coming of their messiah.

The FBI had a surveillance team assigned to several known locations, and was convinced that these locations were just the tip of the iceberg. They were hoping that this group would eventually lead them to other locations and possibly the entire network in order to gather enough information to stop the insurgents from whatever they were planning.

Pete could not discuss the matter with Bill in detail because of security reasons. However, under the circumstances, he was sure he could have Bill cleared by the agency to work on the case.

At the end of the conversation, there was a moment of silence. "Pete, this is my brother, my only brother, we have to protect him." Again, there was silence.

"I understand, Bill. I'm with you on this one. I want you to call your brother and tell him I'm sending two agents to stay with him tonight. I'll meet you at Joe's house tomorrow morning at seven a.m."

"Thanks Pete, see you then."

Bill called Joe and told him what had transpired.

"So, I should expect the FBI to be knocking at my door," Joe said. "Thanks again, Bill."

"Yeah, they should be there within ten, fifteen minutes. I'll see you tomorrow morning at seven."

Just as Joe finished explaining to Tom what had transpired, the doorbell rang.

"I'll get it." Joe said. As Joe opened the door, he saw two large men standing outside waving FBI badges in his face.

"Hi, you must be Joe?"

"Yes. Bill told me to expect you, thanks for coming."

"My name is Matt Johnson, and this is my partner, Harry Kline. We'll be parked about fifty feet down the street in a surveillance truck; it's a black van. I want you to take this two-way radio and place it on a night table next to your bed. Don't panic when it rings; it's loud. You see this black button?"

"Yes."

"If you press it, my phone will ring. You can just start talking and I'll hear you."

"OK, I got it."

"Now, do you see that red button?"

"Yes."

"If the phone rings, push that button. The ring will stop and you'll hear my voice. Of course, we're hoping that nothing happens tonight. But if it does, do whatever I tell you to do, and do it as fast as you can. No thinking! Just do what I say!"

"I understand," Joe responded.

"By the way, Joe, we sent the police car away. They stick out like a sore thumb."

"I understand. Here, let me give you the key to the front door, in case you have to use the facilities."

"Thanks Joe," agent Klein said, "we'll see you tomorrow morning."

The FBI agents went back to their van and drove to an unlit area adjacent to an empty lot, approximately 150 feet from the house. The road beyond that point was a dead end, which meant that any vehicle approaching Joe's house could only come from one direction. There was a lamppost about 15 feet beyond his house, sufficient enough to light up his driveway and the house across from him.

Matt and Harry were seasoned FBI agents, and they were not randomly chosen for this surveillance assignment. They were a part of the team investigating the terrorist group that had recently entered the country.

The night was quiet. Matt and Harry took turns cat napping while the other kept an eye on the house and monitored the satellite surveillance system. They slept two hours on, two hours off, until about two-thirty a.m., when Harry noticed a vehicle on the navigational surveillance system. The vehicle was on a road that ran perpendicular to Joe's street, about three quarters of a mile from his house. As soon as the vehicle made the turn down Joe's street, Harry could visibly see the front lights.

"Matt, Matt. Wake up. We have company." Matt jumped up and grabbed a special piece of equipment that had the ability to X-ray the vehicle. They could see that the vehicle was a white van.

"What do you see Matt?"

"I can't see much. It looks like there are three men in the van. I've got the front of the van. I need a shot of the side!" Just then, before they reached the light pole, the van shut off its lights.

Harry erupted in a silent but excited whisper, "The van is turning into the driveway across from Joe's house!"

MELTDOWN

"Wait. Wait." Matt said in a low voice. "There's a guy in the back of the van with a cylinder in his hand!"

Harry franticly picked up the two-way radio and pushed the black button; he knew the cylinder was a rocket launcher.

After the first ring, Harry screamed, "pick up the Goddamn phone!" At the same time, Matt shot out of the van with an automatic weapon in his hand. Joe picked up the phone as Harry screamed at the top of his lungs. "Get out of the house! Use the back door! Run! Run! Don't stop! Go! Go! Go! Go!" At that very moment, Matt opened fire and sprayed a line of bullets across the van. Two of the men returned heavy fire into the dark. Bullets were flying in all directions, while the third man, who had full cover behind the van, raised the rocket launcher and fired.

The rocket roared into Joe's house, hitting dead center. The explosion was so powerful that it shattered the windows of the surrounding houses, pushing a ball of fire several hundred feet into the air. The house literally disappeared.

Harry jumped out of the van with a weapon in his hand as the white van drove away. Matt continued to fire until they were out of reach. He then turned toward the house, "Holy shit, the house is gone!"

"Yeah, it doesn't look good, does it, Matt?" They immediately radioed for help. As they started to shout for Joe and Tom, three fire trucks roared around the corner followed by four police cars. The people in the surrounding houses started to turn on their lights and opened their front doors to see what had happened.

Bill jumped out of one of the police cars and ran towards Joe's house. He looked at the house with a deep sense of fear in his heart. His eyes started to water as he turned toward Matt and Harry, almost not wanting to ask the question. "Did they get out?" His voice was a little broken, and he tried desperately to control his inner emotions.

"It happened pretty fast," Harry explained. "We had to make sure that the occupants in the white van were not Joe's neighbor. As soon as we confirmed that they had weapons we took immediate action. I did contact Joe and instructed him to leave the house. We told him to use the back entrance, but things happened so fast, I'm not sure if they got out in time."

Bill turned towards his men with as much strength as he could muster, "Get some flash lights and search the back of the house!"

Just then, Matt noticed two men walking down the street. As they passed the light pole, he saw that they were wearing boxer shorts and looked like they had just walked out of a coal bin. He immediately knew who they were. "Bill, you better get back here! You may have to make an arrest! There are two grown men walking down a public street wearing boxer shorts! Family or no family, the law is the law!" Matt and Harry started walking toward Joe and Tom.

As they approached, Harry yelled out, "where the hell did you go?"

"Well, you said run, and we heard the gunfire, so we just kept on running, and if we didn't see the police and fire-truck lights, we would probably still be running." Matt and Harry smiled as Joe continued, "Thanks for saving our lives."

"Well, to tell you the truth Joe, we didn't think you made it out. How the hell did you get out of the house so fast?"

"Fear," Joe explained. "We were motivated by fear."

As Bill joined the four, his eyes were still watery. Joe had a big smile on his face. "Bill, your eyes are a little watery. You're not going soft on me, are you?"

"Well, I could tell you that it was the smoke, but the truth of the matter is that you scared the crap out of me. You have no idea how happy I am to see you."

"I'm glad to see you too, Bill."

Tom took a deep breath and then let it out slowly, and with a bewildered look in his eyes, turned to Joe. "Joe, is this plan C or D?"'

By now, there were more than twenty FBI men on the scene, including Pete. He walked directly over to where Bill was standing. "Bill, we're going to have to get Tom and Joe into protective custody for their own safety until we find out what the hell is going on."

"Do you have any idea who may be involved?" Bill asked.

"Probably the same guys that we have under surveillance."

"Is it possible," Bill asked, "that these guys represent the Mideast oil sheiks, or whatever they call themselves? If Tom's theory is correct, they stand to lose trillions of dollars in oil revenues."

"No," Pete responded, "these guys are pure unadulterated terrorists. They do not negotiate, nor do they associate with anyone that's out of the clan. This was not a scare tactic, this was a hit."

Bill did not respond, he was simply too angry and too upset.

"Look Bill, why don't you just come down to headquarters with me? I'll bring you up to date on the case after I clear you with the agency."

"Thanks, Pete."

Joe walked over to where Bill and Pete were standing.

"I overheard what you said about the insurgents wanting to kill us,"

Joe said. "After my house was vaporized, we didn't have to bring Sherlock Homes in to figure out their intent. What I would like to know is, has your agency come up with a survival plan, noting that my favorite past-time is breathing in and breathing out."

Pete smiled.

"We would like to put you in a federal protection plan," Pete explained. "Of course, this is strictly voluntary. It will assure your safety, and at the same time give us an opportunity to make the connection between your science project and the assassins. You will be free to pursue your science project while under our protection, but you must understand that there is no way we're going to keep the White House out of this one, especially if your scientific findings are substantiated. We are here to help you. The only thing that I ask is that you keep this information under wraps until we get a handle on things."

"Time is not exactly on our side," Tom said.

"I understand Tom, but the fact that these people are after you tells me that whatever you found must have at least some validity, and if it affects national security, we're going to have to run any pertinent information through the proper channels."

"Sounds like red tape to me," Joe said.

Pete didn't respond.

"We have checked your credentials," Pete continued, "and found that you are both notable in your field of science. After two attempts on your life, we are convinced that whatever you're on to has got to be one hot potato."

Tom turned to Joe with the last bit of strength he could muster up for the day. "I think we should take Pete up on his offer. I don't think anyone is going to invite us into their house tonight. Not unless they're looking for a free demolition job."

"Joe, I want you and Tom to go with Pete," Bill urged. "It's for your own safety. I'll keep in touch with you."

Pete asked to speak to Tom and Joe privately. "Tom, now that both your houses were totally destroyed, the question is, can the documentation on your scientific project be reproduced within a reasonable time period, or even better, do you have another set of your research papers in a secured location? And if so, where would that be?"

Tom did not immediately respond, he knew that he gave a full set of documents to his friends John and Phil, but he was determined not to involve them. Tom was well aware of the fact that the FBI had good intentions. He was also convinced that they just wanted to help. However, he remembered the unconditional terms that the four men in the black suits had offered him back in the hotel. At this point, it was obvious that they did not know who Phil and John were, and the last thing he wanted to do was to expose their identity.

Tom's character was impeccable. If you asked him a question, he would give you an honest answer; however, as the situation presented itself, Tom felt justified in not exposing his colleagues. He had already met the bad guys, and he knew that he had to take their threats seriously. Tom was now convinced that these guys were prepared to kill anyone that did not cooperate with their demands.

"I conducted my studies at the University of Pittsburgh where I have a private office and share a workspace with other geologists," Tom responded.

"Where do you keep your research papers?" Pete asked.

"In the office," Tom said. "It's a secured space. The several copies of the study have been copied onto CD-ROMs."

Pete called to one of his agents with a sense of urgency "Matt! I want you to call the Pittsburgh office and tell them to secure the office where Tom Collins conducted his studies at the University of Pittsburgh. Tell them to bring packers. I want everything packed and labeled, and I mean I want everything! Scrap paper, the wastebasket, everything! Have your men ship the material to the secured location."

"Tom, do you have a contact name at the university?"

"Mike Holden is the university chief security officer. He's the person to contact. The night security agent is Jack Kennedy."

"I'll have that information forwarded to the Pittsburgh office."

"Tom," Pete continued, "are you sure that there is no one else involved with this project? You have to understand that these assassins are professionals, and it's not going take them a hell of a lot of time to find out who's involved with the operation."

"The university is where I keep my research," Tom insisted. "All the information concerning the study is in the Pittsburgh office."

Pete felt that Tom was protecting someone. He believed that he had good intentions, but was severely underestimating the organization that was trying to kill him. He continued to believe that Joe and Tom were not the only scientists involved with the study. Pete knew that without the FBI's protection, his friends could run into some serious trouble. He also knew that it was only a matter of time before the insurgents made the connections.

"OK, Tom, we'll let it go for now, but I'm warning you, without our protection, anyone else involved with this operation will be in grave danger. The people that we are dealing with are extremely sophisticated. When they put the pieces together, lives could be at stake."

Tom did not respond. He simply did not want John or Phil involved.

"It's getting late. We had better head out," Pete explained. "You and Joe will ride with Agent Grosso. I'll be in the car just behind you. There will be two additional cars riding in the front and rear of our vehicles. We don't expect any problems, but in the event we run into an unexpected situation, please do exactly what I tell you to do."

"What do you expect to happen?" Joe snapped.

"Like I said, Joe, we are not expecting anything to happen, but in the event that something does come up, it's important that you follow my instructions. Your life may depend on it."

"We have no problem with that," Joe said. "Let me see..." Joe continued. "Four FBI cars packed with agents. Our lives may depend on it! Is there something that you're not telling us, Pete?"

"No! Nothing like that, we are simply taking the normal precautionary steps to secure your safety."

"So you believe that there's a possibility that we may be attacked again tonight?" Joe asked.

"Do you want the absolute truth, Joe?"

"Yes! The truth always works."

"Yes. The answer is yes. We believe that, as long as you and Tom are not in a protected zone, we will be susceptible to an attack."

"Do you believe that there is a price on our heads?" Joe asked.

"No, this is not a contract for money. My guess is that whatever Tom has uncovered out there in those oil fields is somehow compromising whatever the insurgents have planned. However, we're not concerned about that right now, all we know is that these guys are trying to kill you and it's my job to keep you alive." Tom was visibly upset with Pete's continual use of the word "kill."

"Maybe they're just trying to use scare tactics," Tom responded.

"I don't think so," Joe said. "They blew my house to kingdom-come, and I don't believe that they're professional house demolition experts, if you get my drift. If Harry didn't call us, we would be well done by now."

"Look," Pete said. "Why don't you guys concentrate on your science project, and let me handle the insurgents?"

"You have a deal," said Tom, still a little apprehensive.

"I know you're trying to help Pete," Joe explained, "but if you tell us what's going on, we may have a better chance of surviving."

"When I find out what's going on, I promise to tell you, I just haven't figured things out yet. All we really know at this point is that the first bombing was probably initiated to destroy copies of Tom's work. The second bombing, however, was definitely an assassination attempt, and the hotel incident in Washington doesn't seem to have any connection with the insurgents at all. It could be connected to the oil companies, but at this point there's no evidence on the table. Both these groups are heavy hitters but, of the two, the insurgents are the most dangerous.

The fact that these groups are involved tells me that there is something big going on. I don't know what you found in those oil fields, but it's got to be big. I can assure you that Washington is going to want to know what's going on. Right now my priority is to get you to a safe haven as soon as possible."

"Thanks, Pete," Joe responded. "Sorry about the third degree, we appreciate everything that you're doing for us."

"Look," Pete said in a sincere manner, "everything is going to work out. I gave Bill my word that I would do everything in my power to protect you... Right now, we should really get going."

Tom and Joe got into the vehicles and headed out; however, Tom still felt somewhat apprehensive about what their next plan would be, and when that plan would be initiated. It seemed like every time they came up with a plan, they ran into another brick wall.

Tom was visibly upset. Every time we turn around there's another delay, and now we're involved with the FBI and Washington, which equates to a network of bureaucracies and more time lost.

Joe noticed that Tom's eyes were open, but that he wasn't looking at anything. It was as if someone had hypnotized him.

"Tom," Joe snapped, "you're thinking again, aren't you?"

"We are wasting a lot of time here. Now we're involved with the FBI and Washington, a political entanglement ruled by two parties that never agree on anything. It's where the oil company lobbyists hang out. I think this is a big mistake."

"No," Joe explained, "getting killed is a big mistake, because when you're dead time ceases to exist. Do you see how it works Tom? Pete has offered to protect us from the guys who are trying to kill us."

"OK Joe, I get the message, but we do have a problem and we're not going to resolve it if we continue to ride around from one place to another."

"Don't forget Tom, we are not prisoners, we are here voluntarily, and Pete did assure us that we would be able to continue our work."

"I don't mean to sound like a pessimist, but so far nothing has gone our way." Tom took in a deep breath of air and then let it out slowly, "I just hope this is not an omen for things to come."

"That's what I like about you Tom, you're always trying to cheer me up."

Tom smiled.

CHAPTER 4

The FBI team was headed toward a secure military base located in the town of Croton, Connecticut, which was about a forty-five minute drive. It was four-thirty a.m. when Pete received a call from agent Matt Johnson. Joe and Tom had already fallen asleep."Pete. I have very bad news: the office in Pittsburgh...," Matt paused for a moment, "the university."

"What's the matter?" Pete responded.

"It's not there."

"What do you mean it's not there?"

"Someone took half the building out! Tom's office is gone."

"Holy shit, that means we're in trouble!" Pete snapped.

"What do you mean we're in trouble?"

"I have this sixth sense that this same group of terrorist is going to try to take us out tonight!"

"What do you want me to do?" Mat asked.

"I want you to call the agents handling the case, and tell them to secure the site at the university and salvage whatever can be salvaged."

"The area is secured, but trust me Pete, there's nothing to salvage."

"Get a forensics team down there to comb the area. I want a thorough investigation of the entire site."

"That's already taken care of."

Pete paused for a moment in an effort to contemplate their next move. "Matt, listen, I'm on I-95 at exit 42, heading toward the safe house! Get here as soon as you can, meanwhile, I'll call headquarters for backup!"

"We're on our way," Matt said, "probably about twenty minutes."

Pete hung up and called headquarters.

"Hello, this is agent Marchel! I have an emergency! We're heading north on I-95, passing exit 42. I want you to get a couple of choppers in the air, and I also need some ground support. I believe the insurgents are going to attempt to take us out tonight, probably the same group that we have under investigation. I just turned my GPS locator on. Meanwhile, I want you to maintain our position and monitor all north bound traffic!"

"Yes sir."

"You better step on it Tony."

Agent Grosso radioed the other vehicles as he stepped on the gas.

Just then, Pete received a call from headquarters.

"Pete, we just picked up three vehicles on the screen. They're approximately a quarter of a mile behind you and catching up quickly. We have six cars on the way, and the helicopters should be there any minute."

"Joe, get-up and wake your buddy, we might have a problem!" Pete quickly explained the situation to them, including the bombing at the university.

Just in front of them, the driver of an eighteen wheeler suddenly turned the vehicle across the highway and blocked all three lanes. Two other unknown vehicles parked on both sides of the truck, blocking the two outside service lanes, totally sealing off the north bound lane. The first FBI car skidded and turned 180 degrees, running his rear end into the truck. The second car banged off the concrete divider and stopped 60 feet from the truck. Bullets were hitting the car as the agent's emerged from the vehicle fully armed and immediately returning fire.

Tony, knowing that there were three fast-moving cars behind him, hit the brakes and turned the wheel slightly to the right until the vehicle was moving sideways. He then stepped on the gas and ran the car into the woods and down an embankment, stopping just short of a six foot metal fence. The sound of heavy gunfire was deafening.

"Tony, get the automatic weapons out of the trunk!"

As Tony ran to the back of the vehicle, Pete looked up the embankment and saw four shadowed figures standing at the edge of the highway. When they opened fire, everyone hit the deck. He saw flames, and heard the sound of bullets hit the car and everything else around them. Tony and Pete returned fire with a steady barrage of bullets. As Pete moved to his right, a bullet ripped through his flesh. He immediately hit the deck.

"Tony, I'm hit!" Pete yelled. His adrenalin was pumping a million miles an hour as he lifted off the floor and continued to fire.

"Tom! Joe!" Pete snapped, "climb over this fence, and don't look back!"

Tom thought he should stay and help Pete.

"Let me help you Pete, you're bleeding!"

"If they take us, you're dead! Do you hear what I'm saying?" Pete shouted in a commanding voice. "Now climb over the damn fence and get the hell out of here! Stay off the main roads, and call the FBI or Bill when you feel it's safe. Now go! And stay out of sight!"

When the choppers showed up they immediately blew out the two cars to the right and left of the truck. The three vehicles that were following Pete's car fled when they spotted the choppers. The skirmish lasted twenty minutes, taking the lives of two agents and six terrorists.

Tony turned toward Pete and saw blood dripping from his finger tips. He quickly pulled the first aid kit from the trunk, and wrapped a bandage tightly around his arm to stop the bleeding. "How are you doing, Pete?"

"I just got shot, I lost two agents and I don't know where Joe and Tom are! How the hell do you think I'm doing?" There was a pause. Pete turned toward Tony. "Look, forget what I just said, that was the pain talking. You did a great job, Tony. I'm just pissed. You probably saved our lives."

"It's not over, Pete. We'll get these bastards! You get into the chopper and take care of your arm. I'll get some of the agents together and look for Joe and Tom."

"Call me as soon as you find them."

"You got it, Pete."

~~~~~~~~~~

Meanwhile, Tom and Joe were having a hell of a time as they ran through a wooded area in an effort to stay out of site. The night was pitch-dark as they continued to run through the woods, crashing into branches that ripped their clothing and bruised their skin.

"Look," Tom snapped, "there's a light just ahead of us."

"I don't know why," Joe said, "but that doesn't really excite me."

"What do you mean by that, do you think their waiting for us?"

"It doesn't matter Tom, if we continue through the woods in the dark, we'll probably bleed to death."

With only three hours of sleep, and total exhaustion, Tom could not help but to think that the glass was definitely half empty. "If they find us
~~~~~~~~~~

Joe, they're going to kill us. You know that, don't you?"

"Are you trying to cheer me up again?"

"Sorry Joe. Things are just not going well."

"Think about plan D, Tom."

"What's plan D?"

"I don't know, but it has to be a lot better than plan C..."

"Tom, I know where we are now. I have a lady friend I've been seeing on and off for the past six months. She lives about a mile from here. A couple of lefts, a couple of rights, and we're there."

"Joe, do you realize that it is almost five a.m.? Don't you think it's a little early to be dropping in on someone?"

"This is no time to be considerate," Joe said, "remember? The bad guys are chasing the good guys, and if they find us, they're going to kill us! That could be extremely detrimental to our health."

"Well, maybe we should look for a policeman patrolling the area, or even better, call the local police station," Tom suggested.

"Call the police station?" Joe snapped, "there were fourteen FBI agents assigned to protect us, carrying fully-loaded automatic weapons, and we barely escaped with our lives! You don't really expect a local cop carrying a .38 to hold these guys off, do you?"

"I'm just tired, Joe. Let's go to your friend's house. By the way, what's her name?"

"Her name is Angelina Rosselle; Angie for short."

"Is this the same girl that you've been talking about for the past two months?"

"Yeah, she's the one."

Tom smiled.

"You know, Joe, this is the first girl you've talked about since our college years. It sounds like you're in a serious relationship."

"Tom, please don't say anything. We haven't been dating that long, and I don't want to spook her."

"If you really love her Joe, you should tell her."

"She knows I love her. She just hasn't responded yet. I think she needs a little more time."

"I still believe you should tell her, but I do promise not to interfere."

Tom looked like he hadn't slept for a month. His clothes were torn, shredded and stained. They both looked like refugees. Joe smiled when he noticed that Tom was trying to make himself look presentable. You would think he had a date with the Queen of Sheba. He was hand combing his hair, dusting his clothes off, cleaning his shoes on his pants and not looking any better for his effort.

"Wow! You look a lot better Tom, I'm really impressed. Are you planning on stealing my girl?"

"No, no, no, nothing likes that! I was just..."

"Relax, Tom! It's a joke. We're here."

Tom could not believe his present circumstance. Here he was a renowned scientist with leaves in his hair, preparing to meet Joe's girl friend for the first time at five in the morning. What was he going to say to her? Hi Angie, Joe and I spent the night in the woods and decided to have breakfast at your place at five in the morning. I hope this is not an inconvenience for you.

"Tom what are you smiling about?"

"Oh, nothing important. I was just thinking about what to say to your friend. You know, make a good impression."

"You've got to be kidding me."

"Yes, Joe, just kidding."

~~~~~~~~~~

Angie was a nickname that agreed with her. At five-foot-six and one hundred twenty pounds, she had light blue eyes and a body that could stop a clock; she was an absolute beauty. Angie received her law degree at Yale University, and at twenty-nine, she defended clients that for the most part could not afford to pay their bills.

She had fallen deeply in love with Joe, but felt that the relationship was too young for her to reveal such feelings. Additionally, she did not want to scare him off. To her, Joe was a handsome guy with a great sense of humor. He was physiologically in-tune to what was going on around him, and he was always kind and considerate to others. No matter how uptight or frustrated she became, when Joe walked through the door, she knew that everything would be all right again.

Joe's feelings were similar; he was absolutely in love with Angie. The only difference was that he took it for granted that she knew. He felt that Angie liked him, but might not be ready to make any type of serious commitment. This was a relationship that was waiting for the truth to set them free.
~~~~~~~~~~

CHAPTER 5

Joe rang the bell, and waited, and then rang the bell again. Tom noticed a front window curtain moved slightly, as if someone in the house was trying to view whoever was ringing the bell. Five minutes passed. He rang again.

"Joe! Please don't ring the bell again. She already knows you're here."

"What do you mean she knows I'm here?"

"Keep it down Joe, or you'll wake the entire neighborhood. What I mean is that she peeked out of the window about ten minutes ago."

"Then why are we still standing out here?"

"She's probably fixing herself up." Just then, the door opened.

"Hi Angie, I know this is not exactly a good hour for you, but we have sort of an emergency. This is Tom Collins, the fellow I told you about. May we come in?"

Angie was ecstatic. When she looked into Joe's eyes, calmness came over her. She had a soft glaze in her eyes that gave you a sense that she was really happy to see him. Angie simply stood there and stared at him as if he hadn't said anything. At that moment, Tom thought, Joe could have showed up at Angie's house day or night and have been welcomed with open arms. God! She even fixed herself up before answering the door. I think when I get Joe alone, I'm going to hit him over the head with a hammer to bang some of the nuts and bolts back where they belong. This girl is not in love with him, she's madly in love with him.

"It is certainly a pleasure to finally meet you Angie. Joe has told me so much about you. I apologize for the hour and the attire, but as Joe said, we are here because of an unfortunate circumstance."

"Oh! I'm sorry, Tom," Angie said when she realized that Tom was speaking to her. "Please come in."

"Joe has told me so much about you that I feel we have already met."

Angie was happy to hear that Joe was talking about her. She thought that it was a pretty good sign that he really cared.

Joe leaned over and gave Angie a kiss on the lips that lasted just a little longer than the typical peck-and-run kiss that was normally exchanged by married couples.

We are finally in the house, Tom thought, as he sat down in the first chair he could find.

Angie handed Tom a bath towel and a set of casual clothes that had previously been stored in a spare bedroom by Joe. She walked into the kitchen to put on the coffee and make some breakfast while Joe explained to her the events of the past three days. As he completed his story, he noticed that there was a single tear running down Angie's cheek. He walked over to her and held her in his arms. She hung on to him. Angie was unable to say anything for fear of becoming too emotional. Joe looked into her big beautiful blue eyes, which were still watery. "Please don't worry Angie, everything will be all right. Tom and I are well aware of what we are up against. I assure you that we will take every precaution necessary to protect ourselves." Joe paused for a moment. He was not quite sure how much to tell her.

"Why are these people trying to kill you?" Angie said, seeming somewhat perplexed.

Joe walked over and sat beside her. "I don't have all the answers at this point, but I believe it has something to do with Tom's thesis."

Angie stood there not really sure how to interrupt Joe's response.

"Tom has just completed a two year geological study and has definitive evidence that molten lava is moving from the mantle of the planet to the surface of the planet through newly formed cracks in the earth's crust."

"That just doesn't seem like a reason someone would want to kill you."

"I agree," Joe said. He paused for a moment and then responded in a low, calm voice. "Tom's thesis attributes the newly formed cracks in the crust to the extraction of oil over the past one-hundred-years. He further concludes that, unless all future oil extraction is stopped, and the previous resulting damage is not repaired, surface temperatures could reach two-hundred to five-hundred degrees in less than four years. I have personally studied his work in depth and concur with his findings. The only issue that we differ on is the time element. Tom believes we have three or four years before temperatures on the planet become critical, while I believe that we have less than two and a half years."

"And exactly what are we to expect?" Angie asked.

"We'll experience an increased in seismic activity, which will lead to an increase in volcanic eruptions and earth-quakes throughout the globe. In time, molten lava will break through the earth's crust causing severe global warming. This will also cause a meltdown of the caps, rising water levels and more."

Angie was taken aback. She knew that Joe would not exaggerate the facts on such an important issue. Angie stood silent for a moment. She believed what he said, but needed some time to digest the seriousness of the matter. She had a hard time converting Joe's words into any type of emotion.

"Are you alright, Angie?"

"Yes, yes, I'm fine. I still don't understand why anybody would want to kill you. Why don't we simply fix the problem? If it gets a little warmer, we can just turn up the air-conditioning."

"Well," Joe said, "it's not quite that simple." He held her in his arms. She welcomed the affection. "Temperatures could rise to between 200 to 500 degrees if we don't develop a course of action to resolve the problem."

Angie was not happy to hear the bad news, but was grateful for the trust Joe had in her. She was resolved to do whatever she could to help them.

"Thank you for trusting me Joe."

He smiled.

"The first thing we have to do is find a safe haven," Joe explained, "and it's not here! It will have to be a place that we can communicate from without being detected, and the location has to be one that cannot be easily traced. We do not know where that someplace is yet. But one thing for sure, Angie, I do not want you even remotely involved."

"What do you mean you don't want me involved?" She snapped.

"It's just simply too dangerous."

Angie had a look of anger on her face. Her Italian temper really started to flare. There was definitely some seismic activity brewing within her.

"Now let me see if I understand this correctly; you want me to stay here in this house while you go out and save the world? And I'll just go on practicing law knowing that life as we know it may come to an abrupt end? And of course, while you are saving the world, I won't know whether you're dead or alive? That's just a great plan! And don't forget, if you happen to make it back alive, and you want to see me again, you'll have to bring candy and flowers to the mental ward where I'll be recovering from a nervous breakdown! Do you really believe that I have no capabilities?"

"No! That is not what I believe. I just don't want anything to happen to you," Joe responded in a compassionate tone, as he continued to explain himself. "The guys that are after us are cold-blooded killers. It's not like in the movies where the good guys always win. I don't know how this is going to turn out. We don't even have a destination." Joe paused for a moment as he paced the floor, thinking of what to say next. "Angie, two FBI guys are already dead. They blew up our homes, and they're not going to stop until they get us."

She allowed Joe to finish what he had to say, and then calmly responded.

"How long do you think it will take them before they know who I am? A day, a week, maybe even a month? Can't you see Joe? We are in this together. I'll be safer with you than if I stay in this house."

At this point, Joe really felt like crap. He never gave a thought to the fact that they would ever make the connection between him and Angie; however, he knew now that he was wrong. What have I done! I put the woman I love in jeopardy. So many mistakes! How am I ever going to make a plan that could possibly work?

Angie knew that Joe was under a great deal of pressure, and did not intend to further complicate his life. She loved him and wanted to help. Angie was as practical as Joe. Her thought process was simple: first, save the world, then, marry Joe. Besides she thought if by some chance things did not go well, I would at the very least like to spend whatever time I have left with the man I love.

Just then, Tom walked into the kitchen looking somewhat refreshed. "I'm as hungry as a horse! By the way Angie, I really appreciate your hospitality. I'm sorry we had to meet under such adverse circumstances."

She smiled. "I have ham and eggs on the stove, and you're welcome. And if you stop apologizing, I'll allow you to stay!"

"Sorry about that."

Joe laughed.

"Tom you're still apologizing. By the way Tom, Angie is coming with us."

MELTDOWN

Angie was beside herself. She was as happy as any one person could be in a single moment. She ran over to Joe, threw her arms around him and gave him a big kiss.

"Joe, do you really think this is a wise decision. Did you explain the danger, the past events, the..."

"Tom! You don't understand, as soon as they link her to me, she'll be in grave danger. We're dealing with professionals. It will just be a matter of time before they make the connection. I just can't take that chance. We have to take her with us!"

Tom had a somber look on his face.

"Angie I'm..."

"Tom! Remember, we have a deal? No more apologizing."

"Yes, Angie, we do have a deal. I'm really happy to be here, and grateful for your hospitality."

Angie smiled, "More coffee, Tom?"

~~~~~~~~~~

Joe ran off to clean up as Tom finished breakfast.

Angie started to put together the things she thought that she would need for what she knew would be a lengthy trip. She also called an old college friend, Ron Massey, who she had met at Yale. Angie had kept in touch with him through the years knowing that she might very well have been the only real friend he had. She explained the situation to him. At first he was a little reluctant, but he simply could not turn her down. She made arrangements to take Joe and Tom out to his place. Ron assured her that his pad was the safest place on the planet, but more so, she knew that he would be an asset to their project.

Ron was an absolute genius in the field of computer science. He majored in the sciences of ecology, energy and environmental studies. Unfortunately or fortunately, he was a little paranoid when it came to governmental agencies and big business entities. He simply did not trust them. As he saw it, big-business continually destroyed the Earth's delicately balanced environment under the premise of profits first and the environment second. Ron was angry as hell at the government agencies that were protecting these guys. It was simple: big profits equaled healthier stock markets, which in turn, enhanced political funding. The key objective here was reelection, and to hell with the environment! To big business, the environmental damage caused by the burning of fossil fuel, mine striping, the dumping of chemical waste, ocean pollution, the
~~~~~~~~~~

destruction of wetlands, air pollution and deforestation were problems that were over-exaggerated. In his view, they were just a bunch of greedy bastards. From their prospective, they had a responsibility to their stock holders. After all, when someone invests in your stock, they expect to make a profit. The concern was not whether or not their grandchildren and future generations after them would have to deal with catastrophic, and in many cases, irreversible environmental damage to the planet, but rather to protect their bottom line.

Ron concluded that the present generation either did not know, or simply did not care.

He was outraged that a country that contains less than two percent of the world's population could consume almost forty percent of the world's natural resources.

Ron was also an avid fan of astronomy, and spent his leisurely hours looking through his telescope at the great domain of lights that lit up the night sky. When he viewed Mars, he saw a planet that did not have the ability to sustain life. He called it uninhabitable real estate. He believed that, without intervention, the planet we call Earth could suffer the same consequence. He was dedicated to protecting and preserving the environment for all future generations to come.

After graduating college, Ron worked for several environmental groups, but found that the bureaucracy in such organizations inhibited his ability to make a significant contribution in his quest to stop environmental abuse.

When the government offered to auction off several concrete bunkers that were built during World War Two, Ron became a low bidder on a bunker located in New Mexico. He bought it at a fraction of what it cost, and then converted the bunker into a laboratory communication center that included the latest technology in computer engineering, communications systems and geological equipment.

For the past six years, he had published a monthly environmental newsletter that identified environmental damage caused by private businesses and governments throughout the world. Numerous injunctions and lawsuits had been filed against his publication to no avail because the pertinent law enforcement agencies could not locate him. To keep the authorities from tracing his whereabouts, Ron hacked into secured networks such as governmental agencies, military bases, oil companies, banks and a number of other networks to publish his newsletter.

The authorities had been trying to track him down for the past five years without success. They have labeled him an environmental crusader because he never entered any top secret program, injected viruses into the system, stolen documents or transferred funds. However, because he has been hacking into secured networks, the charges against him were extremely serious.

At five foot-ten inches, 130 pounds, Ron looked like he was suffering from malnutrition. He had grown his hair down to his shoulders, and wore thick prescription glasses. He had the ability to hold a conversation on five different subjects at the same time, and if you take more than two minutes to explain your point of view, you lost him.

Ron was somewhat of an introvert and did not make friends easily; in fact, he found most people he met to be extremely boring. However, he had a great deal of admiration for Angie, and considered her his best friend. Ron particularly admired her common-sense-direct-approach method for resolution. He always knew that she would make a great lawyer.

"Joe, can I have a private word with you?" Angie whispered.

"Sure," Joe said as they both walked into the kitchen.

"Tom, why don't you the turn the TV on and see if you can find some news on that I-95 incident. I'm just going to have a word with Angie, we'll be right back."

As they entered the kitchen, Joe looked into Angie's eyes with a big smile on his face.

"What is it Angie, what's the big secret?"

"I called a friend of mine who agreed to let us use his facility. It meets all the criteria you had mentioned earlier."

"Where is it located?" Joe asked.

"The facility is located in New Mexico, just south of Roswell. It is a World War Two bunker that was converted into a scientific communication center and is fully equipped with the most modern equipment available."

"It sounds like it'll work, but why are we whispering?"

"Sorry, Joe," Angie said apologetically, "but I gave my word to Ron that I would not diverge the location of his facility until we arrived..."

"Why is it such a big secret?" Joe asked.

"All I can tell you is that the scientific work that he is involved with is highly classified."

"This guy is not with the Russian mafia or anything like that?" Joe asked, with a big smile on his face.

Angie had a surprised look on her face.

"Just kidding, Angie, it sounds like this could really work for us." Joe gave her a big hug and kissed her passionately on the lips.

Just then they heard Tom yelling out to them.

"Joe! You had better get here," Tom shouted, "the I-95 incident is on the news."

Joe and Angie hurried into the family room where Tom had the TV tuned into the five o'clock morning news.

"The shoot-out on I-95 last night took the lives of two FBI agents and six members of a known terrorist group that had been surveillanced by the FBI for several months. The incident occurred between three and four a.m. this morning.

Agent Pete Marchel, who was in command of the operation, was wounded during the incident, but has now been listed in satisfactory condition and should be release from the hospital late this afternoon."

The news went on to explain how the FBI successfully foiled a major terrorist plot.

Tom breathed a sigh of relief. "That's really good news. I'm glad Pete is all right. I can understand why the FBI didn't reveal all the facts. They would have had to explain why two geologists were involved with a FBI take-down of a terrorist group."

"That," Joe responded, "and not wanting anyone to know that the world was coming to an end."

"Of course," Tom said. "And we're all going to die. Isn't that right, Joe?"

Angie had a worried look on her face, but remained silent.

"Don't worry Angie, we're just kidding. The plan is to find a solution."

"I guess we had better start talking about what we're going to do next," Tom suggested.

"Is there any way for you to duplicate the package?" Joe asked.

"That would be impossible. It would take six months or more to put a new package together. Most importantly, we are not going to have the same freedom and access to oil sites and other equipment necessary to gather the required evidence and proofs."

"Well, I guess that narrows our options down to John and Phil, they're the only ones that have a full copy of the package.

Angie, I'm going to need you to drive us over to Phil's house to pick up the packages. From there, we're going to drive to your friend's place, so we had better pack the van and lock the house down."

"I've already made arrangements with a friend to look after things,"

Angie said, "so whenever you're ready, we can leave."

Tom was a little puzzled.

"Where are we going after we pick up the packages? What's our destination?"

"I'll explain everything to you in the van," Joe said, "I think, right now, it's important that we get started."

They immediately packed the van and headed towards Phil's house. Tom and Joe sat down in back of the van to avoid being identified.

"Do you think we should contact the FBI," Tom asked "to let them know that we're still alive?"

"Not right now," Joe said, "I actually believe we can get more accomplished where we're going."

As they approached Phil's house, Joe asked Angie to wait in the van. "We're just going to say a few words to Phil, pick up the package and leave." Just then, the front door opened and out stepped Phil and John. Tom and Joe were really happy to see them. The four embraced each other as if they had just returned from a war. Phil had a big grin on his face.

"What the hell have you guys been up to? Your houses were blown up. Your lab was blown up and the house bombings have been front page news. Now don't tell me that you weren't involved with that shootout on I-95."

"Yes, we were there," Joe responded.

"I have to tell you," Phil said sounding somewhat relieved, "you scared the crap out of us! We didn't know whether you guys were alive or dead."

By this time, John's emotions were surfacing. "Next time guys, do me a favor, CALL!" Tom tried to calm John down. "You have to understand, John, we couldn't communicate over a public communication system for fear of being traced. The last thing we wanted was for them to know that we were connected in any way with you or Phil. And secondly, we certainly did not want them to know that you were in possession of the only two packages remaining. With the houses and lab blown out, you and Phil had the only surviving documents."

"I understand Tom, it's just that...not knowing where you guys were, or knowing whether you were alive or dead, it was nerve-racking. I mean, there were nights I couldn't sleep. Phil, tell them!"

"Well," Phil responded, "the most important thing is that they're finally here. So what's the next move? Where are we going?"

"What do you mean, 'Where are we going?'," Joe said. "Are you guy's nuts? Don't you realize that they tried to kill us on three separate occasions?"

"We have already committed ourselves to the project," Phil said, "and we're still willing to take the risk."

"Absolutely not," Tom said, "it's just not safe!"

"Tom, they're part of the team," Joe stated, "it has always been their choice."

"Yeah, that was before they tried to kill us."

"No, Tom! They have a right to participate. It has always been the four of us."

"Yes, it has always been the four of us," Tom said reluctantly. "We had better get started."

Joe walked back to the van and told Angie that Phil and John were going to join them. He then turned to John. "What about your wife and kids?" Joe inquired.

"I sent them up state a week ago to her parent's house. I gave Joan enough information for her to realize the importance of this mission. She wasn't overjoyed, but she understood."

"How about you Phil, are there any problems?" Joe asked.

"Not really; I'm single with no obligations."

Tom did not respond. He knew Joe was right, they needed all the help they could get.

"I better ask Angie to come into the house," Joe said, "while you both pack."

"We are already packed," Phil said with a smile.

"We have been packed for days," John added.

"By the way, who's Angie?" Phil asked..

"She's a friend," Tom explained in a low whisper. "A really, really close friend. You see Phil, they both love each other, but neither one knows it."

"Funny, funny, funny," Joe murmured. "OK guys, let's head out."

"Where are we headed?" Phil asked.

"According to Angie, we are heading to a safe house," Joe explained. "She promised me that we would not be disappointed. I'll explain everything to you in the van." Joe looked at his watch as he pulled out of the driveway. It was nine-forty-five a.m. He knew the trip would take thirty hours and take them through nine states.

They pulled out of the driveway and headed for the highway. The plan was not to stop, with the exception of rest areas and gas stations. It was imperative that the team reached their destination without being detected.

CHAPTER 6

Joe brought Phil and John up to date on what had transpired over the past three days. He wanted them to have a clear understanding of the horrendous danger they would be facing.

"Another important issue," Joe explained, "is security. For obvious reasons, it is important that we reach our destination incognito. Angie is pretty much an expert in this field. Please pay attention, this is really important."

"Thank you, Joe," Angie said with a smile. "I'm sure that we can all agree that our adversaries are well-trained assassins, and that the three assassination attempts pretty much confirm their true intent. Extreme conditions call for extreme measures. I have developed a number of precautionary measures that we should take to protect the safety of this team. As a trial lawyer, I have learned how to place witnesses, relevant to a case at a specific location, in a precise time period. First, do not communicate with anyone. Any direct contact that you have with a stranger will enhance that person's memory. At a later date, that person will be able to identify you from a picture, in the event your pictures are posted on any type of wanted or missing persons list. It is imperative that we are not identified! Secondly, no telephone calls. We cannot communicate with anyone, and it doesn't matter whether you utilize a public or cell phone. The telephone numbers you're calling could have been tapped by now, which means, that all telephone calls, regardless of whether they are incoming or out-going, can be traced and time-logged.

So, please keep your cell phones on the off mode."

"Can we receive calls from hard-wired systems?" John asked. "That would at least give us the opportunity to know if a family member was trying to reach us."

Angie smiled. "It's just too risky, John. The surveillance equipment today is simply too sophisticated."

"Other traceable items are credit cards, or any other type of card that has a code on it. This means all transactions must be made in cash. In addition, we must avoid being filmed by public surveillance cameras. These mechanisms are time logged. We must fuel up at gas stations that are not equipped with surveillance cameras, and we absolutely cannot stop at a hotel, motel, breakfast house or any other premise that falls into that category. They all have cameras, and they all require a credit card for check-in. In other words, gentlemen, with the exception of off-the -road rest stops and small-town gas stations, this van must not stop until we reach our destination. And one more thing, we absolutely cannot speed or violate any other traffic ordinance that may potentially put us in contact with the local authorities! A police record, regardless of the violation, is a traceable document. This means that the designated driver must obey the local traffic laws at all times. Even a minor infraction could potentially expose our location, so be sure to stop at stop signs and yellow lights. Oh, and keep your seat belt on at all times. Are there any questions?"

John and Phil both clapped.

Angie just smiled.

After a moment of silence, Joe turned to Angie with a slight grin on his face.

"Thanks, Angie, I think you covered just about everything. Am I to understand that we will be staying in the van most of the time?"

"Yes. I promised Ron that the location of his facility would not be compromised. I had to assure him that we would take every precaution possible."

"I have no objection with Ron's request," Joe said, "but I think we should add a few items to the list."

"What would you like to add?" Angie asked, sounding somewhat apprehensive. "Did I miss something?"

"Nothing to do with security dear, but I think that we should all agree that no one, and I mean absolutely no one, will be permitted to eat beans, garlic, broccoli or any other type of food that can result in, or may cause anyone in this van to have an explosive reaction!"

Angie, who was expecting a serious criticism, broke out into hysterical laughter, which caused the guys to also laugh out loud. Even Joe started laughing. It was apparent that they were all over tired and were simply laughing for the sake of laughing.

The team agreed to break the driving into twelve hour shifts, Joe and Angie taking the first shift. This would allow their buddies to rest in-between shifts. John and Phil, who agreed to take the second shift, decided to take a cat-nap while Tom and Joe discussed possible solutions to the problem.

They had stopped several times for gas and coffee. After twelve hours of driving, and just before reaching Indianapolis, Indiana, they pulled into a small gas station, gassed up, and turned the driving over to John and Phil. It was ten pm. The skies were clear and a full moon illuminated the highway, making it a lot easier for Phil to see the road.

As they were nearing Tulsa, Oklahoma on I-44 West, they saw flashing lights that appeared to be coming from five to six police cars parked just in front of a set of barricades that funneled traffic into a single lane, backing up traffic approximately a quarter of a mile. As they moved closer and closer to the police vehicles, they could see the flashing arrows directing them into one lane.

There were police standing on both sides of the lane, checking each vehicle as they passed. Angie and Joe had already been awake for several hours. They were all a little nervous, especially Angie.

"This is just what we don't need," she whispered.

"Let's not panic," Joe said, "we are in traffic and have no choice except to pass the police line." He then turned to Angie. "As soon as the car stops, I want you to jump in the driver's seat. Phil, I think you should sit back here with us. If they ask you where you're going, Angie, tell them we're heading to Phoenix."

As soon as the car stopped, in what was now stop-and-go traffic, they made the switch.

"It doesn't look like they're questioning anyone," Angie responded. "They're just looking into each car. I believe they're looking for a particular person. I know we are all a little nervous, but please, try to stay calm. The police can spot a nervous face a mile away."

Joe immediately started telling jokes in a loud voice. Just before they passed the police, Tom, Phil, and John almost simultaneously asked Joe to shut up. They passed the roadblock without incident. John then turned to Joe and whispered, "nice distraction." However, Angie was concerned when she caught sight of the police surveillance cameras. She was not quite sure whether they were on or off. Angie decided not to tell the boys. She felt that they had enough problems to deal with. Besides, there wasn't much she could do about it.

Five hours later, they entered the state of New Mexico. Angie was behind the wheel now. As they neared the end of 70-West, she remembered the area. Angie had visited Ron several times before and remembered that once off the highway there were a couple of tricky turns to make on roads that were not marked. She passed the town of Roswell and went south on Route 285, then turned off onto unpaved back roads.

Tom had a big smile on his face. "It looks more like we're going to visit Wyatt Earp and the Dalton gang, or one of those boys. Where the hell does this guy live?"

John laughed.

"He must have coyotes for neighbors," Phil said, scratching his head. "I just can't believe people live out here."

"I wonder what these people do for fun," John said laughing.

"You have a point, John," Phil responded, "it looks like Roswell is the 'Ya-Hoo' town if you're looking for a good time. I'll be hanging with a bunch of people that are waiting for Aldo the Space Cadet to show up." By this time, Joe was smiling from ear to ear.

"Phil," Joe said, "think of the assortment of personalities you'll be able to date."

"Yeah, I can't wait to find out what an encounter of the fourth-kind feels like..."

"It's not encounters of the fourth-kind," John snapped. "It's an encounter of the third- kind."

Phil smiled. "You don't understand, John. I know what an encounter of the third-kind is, and it's just not my cup of tea. I'm more interested in showing some gal what an encounter of the fourth-kind is all about."

"What the heck is an encounter of the fourth-kind?" John asked, "I never heard of that one..."

Phil now had a big fat grin on his face. "John, if you don't know what an encounter of the fourth kind is, it simply means that you are a happily married man!"

"Thanks, I assume that's a good thing."

"We're here, guys!" Angie shouted.

Phil looked puzzled. "Joe? This is it? You have to be kidding me. It's a forty by twenty-five foot shack with steel pipes sticking up out of the ground."

Tom was beside himself. "How are we going to accomplish anything out here? This is just not going to work! We have a giant task to accomplish in a facility that is just not going to meet our needs. Joe, what were you thinking?"

"Relax guys; Angie assured me that this place would well exceed your expectations. Don't extend your lack of confidence any further than you already have, because in about five minutes you will all be apologizing."

Angie pulled the car into the garage, a separate structure about ten feet from the house. She wanted to eliminate the possibility of the car being identified. They were all happy to be somewhere other than in the car.

"This is it boys," Angie said smiling.

"That's what worries me," Tom said, seeming somewhat disappointed, "that this is it."

Angie opened the door and entered the premise with the boys following close behind. The interior looked like it needed a paint job. There was one bathroom, two bedrooms, a kitchen/dining area and a family room with a large fireplace. The place was fully furnished, but did not look lived in.

Tom looked around and said, "OK, now what?"

"The furniture," John said scratching his head, "looks like it was built during the civil war."

Just then, Angie asked everyone to follow her into what looked like a large walk-in closet. She instructed them to stand on a carpet that lay in the center of the floor. They followed her instructions and seemed to be somewhat puzzled, but as soon as she closed the door, the floor started to move downward. They all had a stupid grin on their face as the elevator descended. Joe and Angie were grinning from ear to ear as the elevator reached the bottom.

"Prepare yourselves, gentlemen," Angie said in a happy voice, "you're about to enter the twilight-zone!"

CHAPTER 7

As they looked around, they found themselves surrounded by concrete walls that reached twenty-five feet to the ceiling. Directly behind them was a chrome metal sliding door that stood ten feet high and eight feet wide. Phil nudged Joe with his elbow. "Don't tell me, Joe, Batman and Robin are not imaginary figures; they actually live here?"

"We'll, I don't know about that, but according to Angie, this guy Ron has some pad."

The sliding doors started to open from the center, letting in a bright ray of light.

As they stepped out of the elevator, Joe put his arm around Angie, "Angie, I believe we are in the Land of Oz"

The hallway walls were covered with solid chrome sheet panels. All of the ceilings stood 18 feet high, and were one solid mass of light covered by transparent reflector panels that seemed to enhance the intensity of light. The floors were pure white and seamless. They were made from a non-toxic fire retardant rubber compound that slightly depressed when walked on.

The facility had a sophisticated temperature control and air purification system that was powered by four liquid-hydrogen-fueled generators which ran alternately, providing the necessary power for the entire complex. The sound proofing in the mechanical room was so efficient that noise levels outside the room could not be measured.

There were eight identical bedrooms, each with their own bathroom.

The rooms were equipped with a computer, printer and a 4 x 6-foot movie screen that allowed the occupant to view movie sound tracks from six separate nature scenes. There was also a selection of more than six thousand movies that included documentaries and educational films.

The working lab exemplified the true genius behind the entire complex. The electronic and communication systems were engineered to eliminate the possibility of transmission signals being traced back to the facility. Ron Massey had also permanently tapped into the satellite surveillance camera system, utilizing a network of diversions that automatically changed signal patterns periodically, to avoid detection. He utilized this system to monitor catastrophic events occurring throughout the world and to document man's continual efforts to destroy the environment.

Ron greeted Angie and her guests as they walked off the elevator. He was really happy to see her, and gave her a big hug. "It's so good to see you, Angie."

"It's good to see you too Ron. I'd like to introduce you to my friends. This is Joe Solino..."

"Thanks for having us."

"Tom Collins..." Angie continued.

"A pleasure to finally meet you," Tom responded.

"John Mason..."

"Good to meet you, and thanks for your help."

"And this is Phil Dayne."

"We certainly under-estimated the extent of your facility, I'm really impressed."

After Ron greeted each of his guests, he walked them into a circular part of the hallway that had connecting hallways leading to the bedrooms, dining area and the lab.

"There are eight bedrooms down this corridor," Ron explained, "each of the rooms are identical, so it doesn't really matter which one you choose. After you have unpacked and refreshed yourselves we can all meet in the dining area, which is down this corridor."

They again thanked Ron for his hospitality, then headed toward the bedrooms, that is, all except Angie. She walked to the dining area with Ron.

"I have to tell you Angie, I am really excited about working with your friends. I took the liberty of gathering information on each of them and found that they are all at the very top in their particular fields of study. I also discovered that the FBI has launched a major in-house search for Joe and Tom; however, their identifying summary sheet has a peculiar designation on it that states, 'find and protect.' I also have intercepted messages from what seems to be a terrorist group. Unfortunately, they would like to see your friends terminated."

"How in the world do you pick up coded messages from terrorist groups?" Angie asked.

"That's simple; I enter thousands of decoding sequences with designated target names. If I hit a decoding designation, the message is automatically decoded and printed."

"You will never cease to amaze me."

"Are you trying to butter me up for something that you haven't told me about yet?"

"No, Ron, nothing like that. I'm just kidding." She paused for a moment and then turned towards him. "I know how important your work is, and I know how difficult this decision was for you to make. Thanks for saying yes. They are working on an extremely important project and are going to need your help."

"Let's talk about Joe; what's the story?"

"There is not much to say, except that I really love him."

"Will this love thing affect our friendship?" Ron snapped.

"Absolutely not," Angie said, with a big smile on her face.

"OK," Ron said. "Then as far as I'm concerned, you can continue to love him."

"Well, thanks," Angie responded in an excited voice, "such an outburst of affection."

Ron smiled. "I do tend to get a little emotional at times, don't I? I'm not trying to change the subject Angie, but it's just that I want to participate in whatever your friends are trying to accomplish."

"Ron, you are already an important part of the team. They are going to need you more than you can possibly know. Their only concern is going to be your safety. The people that are after them want them, and anyone associated with them, dead. You'll be putting yourself in a high-risk situation."

Ron looked at her, seeming a little confused. "Did you say, 'High risk situation'? Angie, I'm known in the industry as the 'Environmental Crusader'. I'm not only wanted by the FBI, but there are at least a dozen large corporations out there that would like to see me dead. Adding one more adversary to the list at this point is just semantics."

Ron felt her emotion; she is truly a good friend, "Angie, you are being extremely considerate and I appreciate your concerns. I am not quite sure what your friends are up to, but whatever it is, I know that it's big and I know it's important, but most of all, I know that it has something to do with the environment, and that's what I do, the environment. I want in, and I want you to tell them so."

As Tom walked toward the dining area, he overheard the last part of Ron's conversation.

"You would be more than welcome to join the team, Ron, but first I had better explain to you what our situation is. You may very well have second thoughts."

"I have a pretty good idea what you're up against," Ron explained. "Angie did explain a few things to me, and as a trusted friend, I know that she has not explained to you what I have been doing in this underground mausoleum for the past nine years."

Tom smiled, but did not respond.

"I am known as the 'Environmental Crusader,'" Ron continued in an exuberant manner, "I hack into highly-secured computer systems for the purpose of exposing environmental abuse by mostly mega corporations. I also hack into federal, state and city environmental regulatory agencies to expose internal corruption. In essence, I expose governmental officials that negate the prosecutions of major environmental infractions for political contributions and envelopes filled with cash."

"The point being," Angie said, addressing Tom, "if the FBI finds Ron, he will probably spend the remainder of his life in prison, but even worse, if big business gets a hold of him, well, use your imagination."

"Well, then it's settled," Tom said. Just then, Joe, Phil and John walked into the room. They all looked refreshed.

"Angie," Joe said, "I placed your bags in a room that is the third door down to the left. Why don't you go ahead and freshen up? I promise you won't miss anything."

"Thanks, Joe. By the way, what room are you in?"

"Second door, left."

Angie just smiled as she walked to her room.

~~~~~~~~~~

Tom sat at the head of the table and handed Ron a copy of his study.

"This package contains a documented study that identifies the cause of what could very well be irreversible damage to the Earth's crust. I sincerely
~~~~~~~~~~

believe that the crust of the planet is literally breaking up. It appears that the voids created by the removal of petroleum are causing cracks to occur from the mantle to the planet's surface. I believe that the study will prove that the voids within the planet's crust that were created as a result of the extraction of oil are now causing the seismic plates to become critically unstable. I have identified large cave-ins within these voids that seem to extend past the actual voids. These cave-ins and cracks are now being filled with molten lava from the mantle, and if not contained, this lava will eventually seep to the surface of the planet, but more alarmingly, the flow of lava is also making its way to once dormant volcanoes, and recently unknown fault lines. Presently, the seepage of lava in the oceans is more prevalent than on land because the ocean's crust is much thinner, where in some cases, the crust is actually non-existent." Tom paused for a moment to gather his thoughts, and then continued.

"Unfortunately, this increased movement in seismic plate activity has recently become more volatile, which is seriously accelerating the rate of flow. The bottom line is, unless we can come up with a solution, surface temperature is going to seriously increase over a relatively short time period."

"What kind of temperatures are we talking about?" Ron asked in a serious manner. "Are we talking a few degrees?"

"The planet will be uninhabitable," Tom quickly responded, "within three to four years, temperatures could easily exceed two to three hundred degrees. Even if one were to argue against my theory, I have taken sonar reading that definitively confirmed that lava is presently making its way toward the surface of the planet. I also have scientific proof that there are thousands of newly formed cracks in the voids that appear to have been caused by the extraction of oil. This phenomenon is slowly changing the movement of the tectonic plates, especially over the past twenty years and even more so over the past five years, where the volatility has increased more than three-fold. We even have evidence that several previously uncharted fault lines have produced earthquakes with magnitudes ranging from 4.2 to 5.6."

"How many fault lines are we talking about?" Ron asked.

"There is simply no scientific instrument that can accurately detect the exact quantity of fault lines that have been reopened, but I do have confirmation that molten lava is moving through a certain quantity of these new fault lines, and if this lava flow reaches the surface of the planet, it will raise temperatures that are simply not sustainable to support life."

Ron did not respond immediately. He knew that the plates had shown increased activity, but not to the extent explained by Tom.

"I'd have to see the data," Ron said, "if that is alright with you?"

"Absolutely," Tom responded, "but it's important to note that there have been other scientific studies that partially support my thesis.

Four years ago, a team of geologists from the USGS core drilled through the ice caps at the South Pole to determine the cause of why a large section of ice was slowly sliding toward the ocean. They found that there is compressed water under billions of tons of ice, acting as a continuous ball-bearing, directly causing the ice to slide toward the ocean. A member of that team also informed me that he believes that the water under the ice cap was caused by an active volcano that sits under that particular section of ice. This information has not been made public.

"What I am saying Ron, is that the poles are melting mostly from the bottom up and, only in part, from the top down. In other words, lava seeping through the cracks in the plates is warming the ocean waters, which in turn, is causing the atmosphere to warm.

For millions of years, the Atlantic conveyer belt, which we all know provides the planet with a natural cooling system, seems to be breaking down. There is no argument," Tom continued, "that the burning of fossil fuel is also contributing, in part, to global warming due to the green-house effect; but, it is not the main cause for why the planet is heating up. It is an argument that the oil industry can easily argue against. If the cause of this warming process were to be blamed solely on the burning of fossil fuel, we would have fifty to a hundred years to reverse the process.

" The salt waters are being diluted by fresh water due to the melting of the ice caps. This will eventually prevent the heavier salt water from dropping to the sea floor in the northern regions."

"I'm a little confused," Ron said, "if the Gulfstream ceases to exist, the planet would experience another Ice Age. An Ice Age would be devastating, but they are very survivable." Ron paused for a moment; he was trying to figure out where Tom was going with his theory. "Am I missing something? Are we going to freeze or burn to death?"

"We have a duel problem," Tom explained. "If the warming of the planet's atmosphere were solely caused by the burning of fossil fuel, I would have to agree with you. The Gulfstream would slowly come to a halt, and as you said, it would be preceded by a major Ice Age, but that's not the case. What we have is an accelerated warming condition caused by the extraction of oil that is causing the movement of molten lava to move from the mantle to the surface of the planet. Ron, if my calculations are correct, in a very short period of time, this planet will heat up to temperatures that will literally not have the ability to sustain life. The real problem we are facing has more to do with the time element. In other words, will the atmospheric temperature first reach two-hundred degrees Fahrenheit before we are pushed into an Ice Age?"

"What I'm saying is that before the Ice Age kicks in, the planet could reach temperatures in excess of two hundred plus degrees. In essence, the planet will reach un-survivable temperatures in a much shorter time period then it would take an ice-age to fully emerge."

"And you're saying that all this is going to occur within a three to four year period?" Ron asked.

"Well, my original calculations range between three and four years." Tom paused for a moment as he turned to Joe. "Joe has recalculated the figures, and feels that the critical rise in temperature could occur a lot sooner; however, that is not my concern at this point. My main concern is to get this information out to the scientific world so that some sort of procedure can be developed to resolve the problem."

"This is going to be a hard sell," Ron explained. "The scientific world is both near sighted and far sighted when it comes to theories that tend to navigate in uncharted waters."

"We really don't have a hell of a lot of time," Tom insisted.

Ron did not respond. He knew that breaking down the walls of governmental bureaucracies would be no easy task.

"After Tom familiarizes you with his findings," Joe said with a smile on his face, "we will let you in on plan E."

"What's plan E?" Ron asked.

"You don't want to know," Tom said, as he handed Ron a copy of his study.

"I originally started the study when I had become convinced that the ice caps were melting because of warmer ocean waters. I wanted to know what was causing the rapid temperature rises that were occurring in our oceans. At first, I thought it was directly related to the greenhouse effect, but after completing a number of calculations, I found that there simply was not enough heat being generated by the greenhouse effect to cause such a rise in ocean temperatures. So I continued my research. My calculations proved that it would take an enormous amount of heat to raise the ocean temperatures even a fraction of a degree.

"Well, one day I was in my kitchen boiling a pot of water over a full flame when it dawned on me that there was only one source of heat that could possibly increase ocean temperatures to the degree that they were being recorded: the Earth's mantle.

"I knew that temperatures within the mantle exceeded two thousand degrees, but the big question was, if molten lava was reaching the surface of the planet within the ocean boundaries, what would prevent it from eventually reaching the surface of the planet's continents? I decided to complete a survey of all past major earthquakes and volcanic eruptions, and what I found is that within the past two thousand years, 94 percent of those earthquakes actually occurred over the past one hundred and ten years, and ironically, volcanic eruptions with a VEI of 4 or higher increased by 458 percent within that same time period. The only major event that parallels this phenomenon is the extraction of fossil fuel from the Earth's crust. I surmised that there must be some sort of correlation between the extraction of oil and the increase in seismic activity over that period of time. That's when I decided to conduct my study."

Tom looked visibly exhausted.

"I think from this point on," Joe said, "Ron is just going to have to go familiarize himself with your findings."

"Yes, I agree," Tom said.

"I am anxious to go through the study," Ron responded. "I'll get back to you as soon as I complete my analysis."

"I think that the rest of us should hit the sack," Joe suggested.

"Great idea," Tom said, as he yawned.

They all turned in, with the exception of Ron and Tom.

"If there is any part of this study that is not clear, Ron, please do not hesitate to ask for my assistance. The study is lengthy and may require two or three days of your time. I'm sure that you already know that time is of the essence. I also would like to thank you for your help, and for becoming part of the team."

"I am doing what I always do," Ron responded, "protecting the planet from its inhabitants."

Tom smiled.

"Your input will be appreciated," Tom said, as he walked toward his room. "Thanks again, Ron."

Ron nodded, immediately headed to his laboratory. He was anxious to know what Tom had found.

CHAPTER 8

Tom was an early riser, but more over, was anxious to get started on the project. After a quick shower and shave, he quickly dressed and headed to the kitchen area. As he walked up the corridor, he could smell the aroma of freshly brewed coffee. When he reached the kitchen, he noticed that the digital clock on the microwave oven read five-forty-six. He no sooner poured his coffee when Ron entered the room with Joe walking in minutes behind him.

"Cup of coffee, Joe?"

"Sounds like a good idea."

"Would you like a cup of coffee, Ron?"

"No thanks, Tom. I'm on my fifth cup." Ron looked like he had been up half the night. He had completely digested Tom's study and was truly alarmed at his findings.

"This is an incredible piece of work, Tom. Unfortunately, it appears to be correct. I spent most of the evening transferring your calculations into my data bank. Over the past several years, I have also gathered and documented seismic data and other pertinent information that I believe is relevant to your study. I created several possible scenarios, first utilizing your calculations and data alone, and then making a scenario using both sets of data. I have to tell you, not one simulated program takes us past a two, two and a half year time period. I continued to analyze the information after recalculating some of the figures and could not improve on the numbers. It sure does explain some of the strange geological changes that have been taking place these past few years." The room was dead silent.

Joe looked visibly upset with Ron's analogy.

"I was hoping that I was mistaken," Joe said.

"I'd like to thank you for re-analyzing the data," Tom said, seeming somewhat dismayed over the findings, not that he believed Joe's calculations were in error. It was just that, after Ron's reconfirmation of the facts, everything seemed so much more real. It was almost like he wanted someone to find an error in his work, something that would give them more time. "The strange events you were referring to, that wouldn't happen to be at Yellowstone, would it?"

"Yes," Ron responded. "Let's go into the lab, I have to show you something." Just then, Phil and John walked into the kitchen area.

"The coffee smells good," were the first words out of Phil's mouth.

"Yeah," replied John, "love the smell of fresh coffee!" Joe walked over to John and Phil and gave each a friendly pat on the back.

"Ron was about to show us something important in the lab, so why don't you grab yourself a cup of coffee and join us? He spent the night programming the data into his system. It sounds like he may have come up with some interesting results."

~~~~~~~~~~

Once they settled into the lab, Ron picked up a directional pointer and addressed the team. "What you see in front of you is a system I built to survey and monitor the continuing geological changes that take place around the world almost on a daily basis. The system allows me to tap into the government's satellite surveillance cameras and GPS systems. The data received is then fed into a computerized program where it is deciphered, and then transferred to a three-dimensional time sequence program that has the ability to absorb and register three dimensional images on frame by frame bases in less than a second. The data is then transferred to that eight by eight foot screen just above your head."

The room was quiet and full of anticipation as Ron continued his presentation. "There is a definite correlation between Yellowstone and the increased volatility of the tectonic plates. As a volcanologist, Phil, you will be particularly interested in this model I developed using data gathered over a ten year period.

"Before I light up the screen, there are a few facts that we should all be familiar with. Presently, Yellowstone is the only active super volcano in
~~~~~~~~~~

the world. There are others, but they are presently dormant. However, I now fear that these dormant volcanoes may also become active in the near future. And because they have been dormant, they have not been thoroughly monitored as intensely as Yellowstone or other active volcanoes around the world.

The magma chamber, which lies under the Norris Basin at Yellowstone, was recently measured with the latest sound wave equipment and found to be five miles deep, fifty miles long, and twenty-five miles wide. That's three times larger than New York City. And now for the data that should concern us all..." Ron turned on the viewing screen. "What you are looking at, gentlemen, is a three dimensional view of the Norris Basin taken ten years ago. The elevations of the surface crust, you will notice, are represented in blue. Now, I'm going to slowly move the Norris Basin elevations forward in time. Any change in elevations will be represented in red. As you can see, the new elevations in red are starting to rise above the blue line. I would like you to take particular notice of the rise of the basin in the past two years, versus the rise in the past ten years. The total rise in the past ten years, which encompasses more than a one-thousand square mile area, is 12.78 feet, with a dramatic 9.5 feet occurring in just the past two years. That is a four-fold increase in just the past two years. This indicates that there is an increase in pressure within the chamber itself caused by an increased lava flow, and it appears that the process is continuing to accelerate at a dramatic rate."

Joe was the first to react, "Holy shit! Do you see what I see, Tom? It's happening much sooner than we thought. The Norris Basin is being lifted by magma."

Tom was angry with himself.

"This is not what I expected," Tom snapped, "I contemplated that there would be changes, but not to this degree."

"Relax, Tom," Joe quickly interrupted. "It really doesn't matter. Like you said, the facts are the facts. We simply have to deal with it. And besides, without your initial effort on this project, there would be nothing to analyze. Remember what you always say, 'We have to focus on what we know,' so why don't we just concentrate on plan E?"

"Alright Joe, plan E it is."

Ron turned toward the group and continued, "How many square miles did Saint Helen's initial blast cover, Phil?"

"The pyroclastic blast reached distances of seventeen miles," Phil quickly responded.

MELTDOWN

"And what would be the result of a Yellowstone eruption?"Tom asked.

"Well, taking into consideration the size of the magma chamber that lay beneath the Norris Basin, and the size of past eruptions at Yellowstone, I would say that the eruption would be nothing short of catastrophic

"There are two basic zones in all eruptions. The pyroclastic blast at Yellowstone would cover an area of approximately seventy to one hundred miles, traveling at speeds ranging between three to five-hundred miles per hour, and would have temperatures exceeding seven-hundred degrees Fahrenheit. The heavy ash fall-out would cover an area of approximately six-hundred square miles, and it would take only three weeks for the dust cloud to circle the globe, resulting in at least a fifteen to twenty degree drop in temperature. We would most likely enter into an Ice Age. The domino effect would be food shortages, lack of drinking water, over-crowded medical facilities, and numerous other problems such as housing those that would have to be evacuated. It's not going to be a pretty picture."

"Gentlemen," Ron continued, "not only is the volcano at Yellowstone the most active in the world, but the fact of the matter is this latest data clearly indicates that she has already passed the point of no return. This volcano is going to blow no matter what we do! I believe that the potential explosive power that has already built up under the Norris Basin is now uncontainable.

"The question is no longer how we are going to stop this catastrophic event from happening, but rather, what must be done to mitigate the damage. And will it be enough to save mankind from extinction? Remember, Yellowstone is not our only problem. Lava is moving toward the surface of the planet throughout the entire globe. We have to believe that the same scenario is occurring in other locations around the world." Again, the room grew silent. There were a lot of negatives and no answers. In their minds, each was hoping the other would initiate some sort of resolution.

Tom leaned back in his chair. He did not want to hear that Yellowstone was uncontainable, so he allowed that thought to pass. He knew that any kind of speculation regarding the extent of the damage to the planet would be futile. There were simply no absolutes.

"We have to concentrate our focus on a resolution to the problem," Tom explained in a calm voice. "If we are to stop any further damage from occurring to the planet's crust, we're going to have to somehow convince the scientific world that we have a major problem on our hands. We have to start getting people to listen to us."

Tom expressed his thoughts with the utmost confidence. Everyone just listened and agreed. As soon as Tom completed his presentation, Ron, who had plenty of experience informing the public on environmental issues, enlightened them as to their choices.

"I'm sure that we all agree with Tom," Ron continued. "Our first priority should be to prevent any future damage from occurring to the Earth's crust. And I can assure you, that from past experiences, this is not going to be as easy as it sounds. When I first started my quest to protect the environment, I was naive. I believed that once a violation could be substantiated, the government would automatically step in, issue the appropriate fines, and take the proper cause of action to have the violation corrected, but that wasn't the case. Regardless of the amount of evidence that I produced, the courts favored the violators 132 to 0 on major violations. Yes, there were fines that were issued, and corrections that were made, but nothing substantial enough to discourage the violators. No punitive action was initiated to discourage future violations. These corporations were simply paying a minimal fee for the right to violate and damage the environment to enhance their profits! The next day, it was business as usual."

Joe interrupted, "But Ron, according to Angie, you have accomplished so much through the years."

"Yes, you're right. I simply resorted to their way of thinking. I utilized the same tactics that they used. I resorted to slander, blackmail, and all of the other traits that are attributed to building a successful company. In a sense, I gave them an offer they could not refuse. I threatened to take the information to the public through newspapers, environmental groups, TV news networks, and was not shy when it came to exposing other interested parties. In the beginning, they did not take me seriously, but after a couple of front-page headlines, I had their full attention. You have to understand, I was dealing with corporations that would put toxic waste under their grandmother's bed if they thought it would bring a profit."

"What kind of cooperation did you finally receive?" Tom asked.

"Well!" Ron continued. "One could say that they saw the light."

Tom smiled.

"The biggest problem is the government. Federal, state, or city, it doesn't matter. You're dealing with a bureaucracy. Even if you have documented proof of an environmental disaster waiting to happen, you are looking at years before it makes it through the red tape, and when it does, it's usually watered down. Ninety percent of these guys in Washington are obligated to lobbyists. There are campaign contributors that continually lobby against environmental bills that will have a negative effect on corporate profits! And then there's the public, whom mostly have the attention span of a retarded dog when it comes to these issues. Unless it affects their lives directly, they will not become involved," Ron paused for a moment as he slowly turned toward the group. "Of course, there are exceptions. There are environmental groups that really make a difference. And there are a lot of people who financially support these groups.

This does not mean that the public on the whole are not concerned. It simply means that if it is not in their back yard, on the most part, they do not see it as their problem."

Just then, Angie walked into the room and immediately sat beside Joe, quietly, so as not to interrupt the meeting. Joe greeted her by pressing her hand in his; she smiled.

Joe, who was normally a very optimistic guy, felt that Ron's presentation was somewhat negative. However, he agreed with him. "That's just the way it is. As I see it," Joe explained, "we have only one option. We must take our information public, just as Ron did. If we rely on the government, we will probably be barbequing off the surface off the planet before a resolution is found."

Joe looked to Tom for a response. "What do you think, Tom?"

"Well, the FBI had instructed us not to inform the public. They said it could cause riots and a possible collapse of the world economy. But as I see it, if Yellowstone is going to blow, those issues will not be relevant."

"It sounds like Ron has already gone through a trial and error procedure process," John responded. "There's no reason for us to have to reinvent the wheel. I say we follow Ron's procedures and techniques, it'll save us a hell of a lot of time."

"I agree," Phil said. "Time is of the essence. We should really get this information on the street as soon as possible."

Angie knew that she was part of a dedicated team that had a strong commitment to get the job done. Her personal emotions were mixed between fear and commitment. On one hand, she was ready to do whatever she could to help the team, and on the other hand, she was scared to death, not just for her own safety, but also for the millions of people that would be affected by a Yellowstone eruption. The displacement of families and the pain and suffering that would result was beyond anything she could imagine. These thoughts played heavily on her mind.

"So it's agreed," Ron said. "That is, we are all in agreement, to take the information public."

"Yes," Tom said. "The sooner we start the better."

Ron was off his chair and ready to go. "This is not going to take a lot of time. The data is already programmed into the system. I may need a hand getting this stuff out."

They all volunteered, including Angie.

"OK," Ron said, "This is important. We will be transmitting information through highly sophisticated telecommunication systems. My system utilizes outside networks for transmission. Every twelve minutes, the system will transfer to a new network so as to avoid being traced. There is exactly a two-second time span required when the system transfers to a new network. During that transfer period, you cannot transmit. On each transmission station there is a red and green light. Now this is the complicated part. When the light is red, you cannot transmit. And when the light is green, you can transmit."

Everyone smiled.

"Did you hear that?" John remarked, "Ron does have a sense of humor."

"Ron, is there any way I can call my brother before we get started?" Joe asked. "He's probably a little worried by now."

"Yes," Ron responded. "In your room, there is a red phone. If you dial the numbers 007, you will automatically be connected to an outside line that cannot be traced. You must then dial one, the area code, and the number of the party you're trying to reach."

"So we dial 007 to connect into the system," Joe confirmed, with a big smile on his face.

"By the way Joe, the phone will automatically disconnect in three minutes. Anything longer and we jeopardize being traced back to this location."

"Thanks, Ron." Joe went off to his room to make the call.

"New Haven Police Department," the desk sergeant answered, "who am I speaking with?"

"Joe Solino! I'd like to speak to my brother Bill."

"Hold on, Joe, I'll connect you. By the way, Joe, your brother has really been worried about you."

"I know," Joe responded. "Look, I don't have a lot of time."

"I'm connecting you, hang on."

"Hello, Joe!"

"Hey Bill, it's good to hear your voice, listen, this phone is going to disconnect in two minutes, we don't have a lot of time."

"Are you in a safe place?

"I'm safe, and I'm alright."

"Where the hell are you?"

"You know I can't answer that, Bill."

"Yeah," Bill responded, "I'm sorry about that."

"Bill, listen! Regarding Tom's work, do you remember the package?"

"You mean Tom's study?"

"Yes, the study. Well, anyway, we recalculated the time period and it's not good! Two years, maybe two and a half at best! And it could be sooner. Also, we are pretty sure Yellowstone is going to blow first. I'll send you an email that will explain what you have to do to protect yourself and the family. I'm also going to send you and Pete the new study which includes additional information. Tell Pete that we are sorry that we have to renege on our promise to keep a lid on this thing, but there is no way that we are going to stop the oil companies from drilling unless we go public with the information."

"I trust you, Joe. Do whatever you have to do. I'm behind you all the way, just stay alive! And don't take any chances."

"Thanks, Bill," Joe responded as he paused for a moment. "Bill, they know that you're my brother. Please be careful."

"Don't worry, Joe, that's taken care of."

"I have twenty seconds; say hello to the family. I'll keep in touch!"

"I love you, little brother."

"Same here," Joe said as the phone clicked off.

By the time Joe got back to the lab, hundreds of copies of the revised study had already been sent out. They were sent to every major newspaper in the world, to governmental agencies, scientists, environmental organizations, and major oil companies.

"Well," Ron said, "let's see what happens."

"What are the odds of the information being traced back to this location?" Joe asked.

Ron smiled. "Well, Joe, the FBI, with all of their sophisticated equipment, has not yet been able to trace a single message transmitted from this location. There are chemical corporations and other large manufacturing companies that have hundreds of lawsuits filed against me.

There are also several individuals who have a contract on my life."

"Do they know who you are?" Joe asked.

"No! That's the good part. They don't know who I am or where I am."

"Aside from Angie, how many friends or family members know where you live?" Joe was on a curiosity kick.

"Just you and your colleagues," Ron answered.

Joe was surprised.

"Why would you trust someone you never met?"

"Well Joe, Angie is my closest friend, someone I can really trust. When she called and asked me to help you, at first I was a little skeptical. But when she briefly explained what you were trying to accomplish, it was clear to me that you and your colleagues are the good guys.

We're not talking about, deforestation or water pollution or other environmental tragedies," Ron continued, "which of course are important environmental issues. We are talking about resolving an environmental issue within a two-year period, or facing the total extinction of mankind." Ron paused for a moment as he gathered his thoughts.

"I knew that seismic activity was increasing; I just didn't know why. I feel like I should have known, but there was no clear sign of the cause. Tom's work is nothing short of genius. He put everything into perspective. The real question is whether or not there's a viable solution to the problem."

"Don't think that I haven't thought about it," Joe said. "In all honesty, there is simply no scientific method that has ever been developed to control the flow of lava. I'm not saying that one can't be developed; I'm just saying that it's never been done before."

"It's such a massive and complex problem," John agreed, "that it sounds almost incomprehensible."

"We have no choice," Ron responded. "We must resolve the problem or at least die trying. In any case, I will do whatever I can to help."

"I'm sure," Joe replied, "from what Angie told me, I had no doubt that we came to the right place."

"I overheard what you said," Phil snapped, "the fact of the matter is that we're in uncharted waters. I'm not saying that it's hopeless, or impossible, but to date, we don't even have a theory on the subject."

"Right now, gentlemen," Tom said, "we are concentrating our efforts to convince the world that there is a problem. Like you said Joe, the more people we get involved with this project, the better chances we'll have to find a resolution."

MELTDOWN

"Hey boys," Angie said, as she came bouncing toward them with a big smile on her face.

"You guys have been talking for quite a while, anything interesting?"

"Just shop talk, dear," Joe responded with a big smile on his face.

"Has there been any response yet on the data we sent out?" Angie asked.

"Not yet dear," Joe responded.

"The boys look like they're going through a gloom and doom episode," Angie said, "is everything alright?"

Joe quickly turned and looked at his buddies. "They do look kind of stressed out, don't they? Hey guys, I think that we are over-thinking. Let's try to keep things in perspective. We are scientists. You know geeks? Remember, we resolve problems mechanically."

Before they could respond, a signal bell rang over the loud speaker system.

"Excuse me," Ron said, "perhaps we've got incoming mail. I had better get back to the monitoring system; hopefully we are receiving a response."

CHAPTER 9

Ron pulled out some messages from the monitoring system that were unrelated to Tom's study. "Sorry, guys, it's a force-alarm, but we should be getting something in soon."

Ron continued to monitor the screen, anxiously waiting for a response. Hours passed-by. The anticipation was nerve racking; they did not speculate on a possible result, nor was there any small talk amongst them. To pass the time, they went over all the new data that Ron had added to the study. Aside from some minor discussion on the new study, the room was relatively silent. They were all glued to the lab as Ron continued to scan the different avenues of communication for a response.

Angie had just finished making her fourth pot of coffee.

Joe whispered in Angie's ear. "One more cup of this stuff, and I'll probably overdose on caffeine. If you see me sleeping with my eyes open tonight, don't panic."

Angie smiled; she was content just to be with Joe. The atmosphere in the room was compatible to waiting in a maternity ward. You know the baby is in there, you just don't know when it's going to come out.

"Bingo! I think I've got something... yes!" Ron shouted, "a newspaper in Texas!"

"What does it say?"

"It's not a headliner; it's a third-page article. It starts here:

Tom Collins, an independent and renowned geologist, who is also the author of several books, claims that the world is coming to an end. He even gives a time period of three years or less. When we spoke to geologist Jack Cadwell, representing the USGS, he informed us that they receive numerous predictions from both scientists and over--enthusiastic dooms day seekers.

'We investigate serious studies that are submitted by independent scientists and ignore unsubstantiated claims.'

When asked what category Tom Collins was in, he stated: 'Mr. Collins is a recognized geologist in his field of work, and will be taken seriously.' He also stated that 'Collins' study is an extremely difficult study to analyze. There are a lot of unknowns. It may take months, even years to analyze the study. I am sure that there are merits to be taken seriously, but we must be careful not to encourage a doomsday scenario.'

We reminded Cadwell that Collins' papers estimated a two to three year deadline. We asked Cadwell, under such circumstances, did he believe that taking even one year to analyze the study would be cutting it close? He said that if the USGS were to take every doomsday scenario as an emergency situation, they would have to triple their staff. He said that, 'the planet has been here for billions of years. I have no reason to believe that it won't be here for the next two years.'

The articles continued to come in one after the other. Unfortunately, they were mostly extreme tabloids with headlines that read, "THE END OF THE WORLD!" "DOOMS DAY IS UPON US!" "Tom Collins, a renowned scientist, proves the world is coming to an end!" There was one article after the other. It was the same script over and over again.

Tom just shook his head, seeming somewhat disappointed. "This is not what I expected. These articles demean the seriousness of the study. We're going to have to reevaluate our strategy."

"Relax, Tom," Ron said, "Rome wasn't built in a day. This is good news, not bad news. It tells us the information has been received. I can assure you that there are probably a good number of scientists analyzing the package at this very moment, including the USGS."

"I agree," Phil said, "you really can't expect to get a legitimate response in a day. Damn! It took me three days to totally analyze the package, and this is what I do for a living."

"Be patient Tom," Ron said, "the shit didn't hit the fan yet, but it will. We will know a lot more by tomorrow or the next day. Trust me, Tom, I've been doing this for ten years, this is just the beginning."

Tom looked concerned, "I guess you're right," he said with a worried look on his face. "Joe, if there is any kind of time delay, or a delayed response to the study, I'm leaving the facility. We simply do not have that kind of time. I will do whatever it takes to open their eyes. I'd even go on the Oprah show if I thought it would help."

"Now wait a minute, Tom! If you're going on the Oprah show, I'm coming with you, especially if that psychologist is going to be there. You know, Doctor Phil? He'd probably say, 'Don't fix it if it's not busted.' Actually, I'd just like to know why the hell I became a geologist. In all seriousness, Tom, I've been with you since we were kids. Nothing has changed. We are like the two musketeers!"

"Make that the three musketeers!" John interjected.

"Make that the four musketeers!" Phil roared.

Angie smiled. "I guess that just leaves Bat-woman and Bat-man for Ron and me. So if you need any help, just whistle Joe; now, you know how to whistle, don't you?"

"OK," Joe said, "It's settled. You guys protect the fort, and I get the girl."

"It's important that we give this a little more time," John said, as he gave Tom a gentle pat on the back. "I'm sure things will work out."

"Thanks John," Tom responded. "I appreciate the encouragement."

"There's no sense in everybody staying up all night," Ron said. "Why don't you all hit the sack? I'll continue to monitor the system through the night, and fill you in tomorrow morning."

"Sounds like a plan," John said, "I'm exhausted." "Good night guys."

They all hit the sack, except Joe.

"Well Ron, what do you think?"

"This was the first day, Joe. I have had circumstances where it took more than a week to get a response. We sent out a study, not a novel. What we received today was a cursory review of a complex study. It's going to take time for the scientific world to digest the data."

"I guess you're right, too much anxiety, and not enough common sense. But I believe that Tom is right on one thing."

"And what's that, Joe?"

"We really do not have a lot of time."

"There are some things in life that just take time."

"Well, I hope this thing works out, because if it doesn't, Tom has already made a decision to leave the bunker."

"I know that he's under a lot of pressure," Ron responded. "If he decides to leave the complex, I'll understand, but I'm confident that we will receive a positive response from concerning parties."

"From your mouth to God's ears, because if we leave the complex, we're going to need protection," Joe explained as he turned to face Ron. "We'll probably have to contact the FBI." Joe was concerned about Ron. He is on their most wanted list, Joe thought, and could face life in prison if convicted, but even worse, he has a price on his head. Joe started to smile. It's really not relevant considering the fact that we could be facing dooms day within the next two years. Under the circumstance, life in prison won't be much of an issue.

"What are you smiling at, Joe?"

"I was just thinking about you being on the FBI's most wanted list and our plan to contact them."

"You don't really believe that's funny, do you?"

"No, Ron, no... I was smiling about something else."

"The FBI will not be a problem," Ron said. "They have no idea who they're after."

"That, and the fact that the planet is on the verge of total destruction," Joe added, "may override all other issues."

Ron smiled.

"It's getting late," Joe said as he looked at his watch. "I think I'll hit the sack. Good night, Ron."

"Good night, Joe." Ron immediately went back to his lab to monitor incoming mail.

CHAPTER 10

Agent Pete Marchel was now working out of the New York FBI branch office located in the Jacob Javits Center at 26 Federal Plaza. The investigation was now number one on the FBI list.

The agency had already connected the terrorist group, the Last Jihad, to the assassination attempt that occurred the previous week on I-95. Pete had been assigned to head-up the investigation, and he was at the New York office that morning to brief other leading agents on recent developments.

"Good morning, gentlemen. Let's get down to business. OK, we know that this particular group has been entering the country illegally for more than a year. And for that entire time period, the only physical confrontation that has been confirmed is the attempted assassination on I-95."

"What about the house bombing?" an agent asked.

"We believe that they were involved, but to date, we don't have enough evidence to make the connection."

"It just doesn't add-up," Pete continued, "after a year of surveillance, this group has not been in contact with any of the known leaders in their own organization. They have not purchased materials that could be utilized in terrorist attacks, and there is no evidence that there is anything planned. We believe that there is something bigger going on, and it probably has something to do with Tom Collins' research papers. I believe that the insurgents presently under surveillance are nothing more than a decoy, and that the main core of this operation has to be working underground.

"We now believe that this is not about blowing up buildings, germ warfare, or any other terrorist act that we would normally expect. What we do know is that they really don't give a rat's ass about whether they live or die, and that makes them extremely dangerous.

It is clear that the terrorists became familiar with Tom's work on seismic activity only after he submitted his papers to the convention center in DC. The package was obviously intercepted by someone who had access to the premise. The package then made its way to the terrorist group who must have duplicated the document, and then returned it.

I believe that the DC hotel incident was set up by the oil companies as a scare tactic because there was no real attempt on their lives. They left the package in the room because they really had no intention of assassinating the group. It seems as though the oil companies didn't want the project exposed, at least, not until they had time to analyze Tom's thesis. On the other hand, the terrorists not only want Tom and his colleagues out of the way, they've also attempted to destroy all evidence pertaining to the study.

The fact that Tom and his colleagues are still in hiding tells me that there were other scientist involved with the project." Pete paused for a moment to go over some data, and then continued.

"The terrorist might have confronted Tom and Joe in the hotel, but probably backed off believing that the hotel was being monitored by the agency. They probably thought that the four men who threatened Tom, at the hotel, were agents.

In any event, our assignment is to locate Tom and his associates and bring them back to Washington in one piece, and to continue to monitor the terrorist group to find out what the hell they're up to."

Pete than pointed to a topographical map that highlighted where newly formed cells were located. "The terrorist cells located on this map are in areas that we would normally not expect them to be. I believe that this could be the common denominator that could break this case wide open. We have to find out what these areas have in common with one another. The answer may very well lie with Tom and Joe."

"The question is," Pete continued, "where the hell are these guys? Bill Solino, Joe's brother, and a detective in the New Haven police department, received a call from Joe last night. The call was traced to this office, which means, someone broke into the network. The only person that could possibly fit the I.D. is the hacker that we have coded, 'The Environmental Crusader.' He's the same guy that we have been looking for these past eight years. No matter how many security measures we implement, we can't seem to keep this guy out of the system. The good news is, if that's where Joe and Tom are, the terrorists will never find them, and the bad news is, neither will we."

Pete continued. "It's imperative that Tom and Joe are located, and soon! Everything seems to be tied to them and their work. We still have a lot of missing pieces to this puzzle. Someone must have either sold to the terrorists Tom's work on seismic activity, or they have a mole at the convention center. The question is, why would anyone kill a scientist that developed a theory involving some sort of dooms day scenario? It simply does not add up."

"These guys don't have to have a reason," an agent responded.

Pete continued to instruct the agents. "Our immediate agenda is as follows: locate Tom and Joe. Locate the main core of the terrorist group, and find out what the hell they're up to! And we must identify the person or people that allowed Tom's work to fall into terrorist hands. We must also identify the reason why these insurgents are gathering in specific locations around the world, and why Tom's work is so significant to this group.

Are there any questions?"

"I noticed that the operation has been designated 'high priority.' Is there something more we should know?" an agent asked.

"You'll know soon enough," Pete said, "but right now, all I can tell you is that the national security of this country is in serious jeopardy, and we're quickly running out of time. The White House has a spot light on this operation, so it's imperative that you give this assignment your full attention. Are there any other questions?" There was no response.

"Ok, gentlemen, that's it. The lead agents in charge of each division will brief you on your specific assignments. Good luck, and thank you."

Pete's immediate concern was Tom and his colleague's safety; now that they decided to go public with the information, he wasn't quite sure how the terrorists would react.

Pete completed his instructions to the lead agents, then left the conference room and immediately headed toward John McBride's office. John, who had a great deal of respect for Pete, commanded the New York District FBI Command Center.

"Good morning Pete," McBride said, "please have a seat."

"Pete, we just received orders from Washington that will permit us to work and share information with other international government security agencies and officials that are on this list." John handed Pete the list.

"Thank you sir, this should help us with the investigation."

"What do you think they're up to, Pete?"

"I'd like to believe that it's just about the oil companies and profits, but I think there's more to it. I haven't really put the pieces together yet."

"This case has become a top priority in Washington," McBride explained as he got up from his chair and walked around the desk. "The president is now personally involved with this case. I want a network of information coming into my office on everything that is happening, as it happens! The case is now high-priority, so make sure there are no leaks. After this week, you'll be working out of the DC office, but I'll still be your New York contact."

"Yes sir, I understand."

"Good luck, Pete."

"Thank you sir, I'll get started immediately."

Pete walked back to his office where Agent Mel Carson was waiting. He was second in command of operations, working under Pete's authority.

"Mel! Have you issued your lead agents their orders?"

"Yes, sir," Agent Carson responded. "They have all been thoroughly instructed."

"That's good, Mel." Pete handed Mel a copy of a list that contained the locations of recent insurgent movements previously prepared by the FBI information center. "What I have to know is what these locations have in common. Look at this Mel," Pete continued as he pointed to a number of locations on the list. "The locations are in small towns and villages. With the exception of New York City, the remaining locations are in unpopulated areas." Pete paused for a moment to assure himself that he had not overlooked anything.

"Do you have any questions, Mel?"

"No, sir, I believe I have what I need to get started."

"Oh, one more thing, I want the information to flow into the office as fast as you receive it. The big boys will be watching us on this one."

"You got it, Pete!"

"By the way, who did you assign to locate Tom and Joe?"

"Agents Matt Johnson and Harry Kline."

"That's a good choice, Mel. I want you to tell Harry to put an all-point bulletin on the FBI networks. If the boys are with the Environmental

Crusader, we are not going to find them. They're going to find us, so make particularly sure that the bulletin is friendly."

"I'll take care of it," Mel said, as he left the room.

~~~~~~~~~~

John McBride summoned Pete back to his office. "What is it, sir?"

"Sit down Pete," John looked concerned. "I received a memo from the Attorney General's office in Washington. It appears that oil stocks have started to drop across the board. The stocks have been frozen to prevent a run on the market. The memo attributes the decline to the scientific data sent out by Tom Collins. They're suggesting that we put an all-points bulletin out for his arrest."

"That is not a good idea!" Pete snapped. "Think about it, sir. They were prevented from presenting their work at the convention center. They have been threatened and survived two assassination attempts notwithstanding the death threats that occurred at the DC hotel. If Tom's report was flawed, or incorrect in any way, do you really believe that anyone would have gone to all this trouble to put them out of commission? What we have here, sir, are lobbyists putting pressure on the White House to put these guys out of business. A dooms day scenario is not going to bring the market down. That is, not unless there is some truth to Tom's findings. You have to believe me sir, these guys are on to something. They are not the bad guys. For God's sake, they're not quacks, both men are renowned scientists, and highly respected in their fields of work. If we spook these guys, they'll never come in. It's the oil companies and the terrorists that should be under investigation."

"OK, Pete," John responded, "I got the message. You bring them in and maybe we'll find out what the hell is going on. And don't worry, Pete, I'll take care of Washington. But it's important that you keep me in the loop. I believe this is going to be a hot potato."

"I'll be in touch sir, and thanks."
~~~~~~~~~~

CHAPTER 11

Lou Feldman, the chairmen of the National Studies of Geology and a board member for their annual geological convention in DC, was summoned to Yellowstone National Park by Steve Beldon, the head of the USGS. Jack Cadwell, also a board member, and recognized as one of the top scientists in his field of volcanology, was also requested to join the team at Yellowstone.

Lou had spoken to Richard Harris, who was assigned by the USGS to take charge of the investigation at Yellowstone. Lou detected a serious, and a somewhat nervous, tone in Richard's voice during their initial conversation on the telephone.

"Lou," Richard Harris explained, "I'm calling you on a serious matter up here at Yellowstone. About two weeks ago, the resident geologist noticed some significant changes in seismic activity. Last week, the USGS assigned a team of scientists to investigate the situation. I am now heading that investigation. I believe that the matter is serious; the basin is starting to swell, and the seismic activity, although not critical at this point, seems to be increasing. After studying Tom Collins' work on seismic activity, I tried desperately to contact him, but he is simply nowhere to be found. Lou, we can really use your help out here.

We have high seismicity and extreme and ongoing ground-surface deformation. The geyser basin is severely heating, seriously affecting thermal features, and there are notable earthquake swarms along mapped, and in some cases, unmapped fault lines. The park is literally deforming."

"You certainly have my attention, Richard," Lou said. "I'll arrange to fly out there sometime tomorrow."

"The arrangements have already been made," Richard responded. "We have arranged to have a car in front of your house in three hours. You'll be flown to a military base where there will be a helicopter waiting to take you to the park."

"I assume that all the necessary equipment is already in place."

"Yes," Richard responded. "That has all been taken care of."

"By the way, my associate, Jack Cadwell, will be joining me."

"I read some of his work on volcanology. He would certainly be an asset to the project," Richard enthusiastically responded.

Richard then went into some detail regarding the type of equipment that the geologist at the park had installed. He assured Lou that the park was being monitored twenty-four-seven. Lou had requested some additional equipment.

"We will have everything in place before you arrive," Richard explained. "I'll expect to see you and Jack sometime tonight. Have a good flight. And Lou, thanks for not hesitating to offer your services, we are going to need all the help we can get on this one."

"I'm happy to be part of the team. We will see you tonight...Oh, one more thing, I believe that it might be a good idea to keep the situation under wraps. It's important for us to limit what information is given to the media. The last thing we need is a panic."

Richard agreed, but mentally thought that it would be similar to trying to stop a herd of buffalo with a stop sign. They had managed to fight off the news media for awhile, but with the recent documentaries that were shown on television highlighting Yellowstone as a potential disaster area, and now, with Tom's doomsday scenario plastered all over the media, the story was already headline news.

"All I can say, Lou, is that we have done everything we could to downplay the news at this end. We can discuss this tonight when you arrive. Have a good flight."

"See you tonight."

Richard hung up the phone and turned to his associate, volcanologist Bob Kelso. "This guy, Lou Feldman, sounds like he doesn't have a clue on what the hell is going on. I hope bringing this guy up here is not one big mistake."

"Who assigned him to the project?" Bob asked.

"The big boss got a call from Washington."

"Sounds a little political," Bob responded. "We don't really need this guy."

"Well, let's stay positive and see what happens."

As soon as Lou Feldman hung up the phone, he immediately called Jack Caldwell to brief him on the situation at Yellowstone.

"Hello Jack, Lou Feldman here. I'm calling with regards to Yellowstone."

"Yes," Jack responded, "Richard Harris called and explained the situation to me, I guess we're going to Yellowstone."

"So you have already been informed that they'll have a separate car to pick you up?"

"Yes," Jack responded, "as soon as I hang up I'll be heading home."

"Another thing, Jack, we had better get a copy of Tom Collins' study."

"That's already taken care of, Lou. I received the package yesterday. It's an extensive study, but I did manage to analyze most of the figures. We may have a serious problem on our hands. The study developed by Tom Collins seems to favor a little more fact than theory. We have been theorizing for years that the heat from within the planet mantle might very well be the main cause of global warming. Tom's work puts that theory into a more factual prospective. I have already sent a copy to your home. I think you had better go over some of these figures. I'm going to head home to pack my bags and explain to my wife that I'll be off and running again. This is not going to be a couple of days, we are probably looking at weeks."

"Yes," Lou agreed, "we're probably going to be there for a while. But before we become over exuberant regarding Tom's study, we are really going to have to nail down the facts. The last thing that we want is to create an emergency situation based on a possible dooms day scenario that may never come to fruition."

"I agree, all I'm saying is, read Tom's papers. We can discuss the matter on the plane."

"Jack, I'm sorry if I sound a little demanding regarding this issue, but there are certain precautionary measures that must be taken when…"

"That's all right, Lou. I realize that you have political responsibilities. We will determine the facts, and take it from there."

"Sounds good, Jack. See you at the airport."

~~~~~~~~~~
~~~~~~~~~~

MELTDOWN

Lou and Jack arrived at Yellowstone late that night.

Richard, Bob and several other USGS geologists who had been working around the clock recording and gathering data for analysis, took time out to greet Feldman and Cadwell.

The team was standing just outside several trailers that had been set up as temporary office facilities. They had the landing area for the incoming helicopters lit up with spot lights.

"I can hear the chopper, but I can't see them," Bob said.

"Over to the left Bob, I see the red and green lights flashing. Get on the radio and inform the helicopter pilot that everything is set up for the landing."

As the helicopter approached the landing, the noise became deafening. Bob turned his face away from the dust as the chopper touched down.

As soon as Feldman and Cadwell climbed out of the chopper, Richard and Bob walked over to greet them.

"Welcome to Yellowstone," Richard shouted. "How was your trip?"

"Long," Jack responded. "How is everything going out here?"

As soon as they cleared the landing area, the helicopter departed. "There's not much that we can accomplish tonight," Richard explained, "so what we have done is make copies of the latest readings including the topographical outlay of the park showing where most of the hot spots are. You can familiarize yourself with the information back at your quarters."

"Has the park been sealed off?" Lou asked.

"Yes," Richard responded. "There were four National Guard units assigned to secure all entrances to the park. We also have helicopter units in the air."

"That's good," Lou said, "it's important that we keep the news media out."

"It appears that there's more going on than we had originally anticipated," Jack said.

"The changes are so frequent," Richard replied, "that you can't recognize the place from one day to the next. It's like a time bomb waiting to go off."

"You did sound a little frantic when we spoke on the phone," Lou said, seeming somewhat doubtful that things were as bad as he was explaining.

Richard did not respond.

"It's getting late," Bob said, "why don't you jump in the jeep. I'll take you to your quarters. We can discuss the matter tomorrow."

"Great idea," Jack said, "we'll take a look at these latest data reports and discuss them tomorrow."

"That's all good and well," Lou explained, "but we have to make sure that we keep our finding from the public until we have conclusive evidence that we have a real emergency situation on our hands."

"Good night, gentlemen," Richard said as walked toward his trailer.

Bob drove Lou and Jack to their sleeping quarters and then returned to the trailer.

"Well Richard, what do think?" Bob asked with a smile.

"I think we're going to have problems. This guy Lou is a real asshole."

"What about Jack?"

"I thing Jack is a straight shooter, I like the guy."

"How are you going to handle this guy Lou?"

"How long have you known me?"

"Good night Richard," Bob said with a smile, "see you tomorrow."

"See you tomorrow."

The next day, after going over much of the data, Jack was convinced that Yellowstone was a disaster waiting to happen. There was absolutely no way to predict exactly what the volcano was going to do. The potential magnitude of an eruption was beyond comprehension. Yellowstone National Park looked like another planet. There was smoke, hot ash, visible lava and 1.5 to 2.5 earthquakes registering on the Richter scales with regularity throughout the park. Jack turned to Lou with an almost frightened look on his face and a seriousness that demanded attention. "Lou, this is the largest hydrothermal system on the planet. The plateau volcanic field developed through three volcanic cycles spans more than two million years. It included the largest known eruptions known to man. We are no longer talking about whether Yellowstone will erupt, we are talking about when. What we have here is a super volcano that is following a historical pathway, and there is nothing that we can do to stop it. The evidence is overwhelming, Lou, we may have even past the point of no return. When it goes, the world as we know it will be permanently changed."

"Wait a minute, Jack! Don't you think you're being a little hasty?" Lou interjected. "After all, we have only been here for a day. I believe we should give ourselves a little more time."

"Lou! The Norris Basin has risen more than six feet in the past month. Seismic activity has increased tenfold, there is lava breaking through the crust, and there is a steady increase in ground uplifts throughout the park.

You have to understand, Lou, the USGS has been gathering data for the past two months notwithstanding the fact that they have been monitoring the area for years. You need only compare the past data with data taken these past two months to know that this volcano is winding up its springs. This baby is going to blow! If we don't start moving people out of a six-hundred mile range of this baby, a lot of people are going to die."

"We cannot take this to the public until we are absolutely sure," Lou insisted.

Jack was beside himself. He knew that Lou's decision to postpone a desperately needed "red alert" was predicated on political repercussions, rather than the bare bones facts.

"The evidence gathered at Yellowstone these past six months is insurmountable."

Richard, after listening to Lou's comment, shook his head in disbelief. It was clear that Lou had made a decision to ignore the scientific facts in favor of his political agenda. He was not willing to jeopardize the previously planned funding to his projects. Richard, on the other hand, agreed with Jack. He could not override Lou because of his political connections in Washington, but he was certainly going to speak his mind.

"Lou! I have enough data gathered to recommend an evacuation. Every day lost will only produce more casualties. I have already spoken to my boss, Steve Beldon. Of course, he will make the final decision. He also issued a request to the FBI to locate Tom Collins. We have received information from scientists throughout the world that there are other previously inactive volcanoes that are showing signs of life. Tom must be found."

Lou did not respond. He had already set his mind to gathering additional information in the park before making a decision. He also intended to convince Steven Beldon not to start any evacuation until his investigation was completed. Jack, who was standing next to Richard Harris, whispered his opinion.

"Who told you to bring Lou into this?"

"Steve Beldon."

"That means Lou was sent here by Washington to keep the lid on the situation. Without Tom, we're going to be at a stale-mate unless we can convince Steve that the situation is serious." Jack was not happy with Lou's political agenda. He knew that Yellowstone was a serious situation that required immediate action. There were lives at stake.

"Richard, it is imperative that we find Tom!"

"Thanks for your support Jack, I think I have an idea. It may cost me my job, but under the circumstances, I believe that there is no other alternative. If even a single person died, notwithstanding the millions that will be at risk, I would not be able to live with myself. What I am going to do is, rather than fax the information to my boss, I am going to email it. I am sure that Tom Collins is monitoring all information in and out of Yellowstone. If anyone can light a fire under the fed's ass, it's him."

"You have my full cooperation, Richard," Jack assured him. "I give you my word that I'll personally be by your side when the shit hits the fan."

"Thanks, I really appreciate the support."

CHAPTER 12

"Take a look at this!" Ron said in an excited voice. "Look at what just came over the machine! It's a ten-page report sent out by a Richard Harrison. He's with the head geologist running the show for the USGS at Yellowstone. The report was sent to his boss, Steve Beldon who heads the agency in DC. It's a data report regarding increased seismic activity at Yellowstone. Look at this! Harrison is recommending a complete evacuation. Guys, this is serious!"

"Can I have a copy of that report?" Tom asked.

"I'll make a copy for everyone," Ron said in an excited voice. "But that's not all. Look! There is a second message. This one is from the FBI. Tom, they want you to contact them. They say that it is a matter of national security."

"Let me read the message." Joe reached out to the copy machine and snatched the letter before it fell into the basket.

"Attention: Tom Collins

It is urgent that you contact Agent Pete Marchel immediately. We are aware of the fact that you may be with a person wanted by the FBI whom we have coded 'The Environmental Crusader'. To secure your safety, and hopefully your cooperation, the FBI has agreed to offer your host, the Crusader, amnesty. Attached, you will find a certification that grants a full pardon on all past violations. It is imperative that you do not attempt to leave your present location. The FBI will send adequate forces to assure your safety and the safety of your friends. We have raised our terrorist security levels to red alert. Consider this request to be a matter of national security. Please contact me at the telephone number listed on this document.

It is imperative that we receive your full cooperation."

"The letter is signed by Agent Peter Marchel," Joe said as he turned toward Tom. "Well, Tom, what are we going to do?"

Tom turned to Ron with a serious look on his face. If I call Pete, Ron's operation will be exposed.

"You have certainly been an asset to the operation, Ron, and I just want you to know that we sincerely appreciate everything you've done. The thing is, I don't want to repay you by handing your address over to the FBI. What we could do is leave the bunker sometime tonight and drive to another state before contacting Pete. This will secure your privacy and allow you to continue your operation"

Ron was quiet for a moment as he digested Tom's attempt to be considerate. "Let me see if I got this right," Ron responded, "and stop me if I'm wrong, but the situation, as I understand it, is that this planet might not even be here two years from now, unless someone comes up with a solution to reverse what appears to be a doomsday scenario, and you expect me to stay here and twiddle my thumbs while you and the boys go out and save the world. Does that about sum it up?"

"No, Ron, that was not my intent."

Angie was smiling from ear to ear, she knew that there was no way that Ron would walk away from what had to be the most challenging environmental apocalypse since man walked the planet.

"I appreciate your concerns Tom," Ron said in a calm voice, "but you really don't have to butter the road up for me. If we're going to accomplish anything, with the time that we have remaining, we're going to have to do away with some of the formalities and concentrate on productivity. I have already decided to go the gamut on this one, is there an objection?"

"That's what I like about you Ron," Joe said, "you have a way with words." Joe then turned toward Tom. "Well Tom, what do you think?"

Tom walked over to Ron and shook his hand. "Thanks Ron, we can sure use the help."

"OK, now that we have that settled," Joe snapped, "I believe that we have once again hit a crossroads in our journey. We have a choice of staying here in this safe haven, or heading back to Washington to save the planet. Now what will it be?"

Tom smiled and immediately responded, "I assume that we are all in agreement. That is, to head back to Washington. We are still going to need the cooperation of the oil companies and just about every country in the world, gentlemen, and we're not going reach that goal without the government's help."

"I agree," John said, "this is an international crisis that's going to require the full cooperation of every government on the planet."

"I believe it's the right decision," Phil said.

"Well Joe," Tom continued, "how do you see it?"

"I think we always knew what direction we were headed in."

"Ok, then its settled. Ron, can you connect me to Pete Marchel's office? I think it's time to present our case to Washington."

Ron immediately connected Tom to an outside line and dialed Pete's number. "Hello, this is Agent Pete Marchel speaking"

"Hello Pete, this is Tom Collins."

"Thank God!" Pete responded. "You have no idea how happy I am to hear your voice! Are you and your friends alright?"

"Yes. Well, things could be better, but health wise everyone is just fine, sorry for not calling sooner."

"I understand Tom, but I have to tell you, things have really started to heat up since you went public with the report. Your study is headline news in just about every major newspaper in the world. It's been like a mad house around here. There are people walking around with signs saying that the world is coming to an end, but we are downplaying the story to the general public until we can get a grip on what the hell is going on."

"We were against the wall," Pete continued. "When your report hit the streets all hell broke loose. But that's not really our main concern at this point, now that the cat is out of the bag, you and your friends are in grave danger. The insurgents have an all-out-alert on you and Joe, which is why it is important that we get you back to a secure location as soon as possible."

"The thing is that we are going to need a fully-equipped facility," Tom explained. "Time is running short, and to date, not much has been accomplished toward finding a solution to the problem."

"That has already been arranged," Pete assured Tom. "The White House staff is already making arrangements to meet with the heads of state in all of the oil producing countries."

"That's good news," Tom responded, "we have a mega problem on our hands and at this point, I'm not really sure if the problem is even resolvable. We have reanalyzed the data over this past week and the prognosis is not good. The latest reports out of Yellowstone confirmed our worse fears, and I'm now convinced that Yellowstone is just the beginning of what we're to expect in the days ahead."

"Well, my job is to get you back to Washington in one piece before the insurgents know where you're located."

"I'm really sorry," Tom said in an apologetic tone, "about letting the cat out of the bag."

"I'm not really concerned about that now, although it does make security a little tougher, but I have to give you credit, you certainly accomplished your goal. There are a lot of people studying your report, including the feds. That's why we need you back in Washington."

"I understand, Pete," Tom said, "we are prepared to do what has to be done."

"What I need now is your exact location."

Tom explained in detail exactly where the bunker was located.

"OK Tom, just stay where you are, and do not move until we get there."

"Will I be able to contact you on this same number in the event something comes up?"

"Yes. Also, it would be a good idea if you gave me a contact number where you are, in the event there's a change in the plans."

Ron gave Tom a telephone number to give to Pete. They spoke for a few minutes more and then disconnected.

Tom and his loyal and trusted colleagues were now a little anxious. The atmosphere was filled with a high degree of anxiety. There was a lot of anticipation in the air. Joe and Angie sat in a area that was distant from the group, while Tom, Phil, and Ron studied the ten-page report that was sent to the USGS by Richard Harris.

Joe reached out and held Angie's hand as he looked into her eyes. "I'm really happy that you're with me. You're like a bright light in a dark room. You have no idea how concerned I am for your safety. With all that is going on, I sometimes feel that I have trapped within me an infinite amount of data and information just screaming for resolution. If at times it seems that I'm not giving you the attention you deserve, I'm sorry."

"That's alright Joe, I really do understand, and besides, I'm just happy to be with you. That's how simple it is. I do realize that in between the time that we do spend with each other, there is the 'Save the world' problem. I cannot tell you how proud I am of all that you and the boys have accomplished in such a short period of time."

"Thanks, Angie, you're sweet. You're like a breath of fresh air."

"What are you saying, Joe?"

"What am I saying?" Joe whispered. "I'll tell you what I'm saying!" Joe paused for a moment. He then turned and looked into her eyes, which were resonating with a soft mellow glow. "What am I saying, Angie, is that I have fallen in love with you. I am in love with you. Yes! That's what I'm saying. I am deeply in love with Angelina Rosselle."

If Angie were made of butter, she would probably have melted right there on the spot. There was nothing at that particular moment that could have made her happier. She had been in love with Joe from the very first time she met him. Her only fear was that the love she had for him would never be returned. As she put her arms around him, her eyes started to water.

"I love you too Joseph Solino, from the very first time we met," she said as the tears ran down her cheeks. Joe held her in his arms and gently but passionately kissed her.

Just then, Tom walked into the room and noticed the tears on Angie's face. "Is everything alright, Angie?"

"Yes," Angie said in soft voice, "everything is just fine."

"You have to forgive Tom," Joe said with a smile, "he doesn't yet have the ability to differentiate between happy tears from those that are sad."

"Don't tell me," Tom said, "the cat is finally out of the bag. You mean you actually told her. Well, this calls for a celebration."

"What's out of the bag?" John asked, as he approached them.

"Ok, Tom, let's not make a big deal about this," Joe snapped. Angie just smiled.

"Come on guys," John said, "what's the big secret?"

"This is a momentous day, John," Tom responded with a big smile on his face, "they just found out that they love one other."

"But we've always known that," John said.

"You're right John, but now they also know it."

"Ok, ok guys," Joe said, "you're wearing out the carpet and embarrassing Angie."

"Sorry Angie," Tom said, "just having some fun."

Angie smiled. "When will we be leaving the bunker?" she asked.

"In a couple of hours," Tom responded. "I guess we had better start packing."

"Good idea," Phil said, as he joined the team.

John leaned over and whispered in Phil's ear. "You missed the big event."

"What are you talking about?" Phil said in a low voice.

"Joe and Angie just found out that they love one another."

"What's new," Phil said, "and why are we whispering?"

"I don't know," John said laughing, "but we're going to start packing, Pete's team should be here within the next two hours, and I'm really anxious to get started."

They all headed back to their rooms except Tom who walked to the control room to inform Ron of their plans.

"Tom," Ron said, "I'm glad you're here. Look what's coming over the network."

Tom immediately walked to where Ron stood.

"Almost every major newspaper in the world has a cover story on your study, but so far, we have no conclusive statements or conformation from the scientific world. I suspect that they're going to need a lot more time to develop a thesis."

"My only concerns," Tom explained, "are the negative reports that will be submitted by scientific organizations that rely on financial grants from the oil industry."

"I wouldn't worry too much about that," Ron insisted. "When all of the rhetoric is pushed aside, the only things that will surface are the facts. Remember, we are dealing with scientists that do not rely on crystal balls to prove a thesis."

"That's encouraging," Tom said. "By the way, I wanted to inform you that Pete has arranged to have this complex put under military guard as a security measure to assure that the premise is not compromised. They should be here in a couple of hours. The team is in the process of packing their bags. You may want to do the same."

"I'm going to miss this place," Ron said. "It's been a home to me for more than ten years, but I know that what we are trying to accomplish is a lot more important than this bunker, and besides, if we fail to resolve this problem, all that we believe to be important today will become totally insignificant if we don't resolve this problem."

"Isn't that the truth," Tom said.

"I'm going to secure the facility, and then pack some of the data that I believe will be helpful in our research."

"Good idea," Tom agreed. "Is there anything I can do to help?"

"No thanks Tom, I know where everything is. It'll be a lot easier if I do this myself."

"Well, if you change your mind, you know where to find me. As soon as we finish packing, we can all meet in the dining area."

"I'll meet you there in about twenty minutes," Ron said.

Tom walked back to his room to start packing. No more than fifteen minutes had passed when he heard what sounded like a loud explosion that violently shook the walls and knocked several items off his night table. At first he thought it was an earthquake, or a volcanic eruption of some sort. When he opened his door, there was heavy smoke in the air and several lighting fixtures hanging from the ceiling dangled by the electrical cable attached to a ceiling outlet.

By now they were all in the corridor.

"What the hell is going on?" Phil yelled.

"Feels like an earthquake!" John screamed.

"No, this is no earthquake," Joe shouted seeming a little confused. "It sounded more like an explosion."

"Let's find out what the hell in going on!" Tom snapped, as they all ran toward the dining area.

And then there was a second explosion, and a third, and even a fourth. Ron screamed at the top of his lungs, now standing in the central corridor. "Follow me!" He yelled as he led them to a safety room. Joe held on to Angie's hand as they ran down the corridor. Tom, John, and Phil were steps ahead of them. A two-foot piece of concrete fell from the ceiling, just missing Joe and Angie.

"What the hell is going on?" Joe yelled. "This can't be the FBI!" They made it into the safety room just as another explosion ripped through the bunker.

Phil looked back in an effort to identify the problem. "Shit," he said to himself, "there's daylight coming from the ceiling." Phil immediately realized that the explosions were man-made.

He quickly ran toward the safety room shouting at the top of his lungs, "WE'RE UNDER ATTACK! Ron! Do you have any weapons in this place?"

"In the safety room," Ron yelled, as he opened a metal door to a space that contained a variety of automatic weapons lined up in a neat stack. Phil, who was a former Marine in Special Forces, immediately picked out two rapid-firing machine guns and a bunch of clips. He ran out of the safety room alongside a concrete wall. Through the smoke and dust, he could see ropes being lowered through holes in the ceiling. He then saw men sliding down the ropes with automatic weapons flung over their shoulders. Phil opened fire. Six of the eight men fell to the floor. The other two terrorists made it to the floor safely and were returning Phil's gunfire.

Bullets were flying. A second group of men started down the ropes. A barrage of bullets targeted the corner of the wall that Phil lay behind. He was boxed in and unable to return fire. The two men on the ground had him pinned. Just then, Joe shot out from around the corner and emptied his automatic machine gun in the area where the two men were firing. He pulled the trigger and wouldn't let go. With Joe now covering him, Phil stepped out and unloaded his gun at the men sliding down the ropes. All of the sudden, hand grenades started to fly.

"Joe! Pull back! Hand grenades!" Phil dove to the far side of the wall, out of the range of the exploding grenades.

Meanwhile, Ron was on the phone with the FBI. "We have World War Three outside of our bunker, where the hell are you guys?"

"Shit," Pete yelled, "We didn't figure on this. Listen, Ron, get everybody into a room that can be secured from the inside. Our men should be there any minute."

"Go in a room that could be secured?" Ron screamed. "You have to be kidding me! This place is literally falling apart, concrete is falling from the ceilings. Their converting the bunker into a mausoleum! And guess who's being buried!"

"I get the message," Pete said. "Stay on the line while I contact our forces."

"Where the hell am I going to go?" Ron asked.

As Phil and Joe were reloading, two terrorists shot around the corner, bringing Joe and Phil into their sight. Joe shuffled to get his clip into the gun. Phil was out of ammo as the terrorists moved in on them. "Shit!" Phil yelled as he turned toward Joe. "Hurry up Joe, their moving in!"

"The damn clip is jammed!" Joe shouted as he tried to pull the clip out and reload.

Phil looked up and saw the two terrorists running toward him. He then heard shots from behind him and watched them hit the ground. When Phil and Joe turned around to see who fired the shots they saw John, the mild mannered reporter, with smoke coming out of the automatic weapon he held tight in his hands.

"The 101st infantry is here!" John screamed as he continued to fire.

Joe yelled back. "I love you John! I love you!" John heaved ammo over to Phil and Joe, and then continued to unload his ammo toward the descending terrorists. Suddenly, there was silence. Not a sound could be heard. Phil moved closer to the opening to find out what was happening. He saw the front end of a rocket launcher, turned around, and started to run toward the shelter.

"Rocket launcher!" he screamed, "RUN! RUN!" As they all dove into the room, Tom and Ron closed the heavy metal door and turned the wheel lock. The explosion was deafening, but the door held. Ron immediately gave each of them a thirty-minute oxygen tank. The explosion sucked up every ounce of oxygen from the bunker. Minutes later, they opened the door to make sure that there were no more rope climbers. The dust was so thick that they could not see their feet. They listened, but they couldn't hear a single movement. The room was silent. After about ten minutes, the dust cloud started to settle.

"Do you hear anything Phil?" Joe whispered.

"Yes, it sounds like Aramaic, but I can't see anything," Phil moved a little closer to the hole and noticed silhouettes of men hanging over the hole in the ceiling. When he saw the first rope hit the floor, he again opened fire. Joe and John joined in. The terrorists returned their fire, and then there was silence again. Above the bunker, there were six terrorists laying down flat at the opening of the hole. It looked like they were in the process of replacing the ropes that had been blown to bits by the explosion of the rocket. The insurgents dropped the ropes and then began firing. Just as the terrorists were about to descend into the bunker, twenty Mohawk helicopters thundered over the horizon, fully rigged. Five veered off to the right, five veered off to the left. The remaining helicopters headed straight toward the bunker. It looked like the Normandy invasion. This wasn't a confrontation; it was an annihilation. The terrorists took off in eight different directions. There were three hundred Marines on the ground, and twenty-two FBI agents. The Mohawks took out the group of insurgents around the opening in the ceiling first, and then started to chase down those that were on foot. When Joe, Phil and the rest of the group heard heavy gunfire above the bunker, they knew that help had arrived. The skirmish was over in twenty minutes. The fatalities were thirty -eight terrorists dead, and five captured.

FBI Agents Matt Johnson and Harry Kline walked over to the bunker with a bullhorn. When they looked into the hole, they could not believe their eyes. "Holy shit," Matt shouted, "it looks like it was hit by an atomic blast. It doesn't look good, Harry."

Mat put the bullhorn to his mouth. "Tom Collins, Joe Solino! This is Agent Matt Johnson with the FBI, can anyone hear me?" Joe slowly and cautiously walked toward the hole.

"Matt, is that you?"

"Hey Joe, it's good to hear your voice. Is anybody hurt?"

"No! Well maybe a little diarrhea, a verity of stomach cramps, three migraines, and we are all deaf! Why is it that every time we call the FBI for help we almost die?"

Matt turned to Harry with sort of a blank look on his face.

"You know, Matt," Harry said, "that's a tough question to answer. I've seen more action with these guys in the last two weeks than I've seen in the past two years with the agency."

"Sorry we weren't here sooner, Joe," "Matt said, "but the most important thing is that everyone is all right. We are rigging a harness. Where going to hoist you out one at a time. Leave your belongings behind. We will have everything packed for you later. I have orders to bring you guys straight to Washington without delay."

After they were all lifted from the hole, Matt walked over to where Tom and Joe were standing. "We have orders to take you and Tom to Washington immediately."

"Wait a minute, Matt," Joe snapped, "what about the rest of the group? We're in this together. We're a team!"

"I'm sorry, Joe," Matt replied. "I'm just following orders."

"Well Matt, if they don't go, we don't go," Joe insisted.

"Wait a minute, Joe!" Matt responded in a stern voice.

Tom cut Matt off, "Matt, I want you to call Pete and tell him that there are six of us."

Matt looked at Tom, shaking his head. "OK Tom, I'll call Pete." Matt immediately called him, "Pete, this is Matt. We have secured the area."

"How are the boys?" Pete asked, "are they OK?"

"Aside from being a little ragged and worn, they look just fine. By the way, they brought down twelve of these sons-of-bitches before we arrived."

"They did, did they?" Pete responded, with a big smile on his face.

"Yeah, they fought them off for at least thirty minutes before we arrived at the scene. And I have to tell you, the insurgents didn't have a chance."

Pete was happy that Tom and his friends were all right, but he now knew that there was an in-house security breach. There must be a mole within the agency, he thought. There was no way the insurgents could have possibly found this location without inside help. He was sure that the insurgents had received information from someone within the agency. This was a matter he would have to attend to immediately.

"By the way Pete, Tom and Joe have four additional colleagues that are part of their team. And they want to bring them."

"I knew that there were more of his colleagues involved when I first questioned him about the research papers, I just didn't know how many. It's alright, they'll probably be an asset to the project. By the way, Matt, this mission is now a national security issue. So it's important you get them back to home base as soon as possible."

"I'm on my way, sir. I'll call you if there are any delays."

"The team that you're bringing in may very well be the only group of scientists in the world capable of saving the planet. We cannot afford any more mistakes. The president is anxiously awaiting their arrival."

"I understand, we should have them in Washington early this afternoon."

"That's good," Pete said as he hung up the phone.

"Well, Matt," Tom asked, "what's the story?"

"Pete agreed. We are all leaving in about ten minutes. The plan is to transport the group by helicopter to Area 51 and then fly to DC. There is no necessity for your group to bring anything with them, like I said, everything in the bunker will be packed and brought back to home base. If you have any particular item you want taken back, just make a list and we'll make the arrangements."

"Thanks, Matt," Tom said.

As Joe and Angie walked toward the helicopter assigned to them, he noticed Ron standing alongside the hole that exposed his bunker to the elements. Joe immediately sensed that he was a little emotional about leaving his work behind. Here's a man, Joe thought, who had devoted his life to cleaning up the environment just because it was the right thing to do. There are not many people today that are willing to give everything of themselves and expect nothing back in return. "Hey Ron, are you all right?"

Ron seemed to be in a semi-trance.

"Ron, is everything all right?"

He quickly looked up and noticed Joe standing there.

"It's not easy leaving after so many years with still so much more to be accomplished," Ron explained in a solemn voice.

Joe just listened. He was confident that Ron had already made up his mind.

"Well, Joe, let's go and save the planet."

"Good idea," he said, as they walked toward the helicopter.

MELTDOWN

The team boarded the helicopter that would take them to Area 51, where they were scheduled to catch a transport back to DC.

"Where exactly are you taking us when we hit DC?" Joe asked.

"I don't have the authority to tell you where you and your friends will be staying," Matt explained. "All I can tell you is that you will be working out of a command center. If you have any other questions, I'll be happy to answer them for you."

"I have a question," John responded.

"Yes John, what is it?"

"Do you have any idea when we are going to eat?"

Joe laughed.

"I can't believe it. After all that just happened, all you can think about is food."

"Come on, Joe, you know how it works, after the battle there's the feast."

"Just kidding John, thanks for saving our asses back there."

John smiled. "I'm sure that you would have done the same, if things were reversed."

"We should be on the transport in about twenty minutes," Matt said. "We can all have something to eat at that time." They landed at Area 51 and boarded the transport plane, which immediately departed.

"Well Tom, your report is wide spread, and soon we will have the full cooperation of Washington. I know we're not a hundred percent home, but it's a damn good start."

"Yes!" Tom said in a tired voice. "My only concern now is time. I just don't believe Washington has ever been effective or efficient in any matter requiring an expeditious resolution, to anything; but I agree, it's a start."

"You're not going negative on me, are you?"

"No, nothing like that, Joe, but to date we have not received a serious response from the scientific world, and that concerns me."

"Don't be so pessimistic," Joe snapped. "We are on the threshold of new discoveries every day. There are a lot of brilliant minds in this world and if I had to have my guess, there isn't a single scientist that will refrain from prioritizing this project. It will be a day of reckoning. And besides, Tom, we have plan F to think about."

"What's plan F?" Tom asked.

"I don't know yet, but it has to be a lot better than plan E."

"So we are up to plan F? Is this it, is this the last plan?"

"They say that as long as you have a plan, everything will be all right."

"And who said that?" Tom asked.
"George Washington, of course, when he crossed the Delaware."
Tom smiled.
"You certainly have a great attitude, Joe."
"Yeah, yeah," Joe responded as he yawned, "I think I'll take a snooze."
Totally exhausted, both men fell asleep.

CHAPTER 13

The group arrived in Washington late that afternoon. They were first taken to a preparation room and then to the Security Council meeting.

Vice president Harold Baldwin was sitting at the head of the table. To his right were the Chief of Staff, Joan Dunne, and a number of five-star admirals and generals. To his left was the head of the USGS, Steve Beldon, and sitting beside him was the same Louis Feldman who had just returned from Yellowstone. He was undoubtedly representing the lobbying groups who always managed to get someone in the decision rooms to protect outside interests. There was a formal introduction before the meeting officially started.

The meeting began with Tom's presentation of his study relating to increased seismic activity and the direct effect it would have on the planet. He explained to the council that the polar caps were melting from the bottom up, and not the top down. He went into specific detail about each element of the study in a professional and comprehensive manner. Joe, Phil, and John participated in their fields of expertise. Tom completed his presentation and returned to his chair. The room was silent.

The vice president shuffled a few papers around that were lying in front of him and then turned toward Steve Beldon. "Sounds like a doomsday prophecy from the Bible," the Vice President said with a smile. "Steve, this study was completed over the past two years, is that correct?"

"Yes sir."

"Your research papers indicate that seismic activity at Yellowstone has dramatically accelerated over the past six months, would that be correct?"

"Yes sir," Steve responded.

"It sounds to me," the Vice President continued, "like there may be something to this study, when we consider the fact that I have several reports in front of me put together by some of the top scientists in the world. As a matter of fact, these studies appear to confirm Tom's findings. Now we have, from what I can see, a major problem at Yellowstone. My question, Mr. Beldon, is how has your agency interpreted Mr. Collins' study, and more importantly, are we looking at a Yellowstone eruption in the near future? Now, I want you to really think about this question carefully because these papers in front of me, along with Mr. Collins' and Mr. Solino's presentation, state that the volcano has reached a point of no return. I assume that means that we should have already started evacuating those people that are within, what you have described as, the pyroclastic zone. Exactly what should we expect, Mr. Beldon?"

"Mr. Vice President," Beldon responded, "before I interject our latest findings regarding Yellowstone, I would like to introduce the chairman of the International Geological Conference, and renowned geologist, Lou Feldman, who has just returned from a two week study at Yellowstone National Park. I believe that he can offer a hands-on evaluation regarding the present circumstance that exists at the park."

"Go ahead, Mr. Feldman. I'd like to hear what you have to say."

"Thank you sir, I have just returned from Yellowstone and have observed, first hand, the present seismic changes that are occurring, and have thoroughly analyzed the latest data collected these past two years by the USGS. I put together a preliminary report which indicates that it is too early to conclude that an eruption at Yellowstone is inevitable. Predicting a volcanic eruption is a complex undertaking, and should not be taken lightly, because of the enormous financial impact it will have on the country.

With the present available data, it is impossible to determine whether or not Yellowstone poses an immediate threat to public safety. We simply need more time to effectively analyze core samples, seismic readings, and a culmination of other scientific factors to accurately determine the seismic vulnerability of the volcano.

In the past, we have had many situations when volcanoes have shown signs of activity, and then, have simply gone dormant. Although the pyroclastic zone of this volcano may only be sixty to seventy miles from the eruption, the evacuation zone for the ash fallout is in excess of six-hundred square miles. The economic impact on the country would be irreparable. There would be riots and civil unrest throughout the country if we proceed with an evacuation at this time. The mere chance of moving all these people and then finding out that we were mistaken would be both a financial and political disaster. Mr. Vice President, we need at least two to three months of further testing to confirm and substantiate the facts."

"Mr. Vice President," Tom interrupted in an angry voice, "we do not have that kind of time. You have to evacuate immediately. There is enough scientific data available to confirm that Yellowstone is in the process of an eruption. We may not know exactly when, but 'now' is probably a good guess! Sir, the Norris Basin has risen more than 6 feet in just the last two weeks! This rise is caused by increased lava pressure against the Basin. It's just a matter of time before it breaks through the crust with the fury of a thousand atomic bombs. Sir, the volcano is in the critical stages of a full blown eruption!"

Lou Feldman again interrupted, "Mr. Vice President, this volcano has not erupted in more than six hundred thousand years. If we are motivated by fear rather than common sense, we could very well destroy the country's infrastructure because of an overzealous doomsday scenario. I sincerely believe that we should give ourselves a little more time to complete our evaluation."

The Vice President did not respond to Lou's request, but rather addressed Steve Beldon.

"Mr. Beldon, you do have a team of scientists at Yellowstone?"

"Yes sir," Steve responded in a nervous tone.

"And what report have you received from them?"

Steve paused for a moment. He was well aware of the fact that Richard Harris had sent him a report recommending a complete evacuation.

"Sir, the lead geologist at Yellowstone, Richard Harrison, recommended a complete evacuation. But after I received Mr. Feldman's report requesting more time, I decided to hold off on the evacuation, until I could further evaluate the data."

Just then, a secret service agent came running into the room and handed the Vice President a piece of paper. After reading the document, the Vice President addressed the group with a solemn look on his face. "Gentlemen, I am sorry to have to inform you that there has been a fractional eruption at Yellowstone."

There was total silence in the room. The Vice President paused for a moment and then continued, "Casualties are estimated at more than thirty thousand people, and thousands more injured."

Steve, concerned about his crew, looked at the Vice President with an expression of both anxiety and fear on his face.

"I'm sorry, Steve. I'm really sorry."

Steve sat back in his chair with a look of despair on his face. He attempted to respond, but knew that there was nothing he could say to justify his decision not to evacuate. There was enough evidence to call for an evacuation. Richard Harris pleaded with me to evacuate, what was I thinking? All those people, the hardships, the pain and suffering... What have I done? He asked to be excused and immediately left the room.

The President of the United States, John Hamity, walked into the room and addressed the Vice President. "Harry, I want a complete evacuation at the Yellowstone region! Whatever the radius is, I want everyone evacuated. I want to see Tom Collins, Joe Solino, and their associates in my office immediately."

Lou Feldman excused himself and was escorted out of the building.

When Tom and his associates walked into the corridor, they immediately saw Pete Marchel standing alongside two other men. "Hey Pete, it's good to see you," Joe said in a solemn voice. They were all very emotional about the eruption, knowing that Richard Harris and his team didn't have a chance.

"I heard about Yellowstone," Pete said, "I'm really sorry. Maybe now they'll pay more attention to what you have been trying to convey to these people these past couple of months."

"It's a hard lesson to learn," Phil said shaking his head.

"It wasn't necessary," Tom snapped, sounding mad as hell.

"There's nothing that can be done at this point," Joe said. "It's important now that we give our full attention to the project."

"I agree," John said.

"Well," Pete said, "it is good to see that you're all in one piece after that ordeal at the bunker. I have to apologize for that, but we did find the leak."

"If you're interested in apprehending the rest of these guys," Joe said, "just give them our present location and wait ten minutes."

Pete smiled. Just then, the head of the FBI, Jack Rodrick, stepped out into the hallway with Bill Stallino, the head of Home Land Security. Pete quickly introduced both men to Tom and his colleagues. After congratulating the team for their heroic stand against the insurgents, both men excused themselves.

"So what's the story, Pete?" Joe asked.

"I was asked to come down to Washington to command the security team."

"Does this mean that you will be assigned to this operation?"

"Full time," Pete responded.

"Maybe we should increase our life insurance policies, as a precautionary measure."

Pete smiled, but didn't respond.

"Relax, Pete," Joe said, "If you hadn't gotten there when you did, we'd all be toast."

A little scary, Tom thought. It's seems like every time we're involved with the FBI, we're either jogging through the woods, or shooting our way out of trouble. I know that he's Bill's friend... Ah, why think about it.

"I think we had better head to the conference room, the meeting will start in just a few minutes."

As they entered the President's conference room, CIA agents immediately directed them to their seats.

When President Hamity entered the room, everyone stood up.

"Please be seated," the President said, as he took his seat.

The Secretary of State, Joan Dunne, then rose from her chair and introduced Tom and his colleagues to the President.

"I was informed regarding the unfortunate encounter you had with the insurgents today," the President said, "I guess they didn't realize who they were up against."

"I hope this is not going to be standard procedure," Joe said with a smile.

"No, Mr. Solino, we intend to move your team into a secured location where you will be able to continue your work under the full arm of federal protection. I want to assure you that you will receive the full support and cooperation of the US government from this day forward. We will make available to your team whatever is necessary to expedite a speedy solution to this difficult circumstance we are now facing." The President paused for a moment as he viewed some of his notes.

"Gentlemen, I would like to clear the air before we begin. I do not want to hear any resolutions or suggestions that have been influenced by special interest groups. There are thirty-thousand dead and many more injured as a result of these special interest groups, and when this thing is over, I promise you, I will fight for legislation that will permanently boot special interest groups out of Washington." He stopped for a moment to sip a glass of water, and then continued.

"Gentlemen, there are no words that can measure the magnitude of this problem. We are facing the largest threat to our national security since the signing of the Declaration of Independence.

"We have already closed down the financial markets indefinitely, and have deployed more than fifty-thousand troops to aid in what has to be the largest evacuation in human history. To accomplish this task, I have ordered a complete withdrawal of troops from Iraq and other parts of the world. We have notified the Red Cross and other charitable agencies throughout the country of the circumstance, and they have pledged their full cooperation and support. I have just completed a conference call with the governors located in states that will be least affected by the initial blast. They have already ordered their respective National Guard units to active duty, and are also preparing temporary shelters for the evacuees.

"We are here now to examine the core of the problem. We already know, from the geological data, that Yellowstone is going to erupt. However, it is not clear whether or not the eruption will match the intensity of past eruptions. But if it does, gentlemen, we could be looking at the total annihilation of the human race or, at the very least, life as we know it will be change dramatically.

"I have always known the history of Yellowstone and the fact that an eruption at this point seems to be in line with the time durations of past eruptions, but I believe that people are really never prepared for such an event to actually occur."

"Mr. President," Tom said, "It's important for you to understand that what's happening today has little to do with time periods. As a matter of fact, Yellowstone may not have erupted for another hundred years if it were not for this man caused problem. It must be noted that this phenomenon is occurring throughout the planet, and not just at Yellowstone. The numerous cracks in the planet's crust caused by the extraction of oil over the past one-hundred-ten years has provided these newly formed passageways to move lava from the mantle to the surface of the planet. Sir! In time, if this process in not altered, temperatures on this planet will exceed three hundred degrees Fahrenheit."

"I'm not refuting your findings, Tom; as a matter of fact, I have received similar information from some of the most renowned scientists in the world who have confirmed that your thesis is correct.

However, we have received documentation from several oil companies who have combined their efforts to strongly refute your work. Their findings indicate that there is no correlation between the extraction of oil and increased seismic activity." The President had previously issued Tom a copy of the oil company's data sheets before the meeting.

"Tom, I would like to hear what you have to say about the oil company's findings."

"Mr. President, I reviewed the data with my associates and cannot find anything in the documents that disproves any of the data that I submitted to your office. The documents are simply a general denial of the study. Furthermore, of the several scientists that signed the document, there are two geologists that I had the pleasure to work within the past. I contacted both scientists and spoke to them regarding the results of their findings."

"Mr. President, if I may interrupt," Pete said, "I have some pertinent information regarding the two geologists that Tom is speaking of. If that's alright with you, Tom?"

"Yes, go right ahead Pete."

"Ok," the President responded, "What do you have agent Marchel?"

"I had both of these gentlemen investigated. What we have found is that the oil companies have been issuing general denial letters on any and all issues that affect loss profit. We have written affidavits from both of these men stating that they were not privy to Tom's papers prior to issuing their findings. What they actually did was answer a number of questions issued to them by the oil companies. As it turns out, the questions were not relevant in any way to Tom's findings.

"They also furnished us with documentation showing that the oil companies were well aware of the fact that the extraction of oil had damaged the Earth's crust in numerous areas. Their documents show that the oil companies have had cave-ins at wells where the cavities were extremely large."

The President was visibly angry. "I want the oil company personnel that were involved with this bullshit indicted! I want all the books and records of those sons-of- bitches involved in this cover-up subpoenaed! I want to know what information they have on this issue, and for how long they've had it! And I'd like to know if they have a solution. If we find what I believe we're going to find, I want these bastards indicted for murder! Mr. Redrick, I want you and your boys to get to the bottom of this, and remember, we do not have a hell of a lot of time! We need answers, and we need them now!"

"Yes sir, Mr. President. We are already in the process of subpoenaing the records."

"Tom!" the President said, as he stood up, "I want you and your associate's to meet me in my office." The President walked out of the room with his staff. After a quick briefing session, he joined Tom and his associates in the Oval Office.

"Gentlemen, I want you to know how much we appreciate your efforts regarding this matter. Your resilience and determination has been heroic. I am well aware of what you have already been through. You have risked your lives not once, but several times, to assure that this vital information was brought to the table. I'm happy to have all of you on our team."

"Thank you, Mr. President, but I think we have another problem brewing."

"And what is that, Joe?"

"Yellowstone is not our only problem. I wish it was, but it's not. There is no doubt that the volcano at Yellowstone would have eventually erupted, but like Tom explained, it most likely would not have occurred for decades to come. You see, Mr. President, the phenomenon that is occurring at Yellow Stone will soon be replicated in thousands of locations throughout the globe.

"There are further signs of crust deterioration; two thousand nautical miles southwest of the Canary Islands and three miles below the Atlantic, the crust that separates us from the mantle is approximately three miles thick. Sir, the crust is gone and the mantle is now directly exposed to the ocean waters. Lava is now freely flowing into the ocean! In this region, there is what we call a Globe-Spanning Ridge of undersea volcanoes. These structures are formed when the Atlantic tectonic plates separate and lava surges upward to fill the gap in the Earth's crust. That did not happen this time! Mr. President, the plates are starting to spread apart, allowing lava to flow freely into the oceans. This condition will result in super-warming of the ocean waters and a change in the flow of deep ocean currents. These are the same currents that control the Earth's climate. This is not good, sir!"

"Doesn't that ridge go straight through Iceland?," the President asked.

"Yes sir. The recent volcanic eruptions in Iceland and the present increased volatility is not a coincidence. It's a result of the shifting of the tectonic plates and the recently discovered movement of molten lava through thousands of newly formed cracks in the crust."

The President sat back in his chair in silence. He looked a little overwhelmed. The situation was a lot worse than he suspected. "Thanks

Joe, I believe I have the picture."

"I can assure you," the President continued, "that the government will do whatever is necessary to facilitate a resolution to this problem. I would like you to draw up a preliminary plan on what course of action we should take."

"The question is, where do we start?," Tom responded.

"Our first agenda should be the oil companies," Joe snapped. "Mr. President, the FBI has confirmed that the oil companies were cognizant of the fact that the extraction of oil has severely damaged the crust. But I do not believe that they are aware of the severity of the damage. I have worked with these companies as an independent geologist. It is not an issue that they would normally ignore. I believe that it simply fell through the cracks, or that they simply did not realize the severity of the problem. The federal government is not the only bureaucracy in town, sir. However, after Tom's study fell into the hands of the major oil companies, they became a little nervous. They were well aware that they had past documents indicating that the extraction of oil caused severe damage to the Earth's crust. I believe that when they confirmed Tom's findings to be accurate, the oil companies decided to stop Tom's study from being published. And at a later date, they probably planned to announce the finding themselves. In my opinion, the oil companies were simply trying to cover all the bases. This scenario would eliminate governmental investigations, and at the same time give the company an edge in converting their facilities to produce an alternate source of fuel. It always boils down to profit!"

"Mr. President? If I may add another important issue..."

"Go right ahead, Tom."

"I agree with everything Joe said. There may be some guesswork regarding the latter part of his summation, but I also agree with those same conclusions. The most important issue here is to mitigate the damage; we must immediately halt any further extraction of oil from the ground, and possibly find a way to repair the damaged done to the cavities. One thing more, Mr. President, we are going to need the cooperation of every single oil company in the world, if we are to resolve this problem.

"Our calculations indicate that without intervention, this planet could parallel the atmosphere of Mars in just two to three years. Indictments, subpoenas, and any other type of legal action would be a moot issue under those circumstances, sir. We simply do not have that kind of time. The situation is critical. Not only do we need the cooperation of the oil companies, we will also need the cooperation of every nation on this planet. This must be a global effort if we're to save the planet.

"It's imperative that all parties realize the seriousness of the matter. How much time are we going to waste debating the issue? Mr. President, time is running out. If we..."

"I'm totally cognizant of our situation," the President interrupted, "and we are going to take immediate action. I assure you, Tom, we are not going to sit on this one."

"Thank you, sir."

"Well, gentlemen," the President said, "I believe that we have enough information now to call for an emergency meeting at the United Nations. And I believe that the first item on the agenda will be to immediately order all oil wells to be shut down."

Tom felt relieved. It's not the total resolution to the problem, but it was a damn good start.

"The emergency meeting at the United Nations will be scheduled for the day after tomorrow," the President stated, "and I can assure you that all of the oil producing nations will be present. I have taken the liberty to send each nation a copy of your study although I believe they already have one. I have also decided to assign you and your associates to represent the United States; after all, Tom, you are my new commissioner of seismic and volcano control. By the way, we have converted your study into a computerized visual aid package. Take a copy with you to familiarize yourself with the programming sequence.

"One more thing, Tom, I thought it would be wise if we first have a meeting with the major oil companies prior to addressing the United Nations."

"Yes," Tom agreed, "that would be wise."

"The meeting is set for 9 a.m. tomorrow morning. Representatives of the oil companies have been explicitly instructed to directly address the study without camouflaging the facts. I believe that they are now all aware of the seriousness of the issue. To save time, we will also grant the oil companies full immunity relating to this issue. The immunity will cover any and all illegal activity that may have occurred prior to this date. This should encourage them to be forthcoming with all pertinent information relative to this matter."

Tom was satisfied with the President's efforts to resolve the problem. It was more than he expected. "I would still like to know why the oil companies did not see this coming," Tom said.

The President smiled. "The almighty dollar has a tendency to interfere with common sense, Tom."

. "Are there any questions?" the President asked.

"No sir," Tom responded.

The President continued, "The meetings we have arranged with the oil companies and world leaders will hopefully be the turning point in our efforts to resolve this matter. I'm counting on all of you to get the ball rolling. You will have the full cooperation of my entire staff." The President then rose from his chair and turned to Tom and his colleagues. "You have all done a great job up to now... I believe we can beat this thing."

The President then turned and left the room.

"Do you have a minute?" Pete asked, as he walked to their side of the table. "There is something important I have to tell you."

"What is it?" Joe asked.

"We have additional information regarding the oil companies and the terrorist group that we have had under surveillance," Pete explained. "Further investigation has provided us with additional information that might clear some of the uncertainties. It's true that the men in the hotel room were directly connected to the oil companies. As you said, Joe, they were just trying to buy time. But the house bombing, the attack on I-95, and the recent attack at the bunker were solely initiated by the terrorists. The incident involving the oil companies at the hotel had nothing to do with the insurgents. There is simply no connection between the two. The problem is, we know why the oil companies did what they did, but we haven't got the slightest idea why the insurgents are after you. We just can't figure out what their motive is."

"That makes two of us," Joe said. "So, where do we go from here? Is there a plan to take these guys out, or do we spend the rest of our lives weaving and ducking bullets?"

"For now," Pete said, "you will be under full federal protection. We will move you to a secure area where you can continue working on your project. According to the President, you guys are the most important people on the planet."

"Thanks Pete," Tom responded, "I know that the situation is a difficult one."

"It will be resolved," Pete promised, "the important thing is for you and your team to concentrate on the project, we'll handle the insurgents. I'll keep you up to date on what transpires. If something turns up, or you have any questions, give me a call. I'll see you tomorrow."

"Thanks for the info, Pete," Joe responded.

"See you tomorrow," Pete said as he left the room.

Tom and his colleagues discussed the matter for a short time, then retired for the evening.

CHAPTER 14

Pete had enough evidence to link the terrorist group with the house bombings, and the attack on the bunker, but could not substantiate a motive. There was absolutely no history on when this group was formed or what fanatical doctrine they were following. All he knew is that they seemed to have a strong interest in Tom's work.

Abdul-Aalee, who was in command of the terrorist factor in the U.S., graduated from Boston University with a degree in electrical engineering. He stood six-feet tall and spoke perfect English. Abdul was orphaned at the age of six when a terrorist bomb prematurely exploded, killing both his mother and father. Adopted by his uncle, Ra'ad, a high-ranking official in the sect, he continually reminded Abdul of his birth rite regarding the end-time prophecy. To the sect, their educational program was not the form of brainwashing so often described in TV documentaries and magazine articles. They really believed that they were following a divine doctrine of prophecy. The group had followed the writings that were rejected by mainstream Islamic leaders for so long; the question of authenticity was no longer a consideration.

Unmarried, Abdul hoped someday to be blessed with several virgins as a reward for his sacrificial death.

Abdul offered an impressive outward appearance. He was a well spoken individual and outwardly appeared to be an extremely charming man but behind a thick wall of pretense, he had an angry and uncontrollable disposition, demanding absolute supremacy within the sect through fear and violence. He achieved the position of 'Supreme Leader' for successfully initiating several terrorist missions that took the life of more than four hundred innocent civilians.

When confronted with deviancy or insubordination from other members of the group, Abdul's anger, which lay just below the surface, would erupt in an uncontrollable burst of violence. If diagnosed, he would probably be labeled bi-polar or schizophrenic.

Abdul's second and third in command were Makeen and Naasih. Both men were leaders in the sect and controlled more than two hundred members in each of the cells they commanded.

This was not a group that would negotiate terms and conditions. They were religiously motivated with a martyrdom mentality. Their cause was to the death. They were the most dangerous adversaries a man could face under any circumstance. In their eyes, they were fulfilling a prophecy that was ordained by God.

Abdul Aalee sat across the table from Makeen and Naasih. "Listen carefully! Our mole in the FBI has information that the UN is having an emergency meeting in two days. The two geologists will not only attend the meeting, but have been chosen by the President to represent the United States at the conference. This cannot happen! So far, we do not know how they will be traveling. We must have ground-to-air missiles in the event they come in by helicopter. And if they should decide to arrive by motorcade, we will be prepared."

Makeen listened intently, knowing that he would be assigned to the motorcade.

"And what car, of the dozen or more cars in the motorcade, do we target?" Makeen asked.

"We target all of the cars," Abdul snapped, seeming agitated and angry. "These are the infidels in the prophecy. They must die!"

"Abdul," Makeem responded, "we have received information that the meeting at the UN will be heavily protected. Our brothers in the police department have informed us that they will have a force of more than four hundred police officers on the street. This is without taking into account the federal security agencies that will be involved with the assignment."

"I'm concerned," Naasih said, "we have only two-hundred men."

"No, Naasih!" Abdul snapped. "We will have more than six hundred men fully armed and prepared to die. Izz Udeen's forces have been ordered to participate in this attack. They have been here for the past week and are now awaiting further orders."

The two men smiled.

"That is good," Naasih said, "Izz Udeen is a fierce fighter."

Abdul continued, "Izz Udeen will command one hundred men and initiate an attack at Kennedy Airport with rockets and heavy artillery as a decoy operation. Our adversaries will assume that we were misinformed. We will let them believe that the main attack will be at the airport, but we will have more than five hundred men around the streets leading to the UN building. This will be our main area of attack. We will be successful! After we have fulfilled that part of the prophecy, we will plan our attack on the oil fields. Victory will be ours!"

"And when will we begin to position our forces Abdul?" Makeen asked. "There is not much time."

"We will start positioning our forces late tomorrow and into the morning. Our arms and munitions have been strategically located along the route to the UN and in close vicinity to Kennedy Airport.

"Makeen, these are your orders! They are to be executed only in the event they transport by helicopter! You will also meet with Izz Udeen, who will be leading the attack on Kennedy. I gave him tentative orders last week. He is now waiting for the time sequence. You will meet with him tonight at eight p.m. and give him these timetables." He then turned to Naasih.

"Naasih, these are your orders! The ground attack against the motorcade is laid out. As you can see, there are several possible routes. My guess is that they will be traveling by motorcade. You will meet with the five commanders tonight who are listed on your assignment sheet. They will lead the ground attack. These are preliminary timetables and may change before the initial attack. Be careful not to raise suspicion! Above all, you must protect these orders with your life! We have made arrangements to have additional carriers transport new timetables in the event that there are any changes made to the schedule. Again, protect these orders with your life, and be careful not to raise suspicion. Do you understand?"

"Yes," Makeen answered. "I see that we have positioned three trucks to move across 44th Street towards the UN building. What if 1st and 2nd Avenue are blocked off? Maybe we should position a portion of the men in some of the surrounding buildings. This will at least guarantee some immediate support in the area where the motorcades will enter. We can still bring one truck in with men down 44th Street. This will lessen our risk."

"This cannot be done, Makeen," Abdul responded.

"Why not?," he yelled. Abdul was now physically upset with Makeen.

"Listen to me!" he demanded. "The federal agents have had the area under heavy surveillance for days. They have been monitoring the area around the UN for at least a week. We have to assume that they have placed agents in buildings, on roof-tops, and in places we do not even know! They have already secured a perimeter within a ten-block radius of the target area. If we start sending men into the area, they will be detected."

Makeen did not say anything at first. Abdul was really angry. Makeen had already witnessed an incident where he killed one of his men for defying him.

"My apologies Abdul, the plan has taken everything into consideration. We will come down 44th Street with three trucks. We will defeat the infidels."

This settled Abdul's nerves somewhat. Makeen really did not agree; however, he did not want to die just yet.

"The plan will be carried out in accordance to the timetables that you have been issued. You must take time to instruct your forces on the movement of arms and the positioning of men. If there are any changes in procedures, you will be notified by carrier. Are there any questions?" This time the room was silent. As far as his commanders were concerned, right or wrong, this was the plan.

"We have waited more than fourteen hundred years for the prophecy to be fulfilled; now the time has come! Our victory is at hand! The cleansing will begin! We will die in glory!"

They embraced each other and then left the room to fulfill their assignments. Each went to their designated locations. Both Makeen and Naasih would spend the evening indoctrinating their men and planning what would turn out to be the most daring terrorist attack ever attempted. There would once again be bloodshed in the streets of New York, and once again, the question would be, why? These aimless and random acts of terror only served to fuel the fire of hate, making the civilized world that much more determined to eliminate their ability to function. Everything was now in place. There would be a direct confrontation between the terrorist group and the United States' law enforcement agencies. For the terrorists, it was clearly a suicide mission. They were prepared to die for a cause that the vast majority of main stream Muslims would not condone. When any religious sect adds, subtracts, or misinterprets the scriptures, in any religion, they are no longer acting on behalf of God, but rather, have become God. That's blasphemous in anyone's religion. In this case, the radical religious teaching of this cult had set the stage. There would be no room for reasoning, logic, truth, or other attributes in life that are ascribed to the creation of civilized people. No, there would be no turning back for this cult. The plan was now in motion.

CHAPTER 15

The next morning, Joe was up and ready to go. After taking a long shower, he dressed and headed straight to the dining room, escorted by two CIA agents. To his amazement, Angie came strolling in just two minutes later. "Good morning, Angie."

"Good morning, Joe." Angie was happy to see him.

He walked over to her, put his hand on her chin, and gently kissed her. "You look absolutely beautiful this morning."

"Thank you," Angie said with a smile. No one has ever told me that I look beautiful at 6 a.m.

Just then, Tom and John came strolling in, followed by Ron and Phil. After greeting one other, they all sat down at a single table.

"Anyone for coffee," the waitress asked, as she walked around the table filling each cup.

"I'm as hungry as a horse," John said, as he turned to the waitress. "I'll have pancakes with maple syrup, three eggs over light with bacon, sausage, grits, a bowl of fruit, and a glass of orange juice please. Oh, and three slices of rye slightly toasted, with strawberry jam on the side."

"I think John just ordered for the entire table," Joe said laughing.

"What are you going to 'have-to-go' John?" Phil asked, smiling.

They all laughed.

"Have-to-go?" John asked. "You mean like a box lunch?"

The group was totally hysterical by now, they just couldn't stop laughing.

"No John," Phil responded. "In consideration of what you're having for breakfast, a box lunch is not going to get you through the day. You should probably go with the mini banquet."

"You guys are really hysterical," John said with a big smile on his face. "You had me going there for a minute. And here I was just about to ask the waitress for a box lunch menu."

After a couple of minutes, they all calmed down.

"What are you going to have, Joe?" Angie asked.

"I was going to say, 'Whatever John is having,' but under the circumstance I think I'll just have scrambled eggs on a bun, with coffee."

Angie smiled as she ordered the same.

After the team ordered their breakfast, they brought themselves up to date regarding the latest geological readings at Yellowstone.

"I spent some time with Phil gathering geological data on the internet last night," Ron explained. "The new data, gathered by the USGS regarding Yellowstone, indicates that the magma chamber at the Norris Basin is now increasing at an accelerating rate. I believe that the first eruption was only a belch."

"Yes, I agree," Phil said. "The new geological team has set up their new base in Montana just beyond the maximum pyroclastic flow limits."

"What's a pyroclastic flow?" Angie asked.

"It's a fast-moving current containing rock which is collectively known as teplhra," Phil explained. "This current travels away from the volcano at speeds generally as great as seven-hundred km/h, or four-hundred-fifty miles per hour. The flow normally hugs the ground and travels downhill, or spreads laterally being guided by the force of gravity. The speed depends on the density of the current, the volcanic output rate, and the gradient of the slope. They could reach temperatures of about one-thousand degrees Centigrade, or one-thousand-eight-hundred degrees Fahrenheit."

"How far from the volcano will the flow reach?" Angie asked.

"A Yellowstone eruption will probably produce a pyroclastic flow between seventy-five and a hundred mile radius from the volcano, but the heavier ash fall-out could reach out up to six-hundred miles."

Angie was taken back. She had never realized the devastation a Yellowstone eruption could cause. "Joe," she said in a nervous tone of voice, "there are millions of people in those areas. How are they possibly going to evacuate all those people on-time?"

"Don't worry Angie. The President has already taken steps to evacuate the area. The plan is to evacuate people living within a hundred miles of the volcano first, and thereafter, the remainder of the six-hundred mile perimeter."

Angie did not respond.

"As I was saying," Phil continued, "I spoke to John Conners, who is now in command of the USGS team in Montana. He informed me that the tremors are starting to increase in strength. Readings on the Richter scale have also increased in both volume and magnitude. Some of the readings were recorded as far as sixty miles from the basin."

"I have also completed some calculations," Phil explained. "The basin is continuing to swell and the temperature on some of the surface areas have increased to one-hundred-twenty degrees Fahrenheit. This baby is ready to blow! To date, the USGS can only guess at what the VEI will be, but taking into consideration past eruptions, they are anticipating a VEI of at least seven or greater. The USGS is planning to continue to monitor the system from northern Montana, pending order from the main office to evacuate."

Angie seemed really upset. "Have you been watching the coverage of the evacuation on TV?"

"Yes," John responded, "there is nothing else on TV. Like Joe said, the government is desperately trying to evacuate everyone from the more critical area's first, but the task seems so monumental that I sometimes wonder...." John paused for a moment, not wanting to take a pessimistic view on the situation. "There are just so many people to move in such a short amount of time."

"According to the statistics," Angie responded, "they have to move a minimum of twenty million people out of ten states in less than a month."

"The truth of the matter," Joe added, "is that we really don't know when the volcano will erupt. It could erupt tomorrow, or it could erupt six months from now. All we really know is that an eruption is imminent. There is a very good chance that they will get everybody out in time."

Angie knew that Joe was attempting to lower her anxiety level, but in reality, she would not rest easy until every last person was evacuated from the area. She was convinced that most Americans felt the same way.

"It's a well organized evacuation," Tom explained, "and involves both local and federal agencies. The good news is that the pyroclastic area, known as the dead zone, is less populated then the areas beyond that zone, which will reduce the time needed to evacuate."

"Angie," Ron said in a confident manner, "it's important to know that areas beyond the dead zone are critical but survivable, as long as residents have protective masks, which, from what I understand, are now being distributed. Also, according to the new data, it doesn't appear that the volcano will erupt within the next two months."

"Thank you, Ron," she said, sounding somewhat relieved.

"No need to thank me, Angie. We are all in this together; besides, we have to keep our heads clear for the tough road that we have in front of us."

"That was very considerate of you Ron," Joe whispered in Ron's ear. "You seemed to have calmed her down."

After breakfast, they all walked back to a lounge area to view the latest news bulletins.

"Please stand by for the latest bulletins on the Yellowstone evacuation... This is Bob Miller BNA broadcasting network with the latest news on the evacuation. Evacuees were previously instructed to travel lightly, to take only enough food, water, clothing, and other essential items to last one week, but that is not exactly what is happening." The newsreel zoomed in on cars, vans, and trucks loaded beyond capacity. Bob continued, "The evacuees are taking furniture, refrigerators, and just about everything but the kitchen sink! This is dramatically slowing the evacuation process. Once again, to expedite the evacuation, we urge you to cooperate with the authorities and adhere to the instruction that have been issued by Federal and State authorities.

"Fuel stations have been set up along each route, but it must be noted that there's a limited supply of fuel. If you overload your vehicle, you will consume a lot more fuel, leaving many other evacuees stranded with empty fuel tanks. We understand the hardship you're going through, but it is essential that we receive your cooperation on this matter.

This broadcasting network will be repeating this message every twenty minutes and will provide updated information throughout the day."

Tom and his colleagues felt a great deal of emotion for the evacuees. Some were aware of the fact that the area within the dead zone would not be able to sustain life for years to come, and possibly not in their lifetime. Others leaving the area believed that they would be able to return as soon as the danger had subsided. The evacuees who believed that they would never return to their homes were determined to take whatever they could squeeze into their vehicles. Their instinct to survive had been overshadowed by their need to mitigate the financial setback that they would soon experience. Although the authorities were steadfast regarding the procedures that would allow an expeditious evacuation, they were not judgmental toward those who violated procedures. The National Guard and other officials simply pulled violators over at specific check points and did not permit them to proceed until they reduced their carrying load. Fuel supplies were critically low. To allow these heavily packed vehicles to continue would have compounded the problem. The evacuees were assured that help would be available to them when they reached their final destination.

When the news started to become repetitious, they clicked off the TV.

"Is there something bothering you, Tom?" Joe could look at Tom and immediately recognize when he had moved on to another train of thought. He was still in the same room, but mentally he had moved to another time zone. He is already contemplating his next move, Joe thought, "Well, Tom, what are you thinking about?"

Tom lifted his head and turned to Joe.

"Yes, I do have other concerns. I believe that we are finally on the right road and after the meeting with the President, I believe that things will really start to go our way."

"Yes, they will," Joe agreed. "And it seems like we're going to get the full cooperation of the oil companies, which is what this next meeting is all about."

"We are also going to require the cooperation of almost every nation in the world," Tom said, "especially oil-producing nations. The eruption at Yellowstone will cause dramatic social and economic unrest throughout the world. The standard of living in all nations will dramatically diminish. The question is, will these countries continue to cooperate with us?"

"What choice do they have?" Joe snapped. "In two to three years, the planet could very well terminate the entire human race. This is not a financial issue, it's a survival issue. Nothing else takes precedence. My guess is they're going to do whatever they have to do to survive."

"I guess you're right, Joe."

"Sure there's going to be a downturn in the economy," Joe said, "but that's a moot issue considering the circumstance. When the stock markets reopen, they will probably lose ninety percent of their value. The insurance companies will not have sufficient funds to cover the enormous losses, and after the eruption at Yellowstone, and who knows how many other eruptions will occur around the world, not only will the mid-western farmlands remain barren for decades, but farm lands all over the world will become barren, causing an enormous food shortage. The prime element here, Tom, is not convenience, but survival.

"If the crust of the planet continues to deteriorate, and more and more of the molten lava seeps from the mantle to the surface of the planet, Yellowstone will seem like a firecracker compared to what's coming.

"We have already confirmed the calculations. It has already started. We are now in the first stages of a continental movement of the tectonic plates. This is one time I wish that I were wrong, but the facts are the facts. This is why the future financial outlook doesn't mean a damn thing. Not only are these countries going to cooperate, but I'll bet dollars to donuts that they are working fulltime in an effort to resolve the problem."

"I agree," President Hamity said, as he walked into the room. "Tom, I just received additional reports from the USGS. They have been collaborating with scientists throughout the world for the past twelve hours. The reports are pretty conclusive. Seismic activity around the globe is dramatically increasing. Several volcanoes that have been dormant for years are showing signs of activity. We have reports of earthquakes occurring in Indonesia and Japan registering 6 and 6.5, respectively. Things are starting to heat up.

"We now have enough scientific evidence from top scientists around the world to confirm that your findings regarding the cause of the increased seismic activity are correct. It appears that we are going to receive the full cooperation of the UN in a unified effort to resolve the problem.

"Our meeting with the oil companies," the President continued, "which is in an hour from now, is no longer focused on whether or not they will close down their wells. We received a one-hundred percent vote from both Congress and the Senate last night, in an emergency session, approving a bill that orders the shutdown of all oil wells under the jurisdiction of the United States. Furthermore, ninety-five percent of all remaining wells throughout the world will be shut within the next two days. The remaining wells will be shut down within a week.

"I am not quite sure how much of the planet is salvageable at this point. What I do know is that for the first time since man has inhabited the planet, all nations, regardless of their religious beliefs or political agendas, are unified in a joint effort to protect and preserve the planet.

"The big question at this point is how do we stop and/or reverse the process? We have less than two years, gentlemen. Two years to accomplish what no man has ever accomplished before. We must stop the flow of magma from reaching the surface of the planet." The President paused for a moment to gather his thoughts. "I just do not understand how we allowed this to happen. The planet has been around for billions of years, yet it only took us one hundred years to screw it up! Tom, are we blowing in the wind here? I mean, do you really believe we can find a resolution in just two years?"

"That's a tough question, sir. Even if we succeed, the planet is never going to be the same, at least not in our lifetime. We have some great minds in this world, but the circumstances are not in our favor. The realistic goal here is to mitigate the damage, and the real questions are, how much of the planet can we save?"

"Thank you for your honesty, Tom."

Tom listened to the President intently. He wanted to tell the President that everything would be alright, that they had already developed a plan or method to save the planet. However, he knew that there was nothing on the table. They had not yet developed a method to resolve the problem, and it did not appear that one would be developed anytime soon. He was at a loss for words.

"Unfortunately, sir, there is nothing on the table. We have absolutely no clue about what to do at this point."

"Mr. President!" Joe interrupted. "I believe that God has given us the knowledge and the will to survive. Through our great strides in technology, the human race has managed to resolve just about every problem it has confronted. From putting billions of pieces of information on a chip the size of a pin head to walking on the moon. The problem confronting us, although monumental, is certainly not beyond human capability. I am sure that many of the top scientists in the world are working diligently to find a solution to this problem as we speak."

"Thank you, Joe, you have a great attitude; I hope God was listening," The President said. "We could sure use his help on this one."

"Yeah," Joe said, "a little help from the big guy wouldn't hurt."

The President nodded his head and smiled.

"I'll see you all at the conference room." The President left the room.

Tom walked over to Joe to pat him on the back. "Thanks, Joe, thanks for your input; a little optimism never hurts."

Joe smiled, "Remember, Tom, we have to concentrate on plan G!"

"Plan G, what the hell is plan G Joe?"

"I'm not sure Tom, but it's got to be better then planning F!"

Tom gave Joe a pat on the back as they all walked toward the conference rooms.

CHAPTER 16

The conference room was packed with representatives from just about every major oil company in the world. The dozens of conversations that simultaneously rang through the room sounded like an orchestrated hum.

This would not be an ordinary meeting where argumentative issues encouraged defensive strategies. A bill passed by Congress and the Senate had already closed down the oil wells. There was nothing to debate, argue, or defend.

Tom and his colleagues were escorted to the front of the podium, walking just behind the President and his staff. The representatives of the oil companies gave the President a standing ovation as he entered the room then quietly took their seats. It became so quiet you could have heard a pin drop. Secretary of State, Joan Dunne, was standing at the microphone, preparing to introduce the President.

"Ladies and gentlemen, members of Congress, members of the armed forces, Mr. Collins and his distinguished colleagues, I thank you all for joining us this morning on such short notice. As you well know, the matter at hand is extremely grave and warrants your full cooperation, so without further hesitation, ladies and gentlemen, the President of the United States!"

The President walked to the podium as Secretary Dunne stepped to his left side. The crowd stood up and gave the President thunderous applause. As the ovation continued, he raised both arms in an attempt to silence the crowd and then began to speak as the applause subsided.

"There are no heroes in this room! With the exception of Mr. Collins and his colleagues," the President continued, "there are no heroes in this room!" He paused between his words as if he were disappointed in himself. "Not I, and not a single person in this room. I stand here before you and cannot find the words. How can one day be so different than the next? How could one day offer us business as usual, and the very next day we find that man has damaged the planet to such an extent that there is a strong possibility that the total annihilation of the human race may be imminent? I have posed this same question to the USGS. Isn't there anyone in the entire world that had the insight to recognize that seismic activity had been dramatically increasing over the past one hundred years? Have we become so complacent as not to recognize the severity of the problem? Surely, the oil companies must have known something! The fact is, gentlemen, we had the information and simply ignored it. And to boot, we attempted to silence Tom and his colleagues when they tried to bring this vital information to our attention.

"Well, gentlemen, we have certainly put ourselves in a precarious situation. We are going to have to put forth an enormous effort if we are to circumvent what could very well result in the total elimination of every life form on this planet.

"We are going to require your full cooperation on this project if we're to afford ourselves any hope at all for resolution. The situation is critical, and, unfortunately, time is not on our side."

The President paused for a moment and then continued. "This is not about me! This is not even about us! This is about all of mankind!

"Never before, throughout the history of civilization, have we been faced with such a grim circumstance. We were warned; it's not like we haven't been warned! We simply did not respond! The question is, do we have time to reverse the damage that we have caused, or has time run out? We have literally pushed ourselves into a corner.

"Now we have a problem! The planet that we have been abusing for so many years is breaking up right beneath our feet as I speak. In the past twelve hours, I have received reports that are alarming, to say the least. Vesuvius, Awu, Tambora, Soufriere, Mount Pelee, El Chichon; these once dormant volcanoes now show signs of renewed seismic activity. There are sections of the Earth's crust in the Atlantic that are non-existent! That means that the mantle of the planet's core is actually exposed! We are presently evacuating more than twenty-million people from a six-hundred mile radius around Yellowstone National Park. This is not a drill; it has already been established that the Yellowstone volcano is going to erupt! Ladies and gentlemen, this is not the movies where super heroes fly in from the sky to perform sensational rescues. To date, we have more than thirty thousand dead and scores more injured.

"The impact of this one single eruption will be enormous. We will lose more than 40 percent of our farmlands, and could sustain casualties that will far exceed anything we have experienced in the past. The effects of the fall out will be worldwide. It will take three weeks for the volcanic ash to circle the globe. The results will be catastrophic.

"The message here is clear. Time is running out! The project that we will establish here today, to save the planet, will hopefully circumvent the damage we have caused in an effort to secure the destiny of mankind! If it is not resolved, this entire planet, in the words of our good friend Ron Massey, will resemble the atmosphere of the planet Mars.

"I know that you are all here in full cooperation regarding this project and I thank you for that.

"We have come to the crossroads on this issue. In the past, we have taken the pathways that were self-aggrandizing. We have followed the roads that lead to profit and success at the expense of the environment. We have ignored the warning signs! Our relentless appetite for more has now led us down the path of total extinction. We have to make a decision; the debates are over! There is no longer a need to debate the issues of global warming, water pollution, air pollution, deforestation, the pollutions of our oceans, or any of the other issues that have been slowly destroying the planet's ability to sustain life. These issues are no longer circumstantial conditions; they are events. We have ignored the warnings and now we must face the consequences. As of today, the world must work as a single unit, in full cooperation with one another, or perish. The United States is prepared to join all nations around the world in a solitary pledge that we may act as one nation for the good of all mankind! The time has come when nations divided can no longer control events that lead to what may very well be the total extinction of civilization! It is the responsibility of all of mankind to protect the planet's ability to sustain itself! There is no prejudice in our circumstances. We have allowed our indifferences to circumvent simple visual truths. Now we, as one of the leading nations in the world, hold our hands up high and ask to be heard. Hear our words shouting out to every nation in the world! Unit with us! Together, we shall be triumphant."

Everyone in the room stood up and applauded. The President

continued, "Mr. Collins, who had intended to speak today, has instead requested to meet with you in the presidential conference room immediately after this meeting."

The President then whispered something to Joan and faced the audience. "I have quoted many famous people during my years in politics, but today it seems none fit the cause except for something my mother said to me regularly as I was growing up. She said, 'John, don't tell me you cannot accomplish this, or that, or that the task is just too difficult. Remember, where there is a will there is a way!' So just go out there and do what you have to do!

"Our mission is to save the planet! So let's go out there and do what has to be done! Thank you."

The President received a standing ovation as he left the room.

Tom and his associates retreated to the President's conference room to meet with representatives from the oil companies.

As Tom, Joe and the others stepped out into the corridor, Pete Marchel along with Frank Benit, the head of the CIA security team in the White House, asked to speak with them in an adjacent security room.

Frank, who had been a CIA agent for twenty seven years, had worked on high-security projects for more than twelve years before his assignment as the White House top security agent. He had been married for thirty-five years to his wife, Kerrie, and had two beautiful daughters, Beth and Marian. Frank stood six-foot-four and weighed two-hundred twenty-five pounds, giving him a formidable presence at first site. He had a reputation for being tough as nails, and was well aware of what was going on around him. Highly respected by his peers, he was a man that you would want on your side in the event of a conflict.

Pete sat beside Tom and Joe, while Frank remained standing. Joe seemed somewhat apprehensive, sensing that there was something wrong.

"What's the problem, Pete?"

There was a moment of silence. Pete admired Joe's ability to perceive the intent of others prior to their verbal commitment to a subject.

"I would like you to meet Frank Benit. He's with the CIA and is presently in command of all security at the White House. Frank is responsible for the safety of the President." They each introduced themselves. Joe still seemed a little anxious to know what was going on.

"Frank, why are we here?"

"I have been directed by the President to secure your safety. He admires your courage, your honesty and your uncanny ability to survive. He sees all of you as the true patriots, and I'm inclined to agree with him."

"Well?" Joe asked. "So what's the problem?"

"I like a man who sticks to the point," Frank said. "Well Joe, the FBI, in a joint effort with the CIA, has had the oil companies under surveillance since the assassination attempts. The bad news is that the oil companies are not involved. We have confirmed that the group that goes by the name the Last Jihad is not only acting alone, but they continue to be a serious threat to the operation."

"You're not trying to cheer us up, are you Frank?"

Frank smiled, "I like the way you think, Joe. You answer everything with a question."

"Just trying to find out what your plans are to keep us alive."

"Trust me, Joe, this project has been prioritized. There is nothing in Washington that supersedes the importance of this operation."

"I don't know, Frank," Pete said smiling, "after that bunker incident, I'm not sure if these guys still trust us."

"Yeah," Frank said, "that was one hell of a job they did out there. Anyway, orders are orders. We have assigned a team of security agent's twenty/four/seven to assure your safety. The team will comprise of both CIA and FBI agents, so if you notice that you're being followed to the rest rooms, don't get excited, they've been ordered not to peek. Actually, in most cases, you won't even know they're there. However, once your group is relocated to the command center, the agents will no longer be necessary."

"Why is that?" John asked.

"There are more security agents assigned to the command center then there are personnel who work there."

John smiled. "Well, that's good to know."

"When will we be assigned to the command center?" Tom asked. "That is where we're going to do our research, isn't it?"

"Yes," Frank responded. 'You and your team will be guest at the White House tonight. It'll be the United Nation tomorrow morning, and then late that afternoon, you will all be flown back to the command center."

Tom walked over to Frank and shook his hand. "This is the best news I've heard yet, thanks for everything, Frank."

"I'll be in contact with you as soon as I get the itinerary regarding the time schedule for the UN conference. If you have any questions, Pete has my number."

"Sounds like you're expecting a problem at the UN," Joe said, in a concerned voice.

"It's just a precautionary measure. It's nothing to worry about."

"I've heard that before," Joe snapped.

Pete and Frank just smiled.

"Everything will be just fine," Frank said as he left the room.

"Frank is a pretty thorough guy," Pete said. "Now that he has confirmed what we had already discussed earlier, regarding the ties between the oil companies and the terrorist group, we can more effectively direct our attention toward the terrorist fraction. Right now, I have to meet with Frank in a couple of minutes. If you need anything, just give me a buzz."

"Thanks," Joe said, "See you later."

"We had better get into the conference room," Tom said.

Tom introduced himself and his colleagues to the executive officers representing all of the major US oil companies. They had already given the President their assurance that they would fully cooperate with Tom and his colleagues by offering to provide whatever services and equipment were necessary to resolve the pending problem.

Tom was open and direct about the seriousness of the situation as he addressed the assembly.

"Gentlemen, we are quickly approaching the point of no return. Magma is now moving to the surface of the crust at an accelerated rate. The question is, can it be stopped? What we are up against, according to recent seismic readings, is a tremendous buildup of lava in newly formed cracks, throughout the world. Unless we can find a solution, this magma will break through the surface of the crust; not just in areas of previously known fault lines, but in areas where this type of activity has no historical precedent.

"What we are facing today is a monumental task," Tom continued, "one that puts into question the very existence of life itself. If we fail, we will witness the complete annihilation of the human race! This is not an exaggeration of the facts, gentlemen, and I can assure you that time is not on our side. If not resolved, this planet will revert back to the volatile uninhabitable planet it was billions of years ago, and unfortunately, we are not even close to finding a resolution.

"We are meeting with world leaders at the United Nations building tomorrow morning to solicit their support, which in culmination with the commitment you have made here today, will energize a united effort toward resolving the problem."

Tom paused for a moment as he shuffled some papers around that lay before him.

"We have made a preliminary list of personnel and organizations that we believe will be an asset to the project. These scientists, technicians, and engineers will become part of an international team, who will participate in a continuing effort to save the planet. This does not mean that the list cannot be expanded. Like I said, it is a preliminary list. We have named the project 'Save the Planet,' or STP. The organization will operate as a single unit. What this means is that all scientific information developed by each individual group will be funneled into a single computer program, which will then be automatically logged, deciphered, and categorized. The information will then be categorically separated into specific subject matter and made available for study. Each member of STP will be given his or her own code number to enter the system, making all the scientific information logged-in available to each individual member.

"To enhance the security of the system," Tom continued, "several countries have joined together to develop a coded satellite communication network that not only will allow you to enter and receive information from any place in the world, but it will also permit members to communicate either individually or by conference, twenty/four/seven.

"A group of technicians have already been assigned to install and maintain the system at all locations designated by STP members. You will all be contacted.

"Gentlemen, there is absolutely no room for failure! The entire world is counting on us.

Mr. Ron Massey, who will be in command of this central computer system, will be happy to answer any questions you may have directly after this meeting. Thank you."

As Tom and his team started to walk-away, several oil company representatives stopped to thank him and his colleagues for having such veracity and perseverance, not just for surviving the assassin attacks, but for their ability to cut through all of the political bureaucracy and circumvent the self-centered corporate money mongers, who seldom submit to profit loss under any circumstance.

The three executives representing the oil companies assured Tom that they would be fully committed to the project. The President's staff remained at the meeting to set up a management team. There was much organizing to accomplish in a very short period of time.

As Tom, Joe, and the rest of the crusaders were about to leave the conference room, they were approached by a group of oil company executives.

"Mr. Collins, may we have a word with you?"

"Certainly," Tom responded.

"My name is John Hanson. These gentlemen are my colleagues, Bill Bronson and Lou Banes."

Tom formerly introduced his colleagues to the three oil executives.

"We represent the American Oil Company Association," Hanson explained. "Tom, there is word going around that the oil companies have a contract out on you and your colleagues. I can assure you that it is not the case. That is not how we do business. Also, it has been asserted that we have some sort of connection with the same terrorist group that attacked you at the bunker. I can assure you that we have no such affiliation.

"Some of these tough-guy methods may have existed years ago but such tactics simply do not exist today. When someone makes false accusations against the industry, we simply take them to court, we don't shoot them. I'm not going to tell you that we weren't cognizant of the fact that the damage to the planet's crust wasn't directly related to the extraction of oil: we simply did not know extent of the damage. It was only after we examined your work that we confirmed the severity of damage."

Tom and Joe just listened, but did not respond.

"If you need anything from us," Hanson continued, "please do not hesitate to call."

John Hanson handed Tom his personal business card. Both Bill Bronson and Lou Banes did the same.

"We will assist you in any way possible," Bill Bronson added. "We are presently examining the situation, and have committed all of our resources and personnel to the project. As soon as your satellite system is up and running, we will furnish you with updated scientific data and sonar calculations that will identify both existing and new fault lines, and the progress of these latent conditions in relations with time and distance. This will, at the very least, let us know how quickly the faults and cracks are accelerating."

"Of course," Lou Banes said, "we will also be concentrating on a solution to the problem."

"In any event," Hanson said, "our facilities and personnel will be made available to this operation twenty/four/seven."

"We certainly appreciate your cooperation on this matter," Tom responded.

MELTDOWN

"We'll keep in touch," Bronson said as the men left the conference room.

"Well, what do you think Tom?" Joe asked.

"There was no reason for them not to be sincere," Tom said. "After all, this is not a situation that one can buy them self out of."

"These guys are under the gun," Joe said, "they had no choice except to cooperate, but you really don't believe all that other crap, do you?"

Tom shook his head, but did not respond. He just wanted to resolve the problem, and he knew that he needed the cooperation of the oil companies to do so.

The team went back to their rooms to freshen up a bit before joining each other in the dining room.

Tom and his colleagues were a little restless that evening. Anxieties were high, but so were their expectations. They knew that the next day they would face one of the most important phases of their journey: to join every nation in the world in a united effort to save the planet.

The CIA did not release information regarding the time schedule or the method of transportation for fear of a possible attempt by the insurgents to disrupt the UN conference. The country remained on red-alert.

"I feel pretty confident," Tom said, "that the conference will be the catalyst which will unite every nation in the world toward a common goal."

"They really don't have too much of a choice," Joe said. "Now do they?"

"What do you mean?" John asked.

"It's a choice between living and dying," Phil said with a smile. "Which one would you choose?"

"Ok," John said. "It's late and I'm a little tired."

Just then, Pete walked in. "Are you ready for tomorrow?"

"As ready as we'll ever be," Tom said.

"The UN conference is scheduled to begin at three pm," Pete explained. "Agent Frank Benit and I have been assigned as the leading agents for this operation."

"What do you mean, Operation?" Tom asked. "I thought this was a conference meeting."

"Yeah," Joe said. "It sounds more like you're anticipating the Normandy Invasion. Is there something you're not telling us?"

"No," Pete said, "but we do have to proceed with caution. The insurgents still pose a threat and must be taken seriously. It's just a precautionary measure Joe, and although there may not be an incident, we can't take any chances. The heads of state of almost every nation in the world will be attending this meeting. We're simply following protocol."

"Sounds reasonable," Ron said. "After the bunker incident, a little protection will be more then welcome."

"I second the motion," John said.

Tom smiled. "We understand Pete, and we do appreciate your concern for our safety."

"I'll meet you down in the dining room at five am sharp," Pete said.

"We'll be there," Joe said, "and thanks."

Pete left the room.

"Well, I think we should all hit the sack," Tom said. "We have a big day ahead of us tomorrow."

"Good idea," John agreed, "I'm exhausted."

"Go ahead guys," Joe said, "Angie and I will be right behind you."

They all headed back to their rooms.

"You haven't said much about what's going on, is there something wrong?"

"I watched some of the news commentaries earlier today," she said in a low voice. "It's just heartbreaking to watch. All those families, and not knowing what lies ahead of them." She looked like she was ready to cry. "Joe, most of these people have lost everything. It's just a terrible situation."

Joe walked to Angie and held her in his arms. He then lifted her chin and looked into her eyes. "I have the same compassion for those people as you do, and I have a pretty good idea what they're going through. I know I haven't expressed my feelings openly, but trust me Angie, I do realize what they're going through." Joe paused for a moment and then continued. "That's one of the reasons that I love you. You have so much compassion for others. There may not be anything we can do about the evacuation, Angie, but if we are successful in what we are trying to accomplish, we can, at the very least, offer them a glimpse of hope, something to look forward to."

Angie put her arms around Joe and kissed him passionately. "I love you Joe," she said in a sincere manner, "I love you so much."

"I love you too, Angie. Now do you think we can hit the sack?"

"Yes," she said with a big smile on her face.

Joe put his arms around her and walked her to her room.

CHAPTER 17

The evacuation of 20 million people located within a six-hundred mile radius of Yellowstone National Park sounded more like a pipe dream than a reality. It was the largest evacuation ever attempted. Even the Exodus from Egypt could not compare to the magnitude of this evacuation.

The families were not just leaving their homes behind; they were leaving a life style, a tradition, a way of life. It didn't matter who you were, or your status in life. You could have been a crop picker or the governor of the state, each would be a refugee in his or her own country.

The three or four percent of the evacuees that had family outside the perimeter of the evacuation zone would be somewhat better off than the majority of the evacuees who would be moving into makeshift living quarters, where they would be experiencing water shortages, food rationing, and a number of other inconveniences. The evacuation itself had turned into a nightmare. Aside from fuel stations and limited rations furnished by the National Guard, all the evacuees had left was what they could load into their vehicles. Every town along the way was closed down, which meant that they would not be able to purchase anything until they reached their destination.

The majority of the evacuees came from the heart land of America. They were hard working people with strong family values. These people were a determined group that certainly had the will and the courage to endure such hardships. But the real hardship was the thought that they would never return. After reading the initial newspaper articles describing the magnitude of previous Yellowstone eruptions, the evacuees, for the most part, knew that they would not be returning, at least not in their lifetime. It was a sad day for Americans.

The notice to evacuate was communicated as a red alert. There were no previous warnings. One day it was business as usual, and the next day they were packing their bags. They were instructed to pack enough food, water, and clothes to last five days, and were assured that once they arrived at the makeshift camps they would be provided for.

The first emergency broadcast was very informative. "This is an emergency broadcast! It has been determined by the USGS that the eruption of the volcano located in Yellowstone Park is imminent. The area that is within the six-hundred mile radius of the park will have to be evacuated immediately. The instructions and required restriction for the evacuation, including routes and final destinations, will be broadcast on all television and radio stations continually. Millions of lives are at risk, which means that it is absolutely imperative for all evacuees to explicitly adhere to the evacuation instructions. The National Guard has set up fuel trucks on all routes leading out of the evacuation zone. This fuel will be distributed at no cost to all evacuees. I repeat, this message and the instructions for the evacuation will be repeated throughout the day at thirty-minute intervals."

~~~~~~~~~~

When Mildred Stone first heard the news to evacuate, she became dogmatic. She simply could not, or would not, absorb the initial emergency broadcast as being real. Mildred was waiting for someone to say, 'This is just a drill," or 'This has been a test of your emergency broadcast system.' However, when she changed the channels on her TV set, the message was the same. The order to evacuate was real. Yellowstone is really going to erupt, she thought. Her first concern was to pick-up her four children from school..., or should I start packing? No! I had better go to the store and pick up the things we will need for the trip. The stores will be crowded. That's what I'll do. I better call John. She was frantic by this time, almost hyperventilating. Just then, her husband John walked in the door. She ran over to him and threw her arms around him and started to weep. He held her tight in his arms. She then saw her four children walk into the house. "Oh John, you picked up the children," she cried out, as she attempted to contain her emotions.

The children, ages six to twelve, were carrying boxes of food and
~~~~~~~~~~

water. Mildred, still slightly sniffling and emotionally drained from the news to evacuate, started to realize that everything that she held dear to her was standing right in front of her. "John, I don't know what I would do without you and the children."

John smiled.

"I love you too sweetheart."

Still sniffling, she looked directly into John's eyes.

"I realize now that my biggest fear is the possibility of losing all of you. That is what I fear the most. It's a horrible feeling John. I just don't know what I would..."

"Everything will be all right, Mildred. When we leave, there will be six of us in the van, I promise you. We will even take the dog. Is that all right with you?"

"Yes, John. Yes. Well, we had better start packing."

Within two hours, they were packed and ready to go. John had shut off the electric power and the main water supply to the house. They took one last look at their home and then started on their journey.

Their destination was predetermined by the emergency instructions broadcasted on the television and radio networks.

~~~~~~~~~~

In other situations, entire neighborhoods decided to travel as a single group. There were also entire families, including uncles, aunts, grandparents, and close friends who had planned to make the journey together, thinking that there would be safety in numbers.

There were enormous problems involved with transporting those who were hospital patients, mental patients, those who lived in homes for the elderly, and other patients at facilities of a similar nature.

The millions of personal records and documents kept by the states, cities, and towns would be impossible to transport, notwithstanding the millions of farm animals that could not be evacuated until every last person had reached a safety zone. Then there was the problem of those who decided to stay and ride it out. Some stood behind to protect their net worth, and others simply did not want to leave. Those who decided to stay to protect their financial interest were either inadequately informed or just didn't quite grasp the seriousness of the situation.

The synopsis for the Yellowstone eruption was headline news for weeks before the USGS finally confirmed that another eruption was imminent. The broadcast was clear. "The volcanic ash will move over land
~~~~~~~~~~

at a speed of approximately four-hundred miles per hour, within the first one-hundred miles, heated at a temperature of more than a thousand degrees. The ash fall out will seriously affect residents living within six-hundred miles from the eruption."

Although this was a mandatory evacuation, it would be close to impossible to enforce. The police were not concerned about those who stood behind to loot. Those geniuses would be either immediately cremated, or drown in their own blood when their lungs filled with glass particles from inhaling volcanic ash.

The roads were packed. Every road leading out of the evacuation zone was bumper to bumper. For some people, it was what they had to do to survive. For others, there was emptiness, a feeling of total loss.

~~~~~~~~~~

Chad and Fran Pitt lived in Boulder, Colorado, for the past seven years. He was a carpenter by trade and had been working on and off for the past six months, making it difficult for them to make ends meet. They lived in a trailer home with their two children, Matthew and Martha, aged seven and nine, respectively. They had made numerous friends throughout the trailer park and weren't really too anxious to leave, but when his brother called from North Carolina and offered him steady work, he had no choice but to accept.

After the children had left for school that morning, Chad went off to work to complete a job he had started the day before, while Fran decided to stay home to prepare the trailer for the long trip to the Carolinas. She sat down to finish her coffee and turned the TV on to watch "Good Morning America" and was somewhat taken back when a bulletin flashed across the screen warning of a pending Yellowstone eruption, and further instructing residents to immediately evacuate the area. At first she thought she was watching some sort of documentary, and quickly started to change the channels, but every station was broadcasting the same bulletin. She ran to the door and stepped outside the trailer looking for some kind of assurance that she had misinterpreted the news bulletin.

"Good morning Mary," Fran said to her next door neighbor. "Did you by chance listen to the news this morning?"

Just then, several other neighbors gathered.

"What are we going to do?" Mary asked with tears in her eyes. "We have lived here all of our lives. And Jack with his bad heart, how will we ever make the trip?"
~~~~~~~~~~

MELTDOWN

Mary and Jack are in their late seventies; neither one is in very good health, Fran thought. This is awful; this is going to be a real hardship for most of these people.

"I just can't get myself to believe that this is real," Fran said. "Don't worry Mary, Chad and I will do whatever we can to help."

Other neighbors gathered to offer their support and to discuss the evacuation procedures.

"Some of these trailers haven't been moved in years," one neighbor said. "Who knows if they can make the six-hundred mile trip."

"Maybe it's just a warning," another neighbor Ron insisted. "Maybe she's not going to blow. I think I'll stay and take my chances."

"No," Fran said in a frantic voice. "The bulletin was clear. They said that the eruption is imminent. We all have to leave."

It seemed like everyone was looking for answers, but the reality of the situation remained the same. They would all have to evacuate.

"I have to get Chad to pick up the kids, we can meet later," Fran said as she walked back to her trailer.

Before she reached the door, Chad pulled up to the trailer with the kids in the car.

"I guess we'll be leaving a couple of days early," Chad said, as he got out of the car.

Fran gave him a big hug and then hugged the kids. "We can't leave until we know that our neighbors can also leave."

"You get the trailer ready dear and I'll do what I can to get our neighbors trailers on the road."

Chad worked around the clock the next couple of days and, with the help of others, they managed to get every single trailer in operating condition.

Early the next morning they all gathered together to say their good-byes and wish each other well.

Chad had surmised that this traffic back up would be the worst in history. When they first received the notice to evacuate, they were not concerned because they had previously planned to leave the following week anyway. Chad and Fran had a great deal of empathy for the evacuation victims and included them in their daily prayers. They had lived in the area for more than seven years, and now felt a great deal of compassion for what their friends and neighbors had to face.

Simple, everyday occurrences that were commonplace had come to an abrupt halt. The schools had closed. Little league baseball, planned weddings, family get-togethers, theaters, and other familiar events had simply ceased.

The evacuees were told that they would most likely not return. The banks and the stock markets had been closed one week prior to the date the evacuation notice was issued. This meant that the majority of the evacuees would be short of cash by the time they reached their destination. It was a frightening scenario, to say the least. For the evacuees, plans and aspirations for the future had totally dissipated. For some, there would be despair and uncertainty. For others, there was hope for a better tomorrow.

Chad and Fran had a great attitude in life. They saw this as an opportunity to create a better life for themselves. Although they did not have much, they were determined to help as many people as they could while traveling to the Carolinas.

~~~~~~~~~~

Although each individual coped with the situation differently, families that had been long time residents in the area and who had established even a moderate standard of living were certainly more prone to stress than those that had incomes that fell below the poverty level, such as the migrant workers who mostly immigrated from South America. These people held jobs that were mostly seasonal. They were accustomed to packing their bags and constantly moving from one job to the next. Their hourly rate of pay, in most cases, fell below the standard minimum wage mandated by the federal government. What were they really leaving behind? Going from being poor to being poor was really not much of a status move, and without permanent residency, the only question remaining was, "How do we get the hell out of here before the mountain blows?" Not that they did not have the ingenuity or the ability to move from one place to another; they simply did not have the vehicles.

There were thousands of migrant workers and very few vehicles, and although the subject of illegal immigration was highly controversial in the country, both the state and federal authorities made it absolutely clear that this would not be an issue regarding the evacuation. The orders were to move every single person out of the evacuation zone. When the good news reached the migrant workers, they immediately packed and were ready to go.

Carlos Fernandez, married with five children, and Manuel Gonzalez, married with four children, were both in their early thirties, and they had
~~~~~~~~~~

been best friends since their childhood. Born in a small town in Mexico, they had illegally crossed the border, as did thousands of Mexicans, to seek work in order to support their families in Mexico.

When Carlos and Manuel first heard the news about the evacuation, they were concerned about being deported, or even worse, being arrested. However, when the news stations continued to issue emergency evacuation notices, they both realized that they had to get out of there, and do so as soon as possible.

The migrant workers originally decided not to take the public transportation provided by the government for fear of being identified as being in the country illegally, but Carlos and Manuel convinced them that the immigration problem was no longer an issue.

They decided to return to Mexico to be with their families.

There were many who interpreted the event as the prelude to Armageddon; others just believed that this was a warning sign from God. Still, others reasoned that finding a job in this country during the turmoil, that was about to unleash itself with the fury of a thousand atomic bombs, would be almost impossible.

The more the Mexicans talked about the crises and the more news they read, the more convinced they were that it was time to leave. It would be more advantageous to be poor in Mexico than to be poor in a country that was about to experience the worst disaster since Noah's flood.

The two men arranged to have government buses transport the workers back to Mexico.

~~~~~~~~~~

Ben Hacket, who had just been elected as county sheriff in a small town in Colorado, was angry at the prospect of leaving. He had worked as deputy sheriff for almost eight years under the authority of his good friend, Sam Harris, who had been the county sheriff for more than thirty-five years. A year before the elections, Sam was diagnosed with cancer, and passed on shortly thereafter. Ben was appointed as the temporary county sheriff, which put him in the perfect position for the upcoming elections.

Ben, his wife Judy, and their three daughters, Anna, Linda, and Donna, had previously lived in Tucson, Arizona, where he worked as a police officer. When he was accused of violating civil rights issues regarding Mexicans crossing the border, they decided to relocate. Ben was acquitted of all charges, but the cost of defending himself had drained his savings,
~~~~~~~~~~

and left him in debt. He had a bitter taste in his mouth over the incident, and decided that it was in the best interest of his family to move to an area where this problem did not exist.

Ben had worked hard for almost eight years to secure a position as county sheriff. His aspirations were similar to what any other father's might be: college for his girls, a secured retirement for him and his wife, and the ability to enjoy some of the smaller luxuries in life. Now here it was, coming to a complete end. The instructions were to immediately evacuate and not to plan on returning. He wasn't just angry; he was as angry as hell. At the age of forty-six, he knew that his career as a law officer was finished, which put him in a precarious position. Ben had not worked long enough to receive a pension from his first job in Tucson, and now a volcano was about to terminate his net worth in Colorado. In his mind, God had totally abandoned him. He felt that he had worked really hard to secure financial security for his family's future, and now here I am again, losing all that I have worked for. "I'm a-damn refugee in my own country! It's just not fair!"

"Please Ben, the children," Judy softly responded. She knew that he was fit to be tied. However, she also knew that his anger would not help them get through these crises.

"I'm not like those damn Mexicans that live day to day," he continued. Ben was hot and bothered; his blood pressure was through the roof. "I worked hard to put us in the position we're in!" he screamed. "God felt that things were going too well, so He decided to blow up our town! Maybe we should stay here," Ben continued, "so we can talk to God directly and ask Him what else He has in store for us! That would at least take the element of surprise out of the situation!"

After a short moment of silence, Judy again responded in a soft and gentle voice.

"The Mexicans have nothing to do the evacuation, and neither does God. The newspaper stated that there were twenty million people being evacuated. Did you hear me, Ben? You are one in twenty million that must evacuate. I need you to be with us on this. This is not easy for me or the children." She started to weep as she continued, "I am frightened, Ben." She continued crying. Their three daughters, Anna, Linda, and Donna had tears running down their cheeks.

Ben stood quiet, and then continued in an apologetic manner.

"I'm sorry." He put his arms around her and held her tightly. Then he reached out to his daughters and waved at them to come over. They stood in a circle hugging each other. Judy had reached her breaking point, and he knew it. Ben felt terrible. He had brought tears to the eyes of the four girls that he loved most. He just did not know what to say.

Judy leaned back and looked into his eyes.

"We have each other, Ben. As long as we have each other, everything will be all right." Ben turned to the girls.

"Mom's right; I love all of you, and if I didn't have you here to love, all of the other things that I just complained about would have no meaning. I'm really sorry. I think we had better prepare to evacuate."

Judy knew that Ben was a good man just having a difficult time dealing with past events.

The Hacket's packed their van and headed south to where they had family.

The traffic was slow, but it was moving. Most of the evacuees were traveling east and southeast.

They had not been on the road for more than three hours when they turned around a ridge on a mountain road and noticed loose rocks falling. As Ben watched, several cars swerved out of the way to avoid the rocks. Without warning, a large boulder came from out of nowhere and landed on the front hood of the car with a noise that sounded like a cannon. The engine immediately caught fire as Ben yelled, "Get out of the car!" There were rocks falling from the cliff on Ben's left and a two-hundred-foot canyon on his right. "Get out of the car! Go forward," he yelled, "Move toward the front of the car!"

With the car pushed to the edge of the canyon, there was no room on the right side to stand. Judy, Anna, and Donna scrambled out the left doors. However, Linda, reacting strictly out of instinct, quickly opened the door on the right, and jumped out of the car before she realized that the car was at the edge of the canyon where there was no place for her to stand. She grabbed hold of the car door but could not hold on.

Linda fell down into the canyon that slanted at a thirty degree angle for the first forty feet, then dropped straight down an additional two-hundred feet to the bottom. Ben was frantic. He watched her fall as he screamed at the top of his lungs.

"She fell into the canyon! She fell into the canyon! No God, please! Don't take her from me!" Tears were streaming from his eyes as he rushed to the edge of the cliff. Judy was screaming for help. The girls were crying. Holding onto the car fender, Ben looked over the cliff and saw Linda caught on a tree limb that was protruding from the mountain. He immediately knew that she was unconscious.

As the rocks continued to fall, the other cars on the road had their own problems. Ben had absolutely nothing in his van to make the descent. He was frantic running from car to car for help to no avail. He tried his cell phone several times, but the lines were jammed. "I'm going down to get her!" he screamed.

"No!" Judy yelled. "There is nothing to hold on to!"

An old man, who had pulled over to the side of the road, walked toward Ben to see if he could help. He took one look at the situation and then turned toward Ben.

"Is that your wife over there?"

"Yes," he responded in a frantic voice.

"She's right. You need a rig to get down there. Without a rig, you'll be committing suicide."

Just then, Carlos Fernandez and Manuel Gonsalez, the Mexican farm workers, who had witnessed the accident, jumped off a bus with about thirty of their friends. They did not say anything to Ben. They walked to the edge of the canyon and looked down to see what the situation was, and then, in a calm voice, they started to speak to each other in Spanish. The men were from a mountainous region in Mexico, familiar with this type of terrain. Suddenly, six of the heavier Mexicans lay down in the street and held each other's ankles. The lighter men linked themselves together foot to wrist with belts and proceeded to lower themselves down the mountain, making foot-holds in the side of the mountain as they descended. When they reached the girl, they gently lifted her from the branch and started to lift her up from one man to the next until the last man handed her to Ben. Just then, Linda's eyes opened as she wrapped her arms around her dad. She was a little bruised, but feeling just fine. Ben and Judy attempted to thank the men but most of them spoke very little English. Carlos and Manuel nodded their heads in a friendly manner and disappeared as quickly as they had arrived.

"I think God is talking to you, Ben," Judy said, with tears in her eyes, as she held Linda tightly in her arms.

Ben looked exhausted as he turned to face Judy.

In a quiet voice, he said, "If you ever hear me say anything negative about Mexicans again....," he just shook his head, walked toward his wife and kissed Linda on the forehead.

"I've learned more about life in these last two hours then I have over my entire life."

He then walked over to his car and opened the hood. "I'm afraid the engine is shot."

"What are we going to do?" Judy asked, clutching Linda tightly in her arms.

"Unfortunately, the cars passing us are loaded to the brim. I really don't know what we're going to do."

Just then, the same Mexicans pulled alongside Hacket's vehicle, loaded their belonging onto the bus, and then offered them adjoining seats so that they would all be together.

Ben tried desperately to contain his emotions, but could not as his girls gathered around him. "What can I say?" he said in a low voice. "I can't even thank them because I never learned how to speak Spanish."

"You don't have to," Judy said smiling. "They already know."

Judy was happy. She knew that he really understood. The bitterness that had been within him for so many years was gone. In that one moment she knew that life for them had just started anew, and that everything would be all right.

~~~~~~~~~~

Richard R. Grant, a wealthy financier from Denver, Colorado, tried desperately to have his family evacuated by a private plane or helicopter, but there was absolutely nothing available. The public airports were crowded beyond their safety limits, making it impossible for anyone to secure a flight to any location that was beyond the evacuation zone, much less book an accommodation to an exact location.

The airport personnel instructed all patrons to find alternate means of transportation and asked the National Guard to cut off all the roads that accessed the airports. It was an absolute mad house. One couple offered a ticket holder ten thousand dollars for two airline tickets, and was turned down.

Richard finally decided to take his wife, Sylvia, and their two sons, Ralph and Edward, out by car. They packed just the bare essentials, enough food and water to last that day. With more than forty thousand dollars cash in his briefcase, he was convinced that he would be able to purchase whatever essentials they needed as they made the journey. After a grueling ten hours on Route 70, they had traveled only seventy-five miles. Their food supplies had totally run out and most of their water supply was poured into the engine coolant system, which was seriously leaking. They had run out of water miles from the nearest town, and in
~~~~~~~~~~

spite of visible smoke coming out of the engine, Richard was confident that he would make it to the next town. Before they had traveled a mile, the engine ceased to work. After several attempts to start the engine, he got out of the car and tried to stop other vehicles passing by, but none would give up their spot in the slow-moving lines.

Richard was not born into money; he had a humble start. His father, Jim, was an accomplished carpenter and worked as an independent contractor for the locals. He made enough money to pay the bills and fund his three sons' college educations. His mother, Mary, was a soft-spoken woman. Although she never complained, Richard continually insisted that the day would come when he would make enough money to improve their standard of living. His mother always responded in the same manner, "We already have more than we need, son. The most important circumstance you can create in life is to spend more time with those that you love. Remember, son, happiness is when a person is content with what they have. People who are not content with what they have will never be happy."

Richard's father was somewhat more direct on the subject, "I know that you would like to see your mother and I have a better life, and I admire you for that.

" I don't begrudge anyone for having more, and I don't look down on those who have less, but here's how I see it: In life, we never really own anything, we just borrow it, because when we die somebody else owns it. Do you understand, Richard? Most people stress themselves out over what they have and what they don't have. That is what we die from, stress! History is our best teacher. For instance, everyone born in the year 1800 was no different than the people of today because there's never anything new under the sun. They allowed themselves to be stressed out for the same reasons people stress themselves out today, and today, there's not one of them that's still alive. Do you see the point, Richard?"

"No Dad, what's the point?"

"Everything that they thought was so important has passed on. The material world is temporary, Richard. The only thing that counts on this planet is people. Everything else is secondary. People helping people; it is the only way that we can improve the character of the human race."

Richard never got the message. Both of his parents had since passed on, and he had not spoken to his brothers Steven and Matthew in years.

Sylvia, on the other hand, came from a wealthy family and received her education in the finest schools money could buy. She devoted much of her time to helping charitable organizations, and believed herself to be a gracious, and loving person. She fell in love with Richard when he was young and idealistic. Not heeding his parent's advice, he gave up time for profit, and fell short of being the loving husband and the father that he could have been. She still loved him, but the candle was slowly going out.

"We have a problem Sylvia, the engine has ceased. We are probably about 18 miles from the nearest town. The vehicles that are passing are packed tight and simply do not have room for us. We may have to walk to the nearest town."

Sylvia stood there and listened without responding. She saw Richard as a lost sheep, a fish out of water. There was none of his vice presidents, CFOs, or any of his advisers to whom he could assign a task. Here, he was out of his environment. In an ironic way, she was happy. He had spent more time with her and the children on this one day than he had on any previous day for the past twenty years.

"Sylvia, did you hear what I said?"

"Yes Richard, I heard every word you said, have you ever driven east on this road before?"

"No, I haven't."

"I have!" Sylvia snapped. "It is a mountainous road with very high and low elevations. Not only that, but the sun is about to set. That means that the temperature will drop down into the forties tonight. Walking 17 miles under those circumstances would not be a realistic solution to the problem. The sad part is that we are out of food and water. The car engine is not functional, which equates to no heat, unless we start a fire. And to benefit from a fire, we would have to stay outdoors, which will expose the children to the cold mountain winds. And then there are the night crawlers, the scorpions, and the snakes. Richard! We need help! We need someone to help us!"

Sylvia brought Richard back to reality.

"I know! I know! I know! I am really sorry, Sylvia!" He responded in a nervous tone. "I really screwed up, didn't I?"

Sylvia paused for a moment; she could not speak. She was frustrated with his inability to comprehend that they were really in trouble. Here he is pleading for sympathy, at a time when I really need him. She put her hands over her eyes and started to cry.

"Sylvia! Please don't cry. I'll do whatever you want me to do, but please don't cry. I have cash with me. I can offer cash to anyone willing to help us."

Her eyes continued to water; the emotion that she had tried to hide for so many years was surfacing, and this time there was no holding back. She responded in a whimpering voice as the tears rolled down her cheek.

"I'm sorry, I'm...," she could not control her emotions and continued to cry.

Richard rushed to her side and put his arms around her. "Oh, Sylvia, I'm so sorry. I am so sorry. What have I done?" The children were visibly upset. "I love you, Sylvia. I have always loved you. In my mind, I convinced myself that I was doing everything for you and the children, but I wasn't, was I? I didn't quite get it straight, did I? Will you ever forgive me?"

"I love you Richard, I always have."

She could not stop herself from crying. The enormous amount of emotion that she had held back for so many years was now totally out of control. She had exposed her very soul and could no longer hold back the deep emotions she had held for so many years. Her two sons, who had never seen their mother in this state, ran over to her and put their arms around her. Just then, a tall, thin man stepped out of a trailer home and walked over to where the Grants were gathered.

"Howdy folks, I hope I'm not interrupting anything. My name is Chad Pitt, and this is my wife Fran."

"Hi, pleased to make your acquaintance," Fran said. "This is my son Matt, and this curly-haired gal is my daughter, Martha."

Richard introduced his family as Sylvia turned to wipe the tears from her eyes.

Chad walked over to Richard to see what he could do to help.

"I noticed that you had your blinkers on. Are you having some trouble with the car?"

"Yes, the engine died," Richard explained.

"Shame, such a pretty car."

Richard was standing there in a daze. He could not believe that someone had actually stopped. As Chad leaned over the engine, he asked Richard to turn the key. The engine bailey turned over.

"Yep, the engine is frozen alright."

"Are you an auto mechanic?" Richard asked.

"No sir! I'm a carpenter, but when you live in a motor home, it pays to know a lot about auto mechanics."

"Did you say a carpenter?" Richard asked.

"Yes, I come from a family of carpenters," Chad replied.

Richard looked surprised, but did not immediately respond. He felt like he was experiencing some sort of déjà vu.

"My father was a carpenter, and so are my two brothers."

"Yep," Chad responded, "a humble profession to say the least."

"And you were on a trip when the evacuation was issued?" Richard asked.

"No sir! This is our home."

"You mean you live in this trailer year-round?"

"Yes sir. You don't need much in life to be happy, you know, you just need enough to make sure that you and your family are happy." Richard just stood there mesmerized and totally lost for words; it was as if his father were standing there giving him a second chance. He became overwhelmed with emotion as he turned toward Sylvia. When Sylvia saw his emotion; her eyes started to water, but this time they were happy tears. She knew that he had finally understood.

Richard thought, he's a carpenter, to boot. "I never thanked you for stopping. I sure would appreciate it if you would send someone back to help us when you reach the next town."

Chad just smiled.

"I guess you never heard the story of the Good Samaritan? Sir, we are your help!" Richard was overwhelmed with joy. He could not remember a time in his life when someone offered to help him without expecting a check.

Sylvia walked over to Richard and hugged him with all her strength.

Chad turned to Richard, noticing that the family was somewhat distressed.

"There are certain things in life that can really stress a man out, even change a man."

"You got that right," Richard responded, as they loaded their suit cases onto the trailer.

Sylvia smiled as they pulled out, for the first time in years she knew that tomorrow would be a better day.

CHAPTER 18

Agents Pete Marchel and Frank Benit coordinated the UN operation with the New York City Police department to form one of the most intense security forces ever assembled. They had the entire area around the UN building under satellite surveillance twenty/four/seven. There were also in excess of one hundred and fifty agents assigned to comb the area three days before the scheduled meeting.

Although there was no clear evidence of a pending attack, the federal agencies remained vigilant knowing that Tom and his colleagues were still the primary targets by the terrorists' faction.

The Mayor of New York had instructed the chief of police to cooperate fully with the federal agencies. There were more than four hundred policemen assigned to the task force. Security appeared to be as tight as a drum. Pete and Frank were confident that they had covered all the bases.

The terrorist group, the Last Jihad, had gathered enough information to organize a major assault at the UN and Kennedy Airport. The group had members of its sect employed at several car rental companies based at Kennedy Airport. The plan was to load munitions in a number of the rented cars which would be driven to strategic locations, as instructed by Izz Udeen, commander of the Kennedy operation.

The terrorist also confiscated several trailer trucks that were from nationally-known air freight companies to be utilized as transport vehicles. They unloaded the original freight in the same warehouses where the munitions and personnel would be loaded, in preparation for the final attack. Abdul Aalee turned to his commanders with a look of determination.

"There will be blood in the streets of New York today! The prophecy will be fulfilled. Today, we will rise in glory."

CHAPTER 19

Tom and his associates gathered in the dining area for breakfast at approximately four-thirty the next morning. Angie could not stop herself from yawning, that is, until she spotted Joe sitting at a table next to Tom, with a big smile on his face. Joe immediately pulled a chair out for her. "Good morning Angie. Did you sleep well?"

"A little restless," she responded in a low voice, "I couldn't get my mind off the evacuees."

"I feel the same emotion for them as you do, sweetheart, but under the circumstances there is absolutely no other choice. There's going to have to be some real reaching out to these people. This country has already shown its true colors during the 9/11 crises. Americans have always reached out to help those who were affected by tragedy. There was a real camaraderie following 9/11, not just within the country, but also throughout the world. I have no reason to believe that it won't happen again."

Moments later, John, Phil, and Ron strolled in. After greeting each other, Ron addressed the group with the latest geological readings at Yellowstone.

"I have the latest data on Yellowstone," Ron said. "We can discuss it now or..."

"Now Ron," Joe snapped. "The more information we present at the UN, the better our chances of uniting the assembly."

"Well," Ron continued, "the seismic activity has dramatically increased, the Norris Basin is still rising, and the temperatures in the Calderas has increased by two and one half degrees Fahrenheit. The geologists running the show are refraining from setting any timetables, but the latest statistics and geological data sheets clearly confirm that area has become more volatile."

"Phil," Tom asked, "have you had any news from your colleagues at Yellowstone?"

"Yes," Phil explained, "I spoke to them this morning. The team basically acknowledges what Ron has just explained, but they will continue to monitor the volcano from a location in Montana, until they receive orders to evacuate. Also, the evacuation of the hundred mile pyroclastic perimeter is about seventy-five percent complete and should be completed sometime late tonight."

"Is there any chance of an eruption occurring prior to the completion of the evacuation?" Angie asked.

"No one can really predict when the eruption will take place," Ron said, "but according to the latest data, an immediate eruption is not likely."

"We must pray for them," Angie said.

"Yes," Joe responded, "I'm sure God is listening."

Tom did not respond because he knew that there was nothing that could be done to change the present course of events.

"Well, Joe," Tom snapped, "are you prepared for today's meeting?"

"I have the facts and figures memorized, but I'm a little apprehensive about the trip."

"What do you mean you're a little apprehensive about the trip? What does that mean?"

"Do you really want to know?"

"Absolutely, Joe, you know how much I value your opinion."

Joe paused for a moment.

"Well, if history insists on continually repeating itself, I really don't believe that this is going to be a good day for us! The last couple of times the FBI gave us heavy protection we were forced to do a lot of running, ducking, and hiding. Why should this time be any different? We would be better off sneaking out of the White House, renting a car, and driving to the UN! We can enter the UN building through the servant's quarters as cooks, or window washers, or candlestick makers or..."

"Encouraging words, Joe," Tom snapped, "I'm really happy I asked."

Just then, Frank Benit walked in. "It's time, gentlemen. From this moment on, all communications will be restricted. No calls in and no calls out! Agents Matt Johnson, Harry Kline, and Gary Armstrong will guide you through the proper procedures. Remember, all outside communications, from this time on, are restricted. We are always on red alert when we move the President! Under the guidelines of homeland security, the President has deemed it necessary to put you and your colleagues at a similar security level. So, from this point on, it is imperative that you follow all procedures and instruction that you receive from the agents assigned to you. Although these are precautionary steps that we're taking, we do believe that a confrontation with the terrorist group is possible. So, it's imperative that you follow instructions."

Tom and his colleagues were not happy with the prognosis laid out by Frank, but clearly understood that these measures were necessary.

The thought of being attacked by terrorists inexplicitly played heavy on their minds. Anxieties were high. They felt the same fear that the American soldiers felt moments before landing on the shores of Normandy during World War Two.

Tom turned to Joe with a serious look on his face. "I have a feeling that you're right again, Joe. It may not be such a good day after all. What do you think we should do?"

Joe smiled. "When the time comes," Joe snapped, "run, duck, and hide, with a particularly strong emphasis on ducking!"

"Thanks for your doom and gloom scenario," Tom responded shaking his head, "I feel a lot better now."

Joe laughed. "Relax Tom, it was just a joke. Whatever is going to happen is going to happen no matter what anyone says. What we have to do here, is stick with the plan, and don't forget, this UN meeting is a critical part of the plan. If all goes well, we'll be able to concentrate on finding a solution to this damn problem."

"I agree," John said. "I'm really encouraged by the precautionary measures that Pete and Frank are taking. After all, there's a lot at stake here."

"You're right," Tom said. "We really do have to concentrate on the plan."

"It's time to move out," Agent Benit said.

Tom and his colleagues were led out of the White House through several passageways, and then exited out of a side door where a helicopter was waiting to airlift them to a military base on Long Island. They were on their way.

The helicopter would fly them to an old Army base located in the north shores of Long Island, New York, from where the group would be transported to the UN in unmarked armored cars.

The security team scheduled an alternate route for the President and his staff. They had decided to stay away from all the major airports. The routing plan was not distributed to the NYPD for security reasons. However, the federal security team did inform the local authorities where their critical areas of concerns would be.

The mayor of New York, who was deeply concerned about public safety, set up barricades that would distance the public from potentially dangerous locations around the perimeter of the UN building. He also ordered additional security at all major NYC airports.

All security preparations were complete. The time had finally arrived. There was a strong sense of anxiety and anticipation in the air. Pete Marchel had a premonition that within the shadows of the city, there was an evilness that would attempt to change the course of events. The most dangerous adversary a man can face is one that has no value for human life, an opponent who is ready to die or to kill another without having an emotion for either life. However it is the fear of death that leads to victory. A man will always fight harder to live than to die. That gave the good guys a slight edge.

Frank Benit, on the other hand, was mentally geared up for the worst scenario possible. He never took anything for granted, a formula that he felt was the main catalyst that kept him alive all these years.

"There is nothing to do," Pete said, "except wait."

"It's going to be a long day," Frank said as he sipped his coffee. Pete nodded in agreement.

CHAPTER 20

The helicopter had lifted off. Tom and his colleagues were on their way.

This is history in the making, Joe thought. There is not a single event in past history that could compare to the events that man is now facing, the possible annihilation of the entire human race. Joe had a slight grin on his face as he went through a series of ideological scenarios. Man has been trying so hard to destroy the planet, but just could not seem to get it right. We have polluted the air we breathe and the water we drink, which in combination with deforestation has seriously decreased our oxygen supply. We then polluted that same air with gases and toxic fumes in our continued attempt to choke the human race to death! And still, the planet fought back. It simply refused to relinquish its ability to produce life. Not deterred in his quest for destruction, man camouflaged toxic waste as landfill and spread it throughout the land. He simultaneously destroyed the wetlands, knowing that the wetlands were our only natural water filtering system against toxic waste and other impurities. This would cause a surge in cancer and other pollution-related diseases, not with-standing the wild life sanctuaries that were being destroyed. Of course, this process of killing off mankind was just a little too slow, so man decided to speed things up by raising the planet's temperature. This would melt the icecaps and drown who ever might be left. One thought after another ran through Joe's head as he concocted his own mini-documentary.

Yes, Joe thought, we finally got the planet where we want it! The inability to sustain life! Don't ever let anyone tell you that man is not the smartest life form on the planet; we can kill anything.

"What are you grinning at?" Angie whispered. "Is it my hair?"

"No! No, nothing like that. As a matter of fact, you look absolutely beautiful. What I was thinking was how man has finally managed to bring us to the brink of total destruction. They have finally decided to tune in to the reality network. You know, Angie, the documentaries that have been warning us about man causing irreversible damage to the planet all these years. Now, here we are with an environmental disaster on our hands, and the facts biting us right in the ass. Excuse my language, Angie, but it's the only expression that fits the cause."

Angie admired Joe for his sense of responsibility regarding the environment and his ability to recognize obvious truths. She was angry and confused. She simply did not know why they ignored the warning signs.

Angie asked in a frustrated tone of voice. "Why did they wait until it was almost too late; why does it have to come to this?"

"It's greed, Angie, pure, unadulterated greed. Nothing interferes with the bottom line, the almighty dollar! That is, until now. It's that simple. The possible extinction of the human race has put a damper on the ambitions of materialistic worshipers. Now they simply want to live. Man's instinct to survive has taken over. Even if we somehow survive, life as we know it will be drastically changed."

"What about us, Joe? I want to know that we will have a future. That you and I will have something to dream about..." Angie looked like she was about to cry.

"We will, Angie. Things will never be as they were, but as long as we are together, everything will be all right."

"Yes," she said as she put her head on his shoulder, "as long as we are together. I love you, Joe."

"I love you too, Angie."

Tom, on the other hand, could not help but think back on all that had occurred prior to reaching what he hoped would be their final confrontation. The two long years I spent developing theories into proofs and then not having the opportunity to present my work at the convention in Washington. The many assassination attempts that were made on our lives, the terrorist attack at the bunker, the evacuation at Yellowstone, and still, we continue to be confronted by those who relentlessly and violently sabotage our efforts for resolution. He felt like he was in an action adventure movie that was still running. Could this be the final phase of a long and tiring journey? Would the world really get together in a joint effort to save the planet? What choice would they have?

Tom was prepared to sacrifice his own life in his endeavor to do whatever had to be done to save the planet and he knew that he had five friends that felt the same way. His good friend Joe continually reminded him that it did not matter how many plans they had to develop to accomplish their mission, the only thing that mattered was having a plan. Tom turned to Joe, with a smile on his face. "What is our present plan, Joe?"

"I don't know Tom, but it's probably better than the last one."

Tom smiled. He felt assured that they were heading in the right direction.

Phil, Ron, and John continued to monitor Yellowstone and other parts of the world that were experiencing increased seismic activity. The new calculations were utilized to update Ron's simulated computer programs, affording Tom the opportunity to present the latest data and timetables to the UN assembly.

The helicopter reached its destination at ten-thirty a.m. They were now at the Fort Totton Army Base, just west of the Throgs Neck Bridge in Long Island, New York. The small military base was just a forty-minute drive to the UN building. Tom and his colleagues were escorted into a preparation room, by FBI Agents Johnson and Kline, where they would receive their final instruction.

"To assure your safety," Harry said, "we would like you to put on these bulletproof vests. They have satellite GPS homing devices attached to them. Each of the vests has a nametag located on the upper right hand corner. As a precautionary measure, you will wear these vests until you enter the UN building."

It was obvious now that the group had become seasoned warriors. They received the jackets as if they were common dress attire. As Joe buckled his jacket down, he turned to Harry with a big smile on his face. "Where are the automatic weapons and the hand grenades, Harry?"

"Not necessary, Joe, we have you covered on this one. There are more federal agents assigned to you and your friends than are assigned to the President himself."

Joe smiled. "That's good to know, Harry. So I guess that the bulletproof vest is just the latest fashion in modern attire? You want us to look sharp when we address the UN? Is that it, Harry?"

"Just a precautionary measure, Joe; we're just not taking any chances."

"And of course, the homing devices are also precautionary?"

"Yes, that's right, Joe."

"I guess that will enable you to find us in the event we are captured by bad guys?"

"That's right, Joe."

"And Harry, didn't you also say that these guys are out to kill us?"

"What's the point, Joe? What are you getting at?"

"What am I getting at?" Joe snapped. "If these guys intend to kill us, the only thing these homing devices can be used for is to find our dead bodies."

Harry finally cracked a smile.

"OK Joe, you win. If you get in trouble, I'll throw you a couple of hand grenades."

"That's great Harry, as long as you don't remove the pins."

"Is there anything else?" Harry asked, with a slight grin on his face.

"No, that's about it Harry, that is about as much assurance as I can take in a single day."

Harry really liked Joe. Joe would have made an excellent FBI agent, he thought. He has the ability to see everything beyond his opponent's justifications, and does not settle for what you tell him, but rather see's one's true intent.

"You always get straight to the point, Joe. I like that. How would you like to work for the agency?"

"No thanks, Harry! I think I'll stick to rocks. I work with hammers and shovels. You work with bullets and bombs. Do you see the conflict, Harry?"

"I understand your point, Joe."

Just then, CIA Agents Gary Armstrong and Phil Borman walked into the room. Gary walked over to Tom and his colleagues to give them their final instructions. "We are just about ready to depart. As soon as the command center gives us the green light, we'll be on our way. Agent Kline will issue your final instructions."

"Thanks, Gary," Harry responded, as he pulled the instructions from his brief case. "There will be six separate vehicles in our motorcade. Two of the vehicles will be utilized to transport your group. The remaining four vehicles will be strategically placed in the front and rear of the motorcade. Tom, Joe, and Angie will ride in one vehicle, and Ron, Phil and John, in the other. There will be two agents assigned to each of your vehicles and four agents in each of the security vehicles."

"Again," Harry reiterated, "please follow the exact instructions given to you by the agents assigned to your vehicles. And please, under no circumstances are you to leave your vehicle unless the agent assigned to you, instructs you to do so. Remember, our entire route will be manned with law enforcement agents. Each of you will be given a closed-circuit communication unit that will have a direct network connection to the command center, with a cross link to your assigned security agents."

Harry handed each of them a unit. "To communicate, just push the red button and talk. Are there any questions?" Joe looked around the room and noticed that the entire group looked like they were in a coma. No one was smiling. So Joe decided to break the silence.

"I have a question!" Joe yelled.

This time, Harry was prepared.

"Alright, Joe, what is your question?"

"Do you think we can stop for some pizza on the way to the UN?"

Angie broke out in a hysterical laugh. Tom tried desperately not to laugh, but fell prey to Angie's laugh. John, Phil, and Ron were in the corner laughing uncontrollably. Tears were running down John's eyes. Harry attempted to say "Can you believe this guy?", but the words were almost inaudible as he started to laugh aloud. The remainder of the agents, including Joe, joined in.

"This guy is unbelievable!" Harry said, as tears ran down his cheeks.

Joe did it again, Tom thought. What would we do without him?

The President had already arrived at the UN building safely. It was a common procedure to secure the President's safety, but under the circumstances, he wasn't really the target. It was Tom and his colleagues that the terrorists were after.

The FBI and CIA could not find a motive for the insurgents' relentless and violent aggression toward Tom and his colleagues. They simply had no clue why they were being targeted. Both Frank and Pete were confident that the answer would eventually surface, but that really didn't matter at this point; they were determined to protect Tom and his colleagues at all costs.

Just as Harry and several agents started to escort Tom and his colleagues to the six armored vehicles, an emergency bulletin came over the radio. The group immediately stopped to listen.

"This is a bulletin. There are reports of explosions going off at Kennedy Airport. At this time, we do not have definitive information regarding the cause of the explosions. Wait, there is another report coming in. There are reports of what may be gunfire coming from the north and east end of the airport! We are waiting for...., hold it, we are receiving another report! Kennedy Airport is under attack! It has been confirmed! Kennedy Airport is under what we believe is a terrorist attack! This is unbelievable! There are an unconfirmed number of terrorists who appear to be heavily armed. The fighting is reported as intense. We are sending out the information as fast as we are receiving it. Here's another report! It appears that the terrorists are meeting heavy resistance! We now have video coverage. This is unbelievable! There are a number of pedestrians running from the airport, and others just trying to find cover! There are several vehicles driving up from the far end of the airport. They look like New York City police vehicles, Wait a minute! We now have reports that the NYPD swat team is... yes! They're loading civilians into armored trucks. There are what seem to be several helicopters coming in from the east end of the airport! And now the west end! Wait, it looks like they are coming in from all directions! There must be forty, maybe fifty helicopters or more. It's the Marines! The Marines have surrounded the airport!"

Everyone in the preparation room had their eyes glued to the TV. Harry wasn't really surprised that the terrorists launched an attack. After all, the confrontation was anticipated. He was surprised that they had attacked the airport. Why the airport? Just then, he received a call from headquarters.

"Move them out, Harry! The terrorists have targeted the airport. You should have a clean run."

"Yes sir! We're on our way," Harry responded.

"Get everyone in the vehicles!" Harry shouted. "We have orders to pull out."

They were finally on their way, and although the entire team had mentally prepared themselves to accept any consequences that might arise, the team was still filled with anxiety. They remained fully aware of the dangers they faced, but realized that the meeting was an essential part of the plan. This did not eliminate the fear or the anxieties that are inherent in all of us when facing a life-or-death situation.

"Is everyone comfortable?" Harry asked. "We anticipate arriving at the UN in approximately forty minutes."

"The sooner the better," Tom responded, sounding somewhat concerned.

"Are we going to stop for pizza?" Joe asked.

Harry just shook his head. Tom and Angie just smiled.

Harry called the field command center that was set up by agents

Marshal and Benit, just adjacent to the UN building. "This is agent Kline, the motorcade is on its way and on schedule. What's the status on the security forces along the motorcade route?"

"All security forces are in position, Harry," Pete confirmed. "We will remain on a full red alert status until you enter the UN building."

"What's the status at the airport?" Harry asked.

"The situation is under control," Pete said. "Main Headquarters have taken the position that the terrorists missed their mark when they decided to attack Kennedy. They believe that the risk factor for a confrontation at the UN has been diminished. I just want you to know that this is not going to change our security status."

"That's good to know, sir."

"Don't worry, Harry, we have you on the monitoring screen. If anything changes we'll give you a call." Pete hung up and continued to monitor the screen.

"What was that all about?" Joe asked.

"Nothing to worry about," Harry said. "Main headquarters believes that the terrorists blew it when they attacked Kennedy. They don't believe that there'll be a confrontation at the UN building."

"That doesn't make any sense," Joe said. "There are so many routes that lead to the UN. Why would the insurgents limit themselves to this one location, unless it's just a diversionary tactic?"

"Great analogy Joe, you have an uncanny way of mulling your way through the camouflage. Once again, I agree with you. Why the hell would they target Kennedy and not the UN? Don't worry; the security level is still in the red zone. We are not about to let our guard down."

"That's good to know, Harry," Joe said. "By the way, how is the Kennedy situation going?"

"They have things pretty much under control. The Marines have the insurgents cornered in the northwest section of the airport. There were also some cells scattered in a number of airplane hangars. It's just a matter of time before the area is totally secured. I'm guessing that they have the upper hand on the situation because all CIA and FBI agents at Kennedy have been ordered to join the support team at the UN. Also, there were some civilian casualties being reported, but no definitive numbers have been released."

Tom, Joe and Angie were saddened to hear of the heavy civilian casualties at Kennedy. How some people in this world, Angie thought, could be so idealistically separated from one another at a time when it was so important for the world to become cohesive, to join in an effort to save the only planet that is known to have the ability to sustain life?

Angie put her head on Joe's shoulder closed her eyes and silently prayed for the victims and their families.

CHAPTER 21

The CIA arranged to have an additional two motorcades approach the UN as decoys. The first motorcade would approach from the northbound FDR Drive, and the second from First Avenue. All of the vehicles were completely armored and furnished with non-transparent dark bulletproof windows. This would not afford someone standing in the street the ability to identify a person sitting in the car. The CIA was hoping that the decoy motorcades would expose any insurgents that might be in the area, prior to the arrival of Tom and his colleagues.

Barricades were set up and manned by the New York City Police Department and placed more than two blocks from the UN building. This would prevent the insurgents from using the pedestrians as camouflage or possible hostages. The Coast Guard had been ordered to place several well -armed boats along the East River, adjacent to the UN building. This would cut off the possibility of any attack occurring from the water.

With agents placed strategically along the actual motorcade route, everything was in place for the arrival for Tom and his crew. The plan was to drive the vehicles over the Willis Avenue Bridge and then turn onto 2nd Avenue, a one-way street going southbound. The motorcade planned to make a left at 44th Street and cross 1st Avenue, which would be temporally closed at the precise time the motorcade made its turn to enter the United Nations underground parking garage.

Agent Pete Marchel and his boss, John McBride, planned the motorcade route with CIA Agent Frank Benit. They felt that this route would not draw suspicion. It was important that the two decoy motorcades reached the UN building prior to the arrival of Tom and his colleagues.

Everything was just about ready for the final phase of the trip; however, unbeknownst to the security forces, the NYPD department had moles in their organization who informed the insurgents that there would be two decoy motorcades arriving at the UN as decoys. This still put the insurgents at a disadvantage. Would the actual motorcade that was carrying Tom and his colleagues be the first, second, or third motorcade?

~~~~~~~~~~

Abdul-Aalee, the commander of the operation for the insurgents, decided to wait for the last motorcade.

Abdul, Naasih, and Makeen set up their main headquarters in a building that had a clear view of the streets leading to the UN. And although their plan of attack was well organized, they had no specific information regarding what motorcade Tom and Joe would be arriving in. Naasih and Makeen believed that there could be four, five or even six decoys, but realized that Abdul would insist on making the final decision.

"There are at least three motorcades on their way!" Abdul shouted in a determined voice. "I believe that the first two are the decoys. They want us to expose ourselves! If we randomly fire at the motorcades, we will miss our opportunity to fulfill the prophecy. But we have the advantage. We know the route of the two decoys. We must assume that the last motorcade will be the target."

"I agree!" shouted Makeen.

"I also agree!" Naasih responded. "Why would anyone send a decoy out last? We must remember that the infidels do not know that we have informants. We must wait until we see the third motorcade!"

"And what if there are four?" yelled Abdul, "or five? Or even six? We must know for sure! We cannot fail! We must not fail!"

"Abdul, you are our leader, we will do what you say! You have been chosen to lead us; I ask only that you make your decision on the information that we have been given. I am ready to follow your command."

"And I, too, am ready to follow your command!" shouted Naasih. There was silence as Abdul paced the floor, continually looking out the window toward the UN building. He knew that time was running out, and he also knew that Makeen and Naasih's concerns regarding the number of
~~~~~~~~~~

motorcades was an unknown factor that had not been given serious consideration.

"We will attack the third motorcade," Abdul demanded. Makeen and Naasih both committed their allegiance to Abdul. "Go in peace, my brothers. This day we fulfill the prophecy! Glory will be ours!"

CHAPTER 22

After an intense security sweep of the area by the security units, there was no conformation or evidence that there were insurgents in the area. The surrounding buildings were thoroughly searched, and remained under continual surveillance. However, the feds were still not taking any chances. With NYP monitoring the barricades, and the Coast Guard patrolling the east river, they felt they had all bases covered.

Pete Marchel was somewhat perplexed, as he sat beside Agent Frank Benit, "Is it possible, Frank, that the Kennedy attack was it?"

"I don't think so, Pete. These guys are in the neighborhood somewhere, and when they hit the street, all hell is going to break loose."

"Where the hell are they?" Pete snapped.

"I don't know. It wouldn't surprise me if they came out of the damn sewers!"

"I don't like it Frank; I just don't like it."

"Relax, Pete! There are more surveillance cameras in this one area than there are in the entire city, and that's not counting satellite coverage. We have enough federal agents and police on the street to fight a major war. Trust me; anyone who walks into this area having bad intentions will be committing suicide. Stay with me on this one. We have the area well covered, and don't forget Pete, as long as security hasn't been breached, the two decoy motorcades will lure these sons-a-bitches out of their rat holes."

"What do you mean?" Pete snapped, "If security has not been

breached? What does that mean? I thought we both agreed that security is as tight as a drum."

"Is it as tight as a drum?" Frank asked. "Pete! General Custer lost the war at Little Big Horn because the Indians had more information about him than he had about them! We have three agencies involved in this operation! I consider that a high risk situation."

"Do you believe that there's a mole in the system?" Pete asked.

"I don't know, but the first rule of thumb is to believe that your opponent has as much information about you as you have about them. In our business, underestimating your opponent's capabilities can have a terminating effect."

Pete thought back to the time when the insurgents attacked the bunker. An in-house investigation regarding the incident resulted in one arrest. Could there have been more than one in the system? he asked himself.

"You're right," Pete said. "We did flush a mole out of the system a few..."

"Four days ago to be exact," Frank interrupted.

"How did you know?"

Frank didn't respond.

"Don't worry, Pete, we have already assumed that there was a leak and that they know. But who gives a shit. Even if they show up, where the hell are they going to go? Fort Knox is not this protected!" Frank paused for a moment as he walked toward the window. "I know that you're a little apprehensive Pete, but so am I. We are not in this alone. There are federal agents monitoring the area on both satellite and on-location cameras. We have helicopters in the air, and the United States Marines are standing by ready to be air-lifted in on a moment's notice. There are hundreds of police and federal agents on the street. We have more protection in this one area than we have around the White House and Fort Knox put together. What I'm saying Pete, is if I had a contract to take Tom and his team out, this is not the location I'd choose to do it in."

"I guess you're right."

"Now don't get to confident," Frank said with a smile. "These guys are suicidal, and really don't give a shit whether they live or die. That makes them extremely dangerous adversaries."

Pete shook his head in agreement.

"So we both agree," Frank said with a smile.

"What do you mean, we both agree?"

"That there will be hell, fire, and brimstone on the streets of New York City today."

Pete just looked at Frank, but did not immediately respond; he liked Frank's approach. He simply took all of the guess work out of the situation by predicating his entire plan on the worst scenario possible.

"The decoys should be here any minute," Frank said, "we had better keep an eye on the surveillance screens."

The surveillance screens gave them a clear view of all the streets surrounding the UN, including 1st Avenue and FDR Drive.

"Look Pete, the first decoy motorcade just turned off of the FDR Drive." The two agents just waited and watched.

"It looks like they made it to the UN building without incident," Pete said, seeming somewhat disappointed.

When the second decoy motorcade reached the UN Building, Pete turned to Frank with a worried look on his face."Now what" Pete asked. "Maybe we should stop the motorcade, Frank."

"No!" Frank shouted, in a commanding voice. "I'm sorry, Pete. What I mean is that we don't have the authority to make that call. The President and his security force are in full command of this mission. It is imperative that we follow orders."

Pete was fit to be tied. He was trying real hard not to blow his cool. However, he was also aware of the fact that Frank had direct orders from the White House, and that there was nothing he could say that would influence him to break protocol.

"You know as well as I do, Frank, that their driving into an extremely dangerous situation. The insurgents may have weapons that can penetrate the armored vehicles. Don't you think we should at least inform the President that the decoy motorcades failed to expose the insurgents."

"Trust me Pete, they already know."

Pete was silent for a moment, he simply didn't like the idea of doing nothing, but he knew it wasn't personal. Frank was simply following orders and there was nothing he could say to change his mind.

The third motorcade that Tom and his associates were in had already turned down 2nd Avenue and passed 59th Street.

The atmosphere was filled with anxiety. The street was so quiet that you could have heard a pin drop. Even the dogs stopped barking. Conversation around the UN building and in the motorcade had ceased. There were fourteen large swat-team vans parked in a separate barricade that could be seen from the window of the command center.

MELTDOWN

The commander of the New York Police Department received orders to prepare his men to close down 1st Avenue, and still, there was no sign of the insurgents.

As the motorcade approached 44th Street, Joe put his arm around Angie and asked her to sit low in her seat. He then turned to Tom with a serious look on his face. "Tom, sit low in your seat."

"Do you think something is going to happen?" Tom asked.

"Please, Tom, do me a favor, just get down low until we get into the UN building."

Tom lowered himself into the seat.

They turned the corner and headed toward 1st Avenue. The police had already blocked it off. The fourteen swat-team units moved their vans alongside the motorcade as they approached the barricades. The swat vehicles had the motorcade completely surrounded. The CIA agent driving the front vehicle welcomed the protection; that is, until he heard the voice of his boss, Frank Benit, screaming over the communications system. "What the hell is Swat doing past the barricades?"

Pete quickly jumped to his feet in a frantic posture. "The insurgents, they're in the vans," he screamed, as he grabbed his automatic weapon and ran down to the street with the radio in his hand. "This is a red alert! This is a red alert! The insurgents are in the vans, the Swat vans!"

The driver tried to ram his vehicle through the swat vans, to no avail. They were totally blocked in.

"Hit the deck," Harry shouted, as he saw hundreds of heavily armed terrorists jump out onto the street from the swat-vans.

Federal agents, in the street, immediately opened fire along with hundreds of policemen who were now running into the area. The gunfire from both sides rang through the streets of New York with the sound of a roaring jet engine. When the piercing bullets did not penetrate the armored cars, the terrorists pulled out their rocket launchers.

"They have rocket launchers!" An Agent yelled out. "Hit the guys with the rocket launchers!"

The close-quarter gun battle was deafening. Commands were drowned out by the thunder of gunfire.

As Pete hit the street, he turned to look up 44th Street and noticed four eighteen-wheelers roaring toward the UN building. Still holding a radio transmitter in his hand, he yelled out, "Terrorists in trailer trucks racing down 44th!" He lifted his automatic weapon and began to fire at the front windshield of the moving trucks. Armored military trucks quickly moved toward 44th Street to block off the entrance to 1st Avenue. When the lead truck roared into an armored military unit blocking access to 1st Avenue, it fell over sideways, scrapped across the street and landed between 1st and 2nd Avenue on its side. The other three trucks drove past the first truck and headed toward 1st Avenue. Terrorists from the first truck started to pour out onto the street to join their comrades. The situation was becoming desperate. You could see blood literally pouring down city storm drains.

Harry looked out of his window only to see a terrorist pointing a rocket at his car.

"Shit! These guys have rockets!" Harry snapped. "Do not leave the vehicles!"

"You win Harry!" Joe responded. With a hundred bullets a second hitting the vehicle, there was no way Joe or anyone else was even thinking about leaving the vehicles.

Tom noticed that the guys with the rockets were hit with so many bullets that they would remain standing five to ten seconds after they had already died.

"It doesn't look good, Harry!" Tom yelled.

"What are you worried about Tom? You guys are bullet proof."

Angie was on the floor with her hands on over her ears. Joe held her tight. He wanted to help her, but there wasn't much he could do.

"Stay calm Angie, I think we're winning."

Just then, there was a roar overhead that could have woken up the dead. The sky was literally saturated with helicopters. Some were landing on 1st Avenue and others on 2nd. Hundreds of Marines were on the street. Other helicopters were firing at the terrorist trailers and swat vans. The three terrorist trailers that had attempted to run through 1st Avenue had been destroyed by Marine helicopter rockets. The motorcade was now surrounded by federal agents. The Marines quickly secured areas between 1st and 2nd Avenues, and continued to secure the street leading to the UN building. There was sporadic gunfire, and then total silence.

"I think it's over," Harry said. "We have to stay in the vehicle until we receive orders from the command center."

The casualties were heavy. Of the five hundred terrorists that had participated in the raid, more than four hundred were dead, sixty were seriously wounded, and the remaining were captured. The feds lost twelve agents, with fourteen injured. The men in blue lost eight, with thirty-seven injured. Two marines lost their lives, and eight were injured. There were also four civilian casualties and nineteen injured.

"It's all right, Angie it's over; everything is under control. You can loosen up on the grip, I'm not going anywhere."

As they looked out of the window, all they could see were dead bodies.

Joe gently put his hand on Angie's head and turned her from the window. "Angie, don't look; it's not a pretty site."

Just then, Pete came running up to their vehicle and could not believe his eyes. The outside of the vehicle looked like it was bombarded with hundreds of miniature meteors.

When Joe heard Pete knocking on the door, he immediately lowered the window.

"Is everyone alright?," Pete asked.

"I don't know about alright," Joe said, taking a deep breath and letting it out slowly, "but if you are asking me if we are all still alive, the answer is yes."

"That was a close call," Pete continued, "I'm really happy no one was hurt."

"Nothing that a year or two of therapy couldn't cure," Joe responded.

Pete smiled. "We had better get you inside the building. I'll meet you there as soon as the area is totally secured."

"I can't wait to see what's next," Joe said. "This was a real thriller."

"Bring them into the building, Harry," Pete said. "I'll see you guys inside."

Angie looked physically shaken. She wanted to thank Pete but just couldn't get the words out of her mouth.

Joe leaned over and gently kissed her on the lips.

She felt as if she had just woken up from a bad dream.

"I love you, Angelina Rosselle, and as long as we are together, everything will be alright."

"Yes," she said in a soft voice, as she laid her head gently on his shoulder.

Joe just held her. He even managed to get a smile out of her.

They were all rushed into the UN building and immediately led to a safety room where they were asked to wait until the area was secured.

CHAPTER 23

"How are you guys doing?" Agent Benit asked as he entered the security room. "Is everyone ok?"

"Nothing a month of therapy can't fix," Joe said smiling. "It's not every day you get to sit in a car being riddled by bullets, not knowing whether you're going to live or die; but we do appreciate the Tums, headache pills, and the temporary hearing aids."

Frank smiled, shaking his head. "As soon as we have the area secured, they'll be moving you to private quarters where you can all freshen up. I know that you're all still a little stressed out over the incident and may need some time to calm your nerves. The UN assembly conference has been pushed back an hour or so. You'll be notified of the new schedule within the hour. In the mean time, if you have any questions, or need us for anything, just give us a call."

"Thanks, Frank," Tom responded.

Angie's ears were still ringing from the sound of the gunfire. They were all still recovering from the ordeal, but remained anxious to make their presentation to the UN assembly.

As soon as Pete and Frank left, there was a lull in the room. Each had hoped that the others would say something. Joe felt their anxieties, but wasn't about to let the team fall into a negative mindset, not when they were finally given the opportunity to address the UN.

He walked over to Tom and gave him a pat on the back.

"Everything will be all right, Tom. Destiny has been with us, not against us. This is just another road we had to take, and I can assure you that you won't be walking it alone. It is important that we stay focused; remember, what the insurgents did out there doesn't amount to a hill of beans compared to what's going to happen to this planet if we don't find a resolution."

"It's been one hell of a road," Phil said. "I think I've had it with this protection thing."

"My ears are all screwed up," John said. "All I can hear are the sound of bullets hitting the car."

"How are you doing, Ron?" Tom asked.

"I probably should have stayed in the bunker. I'd just like to know how many more times we're going to have to go through the tunnel of death before this thing is over."

Angie laughed.

"We should be alright for a while," Joe said, "you just have to remember our motto."

"And what's that?" Ron asked.

"Run, duck, and hide," Joe said laughing. "Tom and I use it all the time."

Tom just smiled. He knew that Joe was just trying to calm everyone down.

"On a more serious note," Tom continued "I just want you to know that you have all been loyal friends, and I have not doubted that loyalty, not even for a moment. I really do appreciate the time and dedication you put into this project. I would just like someone to tell me, why the hell are these guys trying to kill us? Didn't anyone tell them that the planet might not be here in two years? Where the hell is the logic; am I missing something?" Tom was fit to be tied.

"Relax, Tom." Joe said, "We're scientists, not psychiatrists. We're here to save the planet, not to cure the mentally impaired."

"I know Joe, I know. But this one was pretty bad. There were a lot more casualties."

Joe paused for a moment before responding. He knew Tom was in one of his serious moods.

"Tom, whoever these people are, they are not our friends. They are fighting against what we are fighting for. That makes them our enemy. The good guys have been fighting the bad guys since the beginning of time. Americans fought the Revolutionary War to establish a free nation, and then there was World War One and World War Two. These were wars that were gallantly fought to prevent maniacs from taking over the world. In all of these wars, tens of thousands of men and women sacrificed their lives to create a safe and free society for all of mankind. What we're doing now is no different then what they did in the past. We are putting our lives on the line to save the planet. The only difference between then and now, Tom, is that we are now the ones on the front-line. We are now the ones that are willing to lay our lives on the line in order to create a safe haven for all of mankind. If we fail, we will not have just failed ourselves, we will have failed all of mankind. You know as well as I do, that this planet, in the volatile state that it's in, can cause more damage in ten minutes than the terrorists can cause in a hundred years."

Pete Marchel had just walked into the room and heard the last part of Joe's conversation. "Don't worry about the terrorists, Frank and I have initiated a major worldwide offensive against the insurgents. We can handle the insurgents, but we can't cool the planet down, it's not what we do. I have a family that would like to know that they have a future. You have to stay focused. There are a lot of people out there counting on this team, please don't let us down."

"I understand Pete," Tom said in confident manner. "Things have really been tough up to now, but we have reached a point when each of us must make his or her own decision whether they wish to continue or opt out, and I wouldn't hold it against anyone if they decide to call it quits." Tom then turned toward to Joe. "Joe said it all, we must do whatever has to be done to save the planet, regardless of the consequences. Those who decide to stay must stay focused, because in reality, we really are in a life or death situation. Thanks, Joe, thanks for putting us back on the road."

"As soon as I make out my last will and testament," John said with a smile, "you can count me in."

"I haven't had this much excitement in years," Phil said, "and besides, I have nothing else to do."

"I'm sticking with Joe," Angie said with a smile, "so I guess I'm still part of the team."

"What are you all looking at?" Ron asked, "You don't really think you're going to resolve this problem without me. Do you?"

The entire team was once again focused on what had to be done, even if it meant risking their lives to complete the mission.

"Well Joe," Tom said in a low voice, "you did it again. You brought reality back into the picture. I believe that we can now prepare ourselves to address the nations."

The team wasted no time. While Phil, John, and Ron updated the latest geological data into the computer program, Joe and Angie helped prepare Tom for his address to the United Nations General Assembly.

As they completed the final draft on Tom's presentation, they were distracted by a commotion that was coming from the corridor, adjacent to the room. When the door opened, they were surprised to see the Secretary General of the United Nations, Christian Friedmann, walk into the room. He was joined by his Safety and Security Manager, Alfred Cabore, and several UN security agents. At first, they thought he might have accidentally walked into the wrong room.

Friedmann was one of Angie's favorite political heroes.

Prior to being nominated as the Secretary General, Mr. Friedmann was awarded the Nobel Peace Prize. He had spent his entire life fighting for peace and justice throughout the world. All nations respected him for his non-discriminatory position on all issues, and his uncanny ability to negotiate settlements between nations that had opposing views.

"Mr. Collins, I would like to welcome you and all of your colleagues to the United Nations. It is an honor for me to be here, having this opportunity to personally thank each and every one of you for your fortitude, courage, and resilience to carry out such a difficult mission, especially given the incident that just occurred. You are all heroes in the strongest sense of the word, and I am truly honored to meet all of you."

"Thank you sir, thank you for your kind reception. It's kind of you to be here," Tom politely responded.

"To date," Mr. Friedmann continued, "you and your colleagues have accomplished what is nothing short of a miracle. I realize that there is an extreme seriousness to the pending problem and that it will require the full cooperation of all nations for resolution. I am here to offer you my full support and cooperation, including whatever influence I may have to encourage others to cooperate toward a resolution to this most difficult situation. Mr. Cabore, who manages our security staff, will be directly responsible for your safety during your stay at the UN. The general assembly meeting has been changed from three p.m. to four p.m., due to the incident." Mr. Cabore gave Tom his personal telephone number and then shook his hand.

"If you need anything," Cabore explained, "just call." Tom thanked both men as they left the room.

Tom and the crew spent the rest of the time updating the latest data into the system and preparing for the meeting.

MELTDOWN

As it drew closer to four p.m., the assembly room became packed. There were more governmental representatives representing more nations at this assembly than any other assembly since the UN was established. The deputy secretary general took the podium to lay down the foundation, rules, and purpose of the assembly. He then turned the podium over to the secretary general, who proceeded to introduce Tom and his associates to the assembly.

"For the greater portion of my life," Mr. Friedmann said, "I have been an advocate for peace. Peace between nations and peace within nations. I am simply opposed to man's quest to destroy man. We would all like to believe that through the centuries, man has become more civilized, and that we now resolve our differences in a more civilized manner. But, of course, history will quickly dissipate that notion. We are a violent society that seeks violent solutions. There are some actions in this world that cannot be put into a recognizable perspective through the attributes afforded to us by logic or reasoning. There are men that simply create a cause as a means to justify an event. The event that occurred outside the UN today is just another example of man's inability to coexist with man.

"We are now faced with a circumstance that can literally annihilate every human being on the planet. The Earth is quickly transforming itself back to the violent planet it was millions of years ago. Within the next two years, this planet may not have the ability to sustain life unless we come up with a solution to repair the damage. Members of the assembly, if we circumvent this issue in anyway, I can assure you that there will be no one left behind to mourn the dead.

"It is imperative that all conflicts throughout the world come to an immediate end and that all of mankind work as a single unit to save the planet. We can no longer afford to be indifferent toward one other. We have come to the crossroads of our very existence. There is now only one road, one cause, and one goal; and that's to save the planet!"

As the secretary general introduced Tom and his colleagues, the entire general assembly rose to their feet and gave them a thunderous applause. Tom attempted to speak above the applause but could not. They continued to applaud for more than five minutes.

The assembly was apparently familiar with Tom's work, and the extraordinary efforts made by him and his associates to expose the truth. It appeared that the majority of the nations had already decided to support the cause. Logically, they had no choice. If the problem were not resolved, the planet would cease to support life.

MELTDOWN

The assembly became silent as Tom lifted his hands. "Secretary General, members of the board and members of the United Nations..." Tom paused for a moment. He did not want to under-estimate or water down the facts. He knew that this was his chance to get the facts on the table in the most serious manner as possible.

"I wish I could stand up here and tell you that everything is going to be all right. But I cannot! I cannot tell you that shutting down the oil wells will resolve the problem. Because..." Tom paused for a moment, "because we may very well have passed the point of no return! Citizens of the world! The extent of the damage is so severe and so extensive that it may very well be irreversible! As we speak, there are thousands of new cracks in the crust of the planet that are connecting the planet's mantle to the planet's surface, and we expect this condition to worsen. There are also large sections of the mantel that are totally exposed in the Atlantic Ocean, and we have reason to believe that a similar condition exists in the remaining oceans. We are dealing with an extreme reversal of the planet's geological composition that is attributing to an increased instability of the tectonic plates.

"As defined in my report, the crust of the planet has been seriously damaged due to the extraction of petroleum over the past one-hundred-ten years. The oil that was confined in cavities within the crust of the planet acted as a natural hydraulic system that somehow, kept the seismic plates reasonably stable. When those cavities were penetrated, and the oil was extracted, the support system dissipated. Over a period of 110 years, this process continued to repeat itself. We are now experiencing severe cave-ins within the crust, which are causing tens of thousands of cracks to occur throughout the planet's crust. It has been confirmed that the average ocean temperatures have increased by 1.2 percent in just the past two months. We also have reports that twenty-eight previously dormant volcanoes have recently shown signs of seismic activity. In the past three months, the ice meltdown at both the North and South Pole caps has increased by of 2.2 percent. Gentlemen! The rate of acceleration of lava flow has far exceeded our original calculations. If the calculations continue to exceed our original estimates, the time remaining will be dramatically shortened. We must take evasive action; and we must take it now!" The general assembly was dead silent. You could not hear a whisper, or see a movement. It looked like a house full of manikins.

"The problem is grave! The message is clear! The planet is attempting to revert back to an atmosphere that existed millions of years ago, an atmosphere that will not have the ability to sustain life as we know it!" Tom paused for a moment and then continued.

"We probably have less than one year to find a way to reverse this process. If we are not successful, this planet will imitate the same atmosphere that exists on Mars. I implore each and every nation in this room to work together as one unit and for one cause, and that is, to save the planet!" The assembly was totally mesmerized. They seemed to be frozen in their seats as Tom completed his address and walked off the podium.

Just then, a messenger ran over to where the secretary general was sitting. As Tom walked back to his chair, Christian Friedmann hurried to the podium. "Members of the assembly, I have just received information that the volcano at Yellowstone Park has just had another eruption. We must pray for the people of this country. And we must pray for the world."

Tom leaned toward the secretary general. "How severe was the eruption?"

"I was told that the eruption has a VEI of 1.5." Tom did not immediately respond.

"I'd like to ask another question."

"What is it Tom?"

"What does it mean, when the General Assembly does not respond to the speaker?"

"Fear, Tom; it's a sign of fear. Reality has set in. They have been scared into reality and they are now praying and hoping that somehow, someway, you and your colleagues can come up with a solution. A quick fix is what they probably have in mind, but I know differently. I know that presently, there is no solution. One does not have to be a scientist to know that man has never had the ability to accurately predict, much less control, seismic events. We have a problem here, don't we, Tom?"

"I'm afraid so, sir. We are going to need every ounce of resource, every scientist from every nation, and most likely, a miracle to produce a resolution. It's pretty simple sir, we either fix it, or the Earth will become a lifeless planet in a very short period of time. The assembly must be made to understand that we need their help. We have set up a scientific informational center that will offer the latest scientific data relative to the pending crisis. Each nation will contribute their very latest scientific findings into the data bank that will be made available to each and every member, in a united effort to expedite a successful resolution to the problem. We have labeled the organization STP, or Save the Planet.

Instructional data for procedures on how to connect to the system has already been sent out to each and every Nation."

"Where are you and your colleagues going from here, Tom?" Chris asked.

"The President has arranged to have us conduct our investigation in a fully facilitated science control center. We were informed that the facility has the latest geological equipment and other required systems capable of monitoring the planet's seismic activity twenty/four/seven. The center will also be the central communication center for the STP data bank. I am hopeful that this joint effort will lead us to a solution."

"What are the real chances of stabilizing the planet?" Chris asked.

"I really don't know. This is new territory, even for a geologist. How do you stop lava, or repair the crust of the planet?"

Chris had a real admiration for Tom. He did not trifle with political dialogue as a means to camouflage important issues. He was more like Davy Crockett, the American legend. He attacked the issues like a bull and did not soften the blow. Chris really wanted to help. In a small way, he wished he were part of the team.

"If there is anyway," Chris responded, "I mean, anything that I can do to help, Tom, please do not hesitate to call me. Please take my personal number."

"Thank you sir, thanks for everything."

"We will win the battle, Tom."

"Yes, we will," Tom agreed. "I had better get to work; my colleagues and I have a lot to do."

"Good luck, Tom."

"Thanks again sir," Tom responded as Friedmann left the room.

"Well Tom, how did it go?" Joe asked.

"According to Friedmann, everything went well. It appears that nations around the world are prepared to cooperate."

"Why is it that you sound so positive, and yet look like the world is coming to an end?"

"I'm not really down, Joe; I'm concerned. Friedmann asked me an important question. He wanted to know if the problem is solvable, and, of course, I told him the truth. We just don't know, Joe. Here we are having this entire power meeting, and yet time is going by and nothing is really being done. If we continue on this path, we will have a lot of philosophical answers and no solutions."

"I understand, Tom; you're a little frustrated. But we are now heading to a command station where we will soon have the opportunity to work on the solution. We just have to stay focused."

"Yes we do," Tom agreed, as they prepared to head back to DC.

CHAPTER 24

The geologists monitoring Yellowstone were convinced that the minor eruptions were just the tip of the iceberg. The general census was that the mega eruption would be between five hundred to one thousand times more powerful than the eruption that occurred at Mount St. Helens.

The evacuees, who had been placed mostly in makeshift camps, never lost hope that somehow, someway, some unforeseen miracle would occur to prevent the volcano from erupting. When the news first came over the emergency communication system that Yellowstone had erupted again, a solemn quietness came over the camps. All the hope and expectations that they had for returning to their homes, had been shattered in a single moment. It was not that the USGS had not clearly confirmed that a main eruption at Yellowstone was inevitable; the information was precise. There were no maybes in their report. It was more like the hope one has when a doctor tells you that someone you love has a terminal illness. No matter how accurate the facts are, you are simply not yet prepared to accept the diagnosis. You hold on to what is inherent in all of us: hope. You are praying that a miracle will occur and somehow change the circumstance; however, that rarely happens. When a person's hope is shattered by the culmination of the many disappointments in life, we experience a sense of hopelessness, a sense of not being in control.

The second eruption at Yellowstone became a solemn moment in time that seemed to last an eternity. When the bad news hit the camps, the evacuees felt that they had emotionally lost something, but they could not quite identify what it was. It was the most severe hopelessness a person can experience, a feeling of complete emptiness. It is a time when people need people. Some men held their wives in their arms to comfort them, and others chose to be alone. Some cried silently, and others were overwhelmed with emotions; many cried openly. In that single moment, they experienced all the emotions of hopelessness, frustration, loss, sadness, need, love and compassion. It was as if they were all one single emotion trying to occupy the same moment in time. The evacuees now knew that they would never see their homes again. Their hopes, dreams and expectations had been abruptly terminated in that one moment of time,

Like in all tragedies, time would be their greatest healer, but there was no doubt that their lives would be forever changed.

The mass evacuation caused by Yellowstone was the first hardship in a series of many more to come. The Northeast and Southern states absorbed the majority of the evacuees. There were already millions of evacuees leaving the camps and entering more populated areas such as New York City, Chicago, Pennsylvania, and Washington DC, including smaller counties and cities that were located in the safe zone. These evacuees were attempting to reestablish their lives. The problem with such a large number of people migrating to these areas, in such a short period of time, could be evaluated by simple math. The massive influx of people seeking employment in areas where the unemployment rate was already off the charts did not sit well with the locals who, themselves, were also seeking employment. There was a lot of resentment and animosity. The residents in these areas had a lot of compassion for the evacuees but with a crumbling economy, people were getting desperate. From the time the oil wells were shut down, the country experienced a twenty-five percent increase in the unemployment rate. Americans were no longer skeptical regarding the volatile state of the planet. The volcano had already experienced two minor eruptions, and with the influx of twenty million people, it didn't look like the situation would improve anytime soon.

Financial institutions and the stock markets remained closed to prevent a rush on the banks, and a sell-off in the markets. Simultaneously, markets around the world were also forced to close, for the same reasons.

In spite of their efforts to save the markets, in just a three-week period, the world economy had quickly moved into a deep recession and shortly thereafter, a full blown depression that would make the 1929 Depression seem like a walk in the park.

The President, who had a great deal more information than the general public, realized that the deterioration of the world economy was insignificant compared to the pending problem they faced. The possibility that the human race could be totally extinct within the next twelve months overshadowed all other issues. He scheduled an emergency staff meeting to evaluate the many issues of concern that were before him, and to prioritize those issues that would expedite a resolution to the pending catastrophe that lay before them. Amongst those attending were Carl Frumskin, Chairman of the Federal Reserve Board; Ben Brodwick, Secretary of the Treasury; Joan Dunne, Secretary of State; Robert Johnson, head of NEMA, and Robert Bates, Secretary of Defense.

When the President entered the conference room, the attendees rose from their chairs.

"Please, remain seated," President Hamity said, "we simply do not have time for formalities." The President looked like he had not slept for days. "All matters discussed in this room will be classified 'Top Secret.' It is imperative that the public not be made aware of the facts until we ourselves know what the hell is going on. Is that understood?" They unanimously acknowledged the President's request.

"I'm sure that you are all familiar with some of the events that have been transpiring over the past several days," the President continued. "I am already cognizant of the fact that the global economy is at the very brink of a total collapse. The financial institutions, banks, and commodity markets across the globe have already closed their doors. My good friends, as devastating and as grim as the financial situation sounds, I can assure you that it is not our worst fear." The President had the staff's full attention.

"Carl," the President said, "I would like you to first summarize the current financial conditions in the U.S. and global arenas. It may have some influence on the decision we make here today."

"Mr. President," Carl Frumskin responded, "I have before me a financial report that incorporates all of the financial data you had requested. There is not much to say, sir. As you can see by the report that lies before you, the world economy is in shambles. Now I can go over each of the items separately with you, or I can give you a general review that will be applicable to the entire report."

"I believe that the short version will be adequate," the President responded.

"The world financial system," Frumskin continued, "is literally disintegrating before our eyes. The world currencies are rapidly devaluating, and in a very short period of time, perhaps months, they will become absolutely worthless. Even commodities such as gold and silver have seemed to have lost their value."

"If there is no method to buy or sell," the President interrupted, "how will people purchase items of necessity such as food, clothes, and medical supplies?"

"They will do whatever they have to do to get what they need, sir."

"It is my understanding," Frumskin continued, "that the people have already started to barter, and I'm afraid that the situation will only worsen."

"I want you to get together with Ben Brodwick," the President suggested, "and devise some sort of federally-controlled monetary system before things get out of hand."

"We have a plan that is almost finalized, Mr. President. We will present it sometime tomorrow."

"Thank You, Carl."

"Bob," the President continued, "how are our oil reserves?"

"The oil reserves are low," Bob Johnson responded, "but if they are properly rationed, the reserves may last twelve to sixteen months. We already have gas rationing in place, permitting just 10 gallons per week per vehicle with the exception of emergency services, such as the fire department, law enforcement, ambulance services and so on.

"It is our estimate that it will take approximately three to five years to completely change over to an alternate fuel source such as ethanol, hydrogen, or battery operated cars. Now as far as electrical power plants are concerned, we can probably convert to coal until we can build enough nuclear plants to handle the load."

"The time element to make the conversion is unrealistic," the President snapped. "I want you to utilize every resource we have to resolve the problem. I want the top engineers and scientists working on this problem twenty/four/seven. Three to five years is just unacceptable."

"Yes sir," Bob responded, "I will do whatever is necessary to expedite the situation."

"I don't understand Bob, why have we not previously implemented a plan to produce an alternate source of fuel?"

"There have been some advancements made in that field, but there has been a lot of political influence from lobbyists, such as representatives of oil producing companies, who vigorously fought against nationalizing a new fuel source. An alternate fuel would have put a big dent in the oil companies' profit margins. Right now, the oil companies have a monopoly, though not in the legal sense, because they are owned by separate and independent corporations; however, there is an unwritten truth that these companies are under a common control system, sort of like a cooperative. The last thing these guys want is a competitive fuel source. In plain English sir, the oil companies have created so much red tape in our political system through lobbyists that it would take decades to untie the knots."

"Well, that is no longer a problem," the President explained, "The oil companies have been shut down permanently. I will send out an executive order to eliminate all referendums that previously block the technology and usage of using an alternate fuel source. Is there anything else you need to get this thing on the road?"

"No sir."

"Good," the President said. I want you to do whatever it takes, Bob. We don't have a hell of a lot of time."

"Yes sir."

"Mr. Bates," the President said, addressing the Secretary of Defense, "the collapse of the monetary system has put the people in this country in a desperate situation. They will fend for what they need to survive, and some may even decide to take the law into their own hands. We cannot afford to have mob rule throughout the country. We are in the process of setting up a federally controlled monetary system as a means to maintain some sort of order, but until that system is in place, it's imperative that we maintain law and order."

"Every National Guard unit in the country is now on red alert, sir," Bates responded. "We are also coordinating our efforts with the military command center and local law enforcement agencies. I believe that we can keep the situation reasonably under control."

"Thanks Robert, I am confident that you will do whatever is necessary to maintain law and order during these critical times."

"Now," the President continued, "I know that you have all been digesting the current headline news that has been saturating the networks these past couple of weeks; not so much about Yellowstone, but more so about Tom Collins' study regarding the volatility of the planet's seismic plates. Well, the general consensus throughout the world today, which I assume has been influenced by the shutting down of the oil wells, is that the cause of the problem has been resolved, and that, in time the planet will return to its natural cycle." The President paused for a moment as he lifted the pitcher of water that stood just to his right side, and slowly poured the water into his glass.

"My friends," the President continued in a serious and concerned manner, "Tom Collins and his colleagues have confirmed that unless a resolution can be found, the seismic plates on this planet will continue to increase in volatility to the point where the plates will literally crumble, permitting molten lava to rise from the planet's mantle to the surface of the Earth's crust."

The room was so quiet that you could hear the faint sound of birds chirping just outside the window.

"Mr. President," Bob Johnson asked, "You're not insinuating that..."

"I'm not insinuating anything, Bob," the President interrupted. "No," he said as he made direct eye contact with each and every single person in the room, "we probably have less than a year before the planet becomes uninhabitable. In plain English, and short of a miracle, all life on this planet will cease to exist unless, somehow, the process of molten lava moving to the surface of the planet can be reversed. The good news is that scientists throughout the world, under the guidance of Tom Collins and his colleagues, have agreed to cooperate in a joint effort to find a resolution.

"What we must do is support that team, and the only way we can accomplish that is by becoming part of the team. From the time we became a republic until this very day, we have always managed to climb to the top of the mountain. Throughout the centuries and against all odds, this republic has fought tyranny at its very doorstep, and changed science-fiction into non-fiction when we put a man on the moon. Now, once again, we are faced with a challenge, and once again, my good friends, we are going to kick this one right in the butt.

"Today we must strive to do our best in order to assure the world that they will see another tomorrow. The people are counting on us..." the President paused for a moment as he lifted from his chair, "they are counting on us to do what must be done, so gentlemen, I'll be counting on all of you to do your very best." He then rose from his chair and faced his staff. "Failure is simply not an option." The President then turned and left the room.

CHAPTER 25

People on the street were already starting to barter. The facts were simple; if you couldn't eat it, drink it, or wear it, it was probably worthless.

Currencies throughout the world became so inflated that in some countries, it took a wheel barrow of money to buy a quart of milk. It became difficult to measure the value of an item in relation to the value of money. A loaf of bread that cost three dollars today could cost thirty dollars tomorrow. If a can of soup previously cost two dollars, in a single day, it would increase to twenty dollars. This scenario of devaluation would rapidly excel to a point when currencies would be absolutely worthless. Even the hard commodities, such as diamonds, gold, and silver were absolutely worthless. Items like food, water, medical supplies, and other necessities, had become the primary items sought after. Merchants who thought they were making a windfall by selling food and other items for ten times their value found that they were not able to buy the same product back for one hundred times the amount that they had previously sold it for. In just days, food and water could no longer be purchased with currency. People were now bartering. Suddenly, everyone had a vegetable garden and a big dog.

The President declared a general state of martial law throughout the country. He ordered every vacant field in the country that was out of the dead zone to be planted. There was a mass effort by the government to produce the necessary food to feed the nation, and until this crisis was over, the food would be temporarily distributed to the nation by way of a point system. To accomplish this task, the government was forced to temporarily take control of all food distribution centers, farms, processing plants, and other entities associated with the food industry. The government developed a point system that would be monitored with government-issued credit cards. If a person volunteered to perform a job, that person would receive a set amount of points. These points would be registered on their credit card account. All merchandise would then be priced in points and made available to those who held government issued credit cards.

Millionaires were now penniless, and had no choice but to participate in the point system. There would be no preferential treatment when it came to the distribution of the necessities needed to live. It did not matter what your status in life had been, at this point, everyone on the planet was now equal.

With the exception of criminal justice cases, the courts were closed down. Cost liability cases were now worthless because of the devaluation of the dollar. Lawyers were basically out of business.

The President decided to turn over the daily job of running the country to the Vice President while he devoted every moment of his time in supporting the efforts to survive the planet. He was determined to help Tom and his associates in every way possible. The President established a special committee to assure that Tom and his colleagues received whatever they might need to find a solution to the problem.

Throughout the country, there were reports coming in of houses that were burglarized for food and water. There were cases in which people were murdered for these simple necessities. The state and federal governments lifted the ban on guns, and requested that every man be given the opportunity to defend their home. Bulletins went out warning looters that people had a right to shoot anyone that attempted to break into their home or cause harm to their family. The President felt that desperate situations called for desperate measures. There simply were not enough law enforcement officers to maintain a safe environment for the public. Some families banded together to protect their interests, forming armed patrols to safe guard their neighborhoods. Times were desperate.

There were special facilities set up to aid those that simply did not have the capability to fend for themselves, such as the mentally ill, the handicapped, the homeless, the elderly, and others who were in similar circumstances.

Nations around the world also volunteered to send food and other items that were desperately needed. Throughout the years, the United States had reached out to many nations in their time of need, and now, these same nations were now reciprocating. The human race had a deep sense of humanity that seemed to surface during catastrophic events. It was what made the human race so unique. It seems that once we shatter the shield of pretence that surrounds us all, we awaken the soul and free the spirit.

CHAPTER 26

When Tom and his colleagues returned to Washington DC, they were immediately escorted to a top-secret underground command center, just under the Pentagon.

"Wow!" Terry said seeming somewhat surprised by the size of the facility. "It looks like a space station from the future."

"Yes," Lieutenant Colonel Earl Roberts said, as he introduced himself. "The command center is the most technologically advanced facility in the world."

"I'm really impressed," Tom said. "I'm really impressed."

The Colonel smiled as he continued. "There are three levels in the main control station that measure three-hundred feet across by one-twenty feet deep, with ceiling heights of thirty feet in the lower section, designated 'Section A', twenty feet in the center section, designated 'Section B', and fifteen feet in the upper section, designated 'Section C'. Each station is separated by bulletproof transparent glass. The glass in 'Section C', of the command center can be darkened just by the push of a button, converting the glass to a one-way vision panel. 'Section C' is called 'the Brain'. It's where all the information is collected and analyzed. What it does is dissect, correlate, and analyze every ounce of information gathered by the facility. It literally absorbs millions of pieces of information an hour and categorizes the information by subject matter and code numbers.

"'Section B', the Colonel continued, "is utilized to gather information from the Earth's crust and the far outer limits of space. It is also our primary asteroid and comet detection system.

"'Section A' is utilized to gather information from the core of the planet to the crust. It basically monitors the planet's pulse on a minute-by-minute basis. That vision screen on the front wall is twenty feet high and two-hundred feet long. The screen projects a live image of the entire planet's surface through a series of strategically placed satellite surveillance camera systems. Every last inch of the planet's surface can be viewed twenty-four/seven. The zoom is so powerful that a person can literally read the fine print of a newspaper lying on the ground.

"The system also has the ability to monitor ocean, lake and river water temperatures, tectonic plate movement, seismic activity, water levels, measurements of the ice cap mass, atmospheric temperatures, and other vital information that may be vital to your research."

The Colonel then walked them over to elevator number seven. "This elevator will take you to your quarter which is located on level four." He then handed them each an electronic card and a sheet of paper listing their room numbers. "The card will get you into the room," he explained.

"Thank you Lieutenant," Joe said. "By the way, where do you keep the Martians that were captured in Roswell?"

John laughed. "You don't really think..."

"No, John," Joe quickly responded.

"Anyway," the Colonel continued, "Sergeant Dick Phillips has been assigned as your guide until you become familiar with the complex. He will introduce you to the heads of the civilian technical staff, who have been assigned to work with you on the project. Are there any questions?"

"Not at this time," Tom said, "but I'm sure we'll have questions as we go."

"Well then," the Colonel responded, "I guess I'll be on my way. Oh, by the way Joe, we keep the Martians in the freezer in the sub-basement."

Joe smiled. "Give them my regards," Joe said, as the Lieutenant left the area.

"He's kidding, right Joe?" John asked. "You don't believe that they really have aliens in the sub-basement, do you?"

Joe just shook his head, but did not respond.

"Don't worry John," Phil said with a big grin on his face, "the aliens are all heterosexuals."

They all laughed.

"Ok," John responded, "let's change the subject."

"Well Ron," Joe said, "what do you think?"

"I feel like I died and went to Heaven. Look at all these computers."

Joe looked over at Tom who seemed to be in a trance. He looks like he's having an out-of-body experience.

"You look like you're spaced out, Tom. What are you thinking about?"

"The time element, Joe, I'm concerned about the time element. In a very short period of time this planet will be so damn hot, we'll be able to cook eggs on the street."

"Does this mean that we are giving up, Tom? Or is the key word here eggs? I know, you haven't eaten yet, and you want eggs. That's it! You're reaching out to me. I give you eggs and we save the planet!"

"Ok! Joe, Ok, I get the message. But the fact of the matter is..."

Joe immediately cut him off. "Tom, let's just get some eggs. We will all do a lot better on a full stomach. We can work out plan H while we are eating breakfast."

"Don't tell me, Joe, you don't know what plan H is, but it's probably a lot better than plan G."

"You never cease to amaze me Tom, such insight."

"OK, let's just get some eggs and maybe a little bacon on the side."

"Now you're talking," Joe said with a smile, as they all headed for the dining area.

When they entered the dining area, Phil noticed that Ron had a big grin on his face.

"What are you smiling at?" Phil asked.

"I actually get to see and work with some of the equipment that I've been hacking into all these years. And it's legal!"

Phil laughed. "You are one in a million, Ron. No, I take that back. There's just one of you. In the government's eyes, you were a rogue wave. You broke every espionage law that ever existed. You tapped into some, if not all, of the most top-secret systems in the world. Not once or twice, but every day for more than ten years, and here you are now, employed by the United States Government in one of the most top-secret facilities in the country. I love it! I have to say Ron, you not only have my attention, but you have my full admiration. You have the balls of a bull and the courage of a lion!"

"Why, thank you Phil, that's the nicest thing that anyone has ever said to me. Especially the part about the bull! But you left something out...,"

"And what's that?"

"They hired me as their chief engineer on level one. Now that's what I call ironic."

"They got a damn good man Ron, and they know it," Phil added.

Everyone lifted their coffee cups as Joe made a toast to Ron.

"Here's to the bull! Hear, hear..., to the bull!" they all shouted. By now, everyone was in a pretty good mood.

Tom was reenergized and raring to go, and apparently so was the rest of the team. He was deeply appreciative of Joe's ability to keep the ship moving, and on course. He knew how to get people back on the road.

"Well," Tom said, "this is the main event. It is the position we fought to be in. It is what we risked our lives for. We must find a way to counteract, or at least slow down the present rate of lava flow. According to the latest statistics, the planet temperatures seem to be accelerating, which means that the data previously entered on the original computer models are incorrect. The planet has taken a violent turn for the worse." "I agree," Phil said, "according to the latest numbers, the volatility has dramatically increased way beyond our original expectations. This is going to dramatically change the time element."

"Yes, but it doesn't change our goal," Joe said. "We're just going to have to roll our sleeves up and do whatever it takes. The only thing that counts are the end results."

"I agree Joe!" Phil added as he lifted himself from the table. "We are geologists. We're not supernatural crystal ball readers, or Casey, or Nostradamus, or any of those guys, not that they really ever knew what the hell is going on. We are geologists that for the most part have an accuracy record similar to that of a weatherman. When it comes to seismic activity, our crystal ball consists of a hypothetical thesis written on toilet paper. You spend months taking readings at a volcano that you know is going to blow. You then predict the approximate date of the eruption and what you believe to be the imminent direction of the blast in an effort to save lives. Unfortunately it's like going to the casino, sometimes you win and sometimes you lose. At Mount St. Helens, we were wrong on both counts. The eruption occurred sooner than we had expected, and instead of a vertical blowout as predicted, the blowout was horizontal. It was a bad day at Black Rock," Phil continued. "A lot of lives were lost, including some of my colleagues and friends. No, Tom, neither you or I, or any of us is going to have the ability to predict the outcome regarding this matter. You said it best, this is the main event. We have risked our lives to be here. And now we have to develop a method to stop billions of tons of lava from reaching the surface of the planet. It's a far reach, and the odds are not on our side. I'm not saying it can't be done. All I'm saying is that it has never been done before."

"That had crossed my mind more than once," Tom said in a low voice. "I also sometimes wonder whether we have taken on an impossible task."

"I'm sorry, Tom," Phil said in sincere manner. "It wasn't my intent to get you into a negative posture. I just don't believe that there is a conventional method of resolving the problem. One of the most fundamental truths in science is that for every action, there is an equal and opposite reaction."

"Exactly, what are you getting at, Phil?"

"I'm not one-hundred percent sure, but, somewhere in the line of reasoning is that one major catastrophic event may very well resolve another."

"That's sure something to think about," Joe said.

"It certainly is."

"Excuse me, may I say something?"

"Go right ahead, Ron."

"In the past twenty-four hours, I have received several possible methods of partial resolutions from contributing scientists. Now, I admit that none of the methodologies that I have studied look workable. But the fact of the matter is that the scientific world is beginning to respond. However, a combination of some of these ideas may very well prove to be feasible. I believe that we should divide our research into several groups. The theory Phil presented is interesting, and should be further investigated. The second study should be to analyze the data we are receiving from the scientific community. We really don't know at this point what's going to work, so it's important that we investigate all possible avenues. The main objective is to get started."

The team spent the remainder of the morning mulling out a plan, and also agreed to meet every evening to update and discuss their progress.

Sergeant Philips introduced Tom and his colleagues to the heads of the technical staff at the command center who had indoctrinated the team on the functional aspects of the equipment. He then introduced the team to the head geologist, Frank White.

"That was a very comprehensive study," Frank said. "I admit I had some doubts at first, but once I got through those sonar readings, it really didn't matter whether it was caused by the extraction of oil or some other source because the readings proved inclusively that molten lava was actually moving from the mantle toward the service of the planet. However, I am now inclined to believe that it was caused by the extraction of petroleum."

"The real problem," Tom explained, "is, how the hell do we reverse the process?"

"Well, if there is a solution to control a lava flow, I can assure you that we're not going to find it in a textbook because it has never been accomplished before. It would be similar to trying to contain a nuclear blast seconds after the explosion."

"A point well taken," Tom said.

"We're here to help," Frank said in a sincere manner. "You tell us what you need and we'll provide it. We have already taken the liberty to download your latest study into the system. What we do here is monitor the very heartbeat of all geological changes that take place throughout the planet. The information received will automatically update statistics and data relevant to your study, including estimated time sequence changes.

"If you have any questions pertaining to the operation of any of the technical equipment that you may not be familiar with, or you're in need of an interpretation of some of the data, you need only ask the technical personnel who have been assigned to this project."

"Thanks, we can use all the help we can get. By the way, Ron Massey has been assigned to coordinate the input of all scientific data that will be transmitted from outside this facility. The rest of the staff, including myself, will spend most of our time computing the information in an effort to develop a resolution, or at the very least, attempt to slow the process down."

"Sounds like a plan," Frank said. "If there is anything else I can help you with, you need only ask. Do you have any questions?"

"Yes," John said, "Is there any place we can pick up a late snack?"

"Now there's a priority that we almost overlooked," Phil said with a smile.

"You know I work better on a full stomach."

"The cafeteria is open twenty-four/seven," Frank said. "It's located on the third floor. Any of the elevators will take you there."

"Thanks again, Frank," Tom said, "We'll see you tomorrow."

"Don't forget. You have a two o'clock meeting with the General tomorrow afternoon. I'll see you then."

The team headed to the cafeteria for a bite to eat, and then retired for the evening.

CHAPTER 27

General Herald Forthworth, chief and commander of the facility, was a hard-core military soldier from the old school who had actively served in Vietnam and the Gulf War. At age sixty-five, the general did not show signs of tiring and had no plans to retire anytime soon. He was married to his wife Mildred for thirty-two years before she had passed on five years earlier. He also had two grown sons, John and Robert, who were both officers in the military. The general did not particularly get along with civilians, but had learned the art of diplomacy. The only real enemy he had was his bullfrog attitude. He talked in a loud and heavy voice that was abrupt and to the point. He did not debate his decisions, but rather, commanded them and seldom expected a response. His underlings would always say that “it was his way or the highway”. The command station was not his idea of the military uniformity that he was accustomed to. Here, he would have to deal with civilian scientists, technicians, and engineers that were as distant from military regimentation as a person could be. When he had first come to the command station, the crew nicknamed him “Bullfrog Herald,” for his deep frog-like-voice. After a few months under his command, they renamed him “Happy Herald,” because he never smiled.

Previous to the two o’clock meeting, the General had gone through Tom’s studies with the head of the USGS, Steve Beldon, and his own staff, to familiarize himself with the technical aspects of the problem. He also met with army engineers who had also been instructed to find a solution to the problem.

Tom and his colleagues arrived at the meeting just minutes before two. The conference room was packed. Mr. Beldon was present with two of his top geologists, along with military engineers and high ranking military personnel from all branches of service.

Tom liked the idea that there were geologists in the room. He and his colleagues were not quite sure what the subject matter of the meeting would be, but were inclined to believe that the conference would have something to do with possible solutions to the problem. They were curious, but remained anxious to know what the government was up to or had planned.

"I have called this meeting to discuss a possible solution we may have to the pending problem," the General said, with a stern look on his face.

It was more like he was commanding a solution rather than suggesting one, Tom thought.

"Our top military engineers, who are here with us today, have come up with a possible resolution that they believe could resolve the problem."

He did not mention Steve Beldon or any of the other geologists, Tom thought.

"What the hell are these guys up to?" Joe whispered in Tom's ear.

"I don't know, but it sounds like he's commanding a solution rather than discussing one. Let's just hear what he has to say."

"General Jack Welsh," Forthworth continued, "Commander and Chief of the Army Engineering Division, will brief you on the details."

General Welsh was a long time friend of General Forthworth, who had served under his command in Vietnam, but unlike Forthworth, he valued the opinion of those that served under him.

"Good afternoon, gentlemen. I'll get right to the point. Predicated on Mr. Collins' evaluation of the problem, we believe that we may have come up with a feasible solution that could possibly limit further damage from occurring to the inner core of the planet's crust. As stated in Mr. Collins' report, large cavities in the earth's crust have previously been filled with pressurized oil, which acted as a hydraulic support system within the cavity. When these cavities were penetrated and the oil was extracted, the support system was destroyed. In time, a number of these cavities caved in, causing thousands of cracks to occur throughout the crust which is now permitting lava to flow from the mantle towards the surface of the planet.

"This data has been confirmed by the USGS.

"In many instances, if we can re-support these cavities we may at the very least stop any further damage from occurring to the crust.

"I know that there is no exact science that can assure us what the result will be, and I'll be the first to admit that this may not be the ultimate solution to the problem, but it may slow down the heating process to a point where life may still be sustainable, or at the very least, buy us some time.

"What we have developed, with the help of some of the largest chemical companies in the world, is produce the hardest compound known to man. What we propose to do, is to mix this chemical with common sand and pressure-feed the mix into the cavities through the existing oil well pipes, at a pressure of six-thousand pounds per square inch. The compound will harden to a solid mass, and have the strength of fifteen-thousand pounds per square inch. We believe that this will eliminate any further damage to the planet's crust, and may possibly repair a small portion of newly formed cracks."

Tom and Joe were still absorbing the information. At first, they were not sure whether this was a good idea, or one that would have long term negative consequences. The oil pipes drilled down to the cavities were the only avenue of access to these areas, Tom thought. If this theory failed, we would have no access to the existing cavities. If we clogged the pipes with a chemical compound, would that effectively limit the damage or, would it permanently seal our fate?

"Joe," Tom whispered. "If the planet continues to heat up after this chemical solution is installed, our options to send other materials into the pipe lines will no longer exist."

Joe thought carefully about the options. He was convinced that they had to decelerate the heating process because of the time element.

"Tom, we already know that the heating process has been dramatically accelerating over the past two weeks. I mean, at the very least, if we can slow the process down it would at least buy us some time."

Tom did not immediately respond.

"We really don't have much of a choice," Joe whispered.

"You could be right, Joe. What if, instead, we used some sort of coolant?"

"With temperatures exceeding two-thousand degrees, do you know how much coolant you would need to cool off the planet?" Joe asked. "There is absolutely no substance known to man that could produce the quantities required to make such a solution plausible."

Ron leaned over toward Joe and Tom. "I have two similar recommendations from a group of scientists located in England and Japan that suggest pumping a concrete mix into the cavities."

"What is your opinion, Ron?"

"Well! We are definitely in unknown territory here, but filling the holes can only help. I have examined their research papers, and I believe that, at the very least, it will buy us some time."

"Mr. Collins," General Forthworth snapped, "can you let us in on your little secret? If you have something of importance to discuss, please put in on the table."

"Sorry sir, we were just gathering options on your proposed solution."

"And what have you come up with?"

"We concur," Tom replied. "We don't believe this to be the total solution, but we do believe that it can possibly slow the heating process down."

General Forthworth was a little taken back by Tom's quick response. "And what makes you believe that this is not a total solution?"

Tom paused for a moment, then addressed the General.

"The problem isn't simply the cavities at this point, sir, but rather, the damage caused by the cavities. The damage to the crust has been occurring over the past one-hundred years, and more so, over the past thirty years. What you have are tens of thousands of cracks that have spread beyond the drilling sites to thousands of previously unknown fault lines throughout the planet."

"Why wasn't this detected?" the General asked. "There must have been signs, or some indication that these events were occurring."

"There were signs," Tom said. "The first signs, which went totally unnoticed, were the dramatic increases in seismic activity over the past thirty years. The second sign, which is extremely informational, is the unprecedented temperature rise in the ocean waters and the melting of the caps and glaciers. Why is this so informational?" Tom continued, "Because the increased temperatures have been accelerating over the past twenty to thirty years, which parallels the increased extraction of petroleum over that same time period."

"What's the bottom line?" the General asked.

"This tells us that there must have been a dramatic increase in lava flow from the mantle to the ocean floor for at least twenty-five years. We have conformation that there are areas in the ocean where the mantle is totally exposed to ocean currents, which I believe has attributed to the dramatic increase in ocean temperatures.

"We have also observed similar lava flows near land drilled wells, which seem to be connecting to previously unknown fault lines. Volcanoes throughout the world that have been dormant for thousands of years are now showing signs of becoming active. This same scenario is occurring throughout the world, Yellowstone being the worst case scenario.

"The point being General, is that you can pour a chemical mix into the oil cavities, but there is no way in hell that we are going to fill up those tens of thousands of cracks which extend way beyond the location of those cavities. We don't even know where some of them are." Tom paused for a moment and then continued. "But I do agree that we should go ahead with the chemical pour. It can only help."

The General now seemed extremely concerned.

"What is your worst fear, Tom?"

"It may be a matter of too little, too late, sir. The readings in the past two months show a dramatic change in global temperatures. The planet's temperatures are accelerating at a rate beyond what we had originally anticipated. I suggest that you install the chemical mix as expeditiously as possible, if we are to expect any positive results at all."

"Thank you, Tom, thank you for your honesty," the General responded in a voice that was completely out of character, almost not knowing what to say next. He absolutely hated dealing with civilians, but somehow he saw Tom and his associates in a different light. He felt their dedication to the project, and even more so, he felt their patriotism.

"I'd like to thank all of you," the General said, "you have the stamina of a soldier and the courage of a patriot, and for what it's worth, you can count on my full support on this project."

"Thank you, sir."

"You heard what Tom said, boys. Let's get the show on the road! I want every oil well on this planet sealed within a month," Forthworth snapped. "We have a big job ahead of us."

General Welsh walked over to Tom and his colleagues, and shook hands with each of them. "I agree with General Forthworth, you did one hell of a job putting this thing together. If there is anything I can do to further assist you, please don't hesitate to contact me directly."

"Thank you, sir."

"What's your personal opinion, Tom? Do you believe this condition can be reversed?"

"Right now, there are no conventional methods to stop or even control the flow of lava. That doesn't mean it can't be done, it simply means that it has never been done before."

"I understand, Tom, maybe this concrete mix will have more of an effect on the damage than may be expected."

"Well, if it can buy us some time, it would have been worth it."

"Good luck," the General said as he left the room.

After the meeting had been adjourned, Tom and his colleagues remained in the conference room to discuss the matter.

"The resolution, being implemented by General Forthworth," Tom explained, "can possibly serve to mitigate further damage to the planet's crust. It doesn't address the lava that is now pushing its way through tens of thousands of cracks in the crust, nor does it address the new fault lines that have become active throughout the planet, but it's a start in the right direction."

"The more lava that enters the crust," Phil explained, "the more volatile the tectonic plates will become, and as you all well know, the volatility of the plates will cause this process to dramatically accelerate. It seems like this man-made cycle of events is now feeding on itself."

"If unchecked," Joe said, "the present rate of deterioration will continue to accelerate the heating process. This would mean that all calculations, relative to time, would have to be calculated on an accelerated basis. Such multiplying factors could severely impact the time remaining to resolve the problem."

"Is this all theoretical?" John asked, "Or am I missing something?"

"I can assure you," Ron responded, "the problem is a lot more severe than is being explained, but we're scientists, not shrinks. We must stick with the facts and the scientific evidence presented if we're going to have any chance for a resolution."

"Have you received any response from the scientific community?" Joe asked.

"There are a number of geologists," Ron said, "that are convinced that the problem is not resolvable because the cracks are too deep within the Earth's crust, and to date, there is no known method to locate the position of these newly formed cracks and fault lines."

"Are you saying that there is no resolution?" Terry asked.

"No," Ron explained, "nothing is impossible. Transmitting a voice over a wire was deemed to be impossible until Graham Bell invented the telephone. The preposterous thought of a man-made flying machine was an absurd idea until the invention of the airplane, and the thought that a man could actually fly to the moon was a pipe dream until Armstrong stepped off that shuttle and walked on the moon."

"So which one is this?" Ron asked, "Would you deem to be preposterous, absurd, or impossible?"

"Actually Ron has a point," Tom responded. "There is presently no existing technology that will allow us to confirm the extent of the damage to the planet. We know that the damage is severe because water and atmospheric temperatures are increasing at a rate never before recorded. What scares me is that the rates of increase are not uniform. An oceanographer from the National Oceanic and Atmospheric Administration has recently confirmed that the depletion of oxygen levels in the three oceans is alarming. In some ocean areas, oxygen levels have depleted 20% in just over the past twenty years and approximately one-third over the past fifty years. When ocean temperatures rise, surface waters act as a cap which interferes with the natural circulation that allows deeper waters, which are already depleted of oxygen, to reach the surface. It is on the surface where depleted oxygen waters are recharged from oxygen in the air. The damage appears to be compounding itself, but the problem is that there is no way to know why. You simply cannot fix something if you do not know what is broken."

Tom continued, "I believe that the crust of the planet is thinning."

"What makes you believe that?" Joe asked.

"We have already found that a large portion of the tectonic plates are missing at the ocean floors. I have to believe that this problem is uniformly spreading throughout all the plates. The exposed mantle in the Atlantic proves that there is some sort of thinning process going on. It was the thinnest crust on the planet, and now there are sections that are completely gone.

"It sometimes appears," Tom continued, "that we're just blowing in the wind."

"Come on Tom," Joe said. "Rome wasn't built in a day. We've only been here for a couple of days."

"I'm not trying to be negative, Joe, but..."

"Tom!," Joe snapped. "We're going to beat this thing or die trying." Joe paused for a moment and then smiled.

"What are you smiling about?" Angie asked.

"I really didn't mean to say 'or die trying'."

Tom just smiled. "Ok, Joe, I got the message."

The team spent the remainder of the day computing and inputting new information into the system. Things were finally starting to click, but Tom was still somewhat skeptical because they weren't even close to a resolution.

"Let's grab a quick bit to eat," Joe said, "we're going to be up late tonight."

"That's a good idea," John said.

Angie smiled.

CHAPTER 28

The next morning, General Welsh met with Lieutenant Colonel Earl Roberts in preparation for a military staff meeting he had scheduled the day before.

"Lieutenant," Welsh explained, "the time line on this project is thirty days. I want you to make damn sure that this project is completed on time."

"Yes sir," Lieutenant Roberts responded.

As they entered the conference room, General Welsh was greeted by Brigadier General William Stratfield, who was in command of the field operation. Also present were Colonel John Brady, the special coordinator under General Stratfield, and several top engineers from the army engineering division.

"Gentlemen," General Welsh said in a determined voice, "the clock is ticking; there is absolutely no time to lose. We must complete this project within the next thirty days.

"General Stratfield," Welsh asked, "what's the status of the operation?"

"The technical advisors were previously deployed to their designated location. They have delivered the necessary specifications and technical data required to complete the installation of the chemical liquid compound into the cavities."

"What about the delivery of the chemical mix?" the General asked.

"The chemical solution required for the mix is also being transported to the designated locations, utilizing a fleet of more than one hundred thirty-five super-tankers. The tankers are in route to their final destination and should arrive within the next forty-eight hours. The entire operation is being coordinated from the Central Command Station, as per your orders. Special high-pressured pumps that were not available, at several of the oil field locations, have already been airlifted to assure that the pumps will be in place prior to the arrival of the chemical mix. It is estimated that the project will be completed within the thirty day time period allotted. All personnel involved with the operation are well aware of the time element."

"Thank you Bill," General Welsh responded, "let's pray to God that this damn thing works."

"Sir," Colonel John Brady asked, "Is there any new data available from Mr. Collins' scientific team?"

"I spoke to Mr. Collins and his team earlier and I can assure you that the situation is critical. According to Mr. Collins, the process is accelerating, which means the time element is critical. The average temperatures around the planet have already increased by an average 3.8 degrees Fahrenheit, and seismic activity around the globe has increased by more than four-hundred percent. There is no doubt that the planet is going through dramatic geological changes.

"If you were thinking that we may have more time, Colonel, Don't! This is one job that we cannot afford to push into overtime."

"Yes sir," the Colonel responded.

"Bill," General Welsh continued, "do you for see any delay on this project?"

"No sir," General Stratfield snapped.

"That's good," the General responded. "I have to meet with General Forthworth in an hour to bring him up to date and finalize the procedures. If you run into any situation that you feel may delay this project, I want you to contact me immediately."

"Yes, sir." General Stratfield responded.

"Ok, let's get this thing on the road," General Welsh said as he left the room.

CHAPTER 29

Frank and Pete were still banging their heads against the wall in an effort to find out what the insurgents were up to.

"So far," Pete explained, "there are absolutely no reports of any unusual activity where the new cells are located. There are no bombings, no suicide runs, and no kidnappings; there is simply nothing on the table to indicate what their next move will be."

"Look at this map," Frank snapped, as they viewed a world map that was pinned to the wall. "All these red flags indicate the location of cells that have been established within the past three months. What do you see as being wrong with this picture?"

"The cells are in mostly unpopulated areas," Pete said in a low voice as if he were asking a question rather than confirming the facts.

"That's right," Frank said. "But what grips me is that there's absolutely no activity, not even a firecracker. I'd just like to know what the hell there up to."

"It seems as though Tom and the boys were their only targets," Pete responded, "and now that they have been moved into a high security area, they've become inaccessible to a terrorist attack."

"That doesn't make sense," Frank said. "These new cells are located all over the globe, which leads me to believe that there is some sort of international thing going on.

"Also, why would a terrorist group pursue Tom and his team when the results of his study had already been made public knowledge?"

"I don't know, we must be missing something, and if we don't find it, we're probably going to pay the price."

Just then, Tom walked into the room.

"Hi Pete," Tom said. "You wanted to see me?"

"Yes, maybe there's something you can help us with."

"Sure, I'll be happy to help in any way possible, what do you have?"

"In the past three months, the insurgents have established hundreds of new cells throughout the world. The location of these cells is marked with a red flag on this map," Pete explained as he pointed, "The question is, do any of these locations mean anything to you?"

Tom viewed the maps carefully, and then stepped back with a surprised look on his face, "These are all of the towns and villages I stayed at while gathering information for my thesis."

"Hold it," Frank said. "Why these locations, why did you choose these locations?"

"Because these locations are adjacent to the oil fields, and of course, the oil fields comprised ninety-five percent of the study."

"Holy shit," Pete yelled. "Did you hear that Frank?"

"Why the oil field?" Frank asked. "What the hell are they up to?"

"It has something to do with Tom's thesis," Pete suggested.

"We have to trace these guys back to find out what doctrine their following, if we're ever going to establish a motive."

Frank picked up the phone and called main headquarters.

"This is Agent Benit, connect me to Mr. Daraine's office, it's an emergency."

"What do you have Frank?""We've just discovered that the new terrorist cells are located adjacent to oil fields; however, we still don't know what their intention is. I would like to know when, why and where this sect was formed. I would also like to know what region in the Middle East they're from. This sect is not even close to mainstream beliefs! I need dates, time periods, and also, I'd like to know specifically if they are following a doctrine other than the Koran. This is extremely important, I need this information yesterday."

"This is probably going to take a little time," Daraine said, "I'll get back to you as soon as I can."

Frank hung up and turned to Pete. "Do you see where I'm going with this thing, Pete?"

"You believe that these guys are following a different doctrine, or maybe, even misinterpreting the Koran."

"It's the only thing that makes sense."

Just then, Pete's phone rang.

"Pete? Jack Redrick. I just received the request for information from CIA head, Ralph Daraine. What is this all about?"

"Actually, this is something that Frank Benit came up with. He has a hunch that the terrorists are predicating their ideology on some sort of religious belief. Think about it, why else would they continue to go after Tom and his colleagues knowing that the information regarding the study had already been made public?

"Not just that," Pete continued, "but why have there been absolutely no terrorist attacks in the past three months? It seems as though they have narrowed everything down to one agenda and it looks like Tom and his colleagues are the targets."

"Ok Pete, I'll do what I can to get the information you need, unfortunately, we're not going to find this stuff in the history books. The only places we're going to find this type of information are in Muslim records and archives."

"Have you interrogated the insurgents we captured from the Kennedy attack?" Pete asked. "If anyone knows anything about the history of this sect, they certainly would."

"The problem is that these guys are not talking, and after that water-boarding incident in Guantanamo, our hands are pretty much tied on what we can and cannot do."

Pete did not immediately respond. "Pete, are you still there?"

"I don't understand," Pete said, "the planet is on the brink of disaster and we're still worried about protocol."

"I'm not arguing the point," Redrick said, "I'm just telling you the way it is."

"How about Iran, how are they reacting to this apocalypse scenario?"

"The leaders in Iran are radical but they're not suicidal, why do you ask?"

"We should send the insurgents to Iran for interrogation. I understand that they have aggressive interrogating procedures. They shouldn't have any problem extracting the necessary information."

Redrick smiled, "Ok Pete, I'll get back to you."

"We don't have a hell of a lot of time," Pete said.

"I understand I'm going to meet with the President in a half-hour. I'll get back to you as soon as I can."

"Well, Pete," Frank asked, "what the hell did he say?"

"He's going to meet with the President and call me back."

"So you told your boss to send the insurgents to Iran for interrogation," Frank said smiling. "I didn't think you had it in you."

"Do you think that was a good idea?" Pete asked.

"I've been with the CIA longer than I would like to remember," Frank said, "after a certain amount of time, you get to develop rules that have a tendency to keep you alive. Well, you know how it is as a federal agent, Pete. When your enemy pats you on the back and tells you he's your friend, the first thing you do is make sure he doesn't have a knife in his hand. However, in the case of Iran, Syria and some of the other Muslim countries that were once hostile toward US, the answer is yes. I think that they are sincere in their effort to save the planet. Will it last? Who the hell knows?"

"I guess we're just going to have wait and see," Pete responded.

Frank just shook his head and smiled. "I still can't believe you suggested sending those guys to the Iranians for interrogation."

CHAPTER 30

The next day, the information that Pete had requested began to be fed into the command computer system. They read page after page of documents, but still could not find a single clue as to why the terrorists had targeted Tom and his crew, or why they were parked adjacent to the oil fields. There was simply nothing in the documents relevant to the assassination attempts.

"Here, Pete!" Frank shouted. "I think we have something here!"

"What do you have Frank?"

"I think this is what we have been looking for. It appears that there was a religious sect, in the year 666 AD, who were condemned to death for forging a religious doctrine that had allegedly been found in the archives at a holy place in Iran. According to the records, the leaders of the sect presented a document in the form of a scroll and claimed it was the writings of Muhammad. The sect claimed that they had found the scrolls in a cave, thirty-four years after the religious leader died. On examining the scrolls, the Islamic fundamental leaders deemed the writings to be forgeries, and found the sect guilty of blasphemy. Look what it says here, Pete! They were condemned to death; however, the leaders of the sect and many of their followers managed to escape into the wilderness and lived as nomads. Throughout this period of time, it seems that the sect managed to hide its identity for fear of being prosecuted. It is theorized that after the original leaders died, the scrolls were somehow past down to other members of the sect as an authentic doctrine.

"Some members of the sect managed to gain enormous wealth these past seventy-five years. They have also managed to gain high positions in the political arena," Frank added. "Apparently, the fundamentalists lost track of the group until recent years. In time, their membership increased dramatically and now pose a serious threat to the world and fundamental Muslims."

Pete and Frank were absolutely positive that the group being investigated had derived from the same sect. Everything was starting to come together. They began to read the English translation of the scrolls.

"Look here," Frank said, "the scrolls contained a series of prophecies that depict the end of days known as 'The Cleansing'. They speak of a time when; 'The Mountain's will roar, and fire and brimstone will flow from their mouths. The Earth will rumble and cities of evil will be consumed. The infidels will be cleansed from the Earth.

"'There will come a time when the waters will boil and the skies will turn black. And before the earth is totally consumed, the prophet will come, riding on a cloud and bringing eternal harmony to the world.

"'When these signs are at your doorstep, there will be many who will try to deceive you. There will be those who will attempt to interfere with the prophecy, and many that will die by your hands. These are the anti-Gods. No man who is against me shall live.

"'There will be many wars and suffering throughout the days before the end comes. These things will come and pass, but you will know the end when the signs of the cleansing are known to all of mankind. When you see fire and brimstone and all the Earth rumbles, you will know it is the end days.

"'For those who are faithful to this prophecy there will be everlasting riches.'"

Pete just shook his head. "Can you believe this crap? They believe that this is the end of days! And look at this part. 'There will be those who will attempt to interfere with the prophecy.' It says that these are the anti-GODS, and that they must be killed. That's why they were after Tom and his colleagues," Frank's face looked solemn. Attempt to interfere with what?

"Pete, we have a big problem! These guys have a forged document that is telling them that these are the ends of days, and that's not the worst of it! They are actually prepared to fight to the death. Apparently, they're prepared to assassinate anyone that interferes with the prophecy. Are you thinking what I'm thinking, Pete?"

"I think so. It's all starting to make sense. For months we've been trying to figure out why they've been setting up cells in mostly unpopulated areas. They know about the operation. They plan on attacking the oil wells," Pete paused for a moment, and then turned toward Frank with a serious look on his face. "We had better notify main headquarters."

Just then the telephone rang. "Pete, this is Jack Redrick, Frank's hunch was right..." there was a slight pause on the phone. Pete heard the shuffling of paper as Jack continued, "Pete, I have bad news. Several large oil well facilities around the world have been taken over by terrorists. We have alerted the military, and the President has been in contact with the heads of state. There are reports coming in as we speak. Reports of terrorist attacks have come in from Iraq, Iran, Arabia, Texas, Kuwait, Alaska, and a slew of other oil producing nations."

"Jack, listen to me!" Pete snapped. "The attacks on the oil fields are predicated on a religious doctrine that had previously been rejected by mainstream Muslims. The terrorists are on a suicidal mission. They are prepared to fight to the death and have no intention of negotiating! You have to take these guys out, and fast, or the plan to stabilize the wells will be lost."

"I am already on the phone with the White House," Redrick explained. "Stand-by for further orders."

Pete waited on the line while Jack relayed the information to the White House and the command center. General Forthworth immediately sent out a field directive to take the terrorists out and to protect the wells, at any cost.

If only we could have figured things out a couple of days earlier, Pete thought. He knew that Frank wasn't a happy man. "Don't frustrate yourself, Frank; there was no way we could have known."

Frank was beside himself, and did not immediately respond. "How is it, Pete, that these guys are always one step ahead of us, and how in the hell do they always know what we are going to do next? We have a damn leak in the system! And if we don't find it, a lot more people are going to die!"

"Calm down, Frank. You're going to burst a blood vessel."

Frank was still angry, but knew Pete was right. Milling over what could have been is not going to do a damn thing for anyone.

"Until we eliminate the terrorist factor," Frank said, "the project to save the planet will remain in jeopardy. The first thing we have to do is clean house. There are moles in the system and we have to clean them out. We will start by further limiting classified information to specific personnel. This has to be a combined effort between both agencies." Pete nodded in agreement. "Secondly, we have to go on the offensive. There has to be a world wide effort to totally eliminate the terrorist threat. This is no longer a political event in which governments take sides." Frank paused for a moment as he turned to face Pete. "We don't have months Pete, we don't even have weeks. We have to take these bastards down now."

"We're going to need the full cooperation of the Islamic nations," Pete explained.

Just then, Frank's cell rang. "Hello, this is Benit."

"Hi Frank, this is Agent Williams. There will be a President staff meeting at one this afternoon which will be held in the presidential conference room. Both you and Agent Marchel have been directed to attend."

"Can you tell me what the meeting is about?" Frank asked.

"They will be discussing several issues," Agent Williams said, "but I believe that the main issue will be associated with the terrorist attacks on the oil fields."

"We'll be there," Frank said as he hung up the phone.

"Be where?" Pete asked.

"Good news Pete, we have been invited to attend the President's staff meeting at one this afternoon. It looks like they're going to address the terrorist problem."

"That's good, Frank. Maybe they're finally getting down to the nitty-gritty."

Frank just shook his head. "We had better get a few things together and prepare for the meeting."

CHAPTER 31

Pete and Frank arrived at the presidential conference room fifteen minutes early and were immediately greeted by FBI Director Jack Redrick and CIA Director Ralph Daraine.

Also attending the meeting was Vice President Herald Baldwin, Secretary of State Joan Dunne, and Secretary of Home Land Security Bill Stallino, Secretary of Defense Robert Bates, Secretary Treasurer Ben Brodwick, and his military staff including General Herald Forthworth.

When the President entered the room, everyone started to get up from their chairs.

"Please sit down," the President said in a brisk voice. "Please, please, take your seats.

"We have called this emergency staff meeting to address the recent attacks on the oil fields. It has been confirmed by Agent Pete Marchel and Agent Frank Benit, who have been the chief coordinators in this operation, that the terrorist group, who has been involved with the most recent attacks against Tom and his colleagues, have apparently predicated their actions on a false doctrine which they believe has empowered them to cleanse the entire planet of infidels. This includes Islamic nations who have openly condemned the sect, and its fanatical interpretation of a doctrine that has been rejected by fundamental Muslims since 666 AD.

"General Forthworth has assured me that the situation is under control, which brings us to the more important issue of global warming.

"The latest scientific data I received from Tom Collins is not encouraging. It seems that the deterioration of the tectonic plates is accelerating more rapidly than they had originally anticipated. This will substantially shorten the time remaining to resolve the problem. That critical time element has been termed 'The Point of no Return', a point by which our ability to reverse the process will be non-existent. My good friends," the President continued, "this means that under no circumstance can we permit this project to be delayed.

"Operation 'Clean-up' has been initiated to totally eliminate the terrorist fraction, by any means necessary. General Forthworth will command the operation and strategically coordinate with Agent Pete Marchel, and Agent Frank Benit will be in full command of the Federal Security agencies, working under the command of FBI Director, Jack Redrick, and CIA Director, Ralph Daraine. You have less than a month to clean house gentlemen, is that understood?"

"Yes sir," General Forthworth said. "Sir, it's imperative that we receive the cooperation of the Islamic nations."

"I agree with the General, sir," Agent Benit said.

"There is no guarantee that we'll receive their cooperation," Bates said in a strong tone of voice. "But under the circumstances, I believe that they will have a tendency to cooperate.

"Desperate times call for desperate measures," the President responded. "My orders are to stop the terrorists at all cost. How that is accomplished will be left in the hands of the General, Agent Marchel and Agent Benit. There are no restrictions to these orders. The choice is simple, we either eliminate the terrorists or the planet eliminates us."

They all understood exactly where the President was coming from.

"Ok," the President continued, "now that we have that straightened out, let's get back to the pending problem. General, what's the extent of the damage to the oil fields and when will the areas be totally secured?"

"Our ground forces are encountering heavy resistance from the terrorists," the General explained. "The last report confirmed that the battles were fierce, and would not end anytime soon.

"We also have confirmation that the Islamic producing oil states have launched a full blown attacked against the terrorists, which leads me to believe that their cooperation to eliminate the terrorist sect will be more forthcoming than originally anticipated. Losses are heavy sir, but we do have the situation under control." The General paused for a moment to go through his latest data reports.

"In other areas of the world, sir, the situation is similar. The fighting is intense. There are oil wells that are being saved, and others that are now burning out of control."

"What kind of delay are we talking about?" the President asked. "When will we be able to start filling the oil wells with the chemical mix?"

"There's no way to tell at this point, sir. As soon as the damage is surveyed I'll have a report on your desk."

Just then, one of Bates' assistants walked into the room and handed him a message.

"Sir," Secretary Bates snapped, "I just received a message that might interest you."

"Go ahead Bob, what do you have?"

"It appears that the Islamic nations had an emergency meeting of their own," Bates explained. "They have voted unanimously to join our effort to wage war against the terrorist fraction. I guess the attacks on their oil field didn't go over too well with them."

"Does that include Iran, Syria and other previously hostile nations?" the President asked.

"Yes sir, the vote was unanimous."

"This is good news," the President said, seeming extremely relieved that something was actually going in their direction. "I guess they finally understand what the hell is going on."

"It sounds like they made a choice between living and dying," Vice President Baldwin said in a determined voice, "It's a good sign."

"I guess we are in new territory," the President responded. "The fighting that is now raging throughout the world are not battles over land, or political gain, nor are they revolutionary. These are the reasons that men used in past conflicts as an excuse to create hardships and cause destruction and devastation to entire civilizations. Men have been killing and maiming each other for unjustified gains since Cain and Abel. Not this time, no! This time the world will be united toward one cause, a single goal, and for one purpose- to save mankind from total extinction.

"The circumstance that lies before the human race today is beyond anything that has ever existed in all the times that have passed. The reality that the Earth could be a lifeless planet has dramatically changed man's thinking patterns. In the past, there were no conflicts that even remotely brought mankind to the brink of extinction."

"That's why," the President continued, "that it is imperative for all nations of the world to put aside their differences, whether they are ideological, political or religious preference; to join together as a single force to save the planet."

The President paused for a moment as he sipped a glass of water.

"Let's turn to the next order of business," the President said, as he addressed Secretary Treasurer Ben Brodwick. "I realize that this may be a mute question Ben, but do you have an undated report on the world economy?"

"There is no economy," Brodwick explained, "We are now one-hundred percent on the point system with each country having a slightly different methodology, but in most cases, similar to the program we developed. The system has allowed people to buy food, clothes, and other necessities. It's full-proof, and appears to be serving its purpose.

"There's not much more to be said, Mr. President."

"Thanks Ben," the President responded, as he turned to address the head of FEMA, Bob Johnson. "My concern, Bob, is civilian unrest, mob rule and other things of that nature. What should we prepare for?"

"Well," Bob explained, "according to previous studies done on human behavior, we should expect some unrest, attempts at mob-rule, and sporadic looting, but in general, there is no study that really covers the present circumstance. I mean, we're talking about the end of civilization here. These people are going through a revelation that makes all other problems and ambitions in life seem insignificant. It could be compared to the same feeling a person experiences when they are on their death bed. Priorities change, and your ambitions and goals for material gain dissipate. Winning or losing an argument, personal status, and even material gain seemed insignificant when death is imminent. Especially when you know that your very existence, in a relatively short period of time, will end. It's probably the one instance in life that actually enlightens a person as to what life is really all about. At that one moment you realize that the only things that count in life are people. Everything else becomes secondary.

"When life becomes terminal, you no longer measure yourself in net worth. You seek compassion, understanding, companionship, and above all, love. These are virtues that can only be given to you by people. All your materialistic ambitions at this juncture of life totally dissipate. The protective shield that we have all built around ourselves starts to fall apart. The reality of our present circumstance greatly diminishes our past justifications. You know what you have given to the people who have passed through your life, and what you have taken from them. For many, there is a lot of sorrow and regret. For others, there is simply a need for companionship. Many will turn to God, but for most people who are facing death, there is a feeling of emptiness. There's a void within them that they can never seem to fill. Things that they thought were so important in life, just days before, no longer seem to matter.

"It is man's instinct to survive, and of course to survive others, that will expose the humanity we all have within us.

"I believe that it is man's will to live that will be the catalyst, and the encouragement, that will energize all of us to survive. Even if we get through the crisis, there will be hardships to face in the aftermath of the event, but most will be grateful just to be alive.

"Within every man there is an unprecedented will to live. It is that same will that I believe will unite the entire world as a single unit of people. Now I can't tell you that the world will be saved. Only God knows the answer to those questions, but I can tell you that any effort to save the planet will be initiated by man's will to live."

"Thank you Bob," the President said, "I just hope you're right. If we can resolve the fundamental problem, I do believe that we'll get through the aftermath regardless of the resulting hardships we will have to face."

They continued to discuss other issues of importance before the meeting was adjourned, but the issue on terrorism remained the main topic that afternoon.

CHAPTER 32

After receiving confirmed reports from his field personnel, General Welsh contacted his close friend, General Forthworth, to update him on the situation. "Jerry, we have just finalized the survey on the damage. It doesn't look good! Almost 60 percent of the wells have been damaged. We have fire fighting teams on the job and additional teams in route. The estimated time to seal the wells is approximately four to five weeks from today. We can start pumping the chemical fluid into wells that are still functional, but cannot start pumping the fluid into the remaining wells until the fires have been extinguished.

"At this point," the General continued, "we cannot confirm whether or not the oil pipes leading to the cavities have been damaged. However, the good news is that the terrorist threat has been totally neutralized. All areas are now secured."

"That's good to know, Jack," General Forthworth responded. "It seems like every time we turn around, we run into a brick wall. I don't have to explain to you the seriousness of the matter. If we don't do something to buy Tom and his colleagues some time, we're going to be shit out of luck."

"Have they made any progress?" General Welsh asked.

"I spoke to Tom late last night," General Forthworth said. "There doesn't seem to be anything on the table at this point, but he assured me that they would continue to work around the clock until the problem is resolved."

"I consulted with Steve Beldon over at the USGS early this morning,"

General Welsh explained, "and the news wasn't good. He didn't quite say that the problem was unsolvable, but he did annotate that past scientific research on the subject is non-existent. Their latest sonar readings have confirmed that there are billions of tons of lava moving toward the surface of the plant which is literally melting the crust as it rises. The team of scientists at USGS have experientially reviewed several aspects of the new data, but they haven't been able to come up with a solution that would feasibly reverse the process."

"The latest data has pretty much confirmed Mr. Collins' latest time table," General Forthworth responded. "We're simply running out of time. Right now, it's important to get the chemical solution down those pipes." The General paused for moment as he took in a deep breath of air. "Jack, be careful out there, we can't afford to lose you."

"Thanks, Harry. I'll do what I can to get those oil wells plugged."

"By the way, Jack, a joint decision has been made by the nations of the world to inform the population of the crises they will be facing within the next twelve months. President Baxter will be broadcasting his statement at two o'clock this afternoon. You may want to tune in."

As soon as General Welsh hung-up the phone, he met with his staff to update them on the latest findings.

At two p.m. General Welsh turned on the TV to listen to President Baxter's announcement.

"My fellow Americans, in the past six months there have been scientific studies that have strongly indicated that dramatic changes have taken place within the planet's tectonic plates. For those who are not familiar with the geological structure of the planet, the very ground we walk on is comprised of thirteen plates that float independently on what we identify as the mantle of the planet. The mantle itself is composed of hot molten lava.

"In the past, the movement of these tectonic plates has caused many earthquakes and volcanic eruptions throughout years in what can be categorized as normal occurrences. However, a recent study that was undertaken by renowned geologist, Tom Collins, has confirmed that the extraction of oil has caused thousands of cracks to occur within crust of the planet, allowing molten lava to flow freely from the mantle to the surface of the planet.

"This man-caused instability in the plates," the President continued, "is presently accelerating at a rate far beyond the cycle of volatility normally experienced, and unless a resolution can be found to reverse this process, the temperatures on this planet will rise to levels that will not support life as we know it.

"This nation in cooperation with all other nations of the world has joined forces in an effort to develop a solution that will reverse this process, or at the very least, prevent the molten lava from breaking through the surface of the planet.

"Scientists in the US have developed a chemical solution, that when pumped into the existing oil wells, will theoretically prevent further damage to the crust of the planet. Unfortunately, there is no way for us to calculate what the results will be.

"In the past, man has overcome many obstacles through its ingenuity and perseverance. Against insurmountable odds, we have made incalculable advancements in medicine, enormous strides in technology, and have even put a man on the moon. Today, we are once again faced with a challenge that threatens our very existence. A challenge that brings us to a new frontier of scientific study, and once again, we will meet that challenge with the same ingenuity and perseverance that has, so often, survived us throughout the centuries.

"It is imperative that we conduct ourselves in a peaceful and orderly manner during this crisis, and that we also extend a helping hand to those who are in need. There will be further bulletins that will explain our method of distributing food and other necessities, including all updates that may be necessary to secure your safety.

"Thank you, and May God bless you all."

As soon as the President completed his statement, the news commentator came on the air. "There will be further updates and information available to the public as they are received. Please stay tuned."

Most people were in shock, they had a difficult time accepting the notion that the world could possibly come to an abrupt end. Some were overwhelmed when they received the news, and other had already surmised that the government was not being forthcoming regarding the cause for the obvious physical geological changes that were occurring throughout the world.

As news continued to be broadcast, the facts became more realistic. Churches, synagogues, mosques, temples and other religious places of worship around the world were packed. The normal everyday life that people had become accustomed to had been totally disrupted. People were really scared. They were looking for some sort of assurance that everything would eventually be all right. There was a need within them to know.

The majority of people continued to turn to God. Of course, there had always been times in life when a person needed a heavy shoulder to lean on, or someone to help them through a difficult time. However, there was never a time in history when that need was so great for so many.

During the first couple of days after receiving the news, people were glued to the communication networks. The news had become a series of repeated stories told in different ways. The public wanted to know what progress was being made to fix the problem. As the days passed without results, anxiety levels increased, and many became frustrated. The world, in a very clear sense, was relying on a hand-full of scientists who did not have the faintest idea of how to resolve the problem.

People were having a difficult time accepting the doomsday prophecy. To most, it was something that you usually watched on the documentary channels. Their thinking patterns were simple; if it's broken, fix it. What's the big deal?

Although facing insurmountable odds, scientists around the world worked long hours in the hope of finding a resolution. They simply were not prepared to throw in the towel.

There were also many heroes during the two-day skirmish against the terrorists, but no one was keeping score. The motto became "One for all, and all for one." The fire fighters became another group that were heroes for the cause. They would work six hours off and eighteen hours on until they secured the oil wells. If hard work, dedication, and fortitude were the ingredients needed for the planet to survive they would surely succeed, and if they failed, it would not be for lack of effort.

The clock was ticking. The shear effort exerted by the fire fighters and the military to save the oil wells was beyond heroic, and yet, it was just one of many efforts that would be needed to ensure the planet's survival.

CHAPTER 33

Back at the command center, Tom and his colleagues had been working fervently to find a viable solution to the problem, and although they worked around the clock, they weren't any closer to finding a solution then they were when they first started.

"We don't seem to be making any progress," Tom said, sounding somewhat disappointed.

"We haven't been at it that long," Joe responded, "and besides, Rome wasn't built in a day. We just have to stay with the program, Tom, and hope the General can buy us some time."

"The chemical solution may prevent further damage to recently drilled wells," Tom replied, "but, it will have absolutely no effect on older wells, where I have sufficient evidence showing lava movement through thousands of cracks and old fault lines throughout the planet. So, I'm not really hyped regarding what effect the chemical solution will have on the overall solution to the problem."

"I'm not arguing the point," Joe said, "all I'm saying is that we're not the first scientists in the world to face a problem that seems almost impossible to resolve."

Tom smiled. "Be careful how you use that word, impossible. Let me lay it out for you, the lava that is flowing toward the surface of the planet is located in areas that are just not accessible. The big problem is that the majority of lava coming to the surface of the crust is beneath the depths of the oceans, where the crust is only three to five miles deep. There isn't a single oil rig in the world that could drill to the required depths to possibly repair the damage. And that's only in the event we find a solution. Even if such a rig could be built, there is no way we could build the quantity of rigs necessary, within a feasible time period; and that's without consideration of the fact that there could be thousands of areas that would have to be drilled at the same time. It's just not possible. So I do wonder at times, whether or not the problem is really resolvable; but to reassure your confidence in me, I have absolutely no intention of giving up."

"I feel like a psychologist," Joe said laughing. "Well I'm sure glad you got that off your chest, if I can be of any further assistance....."

"Ok, Joe," Tom said smiling, "I think we had better get back to the drawing board. Look at this Joe, it's a five-day study just completed by Ron, Phil and a group of technicians and scientists assigned to the project. The data reflects the latest climate changes, and increased seismic activity occurring throughout the planet. It also includes scientific data gathered from scientists around the world." Tom paused for a moment while Joe skimmed over the data.

"It wasn't until the fifth day," Tom continued, "when they realized that the original computer program calculations for projecting future time scenarios were incorrect."

"Ron, why don't you plug the new calculations into the network?"

When the new calculations were plugged in, the news was not good. The large projection screen showing the new data was visible to the entire staff. Ron just stared at the screen, not wanting to believe the results. The entire room of more than two hundred scientists, technicians, and engineers, all of whom had participated in the findings were anxious to see what the new data would reveal. John turned to Phil and Ron with a serious look on his face, almost not knowing what to say.

"Maybe we should reanalyze the findings. We could have made an error. I think we should recheck our figures before we release these findings," John suggested.

"I don't think so," Ron replied. "The calculations have been checked and rechecked. We have already taken into consideration the best and worst scenarios. Nothing is going to change results at this point."

"I agree with Ron," Phil said. "There's no sense in beating a dead horse. With a critical time period of three-hundred-twenty to three-hundred-fifty days, we certainly cannot afford to lose even a day." John seemed somewhat disappointed with the results, but deep down inside, he knew that they were correct. He simply did not want to believe it.

The new calculations seriously diminished the amount of time that remained to correct the problem. Ron was well aware of the fact that the situation had just gone from serious to critical. He asked Phil and John to accompany him to the third level of the command center where Joe and Tom were meeting with scientists to discuss the results.

The team shuffled through the tons of data that they had received from geologists around the world. The majority of information received dealt more with the deteriorating condition of the planet, than with resolving the problem. The resolutions that were received were either incomplete or impossible to accomplish. Tom was convinced that it would take nothing short of a miracle to repair the crust. The mantle of the planet was breached, and soon we'll have to pay the consequences, he thought. What was most discouraging was receiving confirmation from other notable scientists around the world who insisted there was no possibility of controlling the magnitude of lava that was racing to the surface of the planet.

When Ron, Phil and John, entered the conference room with grim looks on their faces, Joe and Tom prepared themselves for another round of bad news.

"Ok, guys, what's up? You look like you just came back from a war and lost the battle. When is the last time you had some shut-eye?"

"That is exactly how we feel," Ron responded. "The new projection, including the new calculations you had asked for on the acceleration rate of the planets deterioration, has been completed. The results are not good. The report confirms that we have a lot less time than was originally calculated. In plain English, global warming is accelerating at a rate far greater than we had anticipated."

"What do you mean, Ron?" Joe asked.

"Well, the original calculations were predicated on a mathematical formula that was incorrect. In other words, the original calculations were additive. That's just not what's happening. The calculation should have been a mathematical formula with a multiplying factor of 1.26. Our original computer model is programmed to calculate time on an additive basis, whereas in fact, it's actually on a multiplying factor of 1.26, and even that may increase."

Tom and Joe immediately understood what Ron was saying.

"Exactly, what did you come up with?" Tom asked.

"Well, there are two ways I can give it to you. I can go over the five days of figures and calculations that include increased seismic activity, water temperatures, increased temperatures at the Earth's crust, and a thousand other calculations. Or, I can just give you the results."

"Just the results; I'm confident that your work is conclusive. You have been right on everything else you've given us. I doubt very much that you would be incorrect on this one."

"This is one time that I wish I was wrong."

By the tone of Ron's voice, Joe already knew that the updated information would shorten the time they had to resolve the problem. He had already started to contemplate what the next move would be.

"Well," Ron continued, "We came up with two projections that take into consideration the best and worst scenarios. You know as well as I do that these projections are predicated on data that is always open to a moderate degree of error. Future calculations can easily change over time because we now know that the calculated multiplying factors are really a variable number. The factor associated with dating and time projections have been substantially decreased."

"What's the bottom line, Ron?" Joe asked.

Ron paused for a moment.

"The first projection gives us three-hundred-twenty days, and the second projection three-hundred-fifty days. These dates represent the point of no return. A time period that will put us on the very edge of extinction."

There was silence in the room as Joe and Tom waited patiently for Ron to continue, but there was really nothing else to say. Joe broke the silence.

"What do you mean three-hundred-twenty to three-hundred-fifty days? What does that mean?" Ron did not know what to say. He knew that they had both understood.

"I'm a scientist, Joe. I gather the hard evidence and then calculate future results through a time-sequence computer program. Let me give you some of the details, it will give you an idea of what we are up against. The average water temperatures have risen an additional 2.2 percent, and atmospheric temperature by 2.6 percent. The water level has raised 3.5 inches worldwide. The volcano Kilauea, on the island of Hawaii, just erupted at a VEI of 4.5. There are several other volcanoes around the world that are ready to blow, including Yellowstone, which is now on a minute-by-minute forecast! And the ice caps are continuing to melt at an alarming rate."

"But Ron, the temperature increases are not that drastic, and neither are the water levels!"

"Joe, these changes have taken place within the last five days," Ron responded.

Joe was a little taken aback. In all his years as a geologist he had never seen anything progress that fast.

"There must be some mistake."

Tom listened quietly and then addressed Joe.

"I don't think so, Joe. I have felt all along that the process has been accelerating, and I believe that deep down inside you came to the same conclusion. All Ron and Phil did is to confirm what we already knew."

Joe was not the give-up type of guy. However, for the first time in his life he felt that the total extinction of the human race was more than just a possibility. Although he knew that the calculations were correct, he had a tough time accepting them.

"And how the hell are we going to find a solution in three-hundred-twenty days?" Joe asked.

"That has been my main concern these last two months," Tom responded.

"That makes two of us," Ron said, "but I'll do everything I can to help."

Joe reached over and put his hand on Ron's shoulder.

"I know you will, Ron. I don't doubt your dedication; I'm just venting. If I offended you, I apologize."

"I'm not offended, Joe, I'm just tired. I think I'll hit the sack. If you have any questions regarding the report, wake me."

"Thanks, Ron."

Tom had listened to Ron intently. He was not really overly surprised. He knew that time was short.

"Joe, listen to me," Tom said. "We have been friends since the beginning of time. You're always telling me that when a geologist cannot explain something, he labels the cause of the event as a natural occurrence. That is not who we are, Joe. We have always dealt with truths and have always confirmed those truths with the facts. Now we have a situation where it really doesn't matter whether we have two-hundred-twenty days or four-hundred days! I'm not even saying that the problem is resolvable. But I would like to believe that we will at least go down fighting."

"OK, Tom, I got the message, my prophecy is coming true, we're all going to die. There is absolutely no hope! But we are going to go down fighting. I think that it's time we start thinking about plan J."

Tom just sat back and listened. He sincerely believed that somehow, someway, Joe would come up with something that would renew their hope.

"Alright, Joe, I'll bite! What is plan J all about?"

"It was Phil who came up with the idea! Do you remember, Tom?" He said, "'For every action there is an opposite and equal reaction'. That's the premise of the plan. That's the theory we have to predicate our research on. We know that the planet is heating up. The question is, what monumental event has to take place in order to cool the planet down?"

Tom just listened; he liked the concept. "We can start working on some theory tomorrow," Joe continued, "right now it's late and we are both exhausted."

"Yeah, I'm pretty tired," Tom responded, looking as tired as he sounded. "We'll work on it first thing in the morning. I'm going to head down to inform the General of these latest figures, I'll see you tomorrow."

"You'll probably ruin his evening," Joe said with a smile, as he headed to his room.

"See you in the morning, Joe."

After receiving a comprehensive briefing on the new time projections from Tom, General Forthworth immediately contacted the President to give him the bad news. President Hamity instructed Secretary of State Dunne to call for an emergency meeting to be held at the command center. The meeting was scheduled for eight a.m. the next morning. The President requested the presence of the Director of Homeland Security, Bill Stallino, the head of the USGS, Steve Beldon, and the President's full staff, including his top military advisers. Tom and his associates were also requested to be in attendance.

When Tom was informed of the meeting, he immediately called each member of the team that evening.

John Mason, realizing that time was short, requested permission to have his wife and children brought to the command center. General Forthworth granted his request.

After Joe had been informed of the emergency meeting, he walked over to Angie's sleeping quarters and gently knocked on the door. Angie who was just dozing off, got up from her bed to answer the door. She was delighted to see Joe standing there. "I know that it's late Angie and I'm sorry if I woke you. I know that the time is unreasonable, but..."

"That's all right, Joe. I'm really happy you're here." She felt Joe's emotions and instinctively knew that something just wasn't right. "What is it, Joe, are you all right?"

"I'm fine, I... it's just that... I'm having..."

"Joe, I know about the bad news."

"I'm just having a difficult time with..."

He seemed a little nervous, and she just wasn't quite sure what he was trying to say.

Joe held her in his arms.

"I love you, Angie!" She looked up into his eyes, sincerely hoping that everything was alright.

"I love you too, Joe."

"Angie, I want you to look at me."

She turned her head and looked directly into his eyes.

"Do you know why I'm here, sweetheart?"

"What is it Joe, what is it that you're trying to tell me?" she asked in a soft voice.

"We just cannot continue to go on this way," Joe said. "It's just not going to work."

"What do you mean, Joe?" Angie became apprehensive and was afraid to ask the next question. She really loved him and was not prepared to lose him. "Well Joe, what is it? Please be honest."

"OK, Angie, here goes. Will you marry me?" Angie immediately turned on the waterworks. The tears flowed down her cheeks and there was nothing Joe could do at this point to shut off the valves. "I don't understand Angie, you cry when you're happy and you cry when you're sad! How is a man to tell the difference? I assume this is a 'yes' cry?"

"Yes, Joe. Yes," she said, as she kissed him passionately. It was truly the happiest day of her life.

"Angie, it's important that you know that we are all committed to finding a resolution to this problem. I did not ask you to marry me because I have contemplated that the world is coming to an end. My intentions are quite the contrary; I intend to enjoy a lifetime of happiness with you, having little Solino babies who like good Italian pizza and maybe some meatballs on the side."

Angie smiled and then laughed.

"I guess I'll have to learn how to make pasta the Solino way," Angie said with a smile.

"I believe that this is going to be the beginning of a beautiful friendship," Joe replied.

This is truly the happiest moment of my life, Angie thought, as they both retired for the evening.

CHAPTER 34

The next morning, Tom arrived in the dining room at five thirty, with Ron walking in just behind him.

"Good morning, Ron," Tom said with a smile, "you look a lot better than you did last night."

"Good Morning," Ron responded, sounding like he wasn't quite awake yet.

"Well," Tom said, "it looks like we are going to have another day to remember."

Ron smiled, "Ever since I joined this group, every day has been a day to remember."

"I know how you feel. It's like being in an action-filled adventure novel, with death and uncertainty around every corner. The only problem is that we are the main characters."

"Yes, we are," Ron said in a low voice. He seemed to fall off into a daze for a moment, and then he abruptly continued, "I've put a lot of time into this project, but I really haven't made a hell of a lot of progress."

"What do you mean?" Tom knew by the tone of his voice that Ron had something on his mind. "What is it Ron? What are you thinking about?

After sitting down at the table, Ron turned to address Tom. He knew that Tom was a dedicated scientist who had spent a great deal of time on his research papers. He was also confident that he could express his views in a factual and confident manner, not having to concern himself with editing his thoughts. Science was measured in truths and proofs; he knew that Tom shared the same sentiment. Ron had a great deal of respect and admiration for the entire team, but he particularly admired Tom's ability to absorb and analyze scientific facts without prejudice.

"Tom, I believe that you already know what I'm thinking."

"That could very well be, Ron," Tom paused for a moment and then leaned towards Ron. "There is really no way we are going to fix this thing, are we?"

Ron took a sip of coffee and bit off a good chunk of his donut. After swallowing his donut with a second gulp of coffee, he responded.

"It is absurd for any scientist to believe that he can control the planet's seismic activity. To alter the flow of lava or to control the movement of the plates is simply beyond man's ability. I don't believe that we all just came to this conclusion; I believe that we already all knew that a man made resolution to this problem is simply not feasible. What I'm trying to say, Tom, is that we have not made any progress because there really are no solutions. Man has set in motion a series of events that has caused the planet to become unstable. In time, the seismic plates will literally split into pieces, allowing lava to freely flow from the mantle to the surface of the crust. Between the carbons in the upper atmosphere holding the heat in, the lava movement in the oceans and the crust of the planet, we will soon be able to fry eggs on city sidewalks. The exorbitant pressure and the momentum of lava rushing to the surface of the planet have the power of a billion atomic weapons exploding at the same time. This is not a controllable situation.

"Pouring the liquid solution into the existing cavities, at this time, is similar to trying to hold up a twenty-ton rock with a two by four. I'm afraid, Tom, that short of a miracle, the planet will continue to deteriorate. I really do not see survival at this point. The planet is reversing back to what its original state was billions of years ago, a hot volatile planet devoid of life, and there is not a damn thing we can do about it."

"Unfortunately, I have to agree, and I do appreciate your candor. I believe that we are all instinctively equipped with the will to survive, to have hope, to remain optimistic regardless of the circumstance. Deep down inside, we are really never prepared to give up, regardless of how terminal a situation may be. It is this same nature, embedded in all of us that has survived man throughout the centuries." Tom paused for a minute and then turned to Ron with a serious look on his face. "But we are scientists, Ron, and I guess it's time to face the music. We simply do not have the technology or the capability, do we?"

"No Tom, we don't."

Everything Ron said, I have already confirmed in my own mind, Tom thought. Phil had also said earlier that we do not have the technology to control seismic activity. I simply cannot understand how the truth could have been so evasive, or was it? We were just fooling ourselves. No one has ever stopped a volcano from erupting or an earthquake from occurring.

"Tom, do you want me to tell them?"

"No, no," Tom said. "I think that I should be the one to tell them."

"I think that they already know," Ron said.

As Tom looked up, he noticed that Joe and Angie had just entered the dining room. They were holding hands and smiling as they approached the table.

"Good morning," Tom said with a smile, "you two look awful happy today! Whatever you're drinking, I'll take a gallon."

"Good morning, Tom," Angie said. "Did you have a good night's sleep?"

"Yes," Tom responded, "I slept like a dead man; all four hours." Tom paused as he looked at Joe and Angie standing before him still holding hands. "Joe, you look like you just robbed the cookie jar! What's up?"

"You really do have great perception, Tom." Joe looked at Angie first, and then turned to Tom. "I have an announcement to make. Last night I asked for Angie's hand in marriage, and she said yes. Well, I think she said yes?" Angie just smiled.

"Congratulations, Joe. I'm happy for both of you. All I can say is that it's about time, I thought you'd never ask her." Tom leaned over and kissed Angie on the cheek.

"Congratulations, Angie."

"Thank you, Tom."

Ron offered his congratulations to Angie with a big hug and a kiss. He then turned to Joe.

"Congratulations, Joe. I wish you both the very best."

"Thanks Ron; thank you, Tom. By the way, Tom, I would like you to be the best man."

"I would consider it an honor, Joe. When will this happy occasion be taking place?"

"In two days," Joe said happily.

"That's great. I am really happy for both of you."

John and Phil walked in shortly afterward and offered their

congratulations as soon as they were informed of the good news.

Tom was really happy about the wedding. He knew that Joe and Angie really loved each other. It is a needed celebration, a celebration that requires a commitment from two people to love and cherish one other for the rest of their lives. Not to remind us that their days may be limited, but rather, to believe that there will be many happy days ahead. However, Tom knew better. He had planned to address the group regarding the conversation he had with Ron, but after learning of Joe's wedding plans, he felt it may be bad timing. But he also felt that they really had to know what was going on.

"Joe, do you have a minute?," Tom asked in a low voice, "I'd like to speak with you privately."

"Sure Tom, what do you have?"

He briefly explained to Joe what he and Ron had discussed earlier.

"I know, Tom," Joe said in an apologetic tone, "we have all come to the same conclusion."

"What exactly does that mean?" Tom asked.

"It means what we all already knew, that the problem is not resolvable. It simply took us this long to admit it. I have already informed Angie that there would be no man- made solutions to the problem. That is not why we decided to get married now."

"Why didn't you say something earlier, Joe?"

"There is nothing I could have told you that you did not already know. You have to understand Tom, in the beginning, we all had a glimmer of hope that somehow we would find a solution. We were also hoping that closing down the oil wells would have stopped, or at least limited, further damage to the crust. But as you had previously explained, it really wouldn't have much of an effect."

"You're a good friend Joe, and there is nothing wrong with having a little hope." Tom was relieved that they were all aware of what was really happening as he continued, "How did Angie take the news?"

"She said, 'I can assure you that God is not going to permit man to destroy what he has created, regardless of how hard he tries. So you had better prepare for the future Joe.'"

"So, I guess as far as she's concerned," Joe continued. "Everything is going to be just fine. She just has this great attitude, Tom."

"She certainly does." We rely on science, Tom thought; she is motivated by her faith. She is certainly a breath of fresh air. "I think I'm going to jump over to her way of thinking. She seems to be on the sunny side of the street."

"Angie has always been on the sunny side of the street. That's why I love her."

After clearing the air, they both walked back to the table where Angie and the group were patiently waiting for them.

"Is everything alright?" Angie asked.

"Yes dear," Joe said with a smile, "everything is just fine."

"Well, Joe?" Phil asked. "Are you going to tell him?"

"Yes."

"Tell me what?" Tom asked.

"Do you like long shots, Tom?"

"Long shots," Tom responded, "what are you talking about?" Tom's spirit was somewhat lifted. He was pretty sure this had something to do with saving the planet.

"Tom, I just want you to know that this is not a one-hundred percent cure-it-all idea."

"Just say what you have to say!" Tom was a little anxious by now.

"OK! We are now all in agreement that there is absolutely nothing that man can do to control seismic activity. However, theoretically, if we could put the entire planet into a giant freezer, at a temperature of minus thirty degrees Fahrenheit, it may be possible to cool off the magma enough to turn the molten lava into solid rock. This process would eventually seal the cracks in the crust, right down to the mantle."

Tom knew exactly where Joe was coming from.

"Yes, Joe! That would work! You are talking about an Ice Age, aren't you?"

Joe, Phil, and the rest of the team were grinning from ear to ear.

"It's still a long shot," Ron explained. "An Ice Age is a natural occurrence. It's like having a baby. It occurs in an exact time sequence. For human birth, it is nine months. And, of course, there lies the problem. It is not a man-caused event, but rather one that must occur naturally."

"This is your brain-storm, Phil," Ron continued, "why don't you explain it."

"I believe that we have a slight edge on this one," Phil said. "But it's still a long shot. The only volcano capable of creating an Ice-Age, within the time period necessary, is Yellowstone. Past history confirms this fact. The problem," Phil continued, "is that the circumstance would have to be almost perfect."

"Yes," Tom agreed, "the eruption would not only have to occur within the next one-hundred-twenty day, but the VEI would have to be 7.0 or larger to cause the necessary Ice Age."

"You have to understand," Phil explained. "We are in unchartered waters. There is no research or scientific proofs available to confirm a positive result. The nearest we could come up with is a highly speculative and an extremely hypothetical scenario."

"Cut to the chase, Phil," Joe said, "we can get into the complexities later."

"Well, like I said, the eruption would have to have a minimum VEI of 7 to 7.5, and it would have to occur within the next 4 to 6 months. We believe that anything past that time period will put us past the point of no return; a discouraging prognosis to say the least.

"The second possibility, of course, would be the melting of the polar caps and glaciers. The caps would have to produce enough un-salted water to disrupt the deep ocean currents. This will cause the conveyor belt to shut down, which in turn, would restrict the warm southern waters from moving to the northern ocean regions, which as you all know, will produce the necessary cooling process. The problem is time. By the time the cooling process kicks in, man would be medium to well done."

If the eruption had to be within a four to six month period, Tom thought, why couldn't we just induce it?

"Ron? What is the possibility of inducing an eruption? I mean, actually causing it to happen? We could penetrate the crust at the Norris Basin with a series of explosions. The configuration and time sequence of the explosive devices would have to be properly placed and timed. This may be a method worthwhile perusing."

Ron's response was immediate. "We need an eruption with an intensity of 7 VEI or greater. If we force an eruption, the VEI magnitude of the explosion will be significantly reduced. As a matter of fact, the reduction of the VEI could be reduced by as much as fifty percent."

Tom quickly agreed. He knew that Ron was correct. As a geologist, Tom never thought that the time would come when he would be participating in a project to induce a super- eruption.

"What the hell are we going to tell the President?" Tom asked.

"If you're asking for my opinion," Ron answered, "don't tell him about Yellowstone. If you do, some general or politician is going to panic and attempt to coerce the President into prematurely nuking the only chance we have for the planet to survive."

"Good advice, Ron."

Ron knew that Tom was upset. "This does not mean that we are giving up Tom. There is always a chance that there is something that we missed."

"No Ron, I don't believe we missed anything. So we agree that a forced eruption will be a last resort."

Phil nodded his head in approval.

"Yes," Ron agreed, "an absolute last resort. I'll start working on the configurations in the event the last resort becomes a reality."

"Good idea," Tom said. "What do you think Joe?"

"I think we had better forget about the last resort idea," Joe explained, "a forced eruption is just not going to give us the necessary VEI required to cause an Ice-age. I mean, even if we have to go beyond the point of no return, the odds will still be in our favor. However, once we inform the General or the President that there's a second option, they're going to take it."

"So you're saying," Tom asked, "not to mention the second option?"

"It's too risky, and it's just not going to work."

"Does anyone have a problem with that?" Tom asked.

"No," Phil said, "I agree with Joe, but I believe that it'll only be a matter of time before they propose the same solution."

"Phil's right," Joe said. "We're going to have to convince them that a forced eruption will eliminate any chance we have of surviving."

"I agree with Joe," Ron said, "the point is going to have to be emphatically emphasized."

"Then it's settled," Tom said. "We'll break the news to the General at the meeting."

They all headed out to the conference room, with Joe and Tom being the last to leave.

"I don't believe that odds are with us on this one," Tom said, "but I do like the idea that the possibility exists."

"Well," Joe responded, "we know that Yellowstone is showing signs of a major eruption, but you're right, there is no way to know if she'll blow on time, nor will we know if the intensity of the eruption will be sufficient enough to cool the planet."

"The most important thing," Tom said "is that we have a plan."

Joe smiled.

CHAPTER 35

Tom and his team entered the conference room and were immediately introduced to the General and his staff.

General Forthworth walked in shortly afterward and took his seat. After greeting Tom, his colleagues, and the military staff, he rose from his chair.

"Ladies and gentlemen, please stand for the President of the United States." The President walked into the room and went directly to the head of the table.

"Please have a seat," the President said, as he greeted those that were present. Also attending the meeting was Steve Baldon, head of the USGS; Joan Dunne Secretary of State; Bill Stallino, Head of Homeland Security, and several cabinet members.

"First," the President said, "I'd like to introduce our guests and renowned geologists, Paul Larson from Cambridge, England, Alexei Ivanov from Russia, and Shoko Okumura from Japan. They are familiar with the circumstances we now face, and are prepared to lend their expertise to the unfortunate situation the world is now facing.

"The good news," the President continued, "is that the terrorist group, aside from a few scattered cells, has been, for the most part, eliminated as a major threat to international security. We especially owe our gratitude to the Muslim nations for infiltrating this terrorist group. It was mostly through their efforts that the world was able to end their reign of terror.

"More than ninety percent of the oil facilities that were on fire are now secure. We have actually started the process of pumping the liquid chemical solution into existing oil well cavities. Our goal is to complete this mission within the next two weeks.

"We are here today to further examine the situation and try to come up with a method to slow down the planet's heating process. I have been informed by Steve Beldon, whom you are all familiar with by now, that the seismic activity around the world is at a critical state." The President paused for a moment and then continued, "It appears at this point, that we do not have the two years that we had originally anticipated to resolve the problem. My good friends, we may have as little as six or seven months, at most, to find and implement a resolution, and unfortunately, during that period of time, the heating process will continue to accelerate."

"General Forthworth, can you clarify these new calculations?" the President asked.

Tom had given General Forthworth the new calculations prior to the meeting. He leaned over and whispered into Tom's ear, "Is there any possibility that these calculations could be wrong?"

"No," Tom whispered.

"The new calculations are a culmination of a five day study performed by Mr. Collins and his team, sir," Forthworth explained. "I think it would be best if he explained it."

"Well, Mr. Collins," the President said, "what do we have to look forward to?"

"The geological data is correct but the time element could be plus or minus ten to fifteen percent. If you examine all of the records, you'll find that there has not been a single scientist that has ever predicted the exact date and time of a major seismic earthquake or eruption. They cannot predict the intensity, and they cannot predict the geometrical direction of the eruption. Geologists at Mount St. Helens, for example, predicted a vertical eruption; but in fact, the eruption was horizontal. Here, with two-to-one odds, they were wrong. Can you imagine the errors that can occur with multiple seismic events occurring throughout the world at the same time?" The President just listened. "Sir, in all honesty, this planet could reach temperatures between one-hundred-twenty and one-hundred-fifty degrees Fahrenheit in just four to six months. Our calculations are based on an acceleration rate that has a plus and minus factor of ten to fifteen percent. Because of the continued acceleration factor we've been experiencing, it seems more likely for the time period to be shortened."

"Mr. Beldon, has the USGS confirmed these new calculations?" the President asked.

"Yes sir," Mr. Beldon responded, "the report is accurate. The planet might reach average temperatures of between one-hundred-twenty and one-hundred-fifty degrees Fahrenheit within a four to six month period, and thereafter, turn progressively warmer. The oceans around the world will rise more than thirty feet, which will cause severe flooding in places like Manhattan, Florida, California, Budapest, Shanghai, the Netherlands, and numerous other areas. There will be crop failures, water shortages, and limited supplies of other necessities that will negatively affect our efforts to survive. And with these deteriorating conditions, we will experience an unprecedented increase in seismic activity."

The severity of the problem was a lot worse than the President had expected.

"It's important to note, Mr. President," Joe explained, "that the detailed calculations were predicted on seismic activity and temperature changes over the past five days, as compared to earlier calculations taken over a six month period. Both the temperature rise and increased seismic activity throughout the planet has been increasing at an acceleration rate. The point being, sir, is that future calculations may be a lot worse than those that have just been presented."

When Joe completed his presentation, the room became silent.

"Mr. Okumura," the President said, "do you concur with these figures?"

"We can definitively confirm the calculations just presented by Mr. Solino. Although not exactly the same, our time periods are similar. Our evaluation has the time remaining to be between five and eight months. However, if we cannot stop the present rate of heat acceleration within the next five months, I believe that we will have passed the point of no return."

"And what does that mean technically, Mr. Okumura?" the President asked.

"It means any effort to change the circumstance after that date will be futile."

Russian scientist, Aletei Ivanov, and Paul Larson, representing England, also confirmed that the latest calculations to be correct.

"The question is no longer, how much time do we have, but rather, is the problem solvable?" Alexei Ivanov explained.

"We will discuss the matter," the President explained, "in a separate secession directly after this meeting."

The President requested to meet with Tom and his associates along with the visiting geologists after the meeting. He also asked the General to join him in this special session. This would afford him the opportunity to fully understand the circumstance, and help him evaluate what course of action to take.

After listening to the geologists' latest calculations, he was convinced that the chemical liquid solution would be similar to trying to fill the Hudson River one glass at a time. The situation looks grim, the President thought. He instructed them to meet in the conference room at one p.m.

Prior to the scheduled meeting with the President, Tom and his associates made arrangements to meet with Shoko Okumura, Aletei Ivanov, Paul Larson and Steve Beldon. Tom knew that they were highly recognized in their specific fields of geological studies and felt that it would be wise to know what their prospective on the proposed Yellowstone solution was. He simply wanted some sort of confirmation that they were all moving in the right direction.

Because of the time element, Tom had pre-arranged to have lunch served in the conference room while they discussed the matter.

When the scientists entered the conference room, they noticed a four inch diameter metal ball on the table suspended over a laboratory burner. Unusual, to say the least, his guests thought.

Tom took the floor. "We have already established the fact that the seismic activity associated with the severe warming of the planet is increasing at an accelerated rate. Utilizing our most recent calculations, we have established similar results regarding critical dates. At this time, I do not believe that we are in dispute over the critical time periods which will establish 'The Point Of No Return'. The range falls between four and seven months. Now, I realize that these numbers are not carved in stone, but they are the latest and most accurate calculations to date. Do we all agree?"

They all nodded their heads in agreement.

"What I am most concerned about, at this time, is that the present rate of acceleration will most likely not remain at a constant. It is anticipated that the rate will continue to change, and I do not believe that these changes will benefit our circumstance. In spite of all the advancements we have achieved in science and technology, we have yet to have the ability to cool down a single volcano, much less the entire planet. To believe that man is capable of resolving this problem would be similar to believing that a colony of ants could build the Brooklyn Bridge. Unfortunately, we are not dealing with a centrally isolated problem. The whole damn planet is heating up, and it will take nothing short of a miracle to cool it down."

"What is it that you propose, Tom?" Okumura asked.

Tom got up from his chair and walked over to the utensil rack to pick up a serving tong. He then walked back to the table and gripped the red-hot steel ball that was heating over a burner, and dropped it in a pitcher filled with ice water. He then lifted the ball out of the pitcher and laid it in his hand.

"My sentiments exactly," Paul Larson, the English geologist from Cambridge commented. "What we most desperately need, my good fellows, is what Tom has so ingeniously illustrated. We need an Ice-Age! My colleagues and I have been observing the situation at Yellowstone in cooperation with geologists from the USGS, as Mr. Beldon can confirm."

"Yes," Mr. Beldon replied. "The USGS has been working with geologists around the world on a program implemented by the White House. Mr. Larson and his colleagues from Cambridge are totally familiar with the circumstances at Yellowstone."

Paul continued, "It has been confirmed that the volcano at Yellowstone is in its final stages before erupting. Taking into consideration past eruptions, and the size of the lava bed beneath the volcano; the intensity of the eruption should easily exceed a VEI of 7. In retrospect, it could be a thousand times greater than Mount St. Helens, but as with all volcanoes that we have observed throughout the years, we do not know when the eruption will take place. It could be today, or it could be in six months or even a year from now. Not knowing when she will erupt can be extremely detrimental towards our efforts to save the planet.

"Some thought has been given to a force eruption, possibly with explosives or other methods that may be available, but I believe that a forced eruption would significantly diminish the intensity of the eruption. Our calculations indicate that the intensity of the eruption will decrease by more than fifty percent. With such a reduction, we would not have the intensity required to sufficiently cool off the planet. It is imperative that we not use this method without first carefully considering the consequences. If we prematurely force the eruption, we could be putting the last nail in our coffin. We would literally be eliminating our last hope to save the planet."

The table was quiet. Aletei Ivanov, the famed Russian geologist, seemed a little uneasy. He was pretty much in agreement with both Tom and Paul, but was still a little concerned about leaving the door open, regarding the forced eruption option, in the event they passed the critical point of no return.

"I am not sure if we should rely on the volcano to do what it must do in a timely manner," Ivanov explained. "Drastic conditions call for drastic actions! There is no way we can accurately predict when the volcano at Yellowstone will erupt. It is a fact that time is not on our side, but we must consider the possibility of initiating the eruption by explosives. If there is no natural eruption within the next six months, we will have lost the battle. Russia cannot permit that to happen. The alternate plan must be used to cause the eruption before it is too late, and hope for the best. We must consider the possibility that the critical time period might pass prior to an eruption. We must talk about this issue."

Shoko Okumura, representing Japan, partially agreed with his Russian friend. "Your viewpoint will be taken into consideration, Aletei. We can consider a provision to initiate the eruption at an agreed-to point in time. However, in my opinion, that would be a last resort."

"I agree with Paul," Tom said, "a forced eruption will not have the VEI necessary to cause the planet to produce the climate change required to cool the planet. Should we have an alternate plan to do so? You can, but to do so would only serve as a psychological pacifier. We will most likely all be well done before the planet's cooling process begins. The tolerance rate of the VEI is only between five to ten percent. These facts cannot be influenced by our decisions, because the decisions that we agree on regarding methods and solutions, cannot influence the truths of science unless they are on a parallel course. If we are forced to cause the eruption, we will have most certainly sealed our fate."

Aletei, who was not totally prepared to relinquish his opinion to cause the eruption, basically agreed with Tom.

"I do not disagree with your findings. I simply believe that we should have a secondary plan prior to being cremated."

"Yes!" Tom agreed. "There does come a time when desperate measures are needed."

Steve Beldon, the director of the USGS, was a dedicated government employee who learned how to use and manipulate the political system at an early age. However, at the present time and in the present situation, he was happy to be sitting with some of the top scientists in the world. Associating with such an esteemed group of scientists totally changed his perspective. Here he would be working with his colleagues to cause a result that would be in total consideration to scientific facts, instead of fighting his way through a maze of paper work and politically-motivated bureaucracies. As far as he was concerned, politics was out. It was important at this time to deal with the reality of the situation. Steve picked up the metal ball that Tom had placed in a dish on the table. He then turned to address his colleagues.

"The facts seem crystal clear," Beldon explained. "If we cause the eruption we are probably not going to save the planet. And if Yellowstone does not erupt with a VEI intensity of 7 or more, the planet temperatures will most likely increase to temperatures that will not sustain life.

"Gentlemen, even if it were possible to place perfectly sequenced and time-controlled explosions in the Norris Basin and attain the necessary Volcanic Explosivity, a consideration that has not been taken into account is that Yellowstone is presently unapproachable.

"With temperatures at the surface of the Norris Basin now exceeding 140 degrees F, any attempt to cause an eruption would have to be made from the air, and I am not quite sure how effective that will be."

"Also," Phil Dayne interjected, "the date of no return that you're predicating your decision on is a calculated figure. We could be off by months. I suggest that when you calculate the critical date, you should calculate the time in seconds, because if we're wrong, and we decide to cause the eruption, we will have initiated the cause of our last days on the planet."

"I concur with Phil," Steve Beldon said. "The USGS has also performed calculations regarding the Volcanic Explosivity needed to cause an Ice Age, and we have concluded that even a fifteen percent to twenty percent reduction in VEI intensity would be critical. In fact, any percentage reduction of the required VEI of 7 would most likely not produce the necessary results."

"We're scientist!" Joe snapped. "We deal with facts and figures. Let's not pretend it to be a second choice, because it's not. With all do-respect to Mr. Ivanov, the idea of a forced eruption should be put on the back burner."

"We will wait until the very last minute," Aletei quickly responded. "We will not use explosives unless the time has passed. Russia will cooperate in any way possible to initiate a successful plan."

"I appreciate your cooperation on the matter," Tom responded, "As I said before, any alternative plan would be strictly psychological. And if that's an important issue to you, we have no argument."

"We have to meet with the President in fifteen minutes," Joe said. "He plans to address the United Nations late this afternoon, so we had better prepare him as best we can."

As they headed toward the main conference room, Joe turned to Tom with a smile on his face. "So," Joe asked, "what are the odds of the volcano blowing on time?"

"I don't really know, but if I had to guess, probably fifty/fifty."

"I think I'll stick with Angie's odds," Joe responded.

"And what is that?"

"What God has created, no man shall destroy; that puts the odds at one-hundred percent in our favor. That's one Hundred percent, with a capital H."

Tom smiled. "We had better get to the meeting."

Minutes after entering the conference room, the President walked in followed by General Forthworth, Joan Dunne, Bill Stallino, and Frank Benit.

The President immediately took a seat and turned toward Tom. "Well Tom, what did you and your boys come up with?"

"Mr. President, my colleagues and I, in cooperation with the USGS, have collaborated with some of the of most recognized scientists in the world in an effort to find an applicable solution to the pending problem, and to date, we are no closer to a solution than we were when we started. There is no existing technology that has the ability to stop billions of tons of lava from rising to the surface of the planet. The fact of the matter is that we have never had the ability to control seismic activity. My colleagues and I have completed a report that contains past and current scientific data indicating the progressive deterioration of the planet's crust. It also contains computerized projections of the planet's continued deterioration relative to time." Tom paused for a moment. The room was silent. "What it does not contain sir, is a solution." The President was not prepared to accept the possibility that the situation was hopeless.

"Are you trying to tell me that there is nothing that can be done to resolve this situation?" The President looked visibly upset. "We have sent men to the moon! We landed a vehicle on an asteroid! You mean to tell me that there is absolutely nothing that can be done?"

"Sir," Tom continued, "the mantle of the planet is pushing billions of tons of lava through tens of thousands of man-caused cracks in the crust with the power of a million atomic weapons. Think of the magnitude of the problem, Sir. We have been corresponding with every known scientist in the world, and they have all come to the same conclusion."

The President was angry. Not at Tom or the findings. He could not accept the fact that the human race was in the process of becoming extinct. "Tom, I cannot go before the United Nations or the general public and tell them that they're all going to die! You see, Tom, once you take the hope out of people, you have effectively already killed them. We cannot just give up. There must be something, anything."

"Sir, I said that there is nothing that we could do to save the planet."

"What does that mean?" the President immediately responded.

"We have calibrated with Mr. Ivanov, Mr. Larson, and Mr. Okumura regarding a theory that may very well lead to a feasible solution to the problem. On the theory that every action has an equal and opposite reaction, we have concluded that an eruption at Yellowstone, having a minimum VEI of 7 or greater, would have the ability to create an Ice Age, lowering temperatures enough to sufficiently turn the molten lava into solid rock."

The President was over whelmed with the prospect. "What's the drawback?" the President asked, "When does this eruption have to take place?"

"Within the next six months."

"We may not have the ability to survive in a one-thousand degree environment," Joe added, "but technologically, we would have no problem surviving temperatures that were thirty or forty degrees below zero."

The President remained quiet for a moment, and then turned toward Joe.

"And what if the eruption does not fall within that designated time period?"

"That is the only drawback sir, we simply don't know. It could erupt today, or it could erupt a year from now."

"Why can't we just nuke the damn thing? Let's blow the damn thing up!"

"No!" Tom responded. "That would only seal our fate for good. If we force the eruption, we will be lucky to reach a VEI intensity of 4 or 5. It is imperative that the magnitude of eruption exceeds a VEI of 7 or greater to have even a remote possibility of attaining the cooling effect necessary. If the volcano were to erupt at a magnitude of 4, 5 or even 6, temperatures would continue to rise up to between two-hundred and three-hundred degrees before the cooling process kicked in. These temperatures are not survivable. The eruption must occur naturally to attain the necessary VEI, and even then, there is no guarantee as to what the final result will be. We are in uncharted waters, sir. Only God knows."

The room went silent; the President almost did not want to ask the next question. However, Tom knew exactly what he wanted to know.

"Sir, we have approximately six months before we reach 'The Point Of No Return'. You must understand sir, even these figures are variable. Thereafter, the planet will be uninhabitable." The President did not immediately respond.

"And I assume," the President asked, "if Yellowstone erupts within that time frame, the planet will survive?"

"Not exactly, sir. The eruption must occur within a six-month period, which will give us a 60 percent chance of surviving." The President looked like someone had just drained every last ounce of energy from his body. He was hoping to hear about some miracle solution. Instead, he was being told that he had to rely on a volcano that had not erupted in more than six-hundred-forty-thousand years. Even he could figure out the math on this one, the odds seemed astronomical.

"Tom, I am going to inform the United Nations and the general public that we are working on a plan to resolve the problem. We will not tell them about the Yellowstone theory."

Joe stood up and turned toward the President with a serious look on his face, "I believe that the people have a right to know, sir."

"Yes, Joe, I agree," the President responded, "but not now, for two important reasons. One, if the terrorists got wind of this time schedule, they would attempt to bomb Yellowstone in an effort to induce a premature eruption, and two, why put the general public into deeper despair at this point in the juncture? Not only will it create chaos throughout the world, but it will have taken away the only thing they had left, 'HOPE'. If all else fails Joe, I will personally inform the public of the circumstance."

"Mr. President, may I speak?"

"Yes, Angie."

"Anticipating that the eruption occurs on time and the planet goes into a deep freeze, will we have the ability to produce enough food and other necessities to survive those who are left? We really do not have much time to develop a plan to produce and store the necessary rations required to sustain the survivors over a predetermined length of time."

"Yes," the President agreed, "our plans must be predicated on a possible survival."

"God," Angie insisted, "is the creator. He simply would not permit man to destroy his creation. God will do for us what he did for Joseph. If you can remember the biblical story, he prepared the Egyptians for seven years of famine during prosperous times, and when the famine came they were able to survive." Joe just stood there smiling.

"We will make that a priority," the President assured her, "Thank you for your input Angie."

The meeting ended. The consensus at the meeting was in favor of the President's decision not to inform the public until all hope was lost. The last thing he wanted at this time was to have to deal with any terrorists that might still exist. However, after Angie's input, he realized that preparing for what might be hard times ahead could only be accomplished in a joint effort with all the nations of the world. He also realized that any public effort to prepare for the survivors would create a positive overtone amongst the public.

The President met with the UN general assembly but did not reveal information regarding the Yellowstone eruption, for fear of media leakage to the news networks. Russia, Japan and England were the only other countries aware of what was really going on.

Tom and his colleagues monitored the geological readings, and continued to collect data on Yellowstone in an effort to more accurately calculate the time element of the pending eruption.

"I have this feeling," Tom said, "that this is going to be the longest six months of our lives."

"I remember when Joan was pregnant with Rose," John said smiling, "it seemed like forever, but at least at the end, God gave me a beautiful loving daughter. In this case, we're not sure what to expect."

"What God did for you, John," Angie said in a soft voice, "he will do for us, you just have to have faith."

"I'm starting to believe," Ron said, "that Angie has all the right answers, or like Tom said, she's seems always to be on the sunny side of the street; and I like the part about having faith. She unconditionally believes that everything is going to be ok."

Angie just smiled.

"Well," Phil said, "at least we know that tomorrow is going to be a good day because Joe and Angie are getting hitch."

"Yes," Tom agreed, "It will be a good day. Joe, why don't you Angie call it quits for tonight, we'll wrap things up. You both have a big day ahead of you tomorrow."

"Thanks Tom, we'll see you guys tomorrow.

MELTDOWN

Tom and his buddies stood around and talked for a while, and then retired for the evening.

CHAPTER 36

Through all the stress and turmoil the day of reckoning had finally arrived, at least for Joe. Wedding bells would ring this day. Angie and Joe were prepared to tie the knot.

The General's wife, Margret, arranged to have the chapel alter decorated with beautiful bouquets of flowers. She also arranged to have a priest perform the ceremony.

The reception was to be held in the cafeteria where the General and his wife arranged to have cocktails and a formal dinner served directly after the ceremony.

Terry had chosen four women that worked in the complex to be bridesmaids and chose Bill's wife, Betty, to be the maid of honor. The bride grooms were of course, John, Phil, Ron and Joe's brother, Bill. Tom had the honor of being the best man.

Because the facility was highly classified, the invitation list was limited to direct family members only. Also attending the wedding were Agents Matt Johnson, Harry Kline, Pete Marchel, and Frank Benit. Other guests were some of the staff members of the facility.

The beautiful white-laced wedding dress was provided by Terry's mom.

"Well," Tom said, "Angie is really a great gal, and I'm really happy for you both."

"Thanks, Tom," Joe said with a smile. "I haven't told you yet, but this is part of plan H."

Tom laughed. "Is this the plan that's going to bring us over the top?"

"I won't be able to give you an answer to that question until tomorrow morning, but I have this sixth sense that things are going to turn out well."

"I'm sure they will," Tom said. "We had better head to chapel, the ceremony starts in ten minutes.

As Joe and Tom made their way to the altar, Agent Harry Kline stepped into the aisle holding a gift in his hand.

"Hi Harry, it's good to see you," Joe said with a smile.

"Congratulations Joe," Harry said, as he shook his hand.

"What do you have in the box, Harry, hand-grenades and a bullet proof vest?"

Harry just smiled.

"I thought that the congratulations weren't given until after the ceremony."

"They aren't," Harry said with a smile. "I'm not congratulating you because you're getting married. I'm congratulating you because you showed up."

Joe laughed. "Look Tom, the man actually has a sense of humor."

"You have a tendency to rub off on people," Agent Matt Johnson responded. "By the way, Joe, that job offer to join the agency is still open."

"I don't know who's funnier, you or Harry."

Just then the organist started playing the bridal march.

"We have to get going Joe," Tom said, "before she beats you to the altar."

As he reached the end of the aisle, his brother Bill approached him and gave him a big Italian hug. "Hey little brother, glade you could make it."

Joe smiled. "Hi Bill, thanks for being here."

"I wouldn't miss it for the world. I just want you to know that we all love Angie."

"Thanks Bill, that's important to me."

Joe stood beside Tom, then turned to look up the aisle. He watched as Terry walked down the aisle, looking more beautiful than he had ever seen her before. When her father lifted the veil from her face, Joe's face lit up like a light bulb. "You are so beautiful," he whispered in a soft voice.

"You can't kiss her until after the ceremony," the priest said, smiling.

After they took their vows, the priest tapped Joe on the shoulder. "You may kiss the bride now, Joe."

Joe kissed Angie as if he were alone with her, while the guest cheered them on.

"You had better let her up for air," the priest said with a smile.

"Congratulations, and may God bless you both."

Angie and Joe thanked the priest, then walked hand and hand up the aisle. The guests congratulated them as they left the chapel.

Tom's toast to Joe and Angie was elegant. It was a good day for the six patriots, especially Angie. She was as happy as any woman could be. They were truly in love with one another, and that's all that mattered.

CHAPTER 37

The nations around the world launched individual survival programs in preparation for the days to come. Large concrete storage houses were built to store food, medical supplies, and other necessities required to survive the aftermath of anticipated catastrophic climate changes to the planet. With the anticipation of losing millions of acres of farm land to volcanic ash-fallout, hydroponic gardening systems were installed as a substitute farming procedure because they did not require soil, but rather a liquid fertilizer that increased the growing time of produce, tenfold.

Manufacturers of electric generators had tripled their output, and wind-powered generator production companies increased to full production. Large water filtering and desalination stations were constructed in the event water supplies became contaminated. This tremendous effort under such severe conditions and adversities only helped to confirm the determination and viability of the human spirit. They were no longer waiting for doomsday; they envisioned a new horizon, a new tomorrow and renewed hope. Some started to believe that everything was going to be alright.

After the first month had passed, the situation on the planet became progressively worse. The average ocean levels had risen four feet, six inches. The beaches in Southern Florida were gone, and the homes on the shore–line were experiencing severe foundation problems. The turbulent waters produced waves that smashed into homes, and the lower sections of high-rise condominiums caused structural damage and electrical failures. The evacuation from these dwellings had already begun, and would continue until all were brought to safety. For the majority of people, this was their only residence, and for those who lived in homes within two miles of the beaches, it was just a matter of time before the rising water levels would force them out. Governmental pamphlets had already been issued informing residents that the water levels would continue to rise. They warned residents in these areas not to wait until the last minute to evacuate.

The estimated relocations that would be required numbered in the millions. The rising waters had become another hardship in a series of many that had passed, and there would be many more that were yet to come. Every TV channel became a news station, and the news was never good. First, there was the news coverage of the Yellowstone evacuation, and then a series of documentaries that described the hardships suffered at the temporary camps where families were forced to relocate. There was the collapse of the world stock markets, followed by the collapse of the banks. Then, there was the progressively worsening situation with food, water, and fuel shortages. The lines were so long at times that family members took turns waiting in line for their rations.

There were many who made it from day to day on pure faith, and others that had a difficult time dealing with the dramatic changes that were taking place in their lives. The very fiber of civilization that had held man together for so long was now breaking apart. In this generation, man was taught to be successful. He lived by the three P's: position, power, and possessions. However, he was now fighting just to exist. There was no distinction in classes, all had to deal with the realities of the times. The big questions now were, how do I stay alive, and how will I eat? Where will I live, and how long will this last? It was clear at this point that some would survive and some would not.

~~~~~~~~~~

The temporary campsites that housed more than fifteen million evacuees were located in states that were considered to be in the safe zones. During the Yellowstone evacuation, Army tents were originally set up with portable latrines. Trailer trucks were brought in to supply food, water, and bath houses. One large tent was set up as a medical facility. Each camp housed approximately fifteen thousand people.

Living in these camps was not mandatory. If you had the opportunity to live with relatives or friends, outside of the red zone, you were
~~~~~~~~~~

considered fortunate.

In time, the camps were upgraded with prefab housing and plumbing. Each residence was attached to the next, with a common wall between them. The interior spaces ranged from six hundred to one thousand square feet, and included a mini-kitchen, a bathroom with a shower, sink, and toilet. Each residence was assigned in accordance to the size of their family.

Going from a tent to a prefab residence became a big deal in the camps. It was almost a celebration. When the government began construction on the new prefab homes, they would pre-assign the homes to evacuees by way of a lotto drawing. When the construction began, those that were assigned to the new homes were so excited that they would monitor the construction each and every day until the home was completed. To move from a tent that utilized a shared shower and latrine to a prefab was like moving from a tenement to a castle. Unlike the big cities where there was rioting and looting, the people at the camps were generally helpful to one another. There was a real camaraderie within the camp. They were all in the same predicament, and they really needed one another. To them, there would be another day. Some called it hope.

CHAPTER 38

Bill Coburn, his wife Mary, and their three children lived in a home located in Stuart, Florida, one mile from the water's edge. At the age of forty-one, Bill had built a successful construction business providing a comfortable lifestyle for his family. Now, everything that he had worked for was just about gone. It was only a matter of time before his house would succumb to the rising ocean waters. Bill was one of the lucky ones. With a sister located in Charlotte, North Carolina, he at least had a place to go.

As Bill watched the ocean waves crest just short of his home, he knew time had run-out. He could no longer procrastinate, or do anything to change the circumstance. Although, emotionally drained, Bill tried desperately to maintain a positive attitude for the sake of his family.

After they had fully packed the bare essentials needed to make the trip to Charlotte, he walked over to Mary and held her in his arms.

"I think it's time to leave," Bill said in a compassionate voice. "The situation is worsening. I know how difficult it is for you to leave your home." His voice was weakening as he tried desperately to control his emotions.

Mary felt his pain and knew he was having a hard time dealing with the situation. In his mind, this was the first time he was taking something away from her. She was grateful for what she had, and knew that his generosity was his way of telling her how much he loved her, but in reality, her love for him had nothing to do with the things he had given her. She felt that she could endure anything as long as she had Bill and the children.

"Bill," she said in a quiet tone, "I was prepared to leave weeks ago." She paused as he walked toward her. "I was just waiting for you to make the decision. And if you could ease up on this bear hug you have on me, maybe I can get my blood to circulate again."

Bill smiled, "I love you."

"I love you too, Bill," she said. "You just have to let go. I know how you feel, but in so many ways, it seems so insignificant compared to all the things that are going on around us. In times like this, the only thing that I really care about are you and the children. Everything else is replaceable."

"I guess you're right, Mary, let's just pack the car and head to my sister's place." They packed the car and headed for North Carolina.

The people in New Orleans, who had already suffered through the hardships brought on by Katrina, were now facing a catastrophic event beyond anything they could have imagined. The waters had risen to just above the levies and were now slowly flooding the city. The city had never really recovered from Hurricane Katrina, and a large percent of the pre-Katrina residents had never returned. The present evacuation had begun more than a month ago. They were not taking any chances this time. With more than ninety percent of the residents already evacuated, and the remainder preparing to leave in the next few days, one of the greatest jazz centers in the world would soon become a memory of the past, or at best, an under-water museum. In a very real sense, it was difficult to imagine a world without the great city of New Orleans. If Yellowstone were to erupt, it would most likely not survive this city that had become such an important part of our culture; Mardi Gras, the jazz, and heritage festivals, and dozens of other events that vividly depicted the very heartbeat of the city's personality would be no more. It is no wonder that the famed trumpet player Joe Holiday and his buddies, Wailing Ronny Brown, Miles Clayborn, Jacky the Sandman Johnson, and a number of other old friends and lifelong residents and musicians of New Orleans, were hanging back, as they put it. They just had to play that one last note in honor of the greatest jazz city on the face of the Earth.

"I find this to be a time of great difficulty," Joe said to his friends. "It seems that the world has dealt us a bad hand.""Yeah, you got that right, Joe." Miles responded. "We are folding our hand for good this time."

Wailing Ronny Brown, who had just celebrated his seventy-second birthday, picked up his saxophone and blew a couple of notes. He looked tired and worn from the years that had passed, but when he played that sax, you had to stop and listen. Wailing, as he was called, had that smooth New Orleans accent, and when he spoke, the words came out slow but free-flowing.

"We here to say good-by to New Orleans; we're not dead. You have to listen to the voice up there. Why, we just movin' on to the next gig. There it is again. Laisez les bons temps ruler (lay-say lay bawn taw rul-lay), 'Let the good times roll'."

"Yeah, I hear it," Joe said, as he picked up his trumpet and started to play.

As they all started to play, those who had not yet evacuated stopped what they were doing and walked out onto the street to hear the old-timers pay homage to the city that they called home. During the two continuous hours they played, the crowd grew larger. There were those who were blocks away who moved toward what they recognized as the sounds of New Orleans. Emotions were high. Some were crying, and others hugging. Those that had never met were shaking hands and saying good-bye. Others were hoping that the music would never stop. This was something that they all needed. Now, they weren't just leaving and going their separate ways. No! Now, they were saying good-bye, not just to New Orleans, but also to each other. The ending was no longer cold and abrupt; it became very personal. Everyone realized at that one moment in time, the very soul of New Orleans had nothing to do with its geographical location. It was what it was because of who the people were. The attitude of the people permeated their life style. It is that life style that made New Orleans what it was; they knew the city would always be within them.

When the music stopped, a Baptist minister, who had been listening to the music with some friends, turned to the crowd. "May God bless you all and keep you safe. May you take with you the joy of life and share it with others."

"And in these terrible times, what will that give them, pastor?" a once prominent businessman asked politely.

"What God has gifted all of us with, joie de vivre, (zhwah duh viv-re), which means, 'the joy of living', 'The gift of life,' my friend." The man shook his head and walked away.

Within the next week, all of the remaining residents of New Orleans had evacuated. By the fourth month, the waters had risen more than eighteen feet, and the atmospheric temperatures in some areas were humming at between one hundred-two to one-hundred-twelve degrees. There was at least one major earthquake a week that registered 6 or greater on the Richter scale, and three volcano eruptions with an intensity of between 2 and 3 VEI. The effect of the increased seismic activity on the people, added an uncomfortable reality that the situation was worsening. The planet was literally deteriorating. The hope and encouragement that was being broadcast on the news networks didn't seem to describe what was really happening.

The communication news networks around the world were issuing one bulletin after another, informing the population of new danger areas.

In Shanghai, the rise in ocean levels had forced more than forty-million people to evacuate, and along the Chinese coast thirty-million, and Bangladesh, another fifty-million.

Food and drinking water had become a major problem throughout the world. It was absolutely impossible for one country to aid another under the circumstance. Even the United States, who had generously aided countries in the past, could not keep up with the devastation that was occurring within its own borders. More than sixty million people were forced to relocate. The majority were forced to live in makeshift camps. The shorelines of the Great Mississippi, Southern Florida, California, lower New York City, New Orleans, and other coastal areas became totally flooded.

Hurricanes and oceanic storms became everyday news on the weather stations. At a time when they were most needed, the cargo ship fleet was unable to navigate the rough seas, which severely affected the much needed food supplies around the world.

The conditions were worsening, and people wanted answers. It was clear at this point that the planet was quickly deteriorating. Governmental officials continued to broadcast information in direct conflict with the actual geological events that were occurring. The people wanted answers, and they wanted them now.

There were a series of violent protests occurring in almost every major city around the world. The lack of food, water, and housing had now reached epidemic proportions. Law enforcement agencies could not handle the riots. The President and other leaders around the world had confided with one another in an attempt to resolve the unrest. They feared that the truth would not resolve the problem. On one hand, the President did not want the terrorists to know that a forced eruption would eliminate the only chance they had to save the planet; yet, he knew that the people were losing confidence in the government, knowing that the news on the networks did not depict what was really happening.

MELTDOWN

The public was well aware of the fact that the planet was physically falling apart. Temperatures and water levels were rising, and category five and six hurricanes were common events. Things seemed to look more and more like Armageddon had arrived.

The President knew that time was running out as they quickly approached "The Day of No Return." He believed that he had to respond to the pressure he was receiving from other nations, especially Russia, who was pushing for a forced eruption. The President called General Forthworth to set up a meeting with Tom and his colleagues to find out what the hell was going on.

CHAPTER 39

"Please don't get up," the President said in a rushed voice, as he took his seat. "In the past two weeks I have received several calls from the Russian President, Nikolai Korcheck, who has vigorously pressured us to give serious consideration to a forced eruption. It seems that things are heating up in Russia in more ways than one. We have learned through intelligence that the Russian military has strategically programmed several of their nuclear weapons to hit Yellowstone. Nikolai has politely suggested that they would launch those missiles at a predetermined time in the event we neglected to make that vital decision."

"They must understand," Tom said, "that the critical date is only an estimate of when the date of no return will occur. The date is not set in stone, sir. It could be months before we reach that critical date, and besides, we already know that a forced eruption is not a viable solution." Tom paused for a moment, seeming really upset with the Russian's insistence of forcing an eruption. "Sir, it is absolutely imperative for you to convince Russia not to force the eruption! It'll be nothing short of suicide!"

"They don't see it that way Tom," the President said. "Their rationality has been overtaken by fear. We have to assume at this point that they have every intention of forcing the eruption."

"That could be a major problem," Joe responded.

"The real point is not what they want," Tom said addressing the President, "but rather, what can we do to stop them?"

"Russia isn't the only country giving us problems," the President explained, "we have received warning from China, and several of the Mid-East Nations. The simple fact is that if we don't make a decision soon, they'll make it for us, and that's the last thing we want to happen."

"What have you decided to do, sir?" Joe asked.

"I've decided to activate our anti-nuclear weapons program, and continue to do everything in my power to prevent anyone from nuking Yellowstone."

"Thank you sir, you won't regret it."

"From your mouth to Gods ears," the President said. "We had better get ready for the White House conference; I'm going to need your input."

The President made one last attempt to convince the Russians that they were making a grave mistake. He received a positive response, but was not totally convinced that they would keep their word.

"Tom," the President said, "I want you to start the conference without me. I have a few important calls to make. General Forthworth has my agenda. I'll be in as soon as I can."

"Yes, sir," Tom responded, as the President left the room.

General Forthworth entered the conference room, followed by the President's staff.

"I understand the President will be a few minutes late," the General explained. "Tom, why don't you bring the committee up to date on the latest geological reading at Yellowstone?"

"Well sir, there's no doubt at this time that the volcano has reached its critical stages. The surface temperatures at the basin are hovering around one-hundred-forty degrees Fahrenheit, and the Norris Basin is continuing to rise. Also, more importantly, seismic activity is continuing to accelerate beyond our original estimate. There is absolutely no doubt that she's ready to blow."

The atmosphere in the conference room was tense, as the General addressed the staff.

"Thank you, Tom. I guess the day of reckoning has finally come." The General paused for a moment as he poured water into his glass from a pitcher lying on the table. "It has been well established, not only by Tom and his colleagues, but also by the USGS, that a force eruption will not have enough VEI to reverse the heating process that is now occurring on this planet. So any prospect of forcing an eruption, as far as the United States is concerned, is simply off the table."

"What if we pass the critical date?" The Secretary of Defense Bates asked. "What would be the harm of a forced eruption?"

"First of all," the General responded, "the established critical date is an estimated time period. There is simply no scientific method of establishing such a date, but the real reason we will not force the eruption is because it simply won't work."

"Mr. Dayne," Bates asked in an abrupt manner, seeming extremely concerned, "I have recently read several of your books on volcanology and am deeply impressed regarding your knowledge on the subject. Can you explain to me why a forced eruption will not produce the necessary VEI?"

"Well," Phil responded, "it has all to do with the inner pressure exerted on the wall of the lava basin prior to the eruption. In other words, the lava will continually push up against the upper wall of the basin until it has built up enough pressure to rupture the planet's surface, and set itself free. This could be exemplified by inflating a rubber balloon. When you blow air into a balloon, the walls of the balloon continue to expand due to the increased air pressure exerted against the wall, until the pressure reaches a PSI that is sufficient enough to ruptures the skin of the balloon. That is called the maximum explosivity prior to an eruption. In this case, it would be the maximum explosivity of that balloon. However, if you were to force the balloon to erupt by pricking it with a sharp object, before its maximum explosivity point was reached, you would severely reduce the maximum explosivity of the ruptured balloon. In the case of Yellowstone, a forced eruption would have the same result. It would reduce the explosivity of the eruption by 2 to 4 VEI."

Bates was clearly disappointed with Phil's explanation, but clearly understood the point.

"Thanks, Phil," Bates said, "I have no more questions."

"Are we all in agreement?" the General asked.

The committee did not respond, suggesting that there were no objections.

"Ok," the General said, "then why don't we take a ten minute break, until the President arrives."

Joe walked into the corridor with Tom and his colleagues to go over a few items. No more than a few minutes had passed when they saw the President walking toward the conference room.

As soon as they got back in the conference room, the Secretary of State, Joan Dunne, stood up to announce the President's arrival.

"Sorry for the delay," the President said, as he shuffled through the data that Tom had sent him earlier that morning. "I just got off the phone with the heads of several nations, including Russia and China, and am not convinced that they are willing to rule out a forced eruption."

"It sounds like," Tom said, "that their simply not paying attention to the scientific data."

"Joe, what am I missing?"

"Mr. President," Joe responded, "The data that you have before you is the latest comprehensive calculation, statistics, and time tables pertaining to the progressive changes in climate temperatures. We believe that the lava rising under the Norris Basin has now reached a critical point, and is at the very brink of an eruption, and if uninterrupted, will produce a VEI of 7 or greater. It is the VEI required to potentially reverse the heating process that is presently threatening the planet. The evidence is overwhelming and to date, has not been disputed. Not even by Russia's renowned geologist, Aletei Ivanov."

Steve Beldon, the head of the USGS responded immediately, "Sir, I am in total agreement with Mr. Solino. The data has also been confirmed by the USGS. There is nothing in the data that is hypothetical. We are in complete agreement with their findings, and also agree that a forced eruption would not produce the required VEI necessary to cool the planet."

"Thank you, Steve," the President said as he continued. "I can assure you that we will do everything in our power to protect Yellowstone from a forced eruption.

"The crises we are facing has already resulted in millions of deaths throughout the world. With constant power outages, even those who are fortunate enough to have air conditioning are now without relief. People around the world are dying from heat stroke, kidney failure, heart attacks, and dehydration. Hospitals are packed beyond capacity, and there does not appear to be any relief in sight.

"The situation has become unreasonable. Logic and common sense have left the battlefield. Law enforcement agencies throughout the world can no longer control the populous. The news regarding the proposed solution to the problem seems to be falling on deaf ears; understanding that, if I now ask the public to believe that a volcano that hasn't erupted in more than six-hundred thousand years must now erupt within the next four months to save the planet, it may be more then they can possibly absorb or believe."

"With Russia holding its finger on the red button," Joe explained, "I believe that informing the public, at this point, would be a wise decision."

"I'll take that under advisement, Joe," the President responded, "I'm sort of heading in the same direction anyway.

"There is no doubt that Russian President Nikolai Korcheck is being pressured by the Russian parliament to keep his option open for a forced eruption.

"All we can do at this point is to keep our anti-missile units on red alert; however, there are no guarantees that we will be successful." The President paused for a moment to recapture his thoughts. "There is not much more to say except God help us all. I believe that we had better start praying for a miracle."

"There is something more we can do," Joe explained. "We can make this latest report available to Russia, and any other nations that may not understand the seriousness of the problem! These people are being motivated by fear instead of fact. There have been rumors circulating in some of the tabloids that a forced eruption will cure the problem. That's what they believe because they simply do not have all the facts. The people are bordering on paranoia and must be brought back to reality."

"My only concern," the President responded, "is the possibility of terrorist interference. There is absolutely no guarantee that we have eliminated all the cells."

"Mr. President," Joe said, "we really do not have a choice. Besides, we already know that the Russians are prepared to push the button at any moment. If that were to occur, it really wouldn't matter what the hell the terrorists did."

The President knew that Joe was right, and it really didn't matter at this point. "How would you like a job as a general, Joe?"

Joe smiled, but did not respond.

Secretary of State Dunne, was taken aback by Joe's fortitude. She had never heard anyone address the President with such voracity. After almost two minutes of silence, the President turned to Joe. "God help us Joe, but I have to agree with you, it's time to let them know what the hell is going on! Unfortunately, the odds are not with us on this one. If one of these assholes nukes Yellowstone, we're finished. We had better put a rush on this one. How long will it take to get the report out?"

"If I may interrupt, sir," Ron said.

"Yes! Ron, what is it?"

"The answer to your question, sir, is sixty seconds; that is, sixty seconds after I make a telephone call and enter a code into the programming system. I have pre-programmed the system to send the report out to all recipients on this list." Ron turned the list over to Joan

Dunne. "If you have additional names that you would like to add to the list, just let me know who they are, and I'll add them to the program."

"Thank you," Dunne said. "I'll try to have something for you this afternoon."

"Well, Mr. President?" Ron asked.

"Make the call. By the way, Ron, make sure Russia is on the top of the list."

"Yes, sir." Ron immediately left the room to initiate the President's orders.

"I'd like to thank everyone in this room for their sincere dedication and commitment to the project," the President said. He then turned to Joe. "I intend to address the general public in about an hour, Joe. Do you have any advice on the matter?"

"No sir, I'm a great geologist and a lousy politician. You simply have a lot more experience than I do when it comes to that kind of stuff."

"If some of these politicians were less political and more practical," the President said, "we would probably get a lot more done around here. I appreciate your support."

Joe nodded his head as the President left the room.

Tom and his colleagues went up to the cafeteria for a bite to eat. They all agreed the meeting was encouraging, but the prognosis for an eruption was still questionable.

CHAPTER 40

The President of Russia, Nikolai Korcheck, called for an emergency meeting regarding the Yellowstone situation. He was being pressured by his cabinet to leave his options open with respect to the Yellowstone situation. Nikolai had already assured President Hamity, that he would not make a decision to force the eruption unless all other avenues of survival were exhausted.

Geologist Aletei Ivanov had strongly recommended not to force the eruption; however, three of Russia's top ranking and extremely influential political leaders, Kikita Parasko, Valdimir Machekha, and Ivan Spevaka, were adamantly in favor of forcing an eruption in the event the critical date had passed.

As soon as Nikolai had entered the conference room, members of his staff rose to their feet. "Please be seated," Nikolai said as he took his seat. "My friends, we are here today to discuss a matter of grave importance. It has been proposed by some members of this staff, that we take the initiative to force the eruption at Yellowstone in the event we pass the day of no-return. However, before we make a decision, I would like you to take into consideration Aletei Ivanov's recommendation on this matter. He has met with the top scientists in the US, England and Japan, and is strongly against a forced eruption."

Aletei immediately laid his papers out on the conference table. "First," he said, "all of the information gathered to date overwhelmingly confirms that a forced eruption simply will not have the necessary VEI to reverse the heating process now occurring on this planet."

"Is the proof one-hundred percent?" Kikita snapped.

"It is conclusive," Aletei responded. "The VEI will not have the explosive force required to cool the planet! Our decision must be predicated on scientific fact, not fear."

"What does that mean?" Ivan interrupted, as he continued to answer his own question, "What it means is that you are not one-hundred percent positive. There is no exact science when it comes to volcanoes!"

Nikolai interrupted, "Aletei! Is the data one-hundred percent conclusive?"

"Yes sir, I have calibrated with some of the most renowned scientists in the world, and have personally reanalyzed the calculations several times myself. We have all concluded that the volcano must have a minimum intensity of 7 VEI or greater to contain temperatures that are survivable, whereas a forced eruption will diminish the intensity of the volcano by 3 to 4 VEI."

"And why will a VEI of 5 or 6 not cool the planet down!" Valdimir snapped.

"It will," Aletei responded with a smile, "but not until temperatures reach 180 to 200 degrees Fahrenheit."

"I do not believe that you know!" Valdimir shouted. "I do not believe anyone knows. We must nuke the volcano now!"

President Korcheck was more inclined to believe the scientific data presented by Aletei, rather than succumb to a bunch of political bureaucrats who were motivated by fear.

Just then, a military officer came running into the room. "Mr. President! Mr. President! We just received this report from Tom Collins and his colleagues labeled, 'Urgent!'. It appears to be the latest scientific data on Yellowstone."

Korcheck quickly viewed the new data, but wasn't quite sure of what to make of it.

"Aletei!" the President snapped. "I want you to go over this report immediately and bring me the results as soon as possible." Nikolai ordered the three political leaders to leave the room.

The data reconfirmed Aletei's original findings.

When Aletei's came back into the conference room, Korcheck was standing by his desk with a serious look on his face. Aletei walked over to where he was standing and handed him his report. He took a few minutes to review the report, then looked up at Aletei.

"We have to wait, don't we?" Korcheck asked in slow, but stern voice.

Aletei shook his head in agreement.

"Thank you, Aletei," Korcheck said, as he slowly sat in his chair. "We may have our grievances with the US, but I just don't believe that they would be this persistent if they believed there was another way." The President paused for a moment and then turned toward Aletei. "We will wait."

CHAPTER 41

News of the latest geological findings had been distributed to every nation in the world. Newspapers, radio stations, television, and the internet quickly covered the story. It became head line news. The message was clear; the people realized that they needed nothing short of a miracle to save the planet from total annihilation. They would have to rely on the natural eruption of a volcano that had not erupted in more than six-hundred-forty-thousand years.

When scientists around the world began to accept the findings as fact, the reality of a terminating planet seemed a little more probable. It was as if someone had just turned the lights on for the first time. The news had both a positive and negative effect. For many, relying on a volcano that had not erupted in more than six-hundred-forty-thousand years, wasn't exactly the news that gave them the confidence they were looking for.

The skeptics that had been lobbying for a forced eruption were no longer anxious to intervene. This wasn't a political issue, nor was it a play for power. There was simply no method or technology that could fix the problem. Man had fractured the delicate and natural sequence of the planets eco-system, and now, ironically, had to rely on a natural eruption of a super volcano, or face total extinction.

The news did not set the people free from their long list of anxieties. It simply made them understand that there was only one method to save the planet, and that there was nothing they would be able to do to influence the outcome. The people were angry. They could not believe that the decision makers, the politicians, and other leaders around the world could allow something like this to happen. The general consensus of the world population had turned to pure unadulterated anger. Where were the regulators, the governmental inspectors, the elected officials that were given the responsibility to protect the public? They were probably all in the pockets of special interest groups, the same lobbyists that controlled the regulatory laws. It amounted to nothing short of mass murder. Yes, the people were angry. Their entire lives had been turned upside down, but all they could do at this point was sit and wait.

The temperatures in most locations were one-hundred degrees Fahrenheit plus, and with major power outages, or at best, sporadic powers being furnished on time intervals just added to the hardships they were forced to endure. Tempers were flaring, but there wasn't much they could do about it.

Those who were religious had filled places of worship, praying for what could only be characterized as a miracle.

It appeared that Russia and China, under the recommendation of their own scientists, had totally changed their position on Yellowstone. However, the President believed that in desperate times people do desperate things, and he wasn't taking any chances. He would keep his military on full red alert.

People continued to crowd into religious places of worship. When it came to praying to God, there was no segregation of religious beliefs. They did what people normally do when facing a circumstance that they had no control over; they prayed for divine intervention.

As the days passed, the seismic activity on the planet worsened. Lava started to sporadically break through the surface in many locations throughout the world. In a very short time period the average temperatures increased between one-hundred-eight to one-hundred-twelve degrees Fahrenheit. The oceans were plagued with major storms on a daily basis, followed by continuous earthquakes and minor volcanic eruptions throughout the world. The distribution of food, water, and other necessities had become a critical issue. Although there were ample supplies stored, those who were assigned to the distribution warehouses were instructed to thinly ration all supplies in preparation for the years beyond the eruption. There would be a time when the planet would not have the ability to produce enough food and supplies to sustain those who managed to survive the initial climate change. There was no way to develop an accurate estimate regarding the number of people that would survive.

MELTDOWN

Hospitals and morgues were filled to capacity. The death toll around the world was off the charts. Some estimated potential fatalities could exceed one billion people, and that was assuming that Yellowstone would erupt on time. The situation continued to deteriorate.

CHAPTER 42

The Last Jihad had been totally decimated by a joint international effort to eliminate the unconscionable terrorist attacks that had plagued the world for so many decades; so many had lost their lives through the unrelenting, brutal, and unjustifiable attacks on innocent civilians. Women and children were murdered without prejudice for a cause that most could not even comprehend. If it were not for the fundamental Muslims, the reign of terror would have never ended. The hard core terrorist leaders and their followers, who did not repent, were condemned to death. However, many of their followers had repented and were rehabilitated by Muslim religious leaders. The false doctrines that they had followed for so many years were destroyed. However, although the sect had been severely disabled, there was concern that a remnant of the sect may still exist.

One major cell of the terrorist group, located in San Francisco, had gone undercover and managed to escape detection. The majority of their contacts were either captured or killed, leaving them totally on their own.

The cell operated independently and had no plans to interfere with what they perceived to be a coming fulfillment of the ancient prophecy. However, when they received the latest technical data from the news media, explaining why a forced eruption would not resolve the problem, the terrorists became convinced that God must have intervened to protect their cell for the sole purpose of fulfilling the prophecy.

"We have been divinely chosen," Al-Azeez, the leader of the San Francisco sect, explained with determination, "to assure the fulfillment of the prophecy, we must force the Yellowstone eruption. It is ordained by God and cannot be altered or stopped by mortal man. After the infidels are destroyed, our messiah will renew the planet. Only then will we be glorified with a rich and eternal life."

The terrorists immediately mobilized their forces and called for an emergency meeting at a warehouse they had rented as a front for their operation. They operated the warehouse as a clothing distribution center, but the seventy-five workers at the plant were all members of the sect.

Al-Azeez arrived at the warehouse at two p.m. and was immediately greeted by his two co-leaders Ad-Daar and Al-Kabeer, who had previously been made aware of the latest development regarding Yellowstone. You could not listen to the radio, watch a news station, or pick up a newspaper without hearing or reading about Yellowstone. The news headlines were similar throughout the world. "Yellowstone: Our Last Great Hope."

Al-Azeez was angry as hell, and although he continued to believe that the volcano would not erupt on time to save the planet, he knew that according to the writings of the prophecy, he would have to intervene.

He stood up and addressed his two associates in an angry voice.

"You know why we are here, do you not?"

"Yes!" They shouted.

"I do not believe that the volcano will erupt on time to save the planet!" Ad-Daar, shouted, "but we are bound by the prophecy." He then picked up the scroll and proceeded to read.

"Listen to these words my friends, 'There will be many wars and suffering throughout the days before the end comes. These things will come and pass, but you will know the end when the signs of the cleansing are known to all of mankind. When you see fire and brimstone and all of the Earth rumbles, you will know it is the end days.'" Al-Azeez paused for a moment and slowly raised his right hand shaking it as he spoke. "These verses describe these times. My friends, these are the days we have been waiting for. We are the guardians of these last days!" He continued to read, "'The guardians of that day shall be faithful until the end. By their hands, there will be a great cleansing, and then the end will come. By our hands," he roared in an angry and determined voice, "there will be a cleansing!' The prophecy is clear! It will be by our hands that we will seal the fate of the infidels. Today we must devise a plan; we will cause Yellowstone to erupt. The Earth will be cleansed and we will be glorified!" Al-Daar and Al-kabeer immediately confirmed their allegiance to Al-Azeez.

Al-Azeez then placed a map of the Mid-western United States on the table, along with a second map that he received from the USGS, showing the topographical view of the Norris Basin. The map showed explicit details of the lava base that lay below the surface of the Basin. Before he laid out the plan of attack, he called a fourth leader into the room who was an expert in rocket power technology and explosives. He had previously led several successful terrorist attacks and was elated to have been chosen for this mission.

"Az-Zahir will lead the mission," Al-Azeez commanded. "He has earned this moment of glory!"

"Thank you," Az-Zahir responded. "I will not fail you."

He had been a member of the sect for twenty-two years, and now, at the age of forty, he would realize his lifelong dream. He would be a main force in the final fulfillment of the prophecy.

"You have done well," Al-Azeez said, "I am truly honored. For me, this will be a day of glory."

"Yes!" Al-Azeez said. "This will be a day of glory for us all."

With the maps before him, Al-Azeez preceded to layout the plan of attack.

"It is important that we avoid detection," Al-Azeez said with a determined voice. "All areas around our target have been totally evacuated. If we run military trucks into the area, we will stick out like a sore thumb."

"That will not be a problem," Az-Zahir quickly responded. "We will position ourselves outside the dead zone until nightfall, and then move into the area. The evacuation limits are approximately 600 miles which will leave us exposed to detection for several hours. It will take approximately eight hours to position ourselves within striking distance of the basin.

"That will be the plan," Al-Azeez responded, "We must now secure the rockets."

"Do not be concerned," Az-Zahir snapped. "Prior to this assignment, I was previously part of a mission that had been assigned to destroy the entire city of New York. The plan was aborted because of this event. The rockets that we smuggled into the country for that mission are now here in San Francisco. They have a one-hundred-fifty mile range and are now stored in two trailer trucks."

"This is destiny!" Al-Azeez shouted. "Everything is falling into place. We will need one additional truck to transport manpower and the required tools and machinery. To avoid detection we will have Red Cross signs painted on the trucks similar to the signs on the trucks transporting water and food to the evacuation camps. The trucks will be moved to within 200 miles of the target at a pre-determined location. And then we will move to our final location at nightfall.

"I have already calculated the exact co-ordinates to be targeted at the Norris Basin. We will pre-program the longitude and latitude headings into the guiding system before we leave. The plan must be executed within three days. There is no time to lose. Are there any questions?" The men all agreed. "This will be our day of glory."

They adjourned the meeting and immediately started to prepare for the journey.

CHAPTER 43

The new reports and scientific data being gathered at the command center were not encouraging. The ice caps continued to melt at an accelerated rate. Lava was breaking through the Earth's crust throughout the planet, and the reports of seismic activity were so numerous that news centers could not keep up with the latest data distributed by the USGS. The planet was heating up at an alarming rate, and the lava movement to the surface of the planet had far exceeded the previously forecasted timetables.

After almost eighteen hours on the database computer bank, Joe was totally beside himself. He could not believe the readings; the rate of seismic activity and the amount of damage it was causing far exceeded anything they had anticipated. He continued to calculate and recalculate the numbers, hoping that somehow the results were in error. Joe was starting to believe that they had already passed the point of no return. He started to have second thoughts about the cooling process. If the volatility of the planet continued to deteriorate at such an accelerated rate, would an eruption still have the ability to cool the planet before the temperature reached uninhabitable levels? Just then, he felt a hand on his shoulder. He turned abruptly, seeming somewhat surprised.

"I'm sorry, Angie. I didn't realize it was you." She looked like she was about to cry. Joe got up and held her in his arms.

"You cannot go on like this, Joe," she said. "You have been in this chair for eighteen hours without sleep. You look like you're ready to drop.

Please, Joe, if anything happens to you..." she was almost in tears, "I don't know what I would do."

Joe looked tired and worn. In his mind, he knew that the situation on the planet had moved into its critical stages. He was no longer convinced that the eruption would occur on time. Joe loved Angie more than he could explain. He wanted desperately to continue his work, and at the same time, he did not want to see Angie in such agony.

"I'm hungry, Angie; let's pick up a couple of box lunches and go back to the room."

"Yes," Angie said in a soft voice, as she tried to control her emotions. "Joe, you have to promise me that you will get some sleep."

"I promise. Now, let's get something to eat."

After picking up lunch, Angie and Joe headed back to the room.

"I'm really scared," she said, as they sat on the couch and laid the food on the table. "Joe, please don't try to shield me. I know there is something that is terribly wrong. I love you so much and I just cannot stand to see you like this."

"Everything will be all right, Angie, trust me," Joe said in a compassionate tone of voice. He searched for something to say that he thought would make her feel better, but he was so tired, he just couldn't seem to get his thoughts together. Joe was just too damn tired. Angie put her arms around him and held her tight. She then kissed him several times on the cheek and then kissed him softly on his lips.

"Do you remember when we took our wedding vows, Joe?" she said in a serious tone.

His heart was broken; he could not stand to see her in such discomfort.

"The words were 'for better or for worse,"' she continued. "Well, that's how I love you and that's how I want you to love me. And if you couldn't abide by the contract," she paused for a moment, "you shouldn't have said 'I do'."

Joe just gave her a big hug.

"Ok. Ok. Angie, calm down. Just relax for a moment. I should have known when I married a lawyer that the first thing that you would do is bring up the contract."

Angie smiled.

"I agree with you, Angie, there should be no secrets between us. After all, we're mature adults and I agree that you should know what's going on. I believe that we have reached a critical point in time. There is even a possibility that we may have even passed the critical date." He paused for a moment. "I checked and rechecked the data to make sure there were no mistakes. Each time, the results were the same."

"Short of a miracle, it seems that we're just not going to make it."

"Yes, we are," Angie said. "It is God who gives life, and God who takes it, and I am just not ready to believe that He is prepared to take it."

Joe smiled.

"You have a great attitude, Angie. Forget about science. I'm with you on this one. It's you and I Angie, until the end of time. It's in the contract." Angie smiled.

"You promised that you would get some sleep."

"Yes," Joe agreed, "but first I have to give Tom the latest data sheets." Angie seemed relieved. "Let me bring these results to Tom." He continued, "I'll call you when I get back to the room."

When Joe entered Tom's station, he saw him working feverishly on his computer. He looks worse than I do, Joe thought. "Hey Tom, how are you doing?"

"I'm not," Tom responded. "What have you come up with?"

"You don't want to know," Joe answered. "The readings are off the charts. If I had to second guess myself, I would have to say that we have passed the date of no return. I've checked the data a hundred times and nothing seems to change. I realize that we are working in uncharted territory and that there is really nothing to compare these figures to, but I have to believe that time is running out."

"Hold on for a minute, Joe, you're making me dizzy. Forget about what's happening around the world; look at what's happening at Yellowstone! She's been on a rampage for the past six hours. I tell you, Joe, this baby is ready to blow."

Joe quickly looked at the data. "Shit! You're right, Tom! Look at these readings. What do you think?"

"I don't want to be too optimistic, but I believe she's close to erupting."

"From your mouth to God's ears," Joe snapped.

Tom did not respond as he continued to check the readings.

"Look Tom, I've been up for more than eighteen hours, and besides, I promised Angie that I would try and get some sleep."

"I understand, Joe. Go ahead and I'll talk to you later."

"Come on Tom, take a look in the mirror, you look like crap. I don't believe she's going to blow in the next couple of hours. Maybe not even in the next couple of weeks."

"You're the optimist Joe; this is no time for you to turn negative on me."

"I'm just tired, and if I don't hit the sack soon, I'll probably fall asleep standing here."

"Go ahead, Joe, get some sleep. I'll be up in just a few minutes. First, I want to run this report over to the general. By the way, I think we should keep Yellowstone under wraps for now."

"I agree," Joe said. "I think I had better talk to Ron and Phil before heading back to the room, just to fill them in on what's going on."

"Good idea," Tom said, as he headed toward General Forthworth's office.

Phil and Ron were busy at their stations gathering data when Joe walked into the room.

"How are you doing, Joe?" Phil asked unenthusiastically. "By the way, you look like shit."

"Thanks," Joe responded, "that makes me feel a lot better."

"I'm guessing that you already know," Ron said.

Joe knotted his head in agreement. 'I just wanted to make sure that you came up with the same conclusion as we did."

Phil just shook his head. "The good news is that Yellowstone has become a lot more active these past six hours. Of course there's no way of knowing when she'll blow."

"There's something going on," Ron agreed, "but in consideration of the new surface temperature readings, I just hope we don't run out of time."

"You're not trying to cheer me up, are you?" Joe said with a smile. "I think I'll spend some time with Angie, she has a much brighter outlook on the situation."

"Sorry, Joe," Phil said, "but these are the facts."

"I know I'm going to head back to the room and take a short nap. If anything changes, please give me a call."

"Don't worry, Joe; we'll call you if anything changes.

"Oh, one more thing, Tom and I believe that it would be wise to keep all new data on Yellowstone under wraps until we know for sure what the hell is going on. The last thing we want to do is create a panic."

"Yes," Phil said as he gave Joe a gentle pat on the back. "Now why don't you get the hell out of here and get some sleep."

Joe left the station and headed back to his room.

CHAPTER 44

After receiving the latest data on the planet's progressively worsening condition from General Forthworth, President Hamity consulted with the USGS to confirm that the new geological data on Yellowstone was correct. Within two hours, the head of USGS, Steve Beldon issued his report confirming that the data submitted by Tom and his colleagues was correct.

Within two hours, after receiving the data, the President called for another emergency meeting to be held at eight sharp the next morning. The Secretary of State, Joan Dunne, was given a list of attendees which included the President's full staff, Tom and his associates, and pertinent military personnel. Also in attendance were the heads of the CIA and FBI.

When Tom and his associates entered the conference room the next morning, Secretary Dunne immediately called the meeting to order.

President Hamity entered the conference room minutes later. "Please sit down," he insisted, as he walked to the front of table and took his seat.

"This is not a good day for our nation!" The President began. "My good friends, this is not a good day for the world. I am not going to spend a lot of time telling you how bad things are. God knows the news media has certainly covered that aspect of this story. The death toll is so high that they can only guess at the numbers. Some estimates are five hundred thousand, and some are as high as a billion." The President paused for a moment, leaned over, and picked up Tom's latest report. "What I hold in my hand is the latest geological report from Mr. Collins, which has also been confirmed by the USGS. The report basically projects a doomsday scenario. If this report is true, and I believe that it is, we could be looking at a world casualty rate of 100 percent.

"My good friends, we have come to a critical hour. We are here today not to discuss whether or not we should force the eruption at Yellowstone, or let destiny take its course. We have done everything possible to survive the aftermath of an eruption, but at this juncture, the actual survival of this planet may be in grave danger."

"Sir," Secretary of Defense, Robert Bates demanded, "After consulting with some of the best minds in the world, and in conjunction with the results of our previous meeting, we have clearly established a course of action. It is clear, Mr. President, that we are most likely beyond the date of no return. It seems that there is absolutely nothing to lose at this point by forcing an eruption!" His voice was filled with anxiety. "We must now make a decision on whether to wait for an eruption that may have already taken us beyond the date of no return, or initiate the only logical remedy remaining, which is to force the eruption.

"We cannot afford to wait one moment more in the hope that a volcano that hasn't erupted in more than six-hundred-forty thousand years will now erupt within the time limits necessary to save the planet.

"Gentlemen! The situation is beyond critical; it is desperate, and I adamantly disagree with any conclusion that deems a forced eruption not to be a feasible solution to the problem. There is just no way to know what the results will be. If we do nothing, the planet will perish."

The President immediately responded.

"We have everything to lose, Bob! An emotional decision will only have a psychological effect; in fact, previous data confirms that a forced eruption will not provide the necessary VEI to reverse the heating process on time. It is not going to improve the situation. If there is a bear behind the door, don't open the door. There is not just one scientific report that favors a natural eruption; we have more than three hundred reports that confirm these facts."

Mr. Bates did not respond.

"I have already made my decision to wait for a natural eruption," the President continued, "so, on a more positive note, let's address what has to be done to survive the world population after the eruption."

The President then turned to Robert Johnson, the head of FEMA. "What do you have to report, Bob?"

"We are continuing to store food, water, medical supplies, clothing, and other needed materials. We believe that we have enough supplies for two to three years, assuming a twenty percent reduction in our present population. The Federal distribution system will be controlled from a central distribution center, with satellite warehouses located strategically throughout the states. All distributions of products will be conducted by the National Guard.

"I have also arranged to convert existing buildings into temporary emergency medical centers to handle the overflow of patients from the existing hospitals.

"The biggest problem that we're going to be up against is lawlessness. That's why it's imperative that we initiate a workable distribution system within days after the eruption. There are other factors that will come into play, but on an overall basis, I believe that we will have the situation pretty much under control."

"Thank you, Bob. The country will remain under martial law throughout the crises. It is imperative for the law-abiding citizens of this country to know that we will maintain law and order, and that violators will be harshly punished. There will be enough hardships to deal with without having to worry about the criminal element. As a precautionary measure, the federal security forces will work in cooperation with the local city and state law enforcement agencies. Are there any questions on this subject?" The room remained silent.

The President continued. "Tom, do you have any additional information that you would like to add?"

"Yes, Mr. President. Our latest calculations at Yellowstone show a dramatic increase in lava build up under the Norris Basin. Sir, I believe that she is on the brink of an eruption. I realize that it's a difficult call, but the recorded lava movement is beyond anything that we have ever recorded. It is conceivable, at this point, that the intensity of the eruption will most likely exceed a VEI of 7."

"That's good news Tom, thank you."

"I want every agency in this government to prepare for the aftermath of the eruption, with a particular emphasis on survival. Mr. Bates, can I count on you to make preparations predicated on a survival outcome to this crisis?"

"Yes, Mr. President!"

"This is not just for Mr. Bates, this goes for every single person in this administration! I do not want anyone to run home to their families to prepare them for the end. This meeting is a survival meeting! Time is running out, and we must prepare this nation for the aftermath of the eruption. Now, let's go out there and do what has to be done."

Bates wasn't quite sure how things would turn out, but what he did realize is that the President's presentation was predicated on the glass being half full, and that was something he could live with.

"Mr. President," Bates said, "I just want you to know that you can count on me."

"I know, Bob," the President said in a sincere manner as he exited the conference room.

CHAPTER 45

The terrorists were once again on the move. It seemed like a never-ending story. They were determined to sabotage the only chance the world had to survive a planet, which was quickly deteriorating. They continued to have this deranged belief that the mass murder plot would not only give them a free ticket to heaven, but that their heavenly home would be embellished with thousands of virgins. Aside from the obvious, what they had not taken into consideration were the millions of Muslims that would also be on their hit list; it just didn't seem like something that God would approve of, or agree with. Compared to the terrorists, Al Capone was a saint; it was not an encouraging analogy.

The terrorists were prepared to carry out one of the most devastating acts against humanity that had ever been derived or executed by man: the annihilation of the entire human race.

The three trucks were painted to look like Red Cross vehicles. The rockets were loaded onto the trucks, along with the necessary manpower and equipment to carry out the terrorist's final assignment. The entire cell had chosen to participate in the operation to assure themselves of the rewards that they would receive for fulfilling the prophecy. They perceived this day to be a day of victory.

Al-Azeez, who decided to drive the van, handed each truck driver their final routes and time schedules. "We will take I-80 to US-50, which will put us in Carson City in four hours or at six this evening. It will take us another nine hours of night driving to reach Idaho Falls. We will arrive at three a.m.

That will put us approximately one-hundred-ten miles from the target." He then addressed Az-Zahir. "What is the time required to prepare the rockets for launch?"

"One hour. The launching units are portable and will take no more than ten minutes to set-up; however, to launch four rockets at precisely the same time there is a series of computerized time sequences that must be accomplished to assure that all the rockets hit their targets at precisely the same time. That should take about one hour to complete."

"Then the launch will be at four a.m.," Al-Azeez responded. "Tomorrow will be a day of glory! We will all be renewed, and the infidels will be no more."

The entire group roared a shout of approval with their guns held high in the air.

"Victory, Victory!"

The trucks and vans pulled out of the warehouse and proceeded to their assigned destination.

As the terrorists approached Mill City, they noticed a roadblock about a quarter mile up the road on Route 80. As they approached, they noticed that there were only six uniformed National Guardsmen at the barricades. Al-Azeez had already given his men an order to kill the Guardsmen on his command, if necessary.

As they approached the barricades, four of the Guardsman confronted the terrorists.

"Sir, this road is closed," the Army private explained.

The driver in the first truck spoke perfect English, and was previously instructed by Al-Azeez to handle any unanticipated incident that may occur on the route to their destination.

"We have an emergency in the towns past Princeton, over the Oregon border, and this is the quickest route," the truck driver explained. "We're taking 80 into 95."The truck driver noticed that the private wasn't quite sure what to do.

"They're really in desperate need of these supplies," the truck driver said in a calm voice.

Al Azeez, thinking that the private seemed suspicious, slowly lifted his two-way radio ready to give the order to kill.

"Let me go back to the sergeant to see what I can do," the private said, as he walked toward the trailer.

The terrorists had their guns in their hands, prepared to kill the soldiers on command.

As the private walked back to the barricade, the terrorists stood fast, prepared to take the necessary action.

"You have permission to pass. The sergeant doesn't believe that the Red Cross has any desire to head toward the volcano. Good luck, guys."

"Thanks," the driver responded, as he stepped on the gas pedal. They were once again on their way to their final destination.

Meanwhile, the sergeant in charge of the military post completed his activity report that documented the passage of the Red Cross vehicles. The report was sent to main headquarters at exactly two-forty a.m.

The report was then logged into the information computer center at two-fifty-two a.m. where it was immediately forwarded to the main headquarters of the FBI and CIA at two-fifty-five that morning. The CIA agent that received the report could not understand why the Red Cross would have initiated an operation in such a remote location. The Agent immediately forwarded the report to the command center under a red alert status. It was labeled, "High Priority- Pete Marchel". The alert was immediately brought to his attention.

When Pete read the report, he panicked. "The Red Cross is driving three eighteen-wheel trucks and seven vans into the dead zone because they have an emergency in a couple of small towns in Oregon? There's something just not right with this report... What the hell are these guys doing there? These areas have already been evacuated. I'd like to know what the hell's going on."

"Agent Roberts, who do we have in Oregon just west of Yellowstone?"

The Agent quickly checked the roster list.

"We have a couple of National Guard units up there, but they're scheduled to pull out in about an hour."

"This is a red-alert assignment," Pete said, "I want you to call the National Guard units in Princeton, Oregon and the surrounding towns to find out if they requested any aid from the Red Cross. Also, I want you to call for an immediate evacuation of all remaining units in the area."

"Yes sir!" Agent Roberts immediately started making the necessary contacts. Meanwhile, Pete alerted the military that he might have a red alert on his hands. He called Commander Frank Philips, who was in charge of the fighter squadrons that were a part of the anti-missile assignment, initiated by the President to protect Yellowstone.

"Frank!" Pete shouted, "We may have a red alert on our hands. Prepare to have your squadron ready to go. I'm not sure if this is a go, but if it is, we're not going to have a hell of a lot of time. It appears that the terrorist group may have crossed one of the barricades, on Route 80 East, which leads to Yellowstone."

"The fighters will be in the air in twenty minutes!" the Commander shouted. "I'll stand by for your instructions."

"Thank you, Frank, I'll get back to you."

~~~~~~~~~~

The terrorists had arrived at the launching site a little before three a.m., and began to set up the rockets. "Think about what we are involved in, Az-Zahir," Al-Azeez said. "We will have the honor to participate in the final fulfillment of the prophecy. This is the greatest honor. We will all be rewarded in the new world. This will be our day of glory."

"Yes!" Az-Zahir agreed. "The rockets are almost prepared."

~~~~~~~~~~

When Agent Roberts received the information on the Red Cross trucks, he quickly turned toward Pete. "It's doesn't look good, Pete. There have been no sightings in Princeton, or any of the other surrounding towns. As a matter of fact, they have confirmed that there has been no outside traffic in the area for the past two weeks. The Red Cross trucks would not be something that they would miss."

At exactly three-forty-eight a.m., Pete contacted Commander Philips. "Frank, it's a go! The best I can guess is near the border lines of Utah and Idaho. Their maximum rocket range is unknown, but knowing their arsenal, I'm guessing between one-hundred to one-hundred-fifty miles. They probably took 80 into 15 North, and may be somewhere between the town of Pocatello, Idaho Falls or one of the other smaller towns in that area!"

"I got it, Pete! I'll get back to you!"

More than forty fighter planes were heading to several locations in the areas that were designated by Pete. Frank had no idea what time element he was working with. The orders were clear and precise: to find and destroy the enemy.

The planes were equipped with night-vision and GPS sensors and would have no difficulty in locating, and destroying, the target.

The terrorists had reached their final destination and were now ready to complete the final preparations for the launch. The time sequence had been completed by Az-Zahir. He immediately turned to Al-Azeez with a determined look on his face, "The launching sequence is complete! The rockets are ready to be launched. My work is now complete," Az-Zahir continued, as he handed Az-Azeez the remote launching device. He held the device in his right hand with his finger on the ignition button as he addressed his men.

"This will be our greatest moment in history! We will all receive great rewards. The time has finally come for us to fulfill the prophecy." Just then, they heard the sound of jet engines roaring overhead.

"They have found us!" Az-Zahir shouted. "Quickly! Push the button!" Az-Zahir screamed at the top of his lungs.

Al-Azeez quickly pushed the button, he screamed, "we must launch the rockets now!" The rockets were launched at exactly four-twenty a.m. "They will hit their target in exactly nine minutes and eighteen seconds!" Az-Zahir yelled. "And they cannot be stopped."

~~~~~~~~~~

The report immediately went back to Commander Philips. The Commander notified Pete, and he in turn notified the President. He also woke Tom from his sleep to give him the bad news. Tom immediately called the rest of the team to explain what had happened and asked that they meet him up at the command center. By this time, Tom was frantic as he threw on a pair of pants and ran up to the command center to personally monitor the intensity of the eruption. The time was four-twenty -four a.m.; he was given an impact time of four thirty. Joe, John and Ron walked in the door just behind him.

"Tell me this is not happening," Joe snapped.

"It's happening all right!" Tom shouted.

"But look at this!" Ron screamed. "There seems to be some lava movement at the Norris Basin! Look at the screen!"

"He's right!" Tom yelled.

"God, this cannot be happening!" Joe said. "Holy shit," Joe screamed as the entire monitoring screen turned red, "it looks like an eruption!" Tom quickly looked at the clock; it was just four-twenty-seven a.m.

Tom immediately knew that the eruption had not been caused by the rockets launched by the terrorists.

"The volcano has erupted on its own!" Tom screamed.

"The rockets never reached their targets!" Ron shouted. "Look at the VEI indicator, it's passing 6.8! Look! 7.2."

"Damn!" Joe yelled. "It just passed 7.4!"

"Let's start monitoring the effects," Tom suggested. They all ran to the
~~~~~~~~~~

main station.

"This is unbelievable!" Tom shouted.

Angie had walked in on time to hear Tom confirming that the eruption had occurred naturally. Tears just ran from her eyes, but this time they were tears of happiness. She didn't interrupt them, realizing that the boys were gathering important data.

"We had better send out an 'all-out-alert' to the news media," John suggested. "They're going to want to know what the hell is going on."

"We should also send the info to Russia and any other country having nuclear armament, just in case they decide to take matters into their own hands."

"I believe they already know," Joe said with a smile, "there's no way their instruments missed this blow-out."

Ron quickly ran to his station and entered the data in his communications network and pushed send.

There was a roar of a thousand thunders that seemed to increase in intensity with each minute that passed. Then, there was an explosion that sounded like a thousand atomic bombs going off at the same time, followed by a light in the sky that had the ability to illuminate the entire planet. Yellowstone had erupted. The rockets never reached their destination. It would be the largest eruption ever recorded in history. The satellite surveillance cameras were transmitting pictures of the eruption directly to the command center's large projection screens. The images were magnificent. "I have never seen anything like this, Joe," Tom said in an excited tone as he viewed the screen. "It's just unbelievable."

"That's exactly what it is," Joe responded. "Unbelievable," Phil and John stood there in amazement.

"It's kind of scary," Phil said.

Joe walked over to Angie, who still had tears in her eyes, and held her in his arms.

"I told you, Joe," Angie said smiling ear to ear. "What God has created, no man can destroy."

"Yes, Angie, you always knew."

~~~~~~~~~~

As the terrorists stood beside their trucks, they first heard a thunderous explosion. They knew the volcano had erupted. Al-Azeez looked at his watch, and immediately realized that his rockets did not cause the eruption. Only six minutes and thirty-nine seconds had passed.
~~~~~~~~~~

They all looked dumbfounded as they continued to look in the direction of the volcano. The sky was lit up like a Christmas tree. First they heard the thundering sound of the explosion, and then they felt the ground rumble. They heard the cracking of trees and the sounds of tornado winds. When the velocity of the five hundred-mile per hour winds, that had been heated to a temperature of more than eight-hundred degrees, overtook them they were immediately cremated.

The terrorist had spent their entire lives following a false doctrine, and in the end, they had died in vain. One could say that it was just another suicide run gone wrong.

~~~~~~~~~~

Within minutes, the entire world knew that Yellowstone had erupted. The magnitude of the eruption was off the charts. Tom calculated the intensity of the eruption to be 7.7 VEI.

Such an eruption should have had the intensity to cool the planet, but in such uncharted territory, nothing is really written in stone. "We must now monitor the heartbeat of the planet," he told himself. Only time will tell."

"It was an absolute miracle," Joe said. "The rockets that were launched by the terrorists came within three minutes from causing a forced eruption. It's just unbelievable."

"It's nothing short of divine intervention," Angie added.

"Yes," Joe agreed, "that's what it was. For months, we attempted to come up with a solution. There were thousands of scientists working on the problem without resolution. Even at the very last minute, man attempted to destroy the only chance the planet had by forcing the eruption, and in spite all of our efforts; it was the natural course of events that saved the planet." Joe paused for a moment. "Just three minutes; that's how close we came from experiencing the total annihilation of the human race."

"You were right, Angie, it was divine intervention that saved the planet."

"We may not be so lucky next time," John added.

"There will be no next time," Tom snapped. "The planet may survive, but look at the damage that we have incurred. There are more than a billion or more casualties that can be directly attributed to this tragedy, and another billion people that have been permanently displaced. This is the worst tragedy in the history of mankind, and we are still not out of the woods."
~~~~~~~~~~

"I agree," Ron said seeming somewhat apprehensive, "there is no guarantee that this is going to work. We are going to have to wait and see. Theoretically, the planet should cool down enough to turn the lava into solid rock, but Tom is correct, we are in uncharted waters. If our calculations are even slightly off, the results could be disastrous. However, I believe that the odds are more in our favor now than they were ten minutes ago."

"We'll know in a few months," Joe said. "I remain optimistic, but we're going have to give this thing time, and let it play itself out."

They were all anxious to get back to work. Their expectations were high, but they did realize that they were still dealing with a lot of unknowns.

CHAPTER 46

In Russia, they were drinking vodka. Nikolai Korcheck made a public announcement regarding the success of the eruption. He also commended Aletei Ivanov for his brilliant work, and congratulated him for standing his ground against such strong political pressure. To the Russians, Aletei was the real hero.

"Mr. Nikolai," Aletei said in a serious manner, "we must remember that we are in uncharted territory. There are no absolutes to how this is going to turn out, but I do believe it will successfully reverse the process. The planet should become bitterly cold in a relatively short period of time. I suggest that measures be taken immediately to protect some of the colder regions of the country. Food, clothing, water, and housing will be in short demand when the freeze sets in."

"Yes, Aletei," Nikolai replied, "We will immediately form a committee to deal with the issue, and you will be commissioned to head that committee."

"It will be an honor, Mr. President."

Aletei sent a wire to Tom Collins, thanking him for including him in the final decision making process, and suggested that an international committee be set up to deal with the oncoming Ice Age. Tom thanked Aletei for his comments and assured him that he would receive his total cooperation in developing a worldwide plan for survival.

~~~~~~~~~~
~~~~~~~~~~

Back at the command center, Tom and his colleagues continued to document the aftermath of the eruption when President Hamity walked into the room with a big smile on his face. He immediately walked over to where they were standing, and congratulated them on a job well done.

"Great job guys," the President said, still smiling. "There are really no words that can express the gratitude we have for the effort you all have made on this project. We are certainly indebted to you. Your persistence and stubbornness on this matter is absolutely commendable. The world is truly indebted to the tremendous effort you put forth, even risking your very lives, to guarantee the preservation of all of mankind. It is nothing short of heroic."

"In all reality," Joe said, "the planet actually saved itself. No, let me rephrase that. As Angie has so often said, 'God will not permit man to destroy what he has created'. With the many scientists that were involved with this project, it was Angie's theology that saved the day."

Angie smiled, but did not respond.

"I guess you're right, Joe," the President said still smiling. "It was nothing sort of a miracle."

"On another note," Tom said, "I communicated with the Russian scientist, Aletei, earlier this morning. We agreed that an international committee should be established, not just to deal with the coming Ice Age, but also to establish an international environmental regulatory agency to permanently protect the planet from its inhabitants."

"I don't believe," the President responded, "that we will receive any opposition on the matter. If man does not alter its present course of action, or take steps to implement international laws to guarantee the survival of the planet, man could cease to exist. We came within three minutes from total annihilation this time. It is imperative that this never happens again.

"I'll make that a priority Tom," the President continued, "and I don't believe that we will receive any resistance from the Nations of the world."

"Not to change the subject," Phil said, "but we're not totally out of the woods yet. We are still in uncharted waters and there's no way to predict how this thing is going to turn out."

"Phil is right," Tom said. "All we can do at this point is monitor the situation and keep you up to date on what develops. It'll take months before we can come to any solid conclusion."

"I understand, Tom," the President said. "Just keep me informed, and above all, make sure that none of this information is leaked to the news media. The last thing we need is panic. If things don't work out, I would like the opportunity to inform the public personally."

"I understand, sir."

"By the way," the President continued, "I have already instructed General Forthworth to instruct his team that all information within this center will continue to be considered classified." The President paused for a moment as he got up from his chair. "Good luck gentlemen, and may God be with you."

After the President left the room, Tom and his colleagues continued to monitor the eruption.

CHAPTER 47

The eruption was catastrophic. To many, it seemed like a doomsday prophesy, or more like Armageddon, than an attempt to save the planet. The initial eruption produced a pyroclastic blast that traveled at 600 miles per hour, with temperatures exceeding 700 degrees F, and totally destroyed all life within a one-hundred mile radius of the blast. Heavy ash fall-out covered an additional 600 square miles, with ash and debris also accelerating for miles into the upper atmosphere caught up in the trade winds. The sun could not penetrate the ash fallout that would circle the entire globe in just a three-week period. These events conjured up inner human emotions that were beyond any fear that most had ever experienced.

As the weeks passed, there did not seem to be any measurable change to the planet's temperatures. Some were skeptical and fearful that the end of the world was at hand. The daily weather reports were not encouraging, and the average global temperatures continued to range between 108 and 114 degrees Fahrenheit, and still rising. The extreme heat caused tempers to flare, and in some areas, rage and violence were simply out of control. However, in other areas, people were tolerant, patient, and hopeful that the promised change would occur.

The distribution of food and water in the United States had been well organized. Yes, there were conflicts. Some people wanted more than their share of rations, which forced the authorities to send a full military escort out with the distribution trucks to protect them from being ravaged. They had orders to shoot any person that threatened the supply trucks. Rules and regulations, relating to the distribution of rations, were continually broadcast over the news stations. The government also distributed informational pamphlets to ensure that procedures were followed. The rules were simple: if an area became riotous, that area would be off the distribution route the following week. This forced unruly areas, with the participation of the local police, to form civilian law enforcement units as a method to assure a safe haven for the distribution trucks. In a very short period of time, these areas became safe for those delivering the needed supplies. People really stuck together.

At this point in time, not a single country in the world had the ability to help another. This was not because of a lack of compassion. They simply had more problems than they could possibly handle in their own country. People around the world were extremely skeptical as conditions continued to deteriorate. The daily news update, reporting these conditions, gravely diminished the hopes and expectations of many, but there was really no way to dilute the facts. The conditions were visible; the deterioration of the environment was more of a personal experience than a far off event. People continued to crowd places of worship. It was one of the few ways they had to maintain some sort of hope or feeling that eventually everything would be alright.

~~~~~~~~~~

The information that was being released by the news media was mixed. Some headlines read, "No signs of cooling," and "Temperature Rises-No Relief in Sight." There were similar articles that had more questions than answers. Scientists continued to monitor the results of the eruption. Months passed, as temperatures continued to rise. The original data gathered by the command center was logged into simulated computer program systems which produced mixed results. Some scenarios indicated that the cooling process would start when the planet reached 112 degrees and others, as high as 180 degrees. Even if it were possible to develop a bunker that could survive such temperatures, all other life on the planet would become extinct.

Scientists involved in the project agreed that the planet might very well reach temperatures that exceeded those that were survivable by man. They were dealing with a lot of unanswered questions. Was the warming process stronger than the cooling process? Was it possible for the planet to heat up to one 150 degrees before the cooling process started?
~~~~~~~~~~

MELTDOWN

As the temperature increased, so did the mortality rate. There seemed to be no end to the torturous heat wave that plagued the entire world.

The rationing of food had become a priority at this point. Even if things turned around, law enforcement agencies knew that a populous without food could turn uncontrollably violent. It would be the survival of the fittest. Rations had already been cut back by most countries. They did not know how long they would have to hold out before the situation improved. As the weeks passed by, rationing would become even tighter.

Scientists, like Tom and Joe, would not comment on the probability of a cooling effect without definitive proof that that the planet was cooling. Unsubstantiated information at this time would further diminish public confidence, which was already at an all-time low.

The death toll continued to rise, especially amongst the elderly. Surviving on a day-by-day basis was a struggle for most. The camp sites housing the evacuees had become a living hell. They had very little relief from the heat. The majority of the camps were located inland where temperatures were higher than in areas close to the water, and without air conditioning, the atmosphere was suffocating.

The government constructed prefab buildings in each camp with air-conditioning for those who suffered from severe heat stroke. The cooperation and compassion that people had for one another helped to make life bearable. The majority of evacuees had come from the Mid-western states where people generally dealt with difficult issues in a practical manner. They spent a lot of time in church, praying for God's intervention. However, they had not lost their sense of humor. When one old man was asked by a news journalist, "What are you praying for?", the old man immediately responded, "to survive the crisis or move in with God, where it will be a lot cooler." Even the answer made him feel better. The journalist included the article in his column that day.

CHAPTER 48

"It's been three months," Joe said in a low voice as he sipped his coffee. "The average temperatures have actually increased by four degrees. I really don't believe these people can take much more."

"There's not much we can do," Ron said. "The problem we have is there's nothing in the past that will even give us the slightest indication of what to expect."

"It seems like the entire world is moving in slow motion," John responded. "Even the airports are closed because of the possibility of engine failure due to the enormous quantity of ash in the atmosphere."

"There's no sense in beating ourselves over the head," Tom said. "All we can do is to continue to collect and process data. The scientists and technicians have been working diligently these past three months, but I sense a feeling of disappointment in the air. There are simply no favorable indicators."

"Theoretically," Joe said, "there should have been some signs of a cooling trend by now."

"My concern is not that there's going to be a cooling trend," Tom responded, "but rather, will it occur prior to reaching temperatures that are unsustainable?"

"According to a recent medical report, temperatures exceeding 120 degrees would be a critical level."

Tom just shook his head, but did not respond.

"The employees at the command center have a great deal of

confidence and admiration for all of you," Angie said in a sincere manner. "They believe that the temperatures will drop because you told them so." She paused for a moment and then continued. "I believe that you should continue to tell the staff at this command center, and people throughout the world, that same message, because all they really have to hang on to is hope. And besides, there has never been a time in history that God has forsaken us."

"There she goes again," Joe said, "still walking on the sunny side of the street."

"Don't worry, Angie," Tom added, "we're going keep the news positive right to the end."

"Thank you, Tom."

~~~~~~~~~~

Another month passed producing average temperatures of 120 degrees Fahrenheit. Tom and his colleagues remained concerned, but did not relay that concern to others. People around the world didn't have to be informed of what was happening; it was an experience. Just to survive on a day by day basis was more than a challenge, and the nights were not much more comforting than the days.

On the morning of the 122nd day after the eruption, Joe, who had an extremely restless night, decided to head down to the command center to check the latest temperature readings. He got down to his station at three-fifty-five a.m. After picking up two cups of black coffee and a cinnamon bun, he headed down to his station. When he gazed at the computer screen, he immediately noticed that the average temperature read 118.8 degrees Fahrenheit. He rechecked the number to make sure that there had not been an error; the numbers came out the same. He continued to check and re-check the monitors until he was absolutely positive that the readings were correct. Then he called Tom, who was still in his room sleeping.

"Hi Joe, don't you think that it's a little early to be calling?" Tom responded as he yawned.

"Tom! Just listen!" Joe shouted, "I just took temperature readings, they're down a little more than a degree."

"Are you sure it wasn't a computer malfunction?" Tom asked, now sitting up on his bed.

"I'm sure," Joe insisted, "I confirmed the data on several different units and the computations are all the same." Tom did not respond. "Tom, are
~~~~~~~~~~

you still there?"

"Yes, I'm still here."

"I'm sorry if I disappointed you; if you give me a couple of minutes, I can call you back with some bad news."

"Ok, Joe, I just wanted to make sure that I wasn't still sleeping. I'll be right down, but please don't say anything to anyone, not just yet." Tom hung up the phone and headed to the command center. When he got off the elevator, he walked directly over to Joe's station and looked at his screen. He could not believe his eyes. "I think we should keep this to ourselves," Tom said. "At least until we can confirm that the temperature drop is not a fluke. We will probably know within a couple of days."

"I think that's a good idea," Joe agreed. "We're probably going to have to monitor the temperatures for at least two or three days to confirm the readings."Tom and Joe met with the rest of the group later that morning and told them the news.

"We must be cautiously optimistic," Tom explained. "The readings over the next couple of days will tell us the story. Until we can positively confirm a downward trend, we must keep this information to ourselves."

They all agreed. The next couple of days would be anxious ones.

By the 125th day, temperatures were down an additional four degrees. The cooling process had started.

Emotions at the command center were high. Tom decided that it was time to make the announcement. When the news rang over the loud speaker, there were loud cheers throughout the command center. They opened bottles of champagne and gave a toast thanking Tom and his associates for their relentless efforts to save the planet. Joe immediately lifted his glass and made a toast to the more than two hundred scientists and technicians involved with the project.

"The first thing I would like to say is if it were not for my colleagues and me, you would never have received all of that overtime."

The crowd laughed.

"I knew that there was something about that guy that I liked," one fellow shouted.

Joe then thanked them for the long hours they had worked, and for their continued dedication to the project. It was a good day.

On the 132nd day, the average temperature around the world had dropped to 82 degrees, and a few weeks later, it had dropped to 32 degrees.

The lava that had broken through the crust of the planet had hardened, and the polar caps had reversed their melting trend and were now increasing in size, but new concerns had surfaced regarding the severe drop in temperature.

"What do you think, Joe?" Tom asked. "We didn't give this much thought, did we?"

"Even if we did, the fact remains that we really don't have a hell of a lot of control over the matter."

"Well," Tom continued, "the President wants to meet at one this afternoon. Steve Beldon and some of his boys from the USGS will be present. He wants to know how low the temperatures are going to drop, before leveling off."

"That's somewhat ironic," Joe said smiling. "Now he's worried about freezing to death. There are really no answers we can give the President, Tom. It would be strictly a guess. We would have better odds picking tomorrow's lotto numbers."

"The big problem," Ron said, "is that the conveyor belt moving warm water to the colder northern regions has slowed down dramatically, and unless it has some way to reenergize itself, the temperatures will continue to drop."

"We had better head to the conference room," John said. "It's almost one."

When they entered the conference room, the President, Steve Beldon, and a number of scientists had already been seated.

"Good morning, sir," Tom said, as he greeted the President, "sorry we're late."

"Good morning Tom, please have a seat."

"Did you get my memo?" the President asked.

"Yes sir, you're concerned about the rapid drop in temperatures."

"I have already consulted with Steve and his staff who have confirmed that there is presently no scientific method to predict when temperatures will level off. I was also informed that past Ice Ages have produced temperatures as low as minus one-hundred degrees, and of course, my fear is that such temperatures are just not sustainable for surviving human life, or any other life forms for that matter."

"Steve is correct," Tom said, "there is no way of predicting when this thing is going to level off. The problem is that the conveyor belt, which normally moves warm waters from southern regions to the colder regions, has slowed down dramatically, and there is no magical repair kit that can speed those currents up."

"So you're saying that there's nothing that can be done to correct the problem."

"We will certainly give it some thought, sir," Tom explained, "but in reality, no one has ever been able to control the weather."

The President paused for a moment, basically knowing that nothing could be done to change the circumstance. "Are there any other suggestions?"

"Yes," Joe said. "I think we should start planning for a cold winter."

The President smiled. "I'll take that under advisement," he said, still smiling.

"Mr. President?"

"Yes, Angie"

"So far, everything has worked out just fine. He just needs a little more time to finish what he has started."

"You know," the President said still smiling, "I think I'm going to go with that answer. It seems as practical as anything else I've heard these past couple of months."

Joe smiled, he just loved her attitude.

"Thanks, Angie," the President said with a big smile on his face. "It's the best news I've heard all day. I promise to relay your message to the people, they'll be anxious to hear it."

Angie smiled as the President left the room.

They all walked over to Angie and gave her a big hug.

"What? Did I say something wrong?" she asked in a surprised tone.

"No Angie," Joe said, "You did exceptionally well. The President was really enlightened."

They all laughed.

"No," Ron said, "It was the best possible answer to what was an unanswerable question."

"Thank you Ron, I'll take that as a compliment."

They all headed down to the cafeteria for a quick lunch.

~~~~~~~~~~

There was not much to do for the next couple of months except monitor the temperatures and the currents at the conveyor belt.

Before the year was out, the temperatures dropped down below 0 degrees F, and would continue to drop for the next two months.

The team was overly excited when the currents at the conveyor belt showed signs of increasing. The planet gradually started to warm, as Angie
~~~~~~~~~~

had predicted. Man would survive, but the days ahead would not be easy.

When the public was informed that the planet had entered its first stages of cooling, reactions were extremely emotional. Grown men cried, and women looked into their children's eyes and for the first time saw a future. Others put their hands on their pregnant stomachs and knew that tomorrow would be a good day. Despair had turned into joy. Strangers were hugging and shaking hands, while others crowded places of worship to thank God. The suffering and hardship that plagued the world from the onset of this crisis would eventually come to an end. They knew now that there would be another tomorrow.

There were celebrations throughout the world. People celebrated the gift of life. There would be hard ships ahead, and the burying of the dead, and the mourning by those who lost loved ones. But all these hardships would soon move into the past. There would be a new beginning; a new tomorrow.

~~~~~~~~~~

When the President learned that the planet had entered a warming trend, he immediately scheduled an International Address to all nations:

"Man tried so desperately to destroy the planet, and then, in desperation, attempted to save it. The planet is enveloped in a complexity of mathematical formulas, and has been given the divine ability to create and recreate life at will. Certainly, a process that will never be totally understood nor duplicated by man, even if given a billion years to do so.

"We were told not to worry, that the environment goes through these cycles. That these occurrences have been taking place for millions of years, and all of this without evidence or proof. We call this, in Washington, salesmanship! Meanwhile, the environmentalists are telling us that there has been more man-made damage to the planet in the last 110 years than since Adam and Eve walked the planet, and they can substantiate their claims with written proof. And whom do we believe; the salesmen.

"It was the planet's uncanny ability to restore itself that continues to afford its inhabitants sustainable life. We spend billions of dollars a year in an effort to find life on other planets, and other terrestrial entities. We speculate that there has to be life on a far- off planet that we will most likely never have the opportunity to visit. And yet, for profit, we neglect the only known planet in our solar system that actually has the ability to sustain life!

"This planet was within three minutes of producing an atmosphere
~~~~~~~~~~

similar to Mars. Citizens of the world, we came within {three minutes} of a total annihilation of the human race. There were plenty of warning signs. Thousands of environmentalists throughout the world spent countless hours attempting to warn us of the unconscionable damage we were causing to the planet. Did we listen to their warnings? No! We were more concerned about our political agenda, catering to lobbyists, and corporate profits.

"Those days are gone, my friends! I do not believe that there is a nation in the world that will not agree with that statement. I welcome all the nations in the world to join the United States in creating a world organization for the purpose of protecting the environment of this magnificent planet: 'THE WORLD ENVIRONMENTAL PROTECTION AGENCY'

"From this day on, self-interests must take a back seat to the preservation of the planet. We must all join together as one force, as a single entity, to assure that this God-given residence called Earth is protected above all other issues, matters, and interests.

"When you glance at the stars tonight, and your eyes survey the billions of stars and galaxies that exists over such vast distances, keep in mind that your feet will be standing on the only sphere in this entire network of heavenly bodies that has been proven to sustain life. Let's take care of her. She's all we've got."

EPILOGUE

Tom and his associates had never thought, in their wildest dreams, that they would be the main driving force in an unparalleled journey to save mankind from total annihilation. They risked their lives at every turn without consideration for their safety and well-being. They continued to sacrifice their own lives, many times over, for the preservation of others. Through adversity, they had a relentless determination to cross the finish line.

Shortly after the President had received the good news from the command center, he summoned the six patriots to the White House, and in a glorious ceremony on the White House lawn, he awarded each of them the Congressional Medal of Honor. The crowd attending the ceremony was so large they could not be counted. Tom and his colleagues were overwhelmed and confused by the extraordinary turn out.

"So many people," Tom whispered to Joe. "They are probably here to pay tribute to the President for his great leadership during these difficult times."

"No!" The President, responded, having overheard Tom's statement. "No, that is not why they are here, but thank you for the compliment. They are here to pay tribute to the six patriots, the six authentic heroes that I have had the honor to serve."

"No, sir," Tom and Joe responded, almost simultaneously.

"It was your encouragement and your optimism that kept these people going," Joe said. "We are not heroes, Mr. President."

The President smiled, "You guys really don't know, do you? There are more than one million people standing in front of you. Ask them why they are here." Before the President could complete his introduction of the six patriots, a dim roar from within the crowd slowly increased into a thunderous applause that totally drowned out the President's introduction. As Tom, Joe, and their colleagues waved their hands, thanking the crowd for such an overwhelming appreciation, the cheers only grew louder. They just could not believe the reception.

The President shook his head, thinking that they really had no idea what they had accomplished. When the cheers diminished somewhat, Tom walked up to the podium in an effort to thank the crowd. "My colleagues and I are extremely grateful for your warm reception." Again the crowd roared for an additional 5 minutes. "We thank you for sharing with us, and the entire world, this day of new beginnings."

At this point, they all had big smiles on their faces as Tom attempted to continue.

"We are truly honored and privileged to have been part of the greatest endeavor ever under-taken since the beginning of time..." Tom paused for a moment as the crowd continued to applaud.

Angie had tears in her eyes, she was so happy to see the guys receiving such recognition.

As the applause continued, Tom realized that his presentation was over. They then held the metals that they had just received above their heads as Tom shouted into the microphone. "We accept these metals on behalf of those who have unselfishly contributed their time and effort to preserve the lives of their fellow man. Yes! We are happy to share this great day of celebration with all of you. Thank you!"

As the crowd continued their celebration, Tom turned to Joe and continued.

"It was plan T that really got us over the hump, wasn't it, Joe." Joe smiled.

When Joe turned to his left, he saw Harry and Matt standing there grinning.

"Congratulations, Joe," Harry said.

"Thanks, Harry. Why the bulletproof vest?"

"I'm selling them as Ice Age warmers."

"Why isn't Matt talking?"

"He's frozen."

"We're going to miss you and the crew," Matt said.

"Yeah," Harry agreed, "not much action since you and your boys froze the planet."

"Well, what can I say, "Joe said smiling, "I hope things pick up soon."

They all laughed.

The team thanked the agents for being there for them when things got rough. They then escorted the six patriots into the crowd where they spent the next hour greeting those that came to honor them. It was a great day for all that were there.

~~~~~~~~~~

Joe had other reasons to be happy; Angie was six months pregnant. There would be happy days ahead. They moved back to Connecticut where they were greeted by marching bands.

Joe and Angie drove directly to Angie's house. When they turned up the street, there were more than five-hundred people waiting to greet them. Joe's brother, Bill, his wife, and their four children greeted the couple with hugs and kisses.

"Hi, little brother," Bill said, as he embraced Joe. "I'm really proud of you, Joe, you're a real hero."

"Thanks, Bill. It's sure great to be home." Joe was really happy to see them all. Angie's mom and dad were both in tears as they embraced their daughter, and were even happier when they found out that she was six months pregnant. They then both walked over to Joe and gave him a warm embrace and officially welcomed him into their family. The crowd just cheered. There were a lot of tears, but they were all happy ones.

John Mason and his family, who lived in a small town just outside of New Haven, loved small-town living. He was extremely grateful for the good will shown to him and his family as they celebrated their homecoming with Joe, Tom, and Angie.

Tom had arrived with Joe and Angie, and was paraded through the streets with his friends.

The President offered Tom the position heading the newly formed International Agency formed to protect the planet. He received a unanimous vote from the nations around the world to head the agency. Tom accepted the position.

John was offered a position by the governor of Connecticut to head the newly formed Environmental Agency. He was extremely grateful and immediately accepted the offer.

Joe was offered several prestigious positions in some of the finest
~~~~~~~~~~

learning institutions in the country. He also had an open invitation to join both the CIA and FBI, but decided that he would devote all of his energy to developing documentaries and lecturing on the subject of environmental protection.

Ron Massey had accepted a full-time job with the government running the command center. He was overwhelmed by the prospect of having all those computers around him.

Phil Dayne was commissioned to head the USGS, replacing Steve Beldon, who had retired because of medical problems. Steve had recommended Phil for the job. They had become good friends.

The economy slowly recovered, and so did the world. Not a single nation was at war. There were those in the world that wondered how long it would take before this tragedy would be forgotten.

The six patriots remained best friends and gathered often to reminisce about their James Bond days.

18079969R00186

Made in the USA
Lexington, KY
17 October 2012